VICTOR

VICTOR

PARA-MILITARY RECRUITER™ BOOK 10

RENÉE JAGGÉR

MICHAEL ANDERLE

THE VICTOR TEAM

Thanks to the JIT Readers

Dave Hicks
Dorothy Lloyd
Wendy L Bonell
Christopher Gilliard
Jackey Hankard-Brodie
Zacc Pelter
Paul Westman
John Ashmore
Jan Hunnicutt

Editor
The SkyFyre Editing Team

CHAPTER ONE

The debating dragons were several hundred feet away, perched on a ledge on the wall of the rocky canyon, but Julie Meadows could easily hear them from where she stood at the edge of the Royal Pavilion.

The smaller of the two was a familiar lithe dragon whose white fur stirred in the breeze as he glared at his opponent. "This goes beyond dragonkind!" Methunoch snarled. "This is about all species across the dimensions. The war could destroy them!"

"*We* could destroy them!" Methunoch's opponent was the size of a brick shithouse. Several brick shithouses. His gray skin moved like plates of armor as he swung his thick neck around to meet Methunoch's eyes, and two thick, curving horns, like those of a rhinoceros, jutted from his nose. They flashed in the sun like polished steel. "It is better for them that we contain our power."

"Our power is ours to control." Methunoch's long tail lashed over his flanks. "We can find a way to go to war and sow less destruction."

The other dragon's brown eyes narrowed. "Perhaps *you* could sow less destruction, mountain mite."

Methunoch's mane rose like hackles and he hissed, showing off his white fangs.

Shit's getting real, Julie observed silently.

The ornate navy service cap studded with gold insignia that was perched on her head responded in a British accent, *It got real as soon as they stopped debating telepathically and started yelling at each other.*

"You can't bait me, Goliason," Methunoch hissed.

"Afraid to fight me?" Goliason roared.

His earth-shaking voice was lost in the chaos of the draconic debate taking place all over the canyon. For as far as Julie could see, the canyon walls and floor were lined with dragons, many locked in telepathic debates. Others were engaged in shouting matches, and clouds of dust marked the places where physical fights had broken out. The thumps of dragon scales against stone and the roars and snarls of battle filled the air.

"Afraid?" Methunoch scoffed, tossing his mane. "I only fear real threats, you fool."

Goliason let out a muted roar and backed up on his stubby legs. His short tail ended in a club studded with bony spikes, and it twitched as he pawed the ground with a forelimb.

Methunoch sat down and curled his tail around his claws like a cat. "Can't fight me intellectually? See if you have any physical luck, then."

Goliason tossed his horns, snorted, and charged. Methunoch jumped aside at the last second and snapped at Goliason's nose. The bigger dragon stumbled and fell to the ground, and Methunoch pounced on him. Scrabbling and spitting, screeching and clawing, the two dragons rolled across the canyon floor and thudded into the wall near the royal pavilion with a force that made it tremble.

"Get back from the edge, young one!"

Behind Julie, Lady Ennowen, the queen of the Deep, was perched serenely on her throne in her humanoid form. The hopelessness Julie had seen in her pale green eyes when they'd first met was replaced by a keen, glittering interest, and her bony hands gripped the stone armrests of her throne.

Julie planted her hands on her hips. "Um, Great Lady?" She unfolded her dragonfly-like wings, which were wider than her arms, razor-edged, and diamond-hard. "I can fly, remember?"

Lady Ennowen's eyes narrowed. "I will take no chances with you for as long as you are bonded to my granddaughter. Now, get *back* from that edge."

Julie wanted to roll her eyes but stopped herself. She bowed sarcastically instead. "Yes, Great Lady." *Grand-smother*, she added in the privacy of her mind.

Well, semi-privacy.

That's the queen of the Deep you're talking about, Hat grumbled.

So? Julie retorted. *She's several leagues more overprotective than my mother. Mom still texts me about my bowel movements from time to time.*

Hat snickered.

Julie flopped onto one of the stone seats near the throne and leaned against the enormous scaly head of the dragon who lay with his body curled around the bases. Alugon's mesmerizing blue, gold, and purple scales were warm and surprisingly comfortable to lean against.

I am not a chair, Julie of the Meadows, he protested quietly.

I'm so done with sitting here. Julie folded her arms. *I feel superfluous.*

Alugon chuckled. *You are simply nervous because the final vote will be cast soon.*

Julie swallowed hard, her belly twisting in anticipation. She glanced up at the glowing golden fungi that grew on the distant roof of this part of the vast subterranean world where the dragons lived. They were beginning to close, so it would be dusk soon. Around her feet, several small pebbles cracked and turned to dust.

You're going to cause an earthquake, Hat grumbled.

Sorry. Julie wiped her sweaty palms on the pressed navy trousers of her dress uniform and took a deep breath. The pebbles stopped moving. *I am nervous, I guess.*

You have every right to be. Whatever the dragons decide, their involvement, or lack thereof, will have a profound impact on the war, Hat admitted.

Julie sighed. *I can't believe it's been eight months since the live test of the Breaker. The dragons know that worshipers of Mordred are involved. How has that not brought us to a much faster conclusion? They could have ended the war by now if they'd only decide to take action.*

I'm afraid that might not happen now, Hat muttered.

Julie glanced at Lady Ennowen. The dragon queen's hands tightened on the armrests again as the fight between Methunoch and Goliason reached a thunderous climax below. Goliason tossed Methunoch into the air with his rhino horns, and when the smaller dragon slammed into the ground, Goliason planted a huge paw on his neck and pinned him to the earth. Trembling, Methunoch held up a claw in a gesture of surrender, and Goliason stepped back. He glanced at Lady Ennowen, and the dragon queen gave him a barely perceptible nod.

Julie's hands clenched into fists in her lap. *I remember when Lady Ennowen told me that to be queen meant either being so stubborn and sharp-witted that no one could outsmart her or so powerful that no one dared to challenge her. Not a beguiling schemer who uses political pressure and owed favors to rule the Deep.*

Don't be cranky just because you miss your boyfriend, Hat lectured.

Heat flashed through Julie's palms. *Excuse me. My annoyance has everything to do with Lady Ennowen having pulled enough strings that none of the dragons will listen to me, even though I'm here as the representative of the Deep's future queen, and nothing to do with Taylor having been away for six weeks.* She sighed, her hands relaxing. *Although, yeah, okay, I do miss him.*

I'm teasing you, Hat admitted. *It's frustrating how she's turned the tide in her favor.*

They watched as Methunoch, head hanging, limped away from the fight and approached a huddled group of dragons perched on the canyon wall. He raised his head to stare at them, but they didn't offer him sympathy. Instead, they took wing with a rustle of scales and flew across the canyon to join the raucous group welcoming the victorious Goliason. Only one hesitated, a white, furry dragon who looked similar to Methunoch. She gazed at him for a few moments before joining the others.

Julie had been watching the dragons debate for long enough to know that Methunoch's defeat in this fight was the final point of his debate with Goliason and that watching him fall had persuaded a whole group of dragons to change their vote.

I don't like being on the receiving end of her political maneuvering; I can tell you that much, Julie muttered.

One can't blame her for not wanting to involve the dragons in war again. Hat paused. *Given what happened to her daughter the last time they went to battle on the surface world.*

Eggy knows that's how her mom died, Julie snapped, *and she's still in favor of the dragons going to war in defense of peace and freedom.*

Eggy hasn't hatched yet, Hat pointed out.

Yes, but you were the one who told me that she already has access to the wisdom of all dragons, Julie returned.

More of the golden fungi had closed, and dusk turned to twilight. Lady Ennowen nodded at Alugon. With a grunt, he rose to his feet and strode to the edge of the pavilion. He sucked in a breath that made flames rush to his chest, then huffed out a mushroom cloud of fire that bathed the canyon in brilliant firelight.

Lady Ennowen rose and stood at the edge of the pavilion. Every dragon in the canyon below went silent, their eyes fixed on their queen. She held up her arms, and her voice surged through the minds of all present.

That concludes the debate on this matter. Her glittering gaze swept through the canyon. *Cast your final votes.*

She returned to her throne as the dragons came forward one by one. Two great piles of smooth stones, one white and one black, stood near the royal pavilion. The first dragon to swoop toward the stones was Goliason. He snatched a white stone, clutching it between his stubby paws, and flew over the empty space between the stone piles and the pavilion. Sixty feet in the air, he let go of the stone, and it fell to the ground with a thump that rang through the canyon.

Julie watched as Methunoch, head hanging and blood soaking into his thick white fur, did the same. He tossed the white stone away as though it revolted him.

He doesn't want to vote against getting involved in the war, she observed.

No, but he doesn't have a choice, Hat told her. *He lost the fight with Goliason. That means that he lost the debate and has to vote the way Goliason, ah, "persuaded" him to.*

Julie folded her arms. *That's screwed up.*

I agree, and that's why the dragons would benefit from a stronger queen to keep them in order, Hat muttered. *Lady Ennowen allowed them to descend into chaos due to her absence. Even her stronger presence in the last eight months has not put an end to the fighting.*

Julie sighed. *It still doesn't seem like the dragon way.*

It isn't, Hat agreed. *But you've learned a lot from the experience of the past few months with her.*

Yeah. Julie grunted. *Namely, how to get what you want when you don't care what the opposition thinks about it.*

The clacks of falling stones and the thumps of wings beating resounded through the canyon as the dragons cast their votes, magic sorting the black and white stones into different piles. Julie clenched her hands into fists, frustration bubbling in her gut as the pile of white stones grew and the black pile struggled to keep up.

"Come on," she muttered. "Come *on*."

Lady Ennowen shot her a furious glance.

Julie flung herself against the backrest of her stone seat and let out a huff as the final dragon dropped his vote on the white pile. Moonlight runes flashed on the stone, then on the ground in front of the stones. Julie didn't have to read the Draconic runes to know that the white pile was far larger.

Lady Ennowen hung her head, her shoulders slumping, and pressed a hand to her face. Julie stared at her. She'd been expecting a smug grin of satisfaction. Instead, the dragon queen kept her head bowed for a moment before she rose to her feet and walked to the edge of the pavilion.

Alugon caught the dragons' attention with another fireball. Lady Ennowen smiled and held up her arms, her gray, white, and green robes rustling with the movement.

The threshold has been reached. The debate is at an end, she announced. *The Lords of the Deep will do nothing to influence the outcome of the war.* She raised her chin, eyes glittering. *The dragons will not get involved in surface issues.*

There was a roaring cheer from the canyon. Julie wanted to punch something. She glared at the ground instead, wisps of smoke escaping between her fingers. Her anger smoldered like a coal in her solar plexus.

<hr>

Julie stormed through the curtain of purple moss toward the nursery chamber, flames licking around her fingers.

Easy, Julie, Hat protested, clinging to her head as she pushed through the rocky, twisting passage. *You don't want to upset the heir.*

Eggy might not be ready for the pressure and responsibility of her political position, but she's curious and ready to handle the information, Julie snapped. *Stay out of this.*

Okay, okay, Hat grumbled. *I'm not the one you're mad at. Don't take it out on me.*

Julie sucked in a breath and relaxed her fingers. *Sorry.*

She stomped into the cavern in which Eggy waited. It was a large space draped with mosses and lichens of different colors. A stone cradle the egg had long since outgrown stood on one side of the chamber, and the niche in which the egg had lain until a few weeks ago still bore the impression of her smooth shape.

Now, the egg lay in the center of the chamber, gleaming obsidian and taking up most of the floor space. She was cradled by a deep bed of moss and lichen. A pulse of moonlight was visible with each slow beat of the unborn dragon's massive heart, illuminating her faint, curled shape, head tucked against her tail, limbs resting on her belly as she lay upside down in her egg. The pulse never seemed to reach her face, and not for the first time, Julie longed to look into her eyes.

The pulse quickened as Julie walked up to her, and Julie made sure that her palm was no longer hot before she rested it on the eggshell. *Hey, Eggy.*

Connection to the unborn dragon's mind was effortless, and joy flashed through it at Julie's touch, followed by frustration. Her mind filled with an image of the conclave and the falling stones, edged with a questioning feeling.

Yeah, it didn't go well. Julie sighed and slumped to the floor with her back to the egg. *They voted against getting involved in Avalonian affairs.*

Frustration thrummed through the dragon's mind, followed by relief, then confusion. A rapid set of mental images reached Julie's thoughts—a mishmash of Julie's memories, memories of the heir's ancestors, and conjurings of Eggy's imagination. Julie saw Fernwood Deep burning. She saw her friend Chester die in battle and felt her anguish doubled in the dragon's heart. Then she saw the Deep, vibrant and colorful and beautiful and safe, and the other dragons living free within it, a world away from the war.

I know you're confused. She stroked the surface of the egg. *I understand. It can't be easy dealing with all this shit.* She sighed, closed her eyes, and leaned her head against the shell. *It's not easy for* me *to deal with all this shit, and I've been, well, you could say hatched, for twenty-one years.*

Eggy's empathy reverberated through her mind. She gently showed Julie one of her memories from the refugee camp in Avalon Town back before the Para-Military Agency got involved, when frightened Fernwood refugees lived in makeshift dwellings and skated on the brink of starvation. Julie would never forget the fear in the eyes of the ogre family she'd helped.

Exactly! Julie slammed her fists on her knees. *This isn't just about the paras dying in battle, Eggy, although Merlin knows there's been enough of those. This is about ordinary paranormals getting forced out of their homes. This is about their children being inducted into Mordred's cult. This is about geasa chaining their minds and their free will.* She sucked in a deep breath, trying to calm herself, but her hands kept smoking. *The dragons could stop it. All of it! They could put an end to it the way they put an end to the Second Pendragon War, but Lady Ennowen is too selfish to allow that. She'll hide in the Deep while Avalon burns.*

The mental images stopped, and Eggy imagined herself curling her body around Julie's in a draconic hug.

Aw, Eggles, I love you, too. Julie turned her head so her cheek pressed against the cool shell. *I just wish you'd hatch. Things would be a lot easier if you could talk to the other dragons yourself.*

A twist of intense frustration flared in the dragon's mind, making Julie's palms pulse white-hot again.

She cuddled closer. *Eggy, baby, I didn't mean it like that. I know you'll only be ready to hatch once you've figured out where you stand. It can't be easy, living with all of the memories of your dragon ancestors and also seeing the surface world from my point of view.*

Eggy pressed her head into the shell near Julie's, helplessness coursing through her thoughts.

Shhh. It's okay, Julie soothed. *Your dragon memories want you to put dragons first, and your bond with me makes you care about Avalon. That's got to be confusing. It's okay that you need more time to figure it out.*

Eggy's frustration scorched Julie's palms. She showed Julie her draconic memories, urging her to put the dragons first and prioritize the people she would soon rule. She saw dragons fall in the Pendragon Wars. Then, almost nervously, Eggy showed her a memory Julie hadn't seen before.

She was a huge dragon, swooping toward a dark castle on a twilit mountainside. A figure swathed in shadow stood on the battlements. She opened her mighty jaws to burn him to ashes with a breath, but he drew a blade that crackled with smoke and lightning.

Julie sat up and opened her eyes to stare at the egg. *Eggy, was that your mother?*

Affirmation flooded the unborn dragon's mind.

I'm sorry. Julie pressed both hands to the shell, remembering too late that they were still hot. The heat did nothing to the shell. Eggy didn't notice anything other than Julie's touch.

The unborn dragon's anger flared. She showed Julie her own memories of the carnage she'd witnessed, the images flashing by so quickly that Julie had trouble keeping up. Mind-controlled yetis. Malcolm Nox bleeding in the front seat of Julie's Mustang. Kidnapped heirs struggling in the Haunted House. Dryad corpses stacked up to build a temple. Captain Jack Kaplan in tiger form, blood soaking his coat during the siege of the Eternal Palace. Blake the werewolf, his front leg torn off by the snallygaster, glassy-eyed and bleeding. Mina Nox, claw marks raking her ribs.

The hollow-eyed refugees. A faerie with a bandaged head, motionless and comatose.

With each image, Eggy grew angrier. Then a pulse of heat shot through the shell and made Julie yank her hands back. Even without physical contact, Julie felt a powerful desire to help the surface world pulsing from the unborn dragon, coupled with her fury that her people would stand by and do nothing. Her last mental image was a stylized imagining of a row of dragons sitting along the mountain called the Maw of the Deep, watching as Avalon Town burned.

When the images stopped, Julie's hands were enveloped in flames. They licked up to her elbows.

"You're so right, Eggy!" she burst out. "It's not right. It's not fair!"

The unborn dragon agreed wholeheartedly. She imagined herself shattering her shell, spreading her wings, and swooping into Avalon, blowing fire at the enemies of the Eternity Throne.

Julie managed a weak laugh, but her hands were still afire. "If you weren't the size of a seven-person SUV, I'd give in and take you to Avalon." She flopped down beside the shell and leaned against it, holding her burning hands up so they wouldn't char her uniform.

The baby dragon was silent, then a new voice spoke in Julie's mind. She hadn't heard it before, yet its lilt and cadence were more familiar than the thump of her heart. It was velvety and, at the same time, held an echoing depth. It rustled.

I think you still can, said the unborn dragon.

Julie sucked in a breath. The flames winked out, and she turned to stare at the egg. *Eggy, did you just* talk?

Yes. Eggy laughed, a melodic sound. *I think our brownie friends would love to have an opportunity to do more than keep you in human groceries.*

Julie grinned.

CHAPTER TWO

Julie couldn't stop laughing. She clapped her hands over her mouth, then pressed them to the egg, then back to her mouth.

"*Eggy!*" she shouted. "You can *talk!*"

Eggy giggled. *I thought we'd established that.*

Julie threw her arms around the egg, or partway around one side of the egg, and pressed her cheek to the shell. *It's incredible to hear you speak so clearly. Not like a human baby learning to talk.*

Human babies aren't born with all the knowledge of their ancestors, the unborn dragon reminded her. *Dragons are.*

Julie blinked back joyful tears. *Oh, Eggy, this is amazing.*

I know. Within the egg, the unborn dragon pressed herself against the shell nearest Julie, and a pulse of moonlight traced Julie's arms. *There's so much I want to say to you. Really* say *to you.*

There's nothing you need *to say to me, moondrop,* Julie murmured.

Eggy's laugh resounded through her mind. *But there is! The first thing is that I love it when you call me moondrop. It's a dragon pet name. I...* She paused. *I like to think Mom would have called me that if she'd had the chance.*

It was hard for Julie to hold back her tears. *I heard a mama dragon call her baby that in the royal gardens a few weeks ago. I thought it was cute.*

Well, I love it. Eggy paused. *I remember the day that you found me. I don't know if you know that.*

I didn't. Julie sat down beside the egg and let her hands fall into her lap as she gazed at the pulse of moonlight running through the unborn dragon, emphasizing the soft curve of her tail where it wrapped over her nose and a wing folded by her side. *Do you remember the Haunted House?*

Only vaguely, Eggy admitted. *I remember that I was scared, and there was no moonlight, and I could feel that I was a long way from home.*

The pulses of moonlight quickened in time with the unborn dragon's heartbeat. Julie pressed a hand to the shell, calming Eggy.

Then everything went dark, Eggy whispered. *The next thing I knew, there you were. A love that woke me.*

Julie leaned against the egg. *I love you, Eggles.*

I love you too, Eggy murmured, and the next pulse was brighter.

Julie laughed. *I guess I have to stop calling you Eggy now.* Her research had shown her that unborn dragons chose their names before they learned to speak.

Yes, the unhatched dragon whispered.

Is it true? Julie asked, her heart quickening. *Can you tell me your name?*

I can. Laughter bubbled under her words.

Well, what is it? Julie gasped.

You already know it, the unborn dragon told her. *The short version, anyway.*

Julie sat back and stared at the shell. *What?*

The unborn dragon laughed. *My name is Eglantine.*

Julie burst out laughing and couldn't stop. It flowed from her, releasing the knot in her solar plexus. She laughed until tears stung her eyes and laid back in the moss beside the egg, still laughing. Eggy's mirth joined hers in her mind.

Oh, moondrop! Julie wiped her eyes and tried to breathe normally. *Alugon is going to shit kittens when he finds out.*

That is part *of the reason I chose this name,* Eglantine admitted.

Julie giggled weakly and pressed her hand to the egg. *I knew I'd like your sense of humor.*

Messing with Alugon is part of the reason, but only part. Eglantine paused. *There's another reason, a more important one.*

Oh? Julie prompted.

I know Alugon doesn't like it when you call me Eggy, but every time you do, I feel more of the love that saved me, Eglantine whispered. *I wanted that love to be part of the name I gave myself.*

Aw, Eglantine. Julie pressed her forehead to the shell. *I love it. I think it's perfect.*

On the other side of the shell, the unborn dragon leaned closer to Julie, and for a few moments, there was no sound except for the dull thud of Eglantine's heart.

Eglantine was the first to move. *Hey, we can't sit here like this all day. You're breaking me out of the Nest, remember?*

Oh, yeah. Julie sat up. *Were you serious about that?*

Absolutely! Eglantine announced. *I'm the Great Lady-in-Waiting of the Deep, aren't I? Well, here's my first royal decree.* She laughed. *Get me out of here!*

<hr>

Julie paced around the edge of the nursery chamber, holding Hat in both hands. It was hard to tell since he didn't have eyes, but it felt like he was avoiding her gaze.

Is this really the time to make rash decisions? Hat grumbled. *She's only just learned to speak.*

Don't try that with me, Hat. Julie's eyes narrowed. *I've spent the past eight months researching dragon development in my free time. I know that the language center of her brain has developed to a point where she can talk. She doesn't need to learn how, and she knows what she's saying. She just needed to grow into the ability.*

I'm just saying that I'm not sure that kidnapping *is the solution to this problem,* Hat hissed.

Can you sense Silversqueaks nearby? Julie demanded, ignoring his protests.

There was no sign of the tiny household dragons who maintained the fortress known as the Nest, but Julie knew from experience that they could pop out of nowhere at any minute.

No, Hat muttered.

Good. We don't need them finding out what we're up to.

Which is exactly why you shouldn't be doing this! Hat retorted. *This could be construed as an act of war, Julie. You could cause conflict between the Deep and Avalon. I'm talking Pompeii here!*

Bullshit. You're being a drama queen. Julie scoffed. *Eglantine made her wishes clear, so it's not kidnapping. I'm following the royal decree of the Great Lady-in-Waiting of the Dragons. I'm just a major in the PMA. How could I refuse to follow her orders?*

There was a long, furious pause, then, *That might actually hold up in court. But still, Julie, even if there are no military or legal repercussions, don't you know what this could do to your relationship with Lady Ennowen?*

What relationship? Julie snapped. *I'm just a pawn in her stupid political game, which has probably already cost thousands of Avalonian lives and will cost thousands more. Now, are you going to put me in touch with the brownies, or do I need to figure out how to do it myself?*

Hat's golden insignias twitched, and his brim drooped. *Fine,* he mumbled. *But for the record, I still think that this is one of the stupidest things you've ever done, which is saying something.*

Julie pulled him onto her head. *Eh, debatable.*

Hat grumbled, but he hummed as he worked. A few moments later, a new voice spoke into Julie's ear. *Hello? Sergeant Droppel-*

heimer? The voice was high-pitched and had a lilting Welsh accent.

Hey, Sally. It's me again, Julie announced.

Oh, hey, Julie! Normally you send an email instead of calling via telechip. What's up? Sally asked.

Julie hesitated. *I need to ask a favor.*

Sure, sure. Taco shells? Pizza bases? Meggie's got a special on Sylthana fish and chips right now.

It's not food-related this time, Julie admitted.

Hat snickered.

Actually, it's illegal, Julie added. *You might get into a shitload of trouble for doing it.*

Sally chuckled. *Sign me up. What do you need?*

Are you sure? Julie asked. *You don't even know what it is yet.*

Of course I'm sure. You changed our lives. Besides, we've been spoiling for a bit of trouble lately. It's been pretty quiet around the Avalon HQ, Sally confessed.

Julie took a deep breath. *Okay. I need you to move a dragon's egg.* She paused. *The heir to the throne of the Deep's egg, to be exact.*

Cool. Where to? Sally asked.

You're not even fazed? Julie wondered.

Sally chuckled. *Girl, I've seen crazier shit than this. So, where are we going?*

Uh... Julie stopped.

Thought this through, have you? Hat mocked.

Before Julie could think of a witty retort, the air crackled and fizzed a few feet away, then shimmered like a mirage. A round magic portal the size of a hula hoop appeared in mid-air, and a hairless cat jumped out of it. The portal closed.

Julie cleared her throat. *I'll get back to you on that, Sally.*

No worries. We'll make our preparations in the meantime. See you soon. Sally ended the telechip call.

"Good morning, Julie," the Sphynx purred. He strolled over to her and arched his bare back against her knees.

"What are you doing here, Horusiris?" Julie asked.

Horusiris sat down in the moss at her feet and curled his tail around his paws. "Oh, I had a feeling there were shenanigans afoot." He chuckled. "You know there's nothing I like more than a good shenanigan."

Do not *tell him,* Hat snapped. *Do you hear me? Don't tell that conniving feline what we're about to—*

"We're kidnapping Eglantine, the dragon heir." Julie gestured at the egg. "At her command, so I'm not sure it's kidnapping."

"It isn't." Horusiris blinked slowly and luxuriously. "It's following orders. Why, may I ask, has she decided she wants to be moved?"

Because "she" is tired of everyone else calling her shots, Eglantine interjected, *and "she" is done with being stuck down here when "she" would like to be with Julie and make a difference in the surface world.*

Horusiris gazed at the egg. "My, my. *She* is quite opinionated." He got up and stretched, flicking up his naked tail. "You could bring her to our temple if you like. It would serve quite well as a temporary nest, and given that it's in a pocket dimension, it exists beyond all jurisdictions. We'll open a portal for some moonlight."

Relief washed through Julie like warm water. "That would be great, Horusiris. Thanks."

I'm going to New York City? Eglantine let out a squeal of excitement. *I can't wait!*

What are you doing? Hat shrieked. *Aren't you going to question his motivations?*

Does it look like I have time for that? Julie demanded.

That doesn't matter! Hat spluttered. *What's in it for those pesky felines?*

Hat, I love you, but shut up, Julie ordered.

"Very well." Horusiris yawned and glanced casually at a spot in the air beside him. A new portal opened. "I'll tell Cleo and Ranubis to be ready for your arrival." He jumped through the portal and vanished.

Julie walked over to the egg and rested a hand on the shell. "Looks like we're going to the human world, Eggles."

Excitement thrilled through Eglantine's mind. *I can't wait!* She paused. *Julie, can you get a few things from the Nest for me? There are some of my mom's things in there. I've seen them in your thoughts and in Mom and Grandma's memories. I would like to take them with us.*

Of course I can, moondrop. I need to get my stuff, too. Julie cracked her knuckles. *The Silversqueaks can't see any of this.*

Eglantine giggled. *Oooh, this is so much fun!*

Ten minutes later, Julie was pressing her back against the floral wallpaper in the hallway upstairs, squashed as flat as possible behind a grandfather clock. She was starting to doubt Eglantine's definition of "fun." There was a soft buzzing of tiny wings as six diminutive dragons flew past, carrying a huge laundry basket between them. Julie let out a breath as they disappeared around a bend in the hall.

I told you this was a bad idea, Hat grumbled.

Eglantine can't take another day here, Julie retorted. *Honestly, neither can I.*

But— Hat began.

I only have two hours left before the brownies get here. Julie cut him off. *I don't have time to keep arguing with you.*

She tiptoed into the large room filled with random knickknacks. *Is this where it was, Eggy?*

Yes! Eglantine confirmed. *I think it's against the wall on your right.*

Julie glanced at a huge glass case containing a pair of leather-like pants. *Please tell me that it's not the Death Underpants.*

Oh, no. Eglantine laughed. *There, on that shelf next to the case.*

Julie glanced around, then padded up to it. The shelf

contained a tiny jade vase, a china shepherdess whose dress was chipped, and a gold brooch in the shape of a rampant dragon.

That, Eggy murmured. *That was my mom's.*

Julie lifted it gently. It was heavy in her palm, and the dragon had a tiny ruby for an eye. She told herself this wasn't stealing since the tiny dragon technically belonged to Eglantine.

Thank you, Eglantine whispered.

Julie slipped the brooch into her pocket. *No problem. Now to sneak into my room and grab my stuff.*

Eglantine giggled. *Don't let the Silversqueaks catch you!*

I know, Eggy. Julie slipped into the dumbwaiter and shut its doors carefully behind her. *I know.*

They'd snitch to Lady Ennowen. If they did, there was no telling what the Great Lady of the Deep might do.

The dumbwaiter took Julie up to the next floor, where her bedroom was. She opened the doors a tiny crack and peered through it.

Really? she growled inwardly. *Today just* had *to be the day the Squeaks polish this floor's chandeliers.*

The crystal chandelier hanging from the stone ceiling was swarming with tiny dragons, wielding cloths and feather dusters in their miniature paws. Julie watched as the nearest one fluttered over one of the crystals and buffed it with a cloth no bigger than a sugar cube. He paused to peer at the crystal, huffed a small cloud of steam onto it, and then polished some more.

See? It's a sign. They've been everywhere you need to be. Time to give up on this madcap idea of yours, Hat grumbled.

Hat, cut it out. Julie looked up and down the hallway. Her room was two doors down to her right. There were more elegant oak doors to her left. One stood ajar, and Julie could just see the edge of the bed, its white sheets enticingly visible.

No, no, no, no! Hat squawked. *That's Egyptian cotton with a fifteen-hundred-thread count! You can't—*

Julie focused. The corner of the sheet burst into flames.

The Silversqueaks panicked. Their feather dusters and soft cloths tumbled to the floor as they swooped toward the room, shouting for water.

Julie slipped out of the dumbwaiter and scampered into her sumptuous bedchamber. She hauled her suitcase out from under the bed and crammed everything inside willy-nilly.

Where's a telekinetic boyfriend when you need one? she spluttered.

I miss him too, Hat muttered. *Maybe he'd talk some sense into your empty head.*

Julie stuffed her last two coats into the case, hangers and all, and sat on it to zip it shut. She hefted it and peered into the hallway again. The Silversqueaks were still occupied.

"You know that isn't going to fit in the dumbwaiter, right?" Hat enquired unhelpfully.

"Shut *up!*" Julie hissed.

She hoisted the suitcase onto her shoulder and opened her wings to lift her boots a foot off the ground. Buzzing as quietly as she could, she flew to the nearest staircase and swooped down to the lobby. In a few seconds, she scampered into the nursery chamber, panting and hauling her suitcase after her.

There you are! A quick pulse of moonlight ran through Eglantine. *I was wondering what was taking so long.*

Eggy! Julie complained. *I'm trying!*

A portal crackled in mid-air a few feet away, and three short rosy-cheeked paranormals wearing red caps tumbled out of it.

"Fiona, Lewis, Sally." Julie's shoulders sagged with relief. "Hi!"

Sally was the ringleader, grinning from under straw-colored bangs. "So this is the egg, huh?"

"This is Eglantine." Julie patted her shell.

"She's a beauty," Sally observed.

Lewis eyed her with some trepidation. "She's got to weigh two tons."

Three, Eglantine told them proudly.

Lewis' eyes widened. "Are we going to get her through the portal, girls?"

"Of course we will!" Fiona scoffed. "We've moved bigger things."

"Yeah, with a *team* of brownies," Lewis muttered.

Sally was already at work, waving one hand in a circle so that a portal sputtered in the air in front of her. "The Sphynx lair, you said, Julie?"

"That's right," Julie agreed.

"Sally? Are you listening?" Lewis pestered. "I don't think it's going to fit."

"We'll make it fit," Fiona retorted.

There was a sudden chorus of squeaking from deeper in the fortress. Julie glanced at the purple moss curtain separating the nursery chamber from the humanoid parts of the Nest, and her toes curled in her boots.

"Uh, guys?" She turned to the brownies. "We kind of need to hurry."

"You heard the fae," Sally barked. "Help me with this portal!"

The other two brownies joined her, each grabbing one side of the portal. They pulled, the aether flexing between them like elastic. Sally's face contorted with concentration, and Julie heard more squeaking as the portal stretched wide enough to admit the egg.

"Lewis!" Sally grunted, grabbing the portal just below Lewis' hands. "Get the TMDs!"

"The whats?" Julie squawked.

Leaving Sally and Fiona to keep widening the portal, Lewis dove for the duffle bag they'd brought with them and extracted three small silver disks with glowing blue runes. "Telekinetic movement devices," he explained and slapped one onto Eglantine's shell near the pointy end.

Hey! Eggy protested.

"Don't hurt her!" Julie squawked.

Lewis rolled his eyes. "It won't hurt her." He slapped on the other two. "It'll make her levitate." He plucked a touchpad remote from his pocket and rolled his finger over it. With a creak, Eglantine rose two feet into the air.

I'm flying! she exclaimed.

"Come on!" Sally exclaimed. "We can't hold it forever."

They'd stretched the portal wide enough to admit the egg. Lewis piloted her to it, the TMDs pulsing, and Eglantine's pointy end disappeared.

"Keep it open, girls!" he barked.

"What do you think we're doing?" Fiona protested.

Oh, balls! Hat squawked. *We've been busted by the squeaks!*

The purple moss curtain parted, and a small cloud of irate silver dragons burst into the nursery chamber, blowing steam and squeaking furiously.

"Get her through!" Julie yelled, grabbing her suitcase.

"I'm trying!" Lewis spluttered.

Eglantine wasn't moving. The widest part of the egg was jammed in the portal, and Sally and Fiona spluttered and pulled, but their faces were purple with exertion, and Eggy wasn't going anywhere.

The Silversqueaks spotted Julie and lunged toward her in a silver arrow of charging dragons.

"Go!" Julie yelled. She flung herself against Eglantine, and the massive egg shot through the portal with a loud pop. Lewis, Sally, and Fiona tumbled after her, and as the portal began to deflate, Julie jumped through. She yanked the suitcase after her. The first Silversqueak had almost reached the portal, but it was shrinking too fast. He'd never make it.

Julie just had enough time to give them a cheeky finger wave before the portal snapped shut.

CHAPTER THREE

The Sphynxes discovered that Eglantine could warm her shell at will. All three of them were curled up in the downy nest they'd built in the corner of their lair, their backs pressed against the giant egg, purring delightedly. A portal swirled directly above Eglantine, pouring full moonlight onto her.

Julie rested a hand on the egg's pointed end. *Looks like you'll be okay here until I get back.*

I'm more than okay, Eglantine told her happily. *It's so good to be somewhere new. Thank you, Julie.*

Julie kissed the shell. *See you soon. I've got to get back to Avalon HQ and tell Kaplan what happened before he catches wind of it from someone else.*

Good luck. Eglantine paused. *Julie, I really hope this isn't going to cause trouble for you. Is it?*

Nothing I can't handle, moondrop. Julie gave the egg a last pat and turned to Horusiris. "Are you too comfortable to open a portal for me, or…"

Horusiris yawned, showing off his sharp white teeth. "That can be arranged." He blinked, and a portal opened right next to Julie. She nearly stepped through it before she realized that there was a gigantic pool of lava at her feet. As she watched, something huge and scaly rose from the lava and opened a giant maw—

"Close it!" she squawked, jumping back.

The portal winked out of existence.

"You said *a portal,*" Horusiris purred. "You didn't say where it should lead."

Julie glared at him. "Avalon HQ. *Please.*"

"Of course." Horusiris took his time stretching before he opened a second portal. Julie peered through it and only stepped through when she recognized the stone courtyard that was the inner ward of Avalon HQ.

The portal closed behind her before she could thank him. Julie took a moment to breathe deeply and look around the walls of the stone fortress.

It's so good to be outside in fresh air and sunlight again, she muttered.

Thank goodness, Hat added. *You're so pale now that you're nearly transparent.*

Thanks, Hat. Nice of you to say. Julie rolled her eyes and strode to the front doors. She'd texted Malcolm Nox earlier and found out that Captain Kaplan was working with her boss, First Sergeant Cadmeus Droppelheimer, at Avalon HQ this week. If she went to Droppelheimer's office, she could tell them her side of the story before Lady Ennowen had a chance to do anything grand-smotherly.

She stepped through the open doors and almost crashed headfirst into a seven-foot-tall humanoid with craggy features, burning amber eyes, and enormous bushy eyebrows.

"Meadows!" Captain Jack Kaplan snapped.

Julie ripped off a smart salute. "Sir!"

Kaplan's brow furrowed as he glared at her. "I'm hearing some *very* interesting reports about you."

Julie's toes curled inside her boots, and she was suddenly and painfully conscious of the copper-inlaid steel armor she wore underneath her dragonscale robes. Her alter ego had become an urban legend in the refugee camp at the edge of Avalon, and she'd always known it was only a matter of time before Kaplan found out who the knight was.

"Sir." She swallowed hard. "I can explain."

Kaplan folded his massive arms, biceps flexing like boulders under his uniform. "Please, Meadows. Enlighten me," he growled.

Julie squared her shoulders. "I was only doing what I believed to be the right thing, sir. It didn't seem like anyone else was going to do it since everyone was so occupied with the war."

Kaplan raised a bushy eyebrow. "So you took it upon yourself to go off on your own, with no support, no backup, and no authorization?"

Julie rubbed the back of her neck. "Okay, I've done smarter things," she admitted, "but I couldn't just stand by and watch, sir. I needed to act."

"Do you understand the repercussions this could have, Meadows?" Kaplan snapped. "Do you understand how you've compromised paranormal relations at a *very* tenuous time for your species?"

Julie cringed. "Sir, I just wanted to help. Those paras—"

She stopped short when a familiar figure, wrapped in blue, gold, and purple robes of shining dragonscale, strode through the busy lobby and stopped beside Kaplan.

"Wait. Alugon?" Julie stared at him. "What are you doing here?"

"What do you think he's doing here?" Kaplan snarled. "Did you think Lady Ennowen would allow her heir to be kidnapped without making any effort to get her back?"

"Is *that* what this is about?" Julie blurted.

Kaplan's eyes narrowed, boring into her. "Have you committed any other acts of war of late, Meadows?"

Julie's toes tried to retreat into her ankles. *Shit. I nearly gave myself away.* "Um, not that I'm aware of, sir."

Kaplan sighed and rubbed a hand over his face.

"How did Lady Ennowen find out where Eggy was so quickly?" Julie asked, turning to the dragon.

Alugon sighed. "I *wish* you wouldn't call her that."

Julie kept her smirk in the privacy of her mind. *Oh, wait 'til you find out!*

"There were not many guesses as to where you took her, young one," Alugon went on. "The Silversqueaks immediately alerted Lady Ennowen as to what had happened. She sent me to bring the heir back to the Deep."

Julie clenched her hands into fists. "You called this an act of war, Captain." She glared at Kaplan. "But it wasn't. I removed the dragon heir at her decree. She asked me to bring her out of the Deep."

Alugon's eyes widened. "She spoke to you?"

"I know there will be consequences." Smoke rose between Julie's fingers. "But I stand by what I did." Her eyes met Alugon's. "If you want to take her back to the Deep, you're going to have to go through me."

Kaplan's lip curled in a snarl. Julie's stomach dropped through her boots. If she had to fight Kaplan to keep Eglantine safe, she would, but the thought made her sick.

"That's what I told Lady Ennowen," Kaplan growled. "She has no right to imprison her granddaughter."

Julie blinked, lowering her hands. The smoke vanished. "What?"

"You're batshit-crazy, Meadows, but you usually have a good reason for your shenanigans," Kaplan grumbled.

Alugon smiled. "What the good captain is trying to say is that he backed you fully when Lady Ennowen contacted him via the scrying screen. He told her that whatever your reasons were, they would be valid and you had his full support."

Julie's jaw dropped. She gaped at Kaplan, who looked away and shuffled his gigantic feet. "You're backing me on this, sir?"

"You've been a good bet so far, Meadows," Kaplan growled.

Julie stared at him. "Sir, that's—"

"Don't make a scene, or I'll change my mind and feed you to the dragons," Kaplan snarled.

Julie grinned at him. *Softie.* She turned to Alugon. "I'm sorry I put you in this position, Al."

"I wish you wouldn't call *me* that," Alugon muttered.

"I know you only have Eggy's best interests at heart, but she's safe and sound." Julie folded her arms. "But I meant what I said. I'm not giving her back. She doesn't want to go."

Alugon spread his hands. "That is why I am not here to take her back, Julie of the Meadows. You did the right thing to bring the unborn heir out of the Deep."

Julie blinked at him. "I did?"

"You did. Lady Ennowen has disappointed all of us, and her influence on the unborn heir is no longer in the best interests of dragonkind." Alugon hesitated. "That is why I have renounced the Deep and will return only on the condition that Lady Ennowen abdicates when the heir hatches."

The dragon turned his face away as he spoke. Julie saw his shoulders droop as he spoke. She stepped forward and put a hand on his arm, feeling his silken strength.

"I'm sorry, Al," Julie murmured. "I know how loyal you've always been to the royal family and that you've been the Augur for centuries. This can't have been easy for you."

"Lady Ennowen and I played in the Royal Gardens when we were mere dragonlings." He let out a breath and hung his head. "I never thought it would come to this, and I tried to stop it, but this is how it is."

Julie tilted her head. "I thought you would be in favor of the conclave's outcome. I know you don't want to get pulled into this fight."

Alugon shook his head. "It is not the outcome that brought me to this decision, young one, but the methods the Great Lady used to achieve it. Dragonkind was leaning toward assisting Avalon. Lady Ennowen forced the vote by barter and intrigue." He spat the words. "Dragons do not do such things. Lady Ennowen has dishonored us all with her actions."

"I'm sorry." Julie lowered her hand. "It can't be easy for you."

"It is not easy, but it *is* right, and that is what matters." Alugon managed a dim smile. "All of this could have been avoided had Lady Ennowen allowed you to present your idea to the dragons at the conclave instead of rejecting it out of hand the way she did."

"You thought it was a good one?" Julie raised her eyebrows.

Alugon met her eyes and gave her a tiny smile. "Julie of the Meadows, I thought it was a brilliant one. It could have united all of dragonkind."

Julie blushed. "Aw, shucks. I wish I could've recorded that, Al."

Alugon sighed. "I wish you wouldn't... Never mind."

Julie laughed. "Where will you stay? I mean, do you have somewhere to go now that you can't go back to the Deep?"

Alugon smiled faintly. "Have no concerns, young one. We will be fine living humanoid lives in Avalon Town for a little while."

"Wait, *we?*" Julie frowned.

"Alugon's not alone in renouncing the Deep," Kaplan chipped in. "He arrived a few minutes before you did with a whole group of dragons."

Julie's jaw dropped. "Who?"

"Some you know, some you do not," Alugon told her. "You will be pleased to note that Methunoch, Minatarva, and Aladabil are among them, as well as Livius and Axl."

"Those two idiots?" Julie grinned. "I'm glad they're making good choices for once."

A tiny cloud of steam erupted from within Alugon's robes. Alugon jumped, and a Silversqueak burst from the wrinkles of his robes.

"Traitor! Traitor!" the tiny dragon squeaked. "It's just as the

Great Lady feared! You traitor!" He jabbed a claw the size of a fishhook in Alugon's direction.

The larger dragon gazed at him calmly. "I wondered how long it would take you to make your presence known."

"You knew he was there?" Kaplan growled.

Alugon shrugged. "I am a dragon, Captain. Would you be unaware of a creature hidden in your clothing?"

"Lady Ennowen will be told of your treachery!" the Silversqueak railed. "You will be punished!" He wheeled around, wings buzzing, and huffed a tiny cloud of steam at Julie. "As for *you*, the Great Lady will see you in court!"

"Court?" Julie asked.

"Yes," the tiny dragon hissed. "She fully expected your foolhardy refusal, and she filed for full custody of the unborn heir even before this traitor left."

The little dragon whirled and spat. Steaming droplets of boiling saliva slapped Alugon's face, and he stepped back with a faint cry, raising a hand to his eyes.

"Al!" Julie grabbed his arm. "Are you okay?"

Alugon straightened slowly, wiping the boiling drool out of his reddened eyes. "I'm quite all right, young one," he murmured. "It is lucky that dragons retain our heatproof properties even in human form."

"Where's that little asshole?" Julie snapped.

"Gone." Kaplan snarled and shifted into a Bengal tiger. "But I'll catch him."

Alugon held out a hand. "No, Captain. Let him go. Let him tell the Great Lady what he has heard." His mouth turned down at the corners. "I only hope that my words will make her reconsider her actions of late."

Julie hoped so too, but remembering the fierce glitter in Lady Ennowen's eyes as the final votes were cast, she doubted it.

* * *

Julie almost skipped through the courtroom doors, over which hung an Eternity Throne banner. Her wings fluttered as she paused at the top of the steps and sucked in the fresh fall air.

The werehorse beside her chuckled, a whinnying sound. "Feels good, doesn't it?"

"Really good," Julie admitted. "Thanks, Aiden. We couldn't have won full custody of the unborn heir without you."

Aiden Harrington, the attorney assigned to Julie, had kindly brown eyes and high cheekbones like those of his father, the Eternity Throne's royal attorney. He smiled. "It wasn't a difficult case, Major Meadows. Our opponent was intimidating, but you know full well that you did the right thing, and draconic law acknowledges an unhatched dragon's right to autonomy."

"Eggy's happy." Julie grimaced. "I just wish it didn't have to come to this. Lady Ennowen was pretty pissed. I'm not sure pissing off the queen of all dragons was a good move."

"Luckily for you, you have the princess of all dragons on your side." Aiden winked. "I'll see you again, I'm sure."

"With my history of getting into trouble, yeah, probably." Julie laughed. "I'd ask if you want to join us for dinner, but my boyfriend is long overdue for a one-on-one date tonight."

"Go and celebrate." Aiden tossed his black mane. "Goodbye, Major Meadows. It's been a pleasure." He trotted back into the courthouse.

Julie stretched her stiff shoulders, sore from another long day in the courtroom, then gazed at First Street in Avalon Town. She felt she could walk it freely for the first time in weeks.

"Yeah, baby!" she whooped and snatched Hat off her head.

Noooooooooo! Hat protested, but it was too late. Julie flung him into the air, and he flew in a graceful parabola before plopping back into her hands.

Sorry. Julie laughed as she tugged him back onto her head. *Couldn't resist.*

It did *make a good photo op,* Hat admitted grudgingly.

Photo op? Julie started down the steps and noticed the reporters for the first time. LEOs, mostly werewolves, kept the path to Julie's car clear, but cameras snapped and flashes popped around her as she hurried to the parking space in front of the court building.

What are they all doing here? Julie fished her keys out of the pocket of her dress uniform overcoat.

What do you think? Politically, this is one of the most important trials since Qbiit's. Like it or not, you've made history, Hat told her.

Julie strode to the muscle car, keeping her head down. The 1971 Mustang Mach 1 had magical upgrades, and she honked her horn cheerfully as Julie approached.

"Keep it down, Genevieve," Julie whispered, petting the Mustang's roof before she unlocked the driver's door. "We don't need to draw any *more* attention to ourselves."

Should have thought of that before you kidnapped Eglantine, Hat grumbled.

Julie threw herself into the leather bucket seat and slammed the door closed. *The court officially decided that it's not kidnapping, so cut that out,* Julie snapped. *I didn't expect all this attention. I just wanted Eggy to be safe and free. So far, she seems to be enjoying the Sphynxes.*

I did tell you about unforeseen consequences. This is one of them, Hat argued.

Julie sighed as she started the engine and heard the V8 Cobra-jet, altered to run on either magic or gas, roar to life. *Well, it's one that I don't have to think about for a little while,* she retorted. *I'm going to a celebration dinner with my boyfriend, and we're not going to think about courts or dragons or politics or wars this evening, okay?*

Don't be cheeky with me, Hat protested. *I'm not the one who got you into this. That was all you.*

Whatever, old man, Julie teased.

She pulled him off and set him on his favorite spot on the dashboard. Genevieve roared down First Street, leaving the reporters far behind. Julie felt the knots in her shoulders relax. She leaned back in her seat and flexed her fingers on the steering wheel, thinking she should call her mom when she got to Meggie's Bistro. Rosa didn't know dragons existed, but Julie had caved and told her she was involved in a court case, and she knew Rosa had been worrying.

The dials on Genevieve's radio twitched of their own accord, and the volume knob twisted. Soothing pipes echoed through the car from the new Fernwood FM radio station.

"Thanks, Gennie." Julie sighed as she eased the Mustang to a halt at a red light. "A little relaxing music is just what I need right—"

A griffin swooped out of the sky, its massive wing shadow eclipsing Genevieve. Chainmail flashed as it descended in front of the car, backwinging with a force that made wind hiss through the open windows, and landed hind-legs-first on the asphalt. A second griffin joined it, and they paced up to Genevieve with leonine grace.

Julie groaned and allowed her head to thump against the seat. "What is it *now*?"

The first griffin raised a talon and tapped the window. Julie scanned his face, hoping it was Shadowsong, the Eternal Guard corporal she'd worked with before. Then a stab of grief ran through her. Shadowsong had died in an assassination attempt on the queen's life last year.

She rolled down the window laboriously. "License and registration?" she quipped.

The griffin blinked amber eyes at her. "What?"

"It's a human world joke." Julie waved a hand. "Was I speeding?"

"Speeding? We're not law enforcement. We don't care," the griffin purred. "But you do have to come with us."

"Have to?" Julie raised an eyebrow. "Says who?"

The griffin studied her expressionlessly. "The Eternity Queen

Esmerelda the Dragonchosen, Ruler of Avalon, Sole Monarch of the Eternal Throne."

"Oh, her? I guess I can come," Julie snarked.

Julie, this is not the time, Hat hissed.

Julie scanned the griffin's face. "Is everything okay?"

"I am not at liberty to divulge more information," the griffin told her. "Follow me, if you please."

The griffin turned and leaped into the air, then brought her wings down. Her companion followed, clawing into the sky, feathered tail swishing behind her.

The light turned green. Julie punched it, pulling back and up on the steering wheel, and as Genevieve rushed toward a horse and cart lumbering down the street in front of her, the Mustang's front wheels left the ground. Her engine roared and she soared into the air, her front wheels missing the back of the cart by inches.

CHAPTER FOUR

Taylor Woodskin's belly felt like it was filled with Silversqueaks. He paced up and down, sweat cooling on his palms as aromatic fragrances filled the little kitchen at the back of Meggie's Bistro. The kitchen was as eclectically decorated as the front of the restaurant: the backsplash was a blue-and-yellow splatter of modern art, the countertops were classic polished wood, and the enamel containers on the shelves labeled FLOUR, SUGAR, STARDUST, and POWDERED MOONSTONE had chicken silhouettes painted on them.

Taylor reached the other side of the kitchen, turned on his heel, and paced back again.

"If you *must* hover in here, Your Highness, could you stop pacing, please?" the weremouse at the stove enquired in her high-pitched voice. "It makes it difficult to concentrate."

"Sorry." Taylor fell into a chair at the large oak kitchen table. "I just…tonight just has to go right, Meggie."

"It will go right in the most important ways, dear." The little old lady turned to him, smiling. "I've seen you two together. You have nothing to worry about."

"I hope not." Taylor swallowed hard.

"Look at the time! It's nearly a quarter to seven. I'll have the first dish ready in fifteen minutes, just as we planned." Meggie patted his hand. "You go and wait for your lovely lady, pet."

"Thanks, Meggie. You're the best." Taylor got to his feet. "You won't forget about the Belgian waffles, right?"

"I won't forget," Meggie promised. "Don't you worry. I practiced them a hundred times after you took me to that food truck in New York City." She chuckled. "What a day that was!"

"Thanks, Meggie." Taylor left the kitchen and sat down at their usual spot, the big wrought-iron table near the window, then stared out at the moonlit garden with its tumult of flowers and tendrils of jasmine hanging down on the other side of the glass.

The first time he and Julie had eaten at Meggie's, his older sister Ilsa and best friend Iris had been with them. Masked assassins had broken into the restaurant and grabbed Taylor and Ilsa to kidnap them. Taylor would never forget the burning rage in Julie's eyes as she fired at the kidnappers. She hadn't gotten her powers yet, but she'd fought tooth and nail to get him and Ilsa back.

His stomach flip-flopped. He *had* to get tonight right.

He glanced up at one of the collection of clocks on the far wall. It had little mice in different poses instead of numbers. The hour hand was a few ticks from a ballerina mouse in mid-pirouette. He tried to figure out how he was going to get through dinner without throwing up.

Meggie bustled out at seven o'clock sharp, bearing a tray containing two goblets of mead imported at great expense from the war-torn Fernwood. Taylor took comfort in the thought that his considerable expenditure on the bottle would support the economy there. They'd drunk much Fernwood mead at Beltane the night they'd recruited the brownies and the faeries. They hadn't been dating at that point, but it was one of his favorite memories.

"There you are, dear." Meggie set the goblets on the table. "She'll be here any second. You'll see."

Taylor glanced at the clock. It was two minutes past seven. "I hope so."

The minute hand ticked onward. The hour hand left the ballerina mouse and headed slowly toward the gymnast mouse doing a handstand.

At five past seven, Taylor's phone rang. He jumped so hard that he nearly knocked his goblet over as he grabbed his phone. The caller ID was Badass Babe.

"Hey, love!" Taylor squeaked into the phone.

"Hey, T." Julie sighed.

Taylor's heart dropped. "Is everything okay?"

There was a long pause. Taylor heard Genevieve's engine rumbling in the background. Julie had called him as she left the courtroom to let him know the outcome of the trial, and Taylor's stomach twisted with nervousness. Had Lady Ennowen somehow taken revenge?

"I don't know," Julie admitted. "I was driving to meet you..."

Taylor stared glumly at the expensive Fernwood mead.

"And two Eternal Guard griffins appeared and told me the queen requested my presence," Julie finished. "I'm on my way to the Eternal Palace now. I'm really sorry to stand you up, babe."

Taylor let out a long breath, crushed with disappointment. "It's okay."

"You sound upset." Julie sighed again. "I'm sorry, T. I really don't have a choice."

"No, don't be sorry. I completely understand, babe. When the queen wants you, you can't say no, right?" Taylor managed a hollow laugh.

"Yeah. I'll make it up to you, okay?" Julie promised.

"Okay." Taylor forced his tone to be cheerful. "Dinner tomorrow, maybe."

"Yeah, let's see what the queen says. As soon as I can. I promise," Julie added fiercely.

Taylor pressed the phone to his cheek, wishing he could wrap his arms around her. "It's okay, babe. You do what you have to do. You know I'm behind you every step of the way."

"I know, and I love that." Julie's voice softened. "I love you."

"Love you, too," Taylor murmured.

He disconnected the call and set the phone on the table, then leaned back and let out a long sigh.

Meggie appeared at his elbow. "Is everything okay?"

"She's not coming, Meggie." Taylor sighed. "Urgent business at the Eternal Palace."

"The palace! Oh my!" Meggie squeaked, her eyes shining behind her round glasses. "How magnificent!"

Taylor smiled. "Yeah, she's pretty magnificent. Don't worry; I'll pay for the full dinner, of course."

"Oh, let's see how we do, Your Highness. There are some things I can sell tomorrow. I'll bring out the first course for you now," Meggie told him.

Taylor shook his head. "It's okay, Meggie. I've lost my appetite."

"You have to eat something, lamb." Meggie patted his shoulder. "How about that Belgian waffle? You need it back anyway."

"Yeah, okay. Thanks." Taylor mustered another small smile.

Meggie disappeared into the kitchen, returning a few moments later with the most majestic Belgian waffle Taylor had ever seen. It was topped with a wild concoction of chocolate sauce, whipped cream, sprinkles, syrup, and wafers, and it reminded him of the waffles they'd eaten from a food cart in Brooklyn on their first recruitment attempts. He'd never eaten anything from a food cart before then.

The memory made him smile. He picked up a spoon and managed to take a few bites of the whipped cream, then gave up on eating and pushed all the toppings aside with his spoon until he spotted it glinting at the bottom. After setting down his spoon, he picked the ring out of the whipped cream and carefully cleaned it with his napkin.

Then he held it up to the light and turned it this way and that, admiring the perfect glint in the heart of the milky moonstone. It had been cut and polished by the Gem Dwarves, the only jewelers in the world who could cut a gemstone into the shape of a dragon only slightly bigger than the head of a pin, brilliantly detailed down to the pattern of its scales.

Taylor closed his hand over the ring and let out a sigh. He tucked it back into the little blue velvet box he'd been carrying in his jacket pocket over his heart for the past month.

"This was a lame idea anyway," he muttered. He picked up the spoon and took a mouthful of syrupy whipped cream. It didn't help, but he kept eating anyway.

He was halfway through the waffle when the iron grille covering the entrance to Meggie's Bistro creaked open. "Taylor! I didn't think I'd see you here."

Taylor dabbed his mouth with his napkin. "Oh, hi, Malcolm."

The slim young vampire, his hair smoothed into an impeccable faux hawk as usual, crossed the room toward Taylor. There were dark circles under his eyes, but his smile was bright.

"How are you holding up?" Taylor asked, pushing his half-full plate aside.

Malcolm shrugged. "Okay, I guess. It's so hard." He looked away. "Sometimes it feels like she'll never come back to us, not really."

Taylor sighed. "I'm sorry. It must be difficult having your aunt back but her health being so poor. Especially since there have been no new leads, and there's still no justice for what they did to her, Mazi, and Sylvie."

"It's like the Mordred cult has gone to ground. They haven't been active of late. Nobody's spotted the drow for months."

Malcolm threw up his hands. "I'm not saying I liked active conflict, but this limbo is worse."

"I hear you. It's like they're planning something." Taylor grimaced. "I'm sorry."

Meggie appeared with a paper bag that smelled promisingly of fish and chips. "Your order, Your Highness," she squeaked and bowed deeply.

"Thanks, Meggie." Malcolm took the bag. "Just grabbing takeout for Cassidy and me," he explained to Taylor. "It's been a rough night with everything that happened in the palace."

Taylor's eyes widened. "What happened in the palace?"

Malcolm raised his eyebrows. "You don't know? I'd have thought your phone would be blowing up with notifications."

"I haven't checked it in the past half-hour," Taylor admitted. It lay face-down on the table where he'd tossed it after Julie's call. He'd muted the apps in an attempt to make sure they would be uninterrupted this evening.

So much for that idea, he thought.

"It's not good, Taylor." Malcolm bit his lip. "There's been another attempt on the Eternity Queen's life."

"What?" Taylor gasped. He clutched the edge of the table, belly lurching with nausea. "An attack?"

"No." Malcolm shook his head. "Her meal was poisoned."

Taylor's fingers relaxed. "Julie was on her way there."

"She's a badass." Malcolm laughed. "I'd be more worried about her opponents even if there *had* been an attack."

"Yeah, I know." Taylor grinned. "But I still worry sometimes. Is the queen okay?"

"She's fine. She didn't ingest the poison, as far as I know." Malcolm raked a hand through his hair carelessly. "I don't have all the details. I just know this was a crappy day, and there's nothing I can do about it except go home to my wife."

"Do that." Taylor smiled. "Give my, uh, undying terror to Cassidy. I think she'd prefer that to my regards."

Malcolm chuckled. "You're not wrong." He dragged himself to his feet and picked up the bag, then shuffled out of the bistro.

Taylor picked up his phone. He longed to call Julie and check if she was okay, but Malcolm was right. His girlfriend *was* a badass.

Text me when you're done.

He got up to pay the bill.

The escort of griffins that surrounded Genevieve took Julie through an opening in the wards that surrounded the Eternal Palace.

From this height, the palace was magnificent now that dusk was rapidly turning into darkness. Its bewildering array of towers, turrets, battlements, and buttresses was pocked by the glow from windows and the brilliant beams of spotlights affixed to every surface. Each courtyard was so well-lit that Julie could make out the details: the manicured shrubbery, the splashing fountains, and the flowerbeds. Even the menagerie was brightly lit. She saw a wyvern curled up in a perfect circle in the corner of his den, nose pressed against his tail like a dog.

He reminded her of Pookie, her late landlady's little dog, and Julie swallowed a lump in her throat.

She pushed her grief aside and landed Genevieve gently in a courtyard at the base of the queen's tower, where three griffins stood guard. Gargoyles on high alert paced the niches set at intervals up the tower. Julie noticed that the queen's stained-glass windows had been replaced with iron bars covered with glowing blue runes.

She stepped out of Genevieve and ducked as a shadow blotted out the nearest floodlight. Flames briefly flared on her hands but winked out when she recognized the humanoid who landed a few feet from her.

"Bee!" Julie grinned. "It's really good to see you, despite the circumstances."

"*Hey*, girlfriend!" Major Bianca Hartshorn crowed. The tall, leggy succubus folded her leathery wings and strode over to Julie, arms wide. Golden curls spilled luxuriously on her shoulders, complementing the gazelle horns that twisted gently from her head.

Julie submitted to a fragrant bear hug.

"I'm guessing you're here for the same reason I am," Julie began.

Bianca stepped back. "Are you here because the queen summoned you out of the blue?"

"Yeah," Julie admitted.

"We're in the same boat, then." Bianca started for the doorway.

Julie followed, jogging to keep up with Bianca's obscenely long legs. "Do you know what's going on?"

"Not a clue," Bianca confessed.

The griffins at the door stepped aside to let Julie and Bianca through. As they climbed the spiral staircase toward Queen Esmerelda's chambers, Julie noticed that every niche in the walls was occupied by a griffin or a gargoyle. All were alert and bristling and stared at Julie and Bianca intently as they passed.

"Something's up," Julie muttered.

Bianca grimaced. "You can say that again." She chuckled and punched Julie in the arm. "I hear you won your court case, by the way. Total power move. Kicked that old lady's ass."

That old lady, Hat reminded them, *is practically the high queen of all dragons.*

"Doesn't mean she was right about Eglantine," Bianca retorted.

They were sweaty and panting when they reached the door to

the queen's chambers. To Julie's surprise, a glawackus was waiting at the door. The huge, furry creature wore matte goggles over her eyes and sat bolt upright at the door, her curly tail wrapped over her back and her round ears pricked. She said nothing but intently sniffed Julie and Bianca before stepping aside to let them pass.

Julie and Bianca exchanged wordless glances. Julie had never seen security so tight around the queen, and judging by the look in Bianca's eyes, neither had she.

They stepped into a large, comfortable bedchamber, its walls inlaid with glimmering crystals of selenite. Arched windows lined one side of the room, overlooking the crenelated wall of the Eternal Palace. Julie missed their pretty stained glass designs. The iron bars made this place feel more like a prison than a bedroom.

"Julie, good evening." Queen Esmerelda lay in the huge canopy bed. "Major Hartshorn."

Julie and Bianca bowed in synchrony.

"Your Majesty." Julie straightened. "You summoned us."

"Indeed I did." Queen Esmerelda summoned a faint smile. The frail Lunar Fae was propped up on a pile of pillows, her velvet covers tucked around her skeletal frame. Julie thought her cheeks were more sunken than the last time she'd seen her.

There was a scrying screen the size of a laptop screen on the ornate nightstand beside the queen's bed. A strikingly beautiful Lunar Fae looked out of the screen, her hazel eyes very serious.

"Morgan Le Fay has been so good as to join us on a scrying call," Queen Esmerelda added.

Morgan gave a little wave. "Hi, ladies."

"Hi, bestie!" Bianca grinned.

Julie's stomach lurched. Morgan looked strained despite her smile. Had something happened to King Arthur, who was deeply asleep under a centuries-old spell?

She turned to the queen. "Your Majesty, what's happened?"

Queen Esmerelda let out a faint chuckle. "Straight to the

point as always, Julie." She sagged against her pillows and let her head tip back, giving Julie a glimpse of the deep lines in her face and the pallor of her cheeks. "When my dinner was brought up to my room this evening, the dear glawackus burst into the room and informed me that it was laced with vampire blood."

Morgan's hands flew to her mouth, and her eyes narrowed.

"Vampire blood?" Bianca arched her elegant eyebrows. "Gross, but why?"

Julie stared, nonplussed.

Queen Esmerelda managed the faintest of smiles. "Major Hartshorn, you must understand that what I am about to tell you is one of the most closely guarded secrets of my species. We have many."

Bianca gave a slight bow. "I'll keep it in the strictest confidence, Your Majesty."

"I know you will. That's why..." The queen paused and flinched, then let out a breath and continued. "That's why I summoned you."

"What is it, Your Majesty?" Julie asked.

Queen Esmerelda opened her eyes. Despite her pallor, they were fiercely bright, her irises shimmering a dozen different colors. "Vampire blood is fatally poisonous to Lunar Fae. Ingesting a single drop means death."

Julie inhaled sharply, and Bianca's wings drooped. On the screen, Morgan was pale.

"Wait." Julie frowned. "This is something only Lunar Fae know, so only a Lunar Fae would have reason to put vampire blood in your food, Your Majesty."

Queen Esmerelda nodded tiredly. "You're correct, Julie. This is evidence that there is a Lunar Fae working against us."

The thought made Julie's knees wobble. She swallowed hard, controlling her breathing to still the tremor in her muscles before it could run into the floor and cause a quake.

"But *who*?" Morgan burst out. "There are so few of us left. Why would someone turn against their own species?"

"There are many reasons, Morgan." The queen sighed deeply. "The question at this moment is not *why* but *who*."

"Maybe they didn't reveal it willingly," Julie pointed out. "A Lunar Fae could have been captured and forced to tell."

Bianca nodded. "Given that we know our enemies are skilled in magic like mind control and geasa, Your Majesty, it's possible that the information could have been extracted against the Lunar Fae's will."

"Good points, but we cannot know for sure." Queen Esmerelda's eyes narrowed. "This is why I summoned the three of you." Her eyes wandered to Hat, still perched on Julie's head, and the corner of her mouth quirked up. "*Four* of you."

Hat stirred uneasily on Julie's head.

"What can we do, Your Majesty?" Bianca asked.

"You can track down the poisoner." Queen Esmerelda raised her chin. "As well as tracing the Lunar Fae involved, whatever their capacity was."

"Why us?" Julie blurted.

Queen Esmerelda's eyes rested on hers. "Because I know I can trust you."

There were two other paras with her, but it felt as though Queen Esmerelda was addressing her alone, and she didn't know how to feel about that.

Bianca broke the awkward silence. "Of course, Your Majesty."

Julie frowned, rubbing the back of her neck as her mind raced.

"Ma'am, you know I can't leave Tintagel," Morgan stated.

Queen Esmerelda nodded. "Of course, but you can still be of great assistance in an investigatory capacity, Morgan."

"Yes, Your Majesty." Morgan's shoulders slumped with relief.

"Do you have any idea where we should start? Any enemies you can think of who are connected to Lunar Fae?" Bianca asked.

Queen Esmerelda shook her head. "There are times when it seems like the entire world is my enemy, Major Hartshorn."

Julie raised her chin. "I have an idea."

Bianca, Queen Esmerelda, and Morgan smiled.

"I think it's going to work, Julie." Bianca spoke quietly as they walked across the courtyard toward Genevieve, surrounded by griffins. "It's a good plan."

"Thanks." Julie grinned. "I think so, too." She pulled out her keys.

Genevieve honked happily and flashed her headlights as they approached.

"There's something I have to do before we can put it into action, though." Julie petted Genevieve's hood, then touched the brim of her cap. "Hat, could you get in touch with Vivienne?"

"Vivienne?" Bianca's lip curled.

"Not your favorite para?" Julie asked.

Bianca shrugged. "I'm not her biggest fan."

That makes two of us, Hat commented. *What on earth do you want to speak to that wrinkled old hag for?*

"You do know that she's one of the sexiest women in Avalon, right?" Julie pointed out.

Hat sniffed. *My question stands.*

I just want to check that she's okay, Hat. Like the queen said, there aren't many of us left. She sighed. *I'm worried Vivienne might be the one who was kidnapped.*

Hat snorted. *Who would kidnap* her?

Julie sighed. *Just make the call.*

Okay, fine, Hat grumbled.

He hummed on Julie's head, and she studied Bianca. The succubus stared at nothing and tapped her manicured red fingernails against each other.

Hat? Julie prompted. *What's going on?*

She's not answering, Hat muttered.

What do you mean? Julie asked. *Are you calling her phone?*

No, I'm calling her telepathically, Hat snapped. *Why would I call her phone?*

Julie raised her eyebrows. *How can you* not *answer a telepathic call?*

Bianca's eyes were wide now. "You have to be unconscious or magically blocked from responding. Or—" She stopped.

Hat added, *You could also simply ignore it.* He didn't sound convinced.

"Yeah, I don't like this." Julie unlocked Genevieve. "I'm going to her house to check on her."

"I'm coming with you." Bianca opened the passenger door.

Julie stared at her over the roof. "I thought you said you didn't like her."

"I'm not her biggest fan." Bianca shrugged. "Doesn't mean I'd leave her in the lurch if she needs help." She grinned. "Or pass up the chance to ride in this baby."

Genevieve flapped her windshield wipers and honked again.

"Okay, Gennie, keep it in your pants." Julie laughed. "Let's go."

When Julie saw wisps of smoke rising from the end of the street, a knot formed in her belly.

"Shit," Bianca muttered.

Julie put her foot down and Genevieve roared down the street, the Victorian lampposts and quiet brick cottages flashing past as they charged toward Vivienne's house.

When they rounded a curve in the road and saw the firetruck, its flashing red-and-blue lights bathing the peaceful neighborhood in chaotic colors, Hat turned ice-cold where his crown pressed against Julie's forehead. Sirens sang, filling the air with their eerie cries as they directed jets of water onto the smoking ruin of Vivienne's cottage.

Julie braked sharply a hundred feet from the firetruck. "What happened here?"

No one in the car had the answer, but the cottage was gone. Only the back wall remained, rebar jutting from the edge of the roof. The rest of the cottage had been reduced to a pile of charred rubble and ash with wisps of smoke still rising from it. Julie spotted a single teacup that had survived the blaze lying in the gutter near the working sirens. It was badly chipped, and half the handle was missing. As Julie watched, one of the sirens hurried to quench a nearby flare-up, and her work boot crushed the teacup.

Vivienne, Hat whispered. Julie had never heard his voice so small and faint.

She pushed open the door and scrambled out of the Mustang after making sure there was room for emergency vehicles to get past. She heard the passenger door slam as she walked off. As she approached the rubble, Bianca right behind her, one of the sirens stepped forward in bulky turnout gear and held up a hand to stop her.

"Ma'am—" she began.

"Major Meadows, PMA." Julie plucked her badge from her jacket pocket and flashed it. "Let me through."

The siren hesitated, then nodded. "Yes, ma'am." She stepped aside.

As Julie and Bianca walked up to the ruin, the acrid stench of smoke was thick in Julie's nostrils. She coughed and stopped where Vivienne's front door had been. It was gone, just a pile of burned shards at her feet.

Oh, Vivienne, Hat whispered.

Bianca turned to one of the sirens. "What happened here?"

The firefighter shrugged. "We got the call for a fully involved structure fire about ninety minutes ago."

"An hour and a half?" Julie looked at Bianca. "That is enough time. The attempt was only…" she checked her watch, "forty-five minutes ago."

Bianca nodded grimly. "Was there anyone inside?"

The siren shook her head. "We found a cat sitting outside the house, and she's been taken to the animal shelter. There were no occupants, ma'am."

"She was taken, and they torched the place to cover their tracks," Julie muttered. "Was this a magical fire?"

"Not currently, but it could have started that way. The arson investigator will be able to tell you later," the siren explained. "Excuse me, ma'am." She hurried over to where two of her colleagues were struggling with another flare-up.

Julie pulled Hat off her head and cradled him in her arms. *Are you okay, Hat?*

Who would do *this to her?* Hat cried. *Where can she be?* His voice broke.

I don't know, but I know who can find out, Julie told him.

Who? Hat whimpered.

Julie held him up to eye level. *The ancient and powerful magical artifact right in front of me.*

Hat was silent.

Vivienne needs you, Julie murmured.

Hat's crown straightened. *I need to see more of the rubble.*

Julie looked up. *I can summon rain, but I don't know if it'll affect the investigation.*

No. Don't. Hat paused. *Throw me.*

What? Julie spluttered.

Just do it! Hat ordered. *Hard and straight across the scene.*

Julie decided this was not the time to doubt him. She drew back her arm and flung him like a frisbee, and for an appalling second, he spun over the smoking rubble, his gold insignias flashing as the firetruck's lights caught them. Then, with a *poof*, he transformed into a boomerang. The boomerang turned and arced back toward Julie.

Julie raised a hand and caught it with a slap.

"That was random yet impressive," Bianca summarized.

Hat *poofed* back into his service cap form. *Good catch.*

Thanks. Did you find anything? Julie asked.

Maybe. Hat paused. *Do you see that broken piece of mirror over there?*

Yeah.

Hat twitched. *I need to get over there.*

The shining fragment lay in a small area so charred that Julie was certain the fire was out. She opened her wings and fluttered over to it, then landed carefully, one combat boot on either side of the piece of mirror.

Careful, Hat told her. *This is an old-fashioned mirror with silver backing. You have to have a permit to have them in Avalon Town.*

Why would Vivienne have a silver mirror? Julie asked.

It was an heirloom. Hat sighed. *Hold me over it.*

Julie held him up, glancing at her reflection in the mirror, which was distorted and warped in the cracked glass. Hat hummed in her hands, and blue light flashed within his crown. The mirror reflected it, and Julie had to close her eyes against the brilliant light.

When she'd blinked away the after-image, the mirror looked the same until Julie leaned over and tried to see her reflection in it. Nothing was visible.

There was a vampire here, Hat muttered.

Vampire blood. A chill rushed down her spine. *Could be a vampire assassin who drew their own blood to poison the queen after kidnapping Vivienne.*

Speculation, Hat spat. *We need more than that to find Vivienne.*

Hey, I know. Julie put him back on her head. *We're going to find it. We just need to keep looking.*

They could kill her, Julie, Hat whispered. *Vivienne is one of the strongest paras I know. I'm not talking about inner strength. I'm talking about shooting fireballs from her fists. Whoever took her? They're dangerous.*

We'll find her, Julie promised.

How? Hat wailed.

Julie was trying to come up with an answer to that when there was a loud rumble from the road. She looked up, grabbing instinctively for her keys, but she'd left them in Genevieve. The Mustang rolled up to the smoking ruin and revved her engine again. She opened and shut both front doors and flipped her windshield wipers on and off.

"Uh, Julie?" Bianca called. "Your car is losing her shit."

"Not now, Gennie!" Julie yelled. She turned back to the ruins. "What about a hellhound? They might be able to track whoever did this."

She should never have lived here alone with no protection, Hat fretted. *She should have listened to me.*

What do you mean? Julie asked.

Genevieve's engine roared. There was a screech of rubber, and when Julie turned around, the Mustang was driving back and forth, gears crunching as she put herself in reverse, then first gear, and back.

"Gennie, cut it out!" Julie shouted. *Hat, seriously, what about hellhounds?*

Genevieve honked her horn, first gently, then a long, echoing blare.

"Let me see what's going on with her." Julie spread her wings, feeling a pulse of energy from the selenite in the armor she wore under her dress uniform, and flew over to Genevieve. When she landed, the Mustang rolled up to her and nudged her firmly in the thigh with her fender.

"Genevieve!" Julie scolded. "What is your problem?"

Genevieve rolled a few feet forward and flung her driver's door open. She honked again.

"I'm not the car whisperer, but I think she wants you to go with her," Bianca observed.

"What are you, Lassie?" Julie asked her vehicle.

Genevieve revved and flipped her windshield wipers.

Julie stared at her, then touched Hat's brim. *Hat, can she somehow track paras?*

Don't ask me about that car of yours, Hat grumbled. *I don't understand half the things she does.*

Genevieve revved again, then honked insistently.

"It's as good an idea as any." Julie threw herself into the driver's seat. The seatbelt fastened of its own accord, and she grinned. "Well, I did promise that the next pursuit was all yours."

Genevieve's engine screamed.

"Bee, get in," Julie yelled.

The succubus scrambled into the passenger's seat.

"Buckle up," Julie suggested. "This is going to get wild."

Genevieve didn't give Bianca the chance. The seatbelt drew itself over her, clipped, and yanked tight, pinning the succubus into the bucket seat.

Bianca grinned. "Oh, I *like* her. Let's—"

Genevieve surged forward, smoke rising from her tires, slamming her passengers back against their seats. The chase was on.

CHAPTER FIVE

Genevieve's steering wheel snapped to the left, almost wrenching Julie's arms out of their sockets. Bianca let out a yelp as the Mustang's emergency brake shot up and rapped her on the elbow. With a long screech of tires—and a long screech from Hat —Genevieve slid into a handbrake turn around a corner, ignoring the blaring of horns and whinnying of horses as she skidded across the oncoming lane.

Julie wished Lillie was here to see this. She could hear the old lady's cackle.

Genevieve dropped the emergency brake, and the gas pedal slammed flat to the floor, yanking itself out from under Julie's foot.

"Hang on!" Julie yelled.

Bianca seized the handle over the window and clung to it as Genevieve plunged forward, engine screaming. The wheel jumped left and right as the Mustang wove through the traffic. Semi-trucks, chariots, and magic carpets flashed past faster than Julie could react. Taillights rushed up to meet them, then disappeared as Genevieve dodged. She glanced at the speedometer once and decided not to do it again when she saw that the needle was pinned to the right.

Incredibly, Bianca rolled down the window. "Yeeeeeeee-ha!" she whooped, her golden curls wild around her face.

Julie managed a breathless giggle, then inhaled when Genevieve lurched over the curb and bounded across the grass, skipping the on-ramp. The Mustang's wheels left the ground for an asshole-puckering moment, then the smooth tarmac of the freeway rushed up to meet them. Genevieve hit the ground with a shriek of rubber, and Julie's forehead nearly smashed into the steering wheel. The seatbelt yanked her back with inches to spare, and the Mustang accelerated.

I think I'm going to be sick, Hat moaned. He'd flown off Julie's head and was rolling around helplessly on the backseat.

You're a hat! Julie protested. *You don't have a stomach!*

Hat responded with a long groan as Genevieve sharply turned right, filling the rearview mirror with a plume of smoke colored bright red by her taillights. The smell of burning rubber permeated her interior. She plunged onto an exit Julie hadn't taken before and roared over the junction, almost crashing into a horse and buggy containing a flock of weresheep. Their panicked bleats faded into the background as Genevieve surged down the country lane, barely touching the ground, her headlights picking out ruts and puddles between stone walls and white-rail fences.

"Where are we going?" Julie wondered aloud.

"Feels like we're heading into the mountains," Bianca observed.

The road forked ahead, and Julie just had time to make out the sign in the middle: a cutesy arrow, its tip in the shape of a heart, pointing to the right and proclaiming Lambhaven Cottage. To the left was a skull and crossbones and messy, wobbly writing that announced, DANGER. NO ENTRY. Genevieve's wheel spun to the left, and they bucked and plunged up a rutted, winding path that headed steeply uphill.

Julie jumped at the slap of rain on the windshield and switched on Genevieve's wipers. The rain intensified as the Mustang climbed the rocky path, now moving slowly. She thought she heard wolves howling.

Bianca hurriedly rolled up the window. Shadows closed in on the path, and in the headlights, through the driving rain, Julie could make out pine trees.

"Oh, I do *not* like this," Hat announced out loud.

"Nobody asked you, old man," Bianca shot back.

Genevieve slowed further. Her tires crunched on rock, and the wind howled against her windows.

"This is creepy," Julie whispered.

Genevieve's headlights switched off. Julie reached for the knob, but the Mustang halted.

"Don't," Bianca whispered. "We must be close."

"Close to *what*?" Julie wondered.

A jagged bolt of lightning was immediately followed by a crack of thunder. Brilliant white light illuminated a mansion on the top of the mountain. Julie only caught a vague impression, but that was all she needed: wrought-iron gates swarming with bats and a huge house with pointed rooftops. Double doors stood open despite the rain, draped with cobwebs, and red light glowed in the windows.

"The decor's cliché if you ask me," Bianca opined, "but to each their own."

"Still creepy as shit," Julie whispered. "Do you think she's in there?"

Genevieve emitted a faint honk.

"I think that means yes." Bianca glanced at Julie. "Shall we?"

Most certainly not, Hat snapped.

Don't you want Vivienne back? Julie reached back and grabbed him.

He sighed. *Of course I do. I'll call for backup.*

"You do that." Julie slipped him on her head.

They stepped out into the pounding rain, closing the car doors quietly. Genevieve reversed off the road and tucked herself away in the bushes.

"Smart car," Bianca commented. "Ugh. I just had my hair done."

Julie put a hand into the rain and concentrated, diverting the drops. They changed direction and pattered to the ground around her and Bianca but not on them.

"A new trick!" Bianca grinned. "Learn it in the Deep?"

"I learned a lot of things in the Deep." Julie returned her grin. "Let's go."

Keeping off the road, Bianca and Julie picked their way to the gates, which were open a crack. Thick spiderwebs shimmered with raindrops between the iron bars. The fluttering of bat wings filled the air over their heads, and Bianca tossed her horns in disgust.

"Ewww! I hate bats," she complained in a whisper.

Julie raised her eyebrows. "You know you have bat wings, right?"

"Just because they have wings like mine, *I* have bat wings?" Bianca hissed. "What if *they* have succubus wings?"

"Good point," Julie conceded.

The garden surrounding the mansion was a thick, wild tangle, and all the plants seemed to be thorny. Bianca and Julie wove through it to approach the open doors at the top of a long flight of concrete steps flanked by worn, cracked lion statues, both of which were missing their faces. Julie clenched her fist and lit a flame in her palm. Tiny wisps of light and smoke escaped. Bianca's fingers were closed too, and red light glowed behind them.

Avoiding the stairs and creepy statues, Julie fluttered up to the doorway. The red glow of firelight emanated from within. She paused, hidden behind one of the wooden doors, and Bianca did the same opposite her. There was no sound from within the mansion.

Their eyes met, and Julie raised her eyebrows. Bianca nodded, and in unison, they burst through the doorway. Julie's hand was enveloped in flames, and she had a fireball ready to launch.

She quickly scanned the room, hand upraised, but it was empty. A red carpet thick with dust covered the floor. Portraits of pale white people lined the walls, some of whom had eerie black eyes that stared right through Julie. Others had claw marks through them, and white canvas showed like flesh. Yet others lacked faces; they'd been ripped out. Cobwebs covered the dull suits of armor and random implements of torture that decorated the walls of the hall. The moldy collection was illuminated by a brass chandelier that contained dripping yellow candles.

"What did I tell you?" Bianca raised her eyebrows. "*Totally cliché.*"

"Shhh," Julie whispered and pointed at the dusty carpet. Two rows of footprints led across the room to a narrow doorway in the back near an Iron Maiden with an open door. One set of footprints was regular and even. The other was smaller, with drag marks.

Vivienne's not far away, Hat whispered. *I can sense her. Maybe in the next room.*

Gotcha. Bianca nodded. *Let's go get her.*

Julie's boots were swift and silent as she hastened across the room, her magic balled up in both hands, ready to launch. The narrow door was open a crack. Bianca nodded at Julie and stepped back to cover her as Julie pressed her back to the wall beside the doorway, then nudged the door open with one foot.

It swung wide with a long, moaning creak that resounded through the house like something was dying. Bianca moved forward swiftly, with Julie on her heels.

No, Julie realized. *The* crypt.

Candlesticks were everywhere, dripping pools of wax on the floor. Their flames guttered as rain lashed the windows. The red drapes were covered with dust, and cobwebs hung from the candlesticks. In here, the floor was tiled in a creepy brown and white pattern. A massive grandfather clock with a cracked face stood against one wall, its sonorous tick like the beating of a heart.

In the middle of the floor, a coffin rested on a small stone dais covered in runes. It was made of brightly polished ebony and had ornate brass fittings, and Julie caught a glimpse of red lining on the edge of the closed lid.

"I thought vampires being undead was a harmful stereotype conjured by fearful humans," she whispered.

Bianca scoffed. "It is. There's no such thing as the undead. Our vamp friend clearly likes to be over-the-top."

There was a soft moan from the shadows on one side of the room.

Vivienne! Hat cried.

The beautiful Lunar Fae lay on her side on the tiles, the skirt of her silky white dress tangled around her legs. One of her shoes was missing, and blood stained her dress. Her head rested on an outstretched arm, her eyes were closed, and she was ashen. Her wings sprawled on the tiles behind her.

"Vivienne!" Julie whispered, running over to her. Bianca stayed by the coffin and kept an eye on the door. Julie fell to her knees beside the motionless fae and touched her neck. It was cold, but she could feel a sturdy pulse. "Vivienne, wake up," she whispered, shaking her gently.

She won't, not without medical help, Hat told her flatly. *This is mesmerism—vampire magic. She's comatose.*

"We've got to get her out of here," Julie muttered. "Bee, can you—"

Bianca screamed.

Julie whipped to her feet. The coffin lid clattered to the ground, and Bianca's cry was cut off as the vampire's bony white hand wrapped around her mouth. His other hand locked around her neck, and blood dripped down her pale skin where his claws had scored long scratches across her throat. The succubus tried to throw her wings open, but the vampire tugged her closer, pinning her against his chest with supernatural strength.

"Let her go!" Julie roared.

The vampire hissed at her, showing long white fangs.

Julie clenched her hands into fists. Flames roared up to her elbows. "Do it!"

The flames made the vampire's eyes widen, then he let out a snarl and shoved Bianca toward Julie. The succubus staggered, and Julie turned off the flames to throw her arms out and catch the other major. She was heavier than she looked, and when her weight slammed into Julie, they both went down hard on the tiles. The back of Julie's head thumped the floor, and stars appeared in front of her eyes. She tried to roll to her feet, but her limbs were numb; when she gasped for breath, only a wheeze passed through her lips.

With a grunt, coughing and gasping, Bianca rolled off Julie and onto her feet. Red light filled the room as Bianca summoned her magic.

"*Stop!*" she screamed.

There was a crackle of breaking glass and the clop of Bianca's high-heeled boots on the tiles. Julie struggled to her knees, finally able to suck in a breath that sent vigor surging into her muscles. She staggered to her feet and reeled across the floor to join Bianca at the window, its edges filled with freshly broken glass.

"Shit," Bianca muttered. "He's gone."

"Where's Vivienne?" Julie croaked.

"He took her while I was trying to get off you." Bianca touched some of the hot blood still dripping from the shallow wounds on her throat. "Sorry. I should have checked the coffin. I didn't think any self-respecting vampire would hide inside one."

"It's cool." Julie swallowed. "Are you okay?"

"Yeah. You?" Bianca asked.

Julie nodded. "Let's get the son-of-a-bitch." She stuck her head out of the window. "Genevieve!"

The Mustang's engine roared in response, and she swooped through the air toward them, her headlights piercing the rain. Genevieve came to a halt by the window, hovering in midair, blue magic oozing from beneath her hood. Her driver's door swung open. Bianca scrambled through the window and into the car first, and Julie winced as her boots hit the seats and dash while she crawled into the passenger seat, but this was no time to be mad.

Can you still feel her, Hat? she called, hauling herself into the driver's seat.

Yes. Due north, Hat called. *She's weak.* Hurry!

The driver's door slammed shut, and Genevieve roared away, engine bellowing, rain thundering on her roof. When a flash of lightning lit the countryside in brilliant white, Julie spotted it: the silhouette of the vampire, clinging to...

"Is that a broomstick?" Julie asked dubiously.

Bianca peered through the windshield, one hand clasped to her throat. The blood had begun to dry. "It is." She groaned. "Can this day get any weirder?"

The vampire was hunched over the broomstick, zooming through the night air. Vivienne's figure was draped face-down over the handle just in front of him. His dramatic black cape, lined with red, snapped behind him in the wind.

"I can probably shoot him down with a good bolt of magic." Bianca clenched her fist. "But I'm not sure I can catch Vivienne in time...or miss her."

"We'll just have to catch up," Julie snarled. She put her foot down, and Genevieve responded with a surge of power.

The rain had stopped. The Mustang plunged through a moonlit night, stars above, silvery fields below. Julie saw the flash of a pale face as the vampire glanced over his shoulder, then leaned over his broom as if to urge it to go faster.

It wasn't fast enough. Trees, fields, homes, and villages flashed past under Genevieve too fast for Julie to make them out. The distance between them began to close, and not a moment too soon. Vivienne was slipping. The unconscious fae's limp wings flashed in the moonlight. The vampire was struggling to maintain his grip on the back of her silky white dress.

They were close enough that Julie could make out the black veins on Vivienne's wings and the twigs at the end of the broomstick. She squeezed the steering wheel and glanced at Bianca. "I've got the vamp," she murmured. "You've got Vivienne."

Bianca nodded. "Done."

Also, Hat, could I have a helmet? Julie added.

Bugger. Sorry, Hat mumbled.

When Julie's steel visor snapped shut, they were level with the vampire. Julie kicked Genevieve's door open, spread her wings, took a deep breath, and plunged out of the flying Mustang.

The vampire looked up before Julie hit him. The broomstick rapped her shins as she tackled him, then they were both falling, the night air howling past Julie's ears. She flung her arms around his body and gripped him against her chest, pinning his arms. His fangs snapped inches from her face as they fell. She tilted her head back and he snapped at her again, white fangs flashing.

"Go ahead, bite me!" Julie yelled in his face. "How well can *you* fly?"

The vampire looked down, his red eyes widening as he saw the ground rushing up to meet them. He let out a high-pitched shriek and squashed himself against her chest.

"Thought so!" Julie snapped in his ear.

She fanned out her wings, stopping their fall, and lowered them slowly. He was too heavy for her to fly with. When she looked up, Genevieve was hovering above them, her headlights shining. There was no sign of the broomstick, but Bianca flew toward her with strong flaps of her leathery wings, Vivienne cradled in her arms.

Julie let out a breath. "I'm going to land now, and if you snap at me, I'll set you on fire. Got it?"

The vampire nodded wordlessly.

She fluttered down to the ground. They were in open farmland, and she landed on the crunchy grass of an empty field. The vampire put his feet down and tensed to run, but Julie switched her grip to his arms and twisted them behind his back, allowing a quick pulse of heat to rush through her hands. The vampire went limp and hung his head, allowing Julie to restrain him.

"Is she okay?" she called.

Bianca landed gently a few feet away. Vivienne's head lolled. "I don't see any major wounds, but her breathing is ragged," Bianca called. "We need to get her to HQ."

"We need to get this asshole to containment." Julie shook the vampire. "He'll have lots to tell us about Queen Esmerelda's poisoning, won't you, huh?"

The vampire said nothing.

"You are one kick-ass boss bitch. You know that?" Bianca grinned at Julie. "Case *closed* in a couple of hours."

Julie laughed. "Right back at you. Hat, have you got in touch with backup yet?"

"I just sent our location to Captain Kaplan. We'll have backup shortly via portal," Hat confirmed.

"You got any magic-nulling cuffs on you?" Bianca asked.

Julie looked for Genevieve and spotted the car's headlights coming toward them, swooping low over the fields. "There are some in the glove box."

The vampire moved so suddenly that Julie hardly had time to react. He lunged forward, wrenching his wrists from her grip. Julie had fire in her hands before he was two feet away. "Stop!" she snarled, raising both fists, ready to shoot a fireball into his ankles if she needed to.

The vampire turned around, his expression twisted with fear. "Mordred for Eternity," he whispered. He reached into his cloak.

"Stop!" Julie ordered, a fireball in her hand.

The vampire tugged something small from his cloak—an amulet no bigger than a coin, Julie thought, although strong concealment magic made it difficult to see. He closed his fist, and there was a crunch of breaking glass.

Blue fire burst from the amulet.

"No!" Bianca cried.

The flames whooshed and engulfed the vampire in a second, filling the night with their blue glow. The vampire screamed, his silhouette writhing in the flames as he burned. Julie summoned rain, but as the cloud was forming over her head, the vampire crumbled and collapsed. The fire winked out, and Julie's rain pattered onto a pile of ashes.

"Shit." Bianca's eyes were huge. "What in Merlin's name was *that?*"

"It looked like Sylthana fire," Julie quavered. The vampire's scream still echoed through her mind.

Bianca stared at the heap of ashes. "He did that to himself," she whispered. "Did you hear what he said? He knew he was going to kill himself."

The air crackled a few feet away from them, then expanded into a portal, and three familiar paras spilled out of it. The vampire, the dwarf, and the Shajara Elf had been part of Julie's unit before she'd become an officer, and they were all in uniform and clutching automatic rifles.

"Julie!" Raven, the vampire, stared at her. "Are you guys okay? We heard you'd found a lead on the queen's poisoning..." Her voice trailed off.

Korin, the Copper dwarf, eyed Vivienne's motionless figure in Bianca's arms. "Did she do it?" she demanded bluntly.

Vivienne's face twisted in pain, and she moaned.

"No, but she was about to be framed for it, and she needs to get to the para-ER right now," Bianca barked. "Let's go."

Julie was hot on Bianca's heels as she strode through the sliding glass doors into the ER at the OPMA's New York headquarters. Vivienne was still in Bianca's arms, twisting and thrashing as if in the throes of a nightmare, giving tiny, strained cries.

Dr. Olena, a tall Sylthana Elf in purple scrubs, was waiting with an empty gurney.

"What happened?" she asked calmly.

Bianca lowered Vivienne onto the stretcher. "Kidnapped by a vampire. There's blood on her, but I don't know where it came from. He used his powers to make her comatose."

"Where is the vampire?" Olena asked sharply. She raised Vivienne's eyelids one at a time and aimed a flashlight at them. The Lunar Fae's pupils didn't respond, but she stirred and let out a strangled cry.

"Dead," Julie chipped in. "He set himself on fire."

Olena stared at her, then turned to the two nurses waiting behind her. "Trauma One," she ordered.

Julie and Bianca trailed behind as Olena and her nurses hustled Vivienne into a nearby trauma bay. One of the nurses wrapped a blood pressure cuff around Vivienne's arm. The other looked for a vein in the crease of the opposite elbow to start an IV. Hat was freezing where he pressed into Julie's cheeks. She pulled him off and cradled him in her arms.

"Come on, Vivienne," he whispered. "Come on."

Olena leaned over the Lunar Fae and placed both hands on the sides of her head. Purple magic oozed between her fingers, wrapping healing tendrils around Vivienne's skull and threading between her thick black braids. The fae's eyes twitched beneath their lids, and she let out a muffled cry.

"She's tachy," one of the nurses announced, looking at a monitor on the wall. "Hypotensive. Sats are stable."

Olena gritted her teeth, concentrating. The purple light intensified, and Vivienne relaxed abruptly. Color returned to her face, and the frantic beeping of the monitor slowed.

Hat trembled in Julie's arms. She hugged him tight.

"BP one-twenty over seventy-eight." The nurse's shoulders relaxed. "HR is returning to normal."

Vivienne's eyelids fluttered. Olena lowered her hands and stepped back as the fae opened her brown eyes. She stared around for a moment before her brow furrowed.

"I'm in...the ER?" she croaked.

"You're safe now," Olena told her. "Julie and Bianca brought you here. Nothing's going to hurt you."

Vivienne relaxed against her pillows.

"Are you all right?" Hat whispered. He transformed in Julie's arms, becoming the blue wizard hat that he so rarely showed her. She let him hop onto the bed and waddle up to Vivienne.

She put her fingertips on his brim. "I'll be fine, Em...Hat." She swallowed, which looked painful.

Bianca glanced at Olena. "Can we ask her some questions? It's important for the safety of the queen."

Olena hesitated, but Vivienne's hands clenched on the covers. "Yes."

"Ma'am, I—" Olena began.

Vivienne silenced her with a glance. Julie hadn't expected her brown eyes to be capable of a glare so sharp. "*Yes,*" the Lunar Fae repeated.

Julie stepped forward. "What do you remember about the vampire who kidnapped you?"

Vivienne opened her mouth to respond. A spasm shot through her body, and every muscle tightened—arms and legs straining to their full extension, head flung back against the pillow, back arched. Her eyes rolled back.

"Vivienne!" Hat cried.

Olena's hands bled purple light.

Vivienne's body relaxed, but then convulsions seized her. Her limbs jerked and twitched helplessly, head slamming against the pillow. A flying arm knocked Hat off the bed. Julie dove to catch him, then retreated as the purple scrubs descended upon Vivienne. The nurses grabbed her shoulders and rolled her onto her side. Olena seized a syringe from a nearby cabinet and slammed its contents into the IV line the nurse had established earlier. Vivienne went limp.

"What's happening to her?" Hat screamed.

"She had a seizure." Olena frowned, her lips pressed into a firm line.

"Why?" Bianca asked.

"Trauma, maybe." Olena met her eyes. "Or, given recent events, the effect of a geas. Little is known about how Lunar Fae respond to that kind of magic. Seizures have been recorded."

"Get her to containment. The sooner Qtana uses the Breaker on her, the better," Bianca ordered.

Olena nodded sharply. "Let's move," she told the nurses. They grabbed the drip stand, detached the monitors, and wheeled the gurney away at speed, leaving Julie, Bianca, and Hat alone in the trauma bay. Bloody bandages and empty wrappers from medical objects littered the floor.

Hat was ice-cold and trembling in Julie's hands. She cuddled him like a teddy bear. "She's going to be okay, Hat."

He *poof*ed into his usual service cap form but said nothing.

Bianca ran a hand through her golden curls, which had survived a high-speed chase and the fight without a hair out of place. The blood on her throat had dried. "This isn't good," she admitted quietly.

"No. I'm sure Vivienne will be able to tell us more when the geas is lifted, but clearly, the enemy now knows we have a geas-breaking machine." Julie met her eyes. "They're willing to sacrifice themselves rather than being freed from geasa and give up their leader."

"That thing he said before he burned himself alive." Bianca shuddered.

Mordred for Eternity. The vampire's hoarse whisper echoed through Julie's mind, and she had to take a deep breath to prevent a quiver of fear from running through her body to the floor and shaking the earth.

Bianca shook her head as though dislodging fearful thoughts. "Well, standing around here isn't much use, is it? We only have a theory—that the vamp kidnapped Vivienne to frame her for the queen's poisoning. Time to go out and prove it."

"What can we do while we wait for Vivienne's geas to be broken?" Julie wondered.

"She can help us with the Lunar Fae angle. Probably." Bianca snorted. "But what about the vampire angle?"

Julie rubbed her chin. "I'd say we should talk to Malcolm or Julius, but I know they'll both be busy with meetings at the Eternal Palace all day tomorrow after what happened tonight." She looked up. "But another member of the Nox family will be home. One who might have inside information, given what she's been through."

"Who?" Bianca raised her eyebrows.

Julie grinned. "Mina."

CHAPTER SIX

A lack of sleep weighed down the corners of Julie's eyes. The morning light that fell over the broad, quiet Staten Island street was pale and fragile, and nothing else moved as Genevieve puttered toward the familiar solid white gates on their right.

Bianca slurped noisily from a Starbucks cup. "You sleep at all last night?"

"A little," Julie admitted. "It wasn't easy to forget that vamp burning himself to death."

"Same, girl." Bianca yawned. "Have you been here since the attack last year?"

Julie shook her head. "Malcolm told me they'd rebuilt, though."

"Yeah. The mansion looks the way it did." Bianca grimaced. "No way of retrieving Julius' plants or books, though."

"Ugh." Julie grimaced. "That sucks. On top of everything else. I mean, those were his passion."

She was still thinking about the beautiful library and the priceless, timeless books it used to contain as she brought Genevieve to a halt in front of the gates, then rolled down the window and pressed the button on the intercom.

"Nox residence." The cool voice belonged to Gerald Perkins, the Nox family's butler.

"Hey, Gerry. It's Bianca and me," Julie announced.

"Oh, Major Meadows! How wonderful to hear your voice." Gerald perked up. "Come on through."

The gates opened, and Julie steered Genevieve into a courtyard lined with rosebushes covered in fragrant white blooms. The mansion towered behind the courtyard, elegant and modern, with floor-to-ceiling windows that reflected the bright sunlight.

"Poor Mina." Julie grimaced. "She's staying up late for us."

Bianca waved her hand. "She was adamant on the phone that we should get some sleep before coming to see her."

"I'm grateful." Julie brought the Mustang to a halt and set the parking brake. "That was one long-ass day."

Bianca unbuckled her seatbelt. "I hear you."

Julie stepped out of Genevieve and closed the door, looking around. "Where's Gerald?"

"Right here, madam." The butler spoke from directly behind her.

Julie jumped a mile, spun, and clapped a hand over her thudding heart. "I am *still* not used to that," she complained.

Gerald wore a top hat with a wide brim, a tailcoat, and a scarf pulled up over his mouth and nose to protect him from the sun. "Good day, Major Meadows, Major Hartshorn." His eyes rested on Bianca. "It is good to see you back so soon. Miss Nox is always glad to have company besides her doctors."

Miss Nox, Julie noted. Not *Councilor* Nox anymore. Gerald didn't get these things wrong.

"Glad to be here, Gerry." Bianca smiled.

The butler gestured elegantly with a gloved hand. "Please, follow me." A smile twitched the scarf. "It is good to see you, Major Meadows."

"I'm sorry I haven't been around much." Julie rubbed her chin. "It's been sort of crazy."

"Ah, yes, the kidnapping of dragons and so on." Gerald chuckled. "This way, if you please."

Julie followed the elegant tailcoated figure, which seemed to float instead of walk, along the path between rosebushes to the front door of the mansion. Bianca brought up the rear.

Gerald made a gesture with one hand as they reached the double doors, and they silently swung open.

"You mentioned doctors." Julie stepped into the gorgeous entrance hall with marble flooring. "Has Mina not recovered from her ordeal at the hands of the drow?"

Gerald shook his head sadly. "Some nights are better than others." He sighed. "Luckily, this was a good night, and she is tired now. It is safe for you to see her."

Julie frowned. "Safe? For who?"

Bianca, now beside Julie as they headed for the nearest of the sweeping staircases, bit her lip. "For us." She grimaced. "I didn't tell you because I knew you were dealing with a bunch of crap in the Deep, and there wasn't anything you could do about it—"

"I sense a 'but' coming." Julie raised her eyebrows.

Bianca spread her hands. "Mina isn't quite herself."

"What do you mean?" Julie asked.

Hat shuddered on her head. *I think I know.*

"Whoever the drow are working for, they hit Mina with so much dark magic that it bonded with her vampire magic." Bianca's mouth turned down at the corners. "She has dangerous moments these days. Her doctors are trying to help her, but it's a complicated issue."

"Merlin's beard." Julie sighed. "Poor Mina. No wonder Malcolm's been looking so peaky."

"It is not common knowledge, madam," Gerald interjected, leading them down a long hallway with a lush red carpet. "We prefer to keep Miss Nox's troubles out of the public eye."

"Understandable." Julie grimaced. "I'm sorry, Gerry."

The end of the hallway was barred by a grille that gleamed

silver. The butler paused several feet from it, head hanging. "It is a great sorrow for the family," he murmured.

And for their butler, Julie thought. "Why the silver?" she asked.

Gerald hesitated. "For the safety of all," he admitted, "Miss Nox is restricted to this wing of the mansion." Keeping his distance from the grille, he grasped an ornamental lamp on the wall nearby and pulled. Something clanked in the wall, and the silver grille rose smoothly and disappeared into the ceiling. Gerald still shuddered when they walked under it.

"If you please." He stopped and gave a faint bow. "We must wait for the grille to return to its place before we may proceed."

The silence was as heavy as the grille as it descended back into position. Gerald shuddered again before leading them down the hallway and through the tall door at the end.

The room beyond was roomy and airy, with a set of high windows at the far end offering a view of the lawn behind the mansion. There used to be a swimming pool there, as well as Julius' greenhouse. Now it was an empty expanse of green. The windows, Julie knew, were designed to filter out the UV rays that fried vampire skin on contact, and the room was bathed in soft light. She spotted bunches of garlic surrounding every one of the window frames.

Mina Nox kept her distance from the windows. The room was furnished with classy cream-colored couches and armchairs surrounding a glass coffee table strewn with books. Mina was curled up on the couch farthest from the windows, wrapped in a plush pink blanket. She'd cut her hair. It was now shoulder-length and draped around her face like a curtain as she stared at her phone despite the TV show playing on the screen against the opposite wall.

"Majors Meadows and Hartshorn to see you, Miss Nox," Gerald announced. Julie saw him slip his hand into the pocket of his tailcoat.

Mina looked up, and Julie braced herself to see madness in her eyes.

The ex-councilor's red eyes were as thoughtful as ever. "Julie, Bianca." She smiled. "It's so nice to see you both and to see you again so soon, Bianca."

She fished a remote from among the folds of the blanket and turned off the TV, then set down her phone. "Have a seat."

Julie's shoulders relaxed. *She doesn't seem so bad.*

Be careful, Hat warned her. *The dark magic's still there. I can feel it.*

It's just Mina, Hat. Look at her. She looks like she always did. Julie crossed the floor and took a seat on the couch opposite Mina. Bianca joined her.

"I'm glad you're home and safe," Julie offered. "Sorry to hear about your troubles."

"I'm grateful to be here." Mina's smile was wan. "I'm hoping the doctors will figure out a solution soon." She waved a hand. "But enough about me! Tell me about the outside world. Have you been back to the Deep recently?"

"I spent a few months there." Julie smiled. "It was good to keep bonding with Eglantine."

"Eglantine." Mina brightened. "That's a pretty name."

Bianca leaned forward, resting her elbows on her knees. "Mina, I'm sorry to break in like this, but I know it's late, and you need to get to bed." She paused. "Something's happened at the Eternal Palace, and I need to ask you a few things about vampires."

Mina's eyes widened, and she sat up straighter, tucking the blanket around her hips. "There's something I can do to help?"

The excitement in her voice made Julie's heart sting.

"There's a lot you can do." Bianca smiled. "Starting with what you're doing right now—resting and healing. But if you don't mind, I'd love it if you could answer some questions."

"Of course. Anything." Mina's eyes shone. "Tell me what happened."

Julie glanced at Bianca and felt the hum as Hat connected them telepathically. *How much do I tell her?* she asked.

Only what she needs to know. We don't need to upset her, Bianca cautioned. *Stick to questions you know she can answer for now.*

Julie turned to Mina. "What do you know about the relationship between vampires and Sylthana Elves?"

Mina ran a hand through her hair. "Historically, the two species coexisted in relative peace under the reigns of the Pendragon kings. Before the Pendragon Wars, there was little contact between them. They mostly left each other alone. But when the Second Pendragon War brought all paras together to bring down—" She stopped and swallowed.

"I know who you mean." Julie smiled reassuringly. "Go on."

Mina nodded and gave a grateful smile. "Well, when that happened and the council was formed, vampires and Sylthana Elves treated each other with some suspicion. Fire has always made vampires nervous." She laughed. "For obvious reasons."

Julie grinned. "I bet." *This is going better than expected.*

Careful, Hat warned again.

"As the centuries passed, though, the two species found themselves seeing eye to eye on numerous issues, especially the independence of their people." Mina paused. "Felix Kushnir is an ass, no doubt about it, and together with the current king and queen of the Sylthana Elves, he's done quite a bit to damage our relationship with the elves. Still, our people tend to get along well enough."

Julie nodded. "Thanks, Mina. That helps."

"It does?" Mina beamed. "I'm so glad."

Bianca spoke quietly. "Mina, the next question is harder." She hesitated. "Tell me if you're not ready to answer it."

Mina's smile vanished, and she hung her head. "Okay."

"I know you remember little of your time with the drow." Bianca's eyes were trained on the vampire.

Mina nodded wordlessly.

"But I need you to try." Bianca paused. "The drow were the ones holding you captive."

Mina's voice was a ghost of its former self, rising from between the curtains of her hair. "Yes."

"I'm sorry, Mina. Should we stop?" Bianca asked.

She shook her head faintly. "No."

"Okay." Bianca paused. "Do you remember any other species of para being present?"

"What are you asking?" Mina demanded flatly.

Careful! Hat cried.

Bianca smiled. "I'm just asking if you saw any other paras. It's okay if you don't remember. We can stop if you—"

"I have a geas on me," Mina whimpered, her voice high-pitched and shaky. "You can't ask me that."

"The geas was removed, Mina," Julie reminded her softly. "It's okay. You're safe."

"You'll make me explode!" Mina exclaimed. "You'll kill me!"

"It's okay." Bianca got up and took a step nearer to her. "You're okay. You're safe."

Julie went to stand.

Stop! Hat gasped.

Julie felt a wave of bitter cold emanating like a ripple from Mina Nox. It swept through her and chilled her bones.

When the vampire lifted her head, her fangs were extended, and her pupils were so small they were lost in pools of red blood. An unearthly shriek echoed from her open mouth, and she lunged.

Julie moved faster. Her shoulder slammed into Bianca, tackling her to the floor. Mina's lunge missed. She landed on her hands and knees a few feet away and scrabbled around to face them, spitting and slavering like a rabid animal. Julie jumped to her feet and stood over the stunned Bianca, summoning flames.

"Mina, stop!" she cried.

Mina was gone. The thing behind her eyes was nothing like the gentle vampire that Julie knew. It was mindless, and it was bloodthirsty. She gathered herself to leap, her claws digging into the carpeted floor—

Before she could leap, Gerald was upon her. He yanked a crystal bottle from his pocket, ripped out the stopper, and seized Mina by the hair. Julie cried out at his roughness as he yanked back her head and upended the bottle over her open mouth. Black fluid splashed her tongue, and she let out another shriek before her body went limp. Gerald threw his arms around her before she could hit the floor.

Bianca scrambled to her feet. "Thanks, Jules," she wheezed. "I didn't see it coming this time."

"I felt it coming." Julie shivered. "What did you do to her, Gerald?"

"What I had to, madam." Gerald's mouth drooped. He cast the bottle aside and lifted Mina. "The potion sedates her deeply. She should be herself again when she wakes."

Bianca and Julie shuffled out of the way as Gerald carried Mina over to the couch, cradling her as gently as a baby.

"That was scary as shit," Julie murmured.

"I know." Bianca's shoulders sagged. "I feel so bad for her. It can't be easy."

"It looks awful. I can't imagine what it's like to go through that." Julie put a hand on Bianca's arm. "I know you two are friends. I'm sorry you have to see this."

Gerald laid Mina on the couch, plumped a pillow under her head, and tucked her pink blanket around her. The vampire's fangs had retracted, and she looked peaceful with her eyes closed.

"Ah, Miss Nox." Gerald sighed, retrieved a silk handkerchief from his pocket, and gently wiped the drool from her chin. He ran the back of one fingertip over her cheek as softly as one would do with a sleeping baby. "Come back to us," he whispered.

Julie clasped her hands together. "Gerald, I'm really sorry."

"I didn't mean to cause her distress," Bianca added.

Gerald looked up at them, smiling sadly. "Don't apologize. It was not your fault." He folded the handkerchief and tucked it away. "The smallest things can make this happen, and you are not to blame." His gloved hands clenched into fists. "The monsters who did this to her. They are the ones who should be punished."

Julie put a hand on his arm. "We'll find them, Gerry."

His eyes met hers. "I hope so, Major Meadows. I truly do." He looked away and shook himself, then took a deep breath.

Julie let her hand fall back to her side.

When Gerald looked up, his usual smooth expression was back in place. "King Julius requests your presence, Major Meadows."

Julie nodded. "Sure."

"I'll head back to HQ. I'd like to check on Vivienne. Meet you there?" Bianca suggested.

"Sure. Take Genevieve if you want." Julie fished for her keys.

Bianca waved her hand. "It's cool. I'll get a taxi."

They headed back down the hall, pausing for the silver grille. Once it was safely back in position, Bianca went down the stairs. Julie expected to be taken to Julius' study, but Gerald led her down another staircase and through the back door to the porch on which Julius had held a council of war more than a year ago, before the war had officially begun.

Julie remembered meeting Georgina and Benedict Woodskin, Taylor's parents, out here for the first time. A pang of sorrow ran through her. They were both dead, as well as two of his brothers.

Gerald bowed deeply. "Major Meadows for you, sire."

Julius Nox had his back to them. As always, he wore a well-cut black suit. This time, he had added a bowler hat, from which hung a stylish black veil that protected his face and neck from the morning sunshine.

"Thank you, Perkins," he murmured.

Gerald disappeared into thin air. Julie took a step forward but didn't bow. "You wanted to see me, sire?"

"I did." Julius pointed. He wore pink and white floral gardening gloves and indicated a little pink watering can on the bench against the wall. "Would you be so good as to water those chrysanthemums, Julie?"

"Sure." Julie picked up the watering can and headed over to a bush that bloomed copiously on a corner of the porch near Julius.

They worked in silence for a few moments. Julius was pruning a tiny twisted bonsai tree that had teeny cherry blossoms on every branch. The vampire king's gloved hands were nimble and gentle on its twiggy limbs.

"I'm really sorry about your greenhouse," Julie offered.

Julius sighed. "The war has made it impossible to get hold of monster flowers. I cannot recreate my monster flower-and-plumeria hybrid."

Julie sighed. "I'm sorry."

"A small sorrow in the face of those far larger that this war has created, but a sorrow nonetheless," Julius conceded. He set down the pruning shears. "Sit with me."

Julie put the watering can on the table near the bonsai, and they sat on a bench overlooking the long green lawn that used to be a swimming pool and tennis court and greenhouse. Julius didn't take off his gloves, but he fiddled with them, tugging at the fingers. Julie had never seen him fiddle before.

She had to break the silence eventually. "You're up late, sire."

"The only time I have for the plants I have left." Julius gestured at the pots on the porch. "My duties as king have been heavier than usual lately."

"I've heard that you've regained control over most of the vampires," Julie observed.

"That much is true, although maintaining that control across two dimensions hasn't been easy." Julius sighed.

"You've taken Mina's place on the council too, haven't you?" Julie asked.

Julius nodded. "I have. It adds to a full plate." He paused. "Malcolm's education has become a priority, too."

Julie didn't like the implication that Julius thought the world would need his heir sooner rather than later. She decided against asking him about it. "Sire, if there's anything I can do to help, I'd love to."

Julius chuckled warmly. "Can you fit me in between causing chaos with the dragons and rescuing your fellow fae from vampires?"

Julie grinned. "I'm sure I have a slot for you somewhere."

Julius patted her knee. "There *is* something you can do, young lady."

"Young lady?" Hat echoed. *The last guy who called you that got a knee to the balls.*

Yeah, well, the last guy who called me that wasn't Julius Nox. He believed in me before anyone else did, Julie reminded him.

She looked at Julius. "What is it, sire?"

Julius met her eyes, his red irises glittering behind the thin veil. "You can find out who you are, break the concealment spell upon you, and come into your full powers."

Julie dropped her eyes to her boots.

"I had hoped," Julius added gently, "that your time in the Deep would have allowed you to do so."

"I was, uh, sort of busy with the dragons," Julie mumbled lamely.

Julius let the silence stretch before answering. "Or perhaps comfortable with your powers and your identity as they are, hmm?"

Julie said nothing.

"You have more power yet to unlock, Julie," Julius murmured.

"It is good to be happy with your growth and, better yet, to celebrate who you are, but none of us are complete. We cannot forget that we are works in progress, becoming daily more and more who we have always been." He smiled. "Some of us in a more literal fashion than others."

Julie managed a sheepish smile. *Maybe Eggy's not the only one who's been avoiding her destiny,* she conceded silently.

Hat said nothing.

"This is not the reason I called you out here, though. You have more important things to do than to listen to the woes of an old vampire." Julius grinned. "I wanted you to know that I am in full support of your actions in the Deep."

Julie stared at him. "Wait, you're cool with me stealing the last burrito? I knew Lady Ennowen wanted it, but I was sort of pissed."

Julius laughed wholeheartedly. "Well, maybe not that. Burrito theft is a serious crime, you know." His features relaxed. "You know what I mean, Julie. I will make it officially known that I think you did the right thing by removing the dragon heir from that environment."

"You...you do, sire?" Julie asked.

"I certainly do. Every monarch should know that we are nothing without our heirs and that our heirs must be free to fly if they are to become our future." He smiled. "Even if I haven't always lived that with my own son."

"I've always thought you're a kick-ass dad, sire, if that counts for anything," Julie told him.

Julius put a floral-gloved hand on her knee. "It does."

"I-I didn't know you knew about me taking the dragon egg from the Deep," Julie admitted.

Julius folded his arms. "Everyone knows, young lady. Lady Ennowen made sure of that." He paused. "Remember this. Your dragon bond must not be severed, no matter what pressures are brought to bear. The dragon heir is the main reason the concealment spell has lifted, even in part. She is the key to helping you become everything you are meant to be. Stay close to her for your sake as well as hers."

Julie nodded. "I'll remember that, sire."

"Good." Julius cleared his throat and rose to his feet. "Now, if you'll excuse me, this bonsai is not going to prune itself."

Julie left him with his plants, glancing back once as Gerald materialized out of thin air and led her to the door. She hadn't expressed how sorry she was about what had happened to Mina, but looking at the vampire king's back hunched over his bonsai, she guessed he knew.

CHAPTER SEVEN

Julie slurped her third espresso of the day as she plodded down the hall toward the portal room at the NYHQ. The corridors were filled with paras hustling every which way. It was refreshing to see all the differently colored uniforms. Julie couldn't help directing nostalgic glances at the recruiters in forest green.

Those were the days, she mused. *I'm grateful I had a glimpse of the paranormal world before the war. Now I know what I'm fighting for.*

Hat chuckled. *It's no wonder you hardly ever wore your green. It's not your color. Navy is far more your speed.*

Shut up, Julie retorted fondly. She took another slurp. *Why do I have the feeling that this day isn't going to be any shorter than yesterday?*

Do you ever *have short days?* Hat enquired.

Julie grimaced. *Valid.*

She pushed open the door to the portal room and collided with Taylor. With a yelp, Julie stepped back and held her coffee cup to the side to avoid splashing him.

"Hey, babe!" Taylor's soft brown eyes lit up.

"Taylor!" Julie couldn't help grinning. She wrapped her free arm around him and pulled him close, then buried her face in the front of his beautifully cut charcoal-gray jacket. As always, he smelled like the earth after rain, and she closed her eyes and breathed deeply.

Taylor kissed the top of her head. "How are you doing?"

"I'm okay. Tired," Julie admitted. She stepped back. "What are you doing here?"

"I stayed at Ilsa's last night. She needed company after what happened at the palace," Taylor explained. "I'm heading there right now. Do you need a ride?" He chuckled. "I realize I'm asking this of a woman who owns a magical shapeshifting Mustang."

"Genevieve's in the parking bay. I didn't have time to drive to Central Park, so Lewis is taking her back to Avalon HQ." Julie grinned. "So yeah, I *could* use a ride."

"Perfect." Taylor reached out a hand.

Julie wrapped her fingers around his, and they walked to the Avalon HQ portal together. "How is Ilsa?"

"She's okay. She's shaken up. You know, attacks on the royal families hit close to home these days." Taylor shrugged.

Julie held her breath as they stepped through the portal and into the basement of the Avalon HQ. She'd never get used to the dizzy nausea that resulted from portal travel. "I bet they do. I saw her on TV last night, giving a statement about the Aether Elves' offer of support to the OPMA to track down whoever tried to poison the queen. She's kicking ass at being queen."

"I know." Taylor grinned. Their footsteps echoed through the basement as they made for the elevator. "She was born for it, literally. I don't think it's easy, but she's exactly the leader we need right now, and I'm proud of her."

Julie squeezed his hand as they stepped into the elevator. "I'm proud of *you*."

"Aw, babe." Taylor tugged her closer and kissed the side of her head. "I'm proud of you, too. Who knows what would have happened to Vivienne by now if not for you?"

"I just wish we'd gotten more answers." Julie sighed. "Olena says Vivienne is going to need a few days to recuperate before they can use the Breaker on her. I was really hoping we'd get answers out of her kidnapper until he set himself on fire."

"That's very worrying," Taylor acknowledged. "It makes me concerned that the Mordred cult really *is* behind all this. It seems like the kind of thing cultists would do."

"Absolutely."

The elevator doors slid open, and they stepped into the motor pool and strolled through the parking bays, stalls, iron cages, and perches. As they passed Genevieve's empty spot, the eight-legged gray stallion in the stall beside it put his head over the door and nickered hopefully.

"Of course I have a sugar cube for you, Sleipnir." Julie fished in her pocket and paused to hold out the cube on her palm.

Sleipnir cheerfully lipped it up and crunched it.

"There's a good boy." Julie rubbed his velvety nose.

Taylor reached out to touch him, and Sleipnir pinned his ears back.

"He's never liked me," Taylor grumbled.

"Oh, Slippy, poor taste is your only flaw." Julie gave the stallion a last pet and headed toward Taylor's Audi.

"How did your visit with Mina go?" Taylor asked, taking his keys out of his pocket. "Malcolm tells me she's not been well since she was rescued."

"'Not well' is an understatement." Julie sighed. "They're trying to keep it quiet, so this isn't official."

Taylor inclined his head. "Of course."

They got into the Audi, and Taylor backed it out of the parking space while Julie explained that the dark magic of the drow had blended with Mina's vampire magic.

"She blacks out sometimes. It's like the dark magic takes control of her," Julie explained. "She attacked Bianca and me."

"Attacked?" Taylor's foot slipped, and the Audi spluttered.

"Don't worry, babe. We're fine." Julie patted his shoulder. "Gerald was there. He hit her with some kind of sleeping potion, and she passed out."

"Wow." Taylor grimaced as he drove out of the motor pool. "That's shitty for all concerned. So that's why no one's gotten any good information from Mina, even after her geas was lifted."

"Exactly. Asking her about what happened is a trigger for her." Julie looked down at her hands, entangled in her lap. "I feel so sorry for Julius. He seems really sad."

"Can't blame him." Taylor paused. "You met with him today?"

"Just briefly." Julie rubbed her wrist. "It was weird, though."

The streets of Avalon slipped past as Taylor drove toward the Eternal Palace.

"Weird, how?" Taylor asked.

"He told me he fully supports me kidnapping Eglantine, which I kind of didn't expect," Julie admitted.

Taylor glanced at her. "Julius has always been in your corner."

"Yeah, but he's the *king*," Julie pointed out. "He's been a champion for unity among all paras forever. I didn't think he'd appreciate that I almost declared war on the Deep. He said it was really important that I never sever my bond with Eggy."

Taylor nodded. "Eglantine helps you with your powers, doesn't she?"

"She's the reason I have *any* powers." Julie gazed at her hands in her lap. She opened her fingers, and tiny flames flickered in her palms. "He said something else, too."

"Something that's weighing on your mind," Taylor observed softly.

Julie rolled her eyes. "Can you quit reading my mind? I already have a telepathic hat to deal with."

They'd reached an open stretch of road, and Taylor put one hand on her knee, grinning. "Want to tell me what it is?"

"Yeah." Julie took a deep breath. "I asked Julius what I could do to help."

"What did he say?" Taylor asked.

Julie closed her fists, and the flames winked out. "He said I could work on lifting the concealment spell and find out who I am biologically."

Taylor stared at her. "What about your wings? Your powers? You look like a Lunar Fae. Doesn't that mean the concealment spell has been lifted?"

"I thought it did," Julie admitted, "but it seems that I was wrong. Julius says I still need to come into my full powers." She frowned. "Remember when the queen told me I was nobility?"

"I do." Taylor nodded.

"Maybe she's found out more about me." Julie bit her lip. "Maybe there's more she can do to find out where I came from. Maybe she can find my birth family after all."

Taylor squeezed her knee, then put his hand on the wheel to make a left turn. "I'm sure she'd have let you know if she'd found out more, babe, but it can't hurt to ask, right?"

Careful, Hat interjected. *That spell will be broken once and for all when your bond with Eglantine is complete.*

When is that, Hat? Julie snapped. *When she hatches? With all the chaos around her, who knows when that's going to happen?* She threw up her hands.

"Easy, babe. Hat's right," Taylor soothed. "Well, Hat *could* be right."

I'm always right. Hat sniffed.

Taylor shot him a look. "Don't push it."

"I'm just saying there are other priorities right now." Hat spoke more gently. "We still haven't found out who tried to poison Queen Esmerelda. If that assassin returns and succeeds, there will be worse consequences than Julie never finding her birth family."

Julie's guts tied themselves in a knot. "Brutal but true." She frowned. "I'm sure the vampires who took Vivienne were responsible for the poisoning. They wanted to frame her."

Taylor grunted in agreement.

Yes, Hat muttered, *but who are they working* for?

The Eternal Palace loomed on the hillside above them, surrounded by smooth green fields. The glawackus cleared them to enter, and Taylor drove to the courtyard in which Julie had stopped Genevieve last night.

"Good luck, babe." He leaned over and kissed her cheek. "Love you."

Julie leaned into the kiss and squeezed his hand. "Love you, too."

As Taylor drove away, Bianca landed lightly on the cobblestones. She waved at Taylor and strode up to Julie. "Hello again. Ready for more shenanigans?"

Julie grinned, pushing thoughts of her identity out of her head. She gave Bianca a good-natured bump with her shoulder. "Always."

"The queen's in the throne room today." Bianca grabbed Julie's elbow and steered her toward the main doors into the palace.

"That's got to be a good sign."

Bianca shrugged. "Or Her Majesty wants to show everyone she's still strong."

Julie grunted. "How's Vivienne?"

"She's...okay. Still pretty out of it," Bianca explained as they headed for the massive arched doorway. Its selenite-inlaid copper gates were standing open, and six griffins guarded it, their armor shining in the mid-morning sun. "They lifted the geas without damage to her mind, but she's exhausted."

"Understandable. Her mind has been through a lot," Julie acknowledged.

Bianca nodded. "She wasn't able to tell me much. Her memory's still coming back. Doc said that that was normal and it'll return, given a little time. She did remember a bunch of vampires attacking her home. She killed some."

Julie grinned. "She's a Lunar Fae. We're pretty badass."

Bianca snorted. "Not to toot your own horn or anything."

Julie raised her hands and shrugged. "It's not tooting if it's true."

Hat snickered.

Bianca laughed. "There's a fart joke in there somewhere, but I'm going to be the bigger person and not make it."

"Did she remember how they overpowered her?" Julie asked.

"She remembers a firestorm that came from nowhere." Bianca glanced at Julie. "That's Lunar Fae magic. She thought it might have been stolen."

They'd passed through the gates and into a vaulted hallway that was wide and tall enough to admit a dragon in his true form. There were no decorations or tapestries on the walls, only stained-glass windows letting in shafts of multicolored light. The banners of the seven royal families hung on the pillars, interspersed with the banner of the Eternity Throne. It was peaceful and silent except for the clops of their boots and quiet purrs from the griffins who sat as upright as statues at regular intervals. Julie felt like an ant moving across the polished marble floor.

Julie frowned as they approached the arched doorway at the end of the hall. "Stolen? Isn't it more likely that a Lunar Fae was working with the vampires? Also, I cannot *wait* to be able to command a firestorm."

"Right?" Bianca chuckled. "I guess you're not wrong, although it's hard to imagine why a Lunar Fae would work against Her Majesty."

Julie thought about the horrific wound in King Arthur's side as he slumbered in a glass casket at Tintagel. "It wouldn't be the first time Lunar Fae made war on one another at the expense of both worlds."

Bianca inclined her head. "You're right. I agree with you."

"Did they ask Vivienne for information?" Julie asked.

Bianca shook her head. "It doesn't seem that they had time to do so. Certainly not before the poisoning."

Julie nodded. "So they didn't kidnap Vivienne to get information about how to poison the queen like we originally thought."

"No." Bianca bit her lip. "They kidnapped her to frame her. Would have worked, too, if you hadn't called Vivienne to check on her." She grinned and gave Julie a good-natured poke in the shoulder. "Brilliant as usual, girlfriend."

Julie laughed.

They stepped into the throne room, and Julie's breath caught. An enormous dome of stained glass formed the ceiling and sunlight poured down in shimmering rainbow patterns on the floor, which was shining white marble shot through with streaks of gold and selenite.

Griffin guards lined the round room, sitting still and straight between the sandstone pillars that supported the magnificent roof. Rows of curved wooden seats with purple velvet cushions surrounded the dais at the very center of the room, where a sheet of plain glass shaped like a crescent moon cast a shaft of sunlight on the Eternity Throne.

Given the splendor surrounding it, Julie had half-expected the throne to be covered with precious metals and glimmering gemstones. It was ancient and worn and roughly carved from cold gray stone. Its chipped, ragged edges suggested a time before even paranormal hands could shape stone with any kind of finesse. Rough chunks of selenite, neither cut nor polished, had been forced into crumbling channels in the back and armrests.

The purple cushions that padded the throne stood in sharp contrast to the stone seat. Queen Esmerelda sat upright upon them. Her wings were open, and though their veins were gray and faded and scars marred their gleaming surface, they were enormous and impressive as they spread out on either side of the throne. She wore a chainmail gown that artfully curved to hide her bony hips and a shimmering silk cloak that trailed down the throne on either side of her, framing her in purple and gold.

Julie realized Bianca was bowing while she stood there with her mouth open. She hastily copied Bianca's formality.

"Julie, good morning." The tiniest tremor underlined the queen's words. "Major Hartshorn. Please rise."

Julie and Bianca straightened.

"I assume you have news for me?" Queen Esmerelda asked.

Julie glanced at the seats surrounding the dais. Paras of different races, all dressed like royalty, occupied them. Most were glaring at Julie.

"I do, Your Majesty, but it's sensitive," Julie announced.

Queen Esmerelda raised a bony hand. "Leave us, all of you," she ordered.

A Sylthana Elf jumped to his feet. "Your Majesty, I—"

Queen Esmerelda turned her eyes on him. She did not raise her voice, and she didn't need to. "I asked you to leave us, sir."

The elf shrank under the power of the queen's gaze. "Yes, Your Majesty," he mumbled.

The throne room emptied with a shuffling of feet and a battery of glares. The griffins shut the doors behind them.

Bianca strode up to the throne, but Julie hung back, glancing at the griffins. *Can we trust them?* she wondered.

These are griffins, Julie, Hat reminded her. *Caring for the Eternity Queen is who they are. If you trust anyone, trust the griffins.*

What, you're encouraging me to trust other paras? Are you feeling okay? Julie teased.

Hat huffed as she hurried to catch up with Bianca. They stopped at the edge of the dais and bowed again.

Queen Esmerelda smiled and waved a weak hand. Up close, she was far paler than she had looked when they came into the room.

"What news?" she asked. "I was relieved to hear of Vivienne's rescue but feared the reason for her involvement." She hesitated. "I am saddened to hear that our enemies will choose death over surrender."

"It's a complication, Your Majesty," Bianca agreed, "but we think we got some solid information."

"Vivienne was briefly placed under a geas when she was kidnapped, but it was safely lifted," Julie added, "and she's going to be okay. She was able to tell us a little about her kidnapping. While there were several vampires involved, including the one who ultimately took her to his, uh, lair, it was Lunar Fae magic that overwhelmed her."

"A firestorm," Bianca clarified.

Queen Esmerelda frowned. "What do you surmise, then?"

"We think Vivienne was kidnapped to frame her for the poisoning, Your Majesty." Julie folded her arms. "We believe she's innocent, but that means that there's another Lunar Fae involved."

Queen Esmerelda sighed heavily. "In that case, the task I gave Morgan is even more important than I thought."

"Your Majesty?" Julie raised her eyebrows.

The queen reached down. Her thin body left plenty of space on the throne on either side of her, and she lifted a tiny casket from the cushion beside her. It was inlaid with gold and selenite, which glowed softly as she held the casket out to Julie.

Julie accepted it. "What is this, Your Majesty?"

"Something you must guard with your life," Queen Esmerelda murmured. She still gripped the casket, though Julie had wrapped her hands around it. "I have asked Morgan to conjure a spell that will show her the whereabouts of all Lunar Fae in Avalon and on Earth. I was concerned that Vivienne was not the only fae who was forced to work with the enemy against her will." She sighed. "It seems that whichever fae are involved, they're seeking to kill me willingly, but Morgan's spell will locate them nonetheless."

Her eyes met Julie's. "We have discussed this spell for some time. There are so few of us left, and we must take care of our own, Julie."

Julie nodded. "Yes, Your Majesty."

Queen Esmerelda let go of the casket. "Morgan's magic is complicated. She will need that." She nodded at the casket. "It will be good for you to witness this, Julie, and good for Morgan to have Lunar Fae help if she needs it. Go to Tintagel right away, both of you. Remember, guard this with your lives until Morgan takes it from you." Her brow creased. "I dread what might become of us all if it falls into the wrong hands."

Julie's gut clenched, and her grip tightened on the casket. "Yes, Your Majesty."

Queen Esmerelda slumped on her throne. "Go," she murmured.

———

Neither Julie nor Bianca said anything during the long walk out to the courtyard. Julie stared at the casket, clutching it so tightly that her knuckles turned white.

She finally broke the silence when they were outside and away from listening ears. "What do you think is in it?" she whispered.

Bianca shrugged. "A powerful amulet if Morgan needs it for her spell." She grinned. "I was hoping to visit my bestie sooner or later in this little adventure."

Julie laughed. "I hope her spell works and gives us answers."

"How do you want to get to Tintagel?" Bianca asked. "It's a bit far to fly ourselves."

"We can take Genevieve," Julie suggested. "I took her there last time, and it was quick."

"She's at Avalon HQ, isn't she?" Bianca asked.

"Not for long." Julie tugged Hat off her head, still holding the casket tightly in one hand. *Hey, Hat, can you call Genevieve for me?*

Call? Hat groaned. *You're aware that I work* telepathically *and that Genevieve is a car?*

"You always say she's got powers you don't understand." Julie raised her eyebrows.

I suppose I could try, Hat muttered. *But you'll have to meet her outside the grounds. She's never going to get through security on her own.*

Julie put him on again, and they set off for the gates. Hat hummed busily for a few moments, then exclaimed, "Bloody bugger!"

"What?" Julie asked.

"She *answered!*" he exclaimed.

When they left the Eternal Palace and walked down the long road through the field beyond the walls, Genevieve's gleaming shape was swooping over Avalon Town. By the time Julie and Bianca stepped through the ward and stood waiting on the grass, she could see the black stripes on the Mustang's pewter bodywork.

Engine purring, Genevieve landed with barely a crunch of tires and rolled up to them. Her front doors swung open, and she gave two cheerful honks.

"Your car officially rules," Bianca announced.

Genevieve flashed her headlights and honked again.

"I think she says thank you." Julie laughed and held out the casket to Bianca. "I'll drive."

Bianca took it. "Can we stop for snacks? It's not a road trip without snacks."

Julie giggled. "I guess that could be arranged."

"Also, I'm the DJ. No arguments," Bianca added.

Julie shrugged. "That's fine by me."

An hour later, Julie regretted her decision.

She eyed the radio, which Bianca had set to a station that played angry succubus rap. It pounded against Genevieve's windows in sharp contrast to the beautiful day outside. They floated calmly through a sunny sky, fluffy clouds like tufts of cotton drifting below them. They weren't far from Tintagel, and the clouds cast fast-moving shadows on the heather-clad hillsides as they approached the moor.

It would have been pleasant apart from the music. And the snoring. Bianca had reclined the seat as far as it would go, and she sprawled in it, head tipped back, mouth open, snoring like an army of dwarves using a chainsaw to cut an angry dragon in half. It was only vaguely preferable to the crunching. Snack detritus was strewn over the backseat.

"She's going to vacuum you when this is over, Gennie," Julie whispered, petting the Mustang's dash.

"You are aware that you have brownies for that, right?" Hat pointed out.

Julie scoffed. "It's the thought that counts." She reached toward the radio's dial, but when her fingers touched the knob, Bianca stirred. Julie hastily returned her hands to the wheel. Bianca rolled onto her side, head pillowed on her arm, and snored at a more annoying pitch.

I love her, but remind me never to go on a road trip with her again, Julie hissed.

I'm not sure this is a road trip, considering we are not going by road, Hat observed.

Julie shrugged. *We're in a car. Close enough. Do I make a left here?*

No, wait until you see the ocean, Hat corrected. *It's not far. Half an hour at this speed.*

Cool. Julie settled into the seat and lowered her hands to her lap, in which the casket rested. She ran her fingers over it, feeling the cool threads of selenite inlaid in its surface, and wondered what was so important that—

Julie! Hat screeched. *Look out! Three o'clock!*

Bianca sat bolt upright with a snort, red magic glowing in her fists. Julie's head whipped to the right.

A shadow soared through the sky toward them.

Julie looked up, but there were no clouds. There was nothing between the shadow and the sun. It surged through the air like something physical, a flat patch of darkness moving quickly toward Genevieve.

Julie summoned fire to her free hand, tightening her grip on the casket. "What *is* that?" she hissed.

Bianca took a sharp breath.

Julie realized there was more than one shadow as it sped nearer. There were three, each roughly the size and shape of a two-dimensional surfboard.

Each was occupied by a squat, pointy-eared humanoid.

"Shit," Bianca muttered. "It's the drow."

CHAPTER EIGHT

Julie uttered something profane about Merlin's nether regions.

Hat gasped. "Julie!"

The drow sped nearer, surfing the sky on their shadows. Two male, one female. All three had skin the color of wet charcoal, short white hair that stood up like flames, and a scimitar in each hand. Their blades flashed in the sun but did not reflect in the shadows they rode.

"Hat, we're going to need backup." Julie made a decision quickly. She opened the glove box and shoved the casket inside, then wrenched Hat off her head and tossed him on the dash.

"Where do you think *you're* going?" Hat demanded.

"Genevieve, get the casket to Tintagel," Julie ordered. "Fast as you can. Hat, make sure it gets there."

"Julie—" Hat began.

"What about us?" Bianca asked.

Julie met the succubus' eyes. "We're going to slow down the drow."

Bianca nodded. "Got it."

"*Julie!*" Hat protested.

She ignored him, shoved Genevieve's door open, and stepped

into thin air. The air *was* thin up here. She had to breathe faster, and sweat broke out on her forehead. Her wings hummed, and she summoned fire to both hands, the flames licking up to her elbows.

Bianca hovered beside her, beating her wings. "Go, Genevieve!" Julie ordered.

The Mustang's engine roared, and she shot forward.

The drow sped up.

"Let's go get them!" Bianca bellowed.

Julie called a fireball to each hand and stirred her wings from a hum into a high-pitched whine. She charged the drow, letting out a wordless yell of fury, and flung both fireballs at once. One slammed into a male drow's shadow, and it burned up and disintegrated like paper set alight. He screamed and tumbled, arms flailing, but the female drow grabbed the edge of her shadow and flipped. The fireball crackled harmlessly past her, and her white eyes found Julie's. She drew back her lips from pointed gray teeth and hissed.

Bolts of red magic plunged past Julie, keeping the other male drow occupied, and Julie summoned two more fireballs. Both missed as the female drow charged her, dodging with a fierce grace, scimitars flashing in the sun.

"Come and get me, bitch!" Julie shouted.

Thunder bellowed over her head. She allowed the flames to vanish and reached for the thought of her father's grave, and a black cloud spread above her. Julie felt the lash of the wind and cold rain on her skin and held out both hands. The drow was mere yards away when she gripped a fistful of whirling rain and air, a handheld tornado, and flung it like a javelin. The drow dodged, but the air swirled around her, making her wobble. She cried out and dropped to her knees to avoid falling off her shadow.

"How do you like that, huh?" Julie yelled.

The drow's eyes narrowed. She had a square jaw and a

pointed nose, with a barrel chest, bowed legs, and heavy shoulders. Julie had never seen an elf like her.

"Want more?" Julie called, forming tiny tornadoes in each fist.

The drow made a scything motion with one scimitar and light flashed below Julie, grabbing her attention. She glanced down just long enough to see that her thundercloud cast no shadow and the rain was tumbling into bright sunshine. Fear stabbed through her gut, and something solid slammed into her back.

Julie would have screamed, but all the air had been knocked from her lungs. Numb pain spread through her wings. The tornadoes vanished from her hands, and her fists closed on nothing.

Then she fell.

Her arms and legs flailed helplessly, air shrieking in her ears. Julie's vision was a mad tangle of moor, sky, clouds, the red pulses of Bianca's fight with the other drow, and the shadow. Her thunderstorm formed into a charging monster, straddled by the female drow like a horse, and dove after her.

Julie gathered her scattered thoughts. Her wings only responded feebly, and the land was rushing up to meet her, but the shadow would catch her before gravity did. She could see the drow's gleaming eyes as she spurred the shadow on.

Taking a deep breath, Julie forced down her fear and summoned rage. Fireballs filled her hands as the shadow pounced. It opened a black maw, and her world filled with darkness. Julie let out a despairing yell and shoved both fireballs into its mouth.

Someone screamed, and she smelled burning hair. Then light filled Julie's world, and her wings responded. The shadow shriveled and vanished, and Julie and the drow fell. Julie's wings hummed, and she kicked to right herself but succeeded only in breaking her fall. She hit the ground feet-first and remembered at the last second to bend her knees and throw her arms over her head. Her momentum threw her flat, and she tumbled through the heather. The impact jarred every bone in her body. Every body part slammed into the earth—back, head, knees, shoulders, and back again.

When she finally stopped rolling, Julie's vision was blurred. She found her way to her hands and knees despite the way the earth pitched and rolled under her and saw twin silver blades flash. Julie flung herself to the side just in time. Both of a male drow's scimitars stabbed into the dirt where she'd been a second before.

She dragged herself to her feet and summoned flame, painfully conscious of the blood that dripped into her left eye. "Come on, then," she rasped, flames billowing in the cool breeze. "Come and get me."

The drow hissed and came at her in a series of strikes that were as swift and graceful as storm winds. Julie fired flames at him, but each missed its mark, and with each slash, the edges of the scimitars hissed closer and closer.

She blasted a fireball at his head, but he spun with smooth grace, ducked, and in the same movement, brought one scimitar up in a sweeping motion that ended with the blade striking her dwarf-made breastplate. The impact drove her back and almost knocked her off her feet. She felt the dwarf steel yield, and the tip of the scimitar pierced her chainmail and planted a kiss of burning pain on her skin.

The drow's eyes met hers, and he grinned, flashing gray teeth. That was a mistake.

"That was my favorite armor, bitch," Julie hissed and slammed her burning hands into the sides of his face.

Selenite flashed in her bracelets, then flickered, and Julie gasped with the sudden weakness that flooded her muscles. But the drow fell back, screaming. He flung down his scimitars and raised his hands to his eyes as flames spread through his hair. His shrieks reached a pitch that hurt Julie's ears, then stopped abruptly. Still burning, the drow fell to the ground, dead, the smell of his blazing corpse filling the air.

Julie took a step forward. Her legs wobbled, and she fell to her hands and knees, nausea boiling in her gut. She longed to fall face-first onto the dirt and take a long nap, but she forced herself to look up.

Genevieve was a shimmering pewter speck in the distance, still pursued by a shadow.

"No!" Julie rasped, struggling to her feet.

Above her, bursts of red light and shadow filled the air as Bianca and the other male drow battled. A hundred feet away, the female drow had summoned another shadow-beast that was galloping across the heather, carrying its rider after the fleeing Mustang.

Darkness fell over the moor. Julie looked as the red light winked out, and Bianca fell, unconscious, her wings and golden hair streaming above her.

Julie forced her wings open and broke into a run. It was a long few moments before they had the strength to lift her into the air, and she pinned her arms to her sides, striving toward the falling succubus as the victorious drow formed his shadow into another surfboard. He crouched, ready to shoot after his companion, and Julie fired a last despairing fireball before she quenched the flames and threw out her arms. She heard the drow shriek, then Bianca fell into her arms with a meaty thump.

"Bee!" Julie yelled, losing height as she struggled to keep her grip on the limp succubus. "Bee, wake up!"

Bianca moaned.

Julie's boots hit dirt and she stumbled, half-dropping Bianca. When she glanced up, the drow female had urged her shadow into the sky and was closing on Genevieve.

"Bianca!" Julie screamed.

A huge shadow blotted out the sky. Julie threw herself over Bianca, waiting for an army of drow to descend upon her.

Instead, she heard the thump of dragon wings. Julie looked up. A sinuous dragon soared above her, borne by three pairs of wings, smoke pouring from his nostrils.

"Livius!" she cried.

The dragon shot after the drow like an arrow. Julie thought she saw someone huddled on his back.

There was a shriek and a clash of steel. Julie sat up as the male drow charged her, limping but furious, scimitars upraised and teeth bared. There was no strength left in her selenite; it just fizzled when she tried to summon fire. Julie yanked the Bowie knife from her boot and held it up, snarling wordlessly, ready to accept whatever fate awaited her.

The earth leaped under the drow's feet. He stumbled on one foot, used the other to launch himself into the air, and turned a graceful somersault, but when he landed running, Malcolm Nox was upon him. The vampire slammed his claws into the drow's chest and slashed at the drow's throat with his fangs. With a shriek, the drow whipped around, raising those gleaming scimitars, and Malcolm fell back with a scream like he'd been burned.

"Leave them alone!" a dragon thundered.

The earth trembled as Axl charged, his sandstone skin flashing in the sunlight and his good-natured face twisted into a snarl of fury. The drow slammed both scimitars into Axl's face… and they bounced. Fingers cracked like twigs as the scimitars rebounded and left the drow's hands. Axl flung him to the ground, then pinned him there with an enormous paw.

"Go after the other one!" Julie screamed. Leaving Bianca slumbering on the ground, she stumbled to Axl, Bowie knife drawn. "I'll keep him down!"

"Julie. *Julie!*" Malcolm grabbed her arm. "It's okay. They've got her."

He turned her gently but firmly. Livius was flying toward them, the limp figure of the female drow clenched in his jaws. Cassidy, Malcolm's beautiful-yet-crazy wife, was perched on the dragon's back. The drow female's eyes glowed with red vampire mesmerism as Livius landed lightly a few hundred feet away and unceremoniously dumped his prisoner on the ground.

"Oh, thank Merlin." Julie realized she was trembling.

"Are you okay? Are you hurt?" Malcolm's eyes widened as Julie's knees buckled.

"No, I'm okay." Julie sank to the ground and covered her head with her hands. "That was balls to the wall."

Bianca sat up abruptly, color returning to her cheeks. "Where's that son-of-a-bitch?" she spat.

"Here," Axl announced helpfully. He closed his claws around his prisoner and held him upside-down. The drow squealed at the indignity.

"Good!" Bianca hauled herself to her feet, swayed, then stumbled to the indignant drow. "You *will* be prosecuted, asshole," she spat, jabbing a finger in his general direction. "You and your little friend are *going* to spill your guts about your boss, and then you will never see the light of day again, you hear me?" She leaned closer, eyes flashing. "I lost good paras in Germany."

The familiar roar of a V8 Cobrajet engine drew nearer, then Genevieve bumpily landed nearby. Her window rolled down, and Hat launched through it and onto the ground at Julie's feet. *Julie! You're bleeding,* he told her urgently.

Julie grabbed his brim. *Where's the casket?*

Safe in the glove box, but we'd better get to Tintagel before more drow show up.

Julie dragged herself to her feet and put Hat on. "Take the drow back to Avalon HQ for questioning," she ordered. "We're going to Tintagel."

"Gladly," Cassidy growled. "We'll call for a portal."

Livius spat out his prisoner, who lay limply on the ground, still under Cassidy's control. "Julie of the Meadows, we will go with you."

"It's okay, Livius, thanks. I have Bianca—" Julie reached out to steady her friend, who was swaying violently.

Livius raised a craggy brow at her.

"Okay, point taken. Bee, go back to Avalon HQ with the Noxes," Julie suggested. "Make sure the drow get there safely."

Bianca's eyes were still glassy, but when she clenched her fists, the red magic that glowed between her fingers was strong. "Gladly," she spat.

Cassidy hopped down from Livius' back and grabbed the unconscious drow female by both ankles. She dragged her unceremoniously across the ground. Malcolm was on the phone with the OPMA.

"Go," Bianca growled, grabbing the drow male's arms. "We've got this."

Julie didn't doubt it.

When Genevieve touched down in front of the portcullis at Tintagel, it was open. The twin towers of the castle straddled two hills, and the sea rumbled against the nearby shore. Afternoon sunshine bathed the castle's sandstone walls in gold.

Morgan Le Fay was a tiny winged figure in the gaping portcullis, but both dragons, who were sitting in Genevieve's back seat, whimpered softly as Julie drove up to her.

"What's the matter, boys?" Julie asked, grinning into the rearview mirror. "Scared of a little slip of a maiden like her?"

Livius' thin, pinched face flushed, and he let out an annoying high-pitched chuckle. Axl's gorgeous, chiseled features were, as usual, blank. Sometimes Julie thought she could hear the wind whistling into one ear and out through the other.

She brought Genevieve to a halt a few feet from the portcullis and grasped the casket, which had ridden safely on her lap to

Tintagel. When she stepped out of the car, Morgan hurried toward her.

"Julie!" the fae exclaimed. "I felt a burst of dark magic. Darker than I've felt in these parts for a long, long time." She shuddered. "What happened?"

"We were attacked by three drow." Julie held out the casket. "Queen Esmerelda said to give you this. It's hugely important. One of the drow died trying to get hold of it."

"It *is* important." Morgan took it and held it close to her chest. "Let's get inside. The drow won't approach Tintagel. I spend my time ensuring that this place is all but impervious to dark magic."

"Sure." Julie turned to the car. "Livius, Axl, come on."

The two dragons slunk out of Genevieve. Livius glanced everywhere, plucking at his robe. Axl wore his robe better, but not his nervousness. He gawped at Morgan, open-mouthed.

"These are my, uh, bodyguards," Julie offered lamely.

Morgan raised her elegant eyebrows. "Okay." She cleared her throat and drew herself to her full height, fanning out her wings to look taller. "I am Morgan Le Fay," she announced, her voice soft yet resounding. "Steward of Tintagel Castle and keeper of the Quest."

I was waiting for her line, Julie snarked.

Hat snickered.

"Nice to meet you, ma'am. Morgan, I mean, ma'am," Axl squeaked, then bowed deeply.

"We can wait outside," Livius blurted. "Since you're safe here, Julie of the Meadows."

Morgan smiled. "You have my permission to enter, honored dragons, but do not approach the orchard in which King Arthur rests, or the consequences will be more dire than you can imagine."

"We'd never hurt the Once and Future King, Your Morgan-ness," Axl assured her.

Morgan's eyes narrowed. "Forgive me for the lack of clarity. The consequences will be dire for *you*."

Axl whimpered and hid behind Livius, an epic failure since he was roughly twice his brother's width.

"Where should I park Genevieve?" Julie asked.

Morgan grinned. "She can do whatever she wants."

Genevieve honked twice.

"Love the new robe, by the way," Morgan added.

Julie smoothed her hands over her bone-white dragonscale robe. "Thank you! They'll take on color when the egg hatches, Alugon said."

"They will indeed, but that's not why I like them." Morgan smiled. "I've seldom seen dragonscale robes, but there's no better protection than a dragon's scales. Powered by a dragon's heart, they can repel even the darkest magic. I don't know if the robe works the same, but they've got to be good protection."

They strode under the portcullis, and Genevieve contentedly rolled into the inner ward and parked under the statue of King Arthur holding Excalibur. As always, Morgan gave the statue a longing look as they walked across the ward. Livius and Axl trailed in their wake.

Julie took a sudden breath and pressed a hand to her chest. "Oh, wow. That's a lot better."

Morgan raised an eyebrow. "What is?"

"I was drained after fighting the drow," Julie told her. "Like the magic had been sucked out of me. Even the selenite in my bracelets wasn't working." She held up the bracelets and shook back her sleeves to reveal the crystals, which glowed brightly. "Until I walked under the portcullis. I feel fine now."

"Tintagel is imbued with moonlight even on the brightest day." Morgan smiled. "That's how I maintain the spell on King Arthur."

"Why did the drow make me feel so drained, anyway?" Julie asked.

"They command the most powerful dark magic in the universe. Little is known about them apart from that," Morgan explained. "You're all lucky to be alive. Did you capture any of them?"

"Two," Julie told her. "I killed the third."

Morgan's eyebrows shot up. "*You* killed a drow? On your own?"

"Sort of," Julie admitted.

Morgan grinned. "Not many paras out there can do that."

Both dragons cheered up after Morgan gave them directions to the dining hall in the second tower. They scampered off, and Morgan led Julie up a spiral staircase to the topmost room in the first tower.

Julie tried not to stare after they entered the round room, but it was difficult. In the center of the floor was a glass window that looked down on the ever-blooming orchard in which King Arthur lay in his enchanted sleep, enclosed in a glass casket. The roof had a circular skylight that allowed shafts of sunlight to reach the orchard. It took Julie a second to remember that it was afternoon, and the sun couldn't be shining straight down into the orchard, but eternal midday reigned where the king slept.

The rest of the floor was covered with a purple wool carpet. The curving walls were lined with desks, most of them covered with velvet, all featuring dozens of drawers. The drawers were labeled in glowing gold letters: Obsidian, Basilisk Antivenom, Unicorn Hippomanes, Batteries, Gleipnir Iron, Selenite, and Buttons.

"Buttons?" Julie enquired.

Morgan gestured at the back of her long green dress. "Never know when you might need one."

Whiteboards had been tacked up on the walls and were covered in runes Julie didn't recognize. A huge book lay open on a nearby table, its runes flickering like flames. Next to it, a tiny brass cauldron rested on a Bunsen burner, the small blue flame hissing. Steam in rainbow colors puffed out of the cauldron.

"There's a lot of magic in here." Julie rubbed the goosebumps on her arms.

"Keeping Arthur both asleep and alive is no small matter," Morgan admitted. "Tea?"

"More of a coffee person." Julie grimaced. "Sorry."

Morgan started an electric kettle on a plain table by the back wall. "Bee's the same. How American of you." She chuckled and set the casket on the table by the tiny cauldron.

Julie came over and peered into the cauldron. Rainbow colors swirled and bubbled within. "What's in the casket, if I may ask?"

"*May* ask? You *must* ask, Julie." Morgan smiled. "That's why Esmerelda sent you. She wants you to learn more about fae magic."

"Sounds good to me." Julie shrugged. *I'd rather learn more about my identity than fae magic, but okay.*

Julie! Hat chided.

Morgan looked at her searchingly.

Julie gave her a big smile. "So, what *is* in the casket?"

"The last thing I need to complete my location spell and find all of the Lunar Fae." Morgan pressed her fingertips to two of the selenite crystals on the casket, and it snapped open. She reached inside and drew out a tiny glass vial with an ornate obsidian stopper. It contained a dark fluid.

Julie drew a sharp breath. "Is that blood?"

"It is." Morgan closed the casket. "It's Queen Esmerelda's blood."

Morgan gently set the vial in a wooden test tube rack, then bent over the cauldron. "Let's begin. This spell is going to take time and energy."

Julie glanced through the window at her feet. She could just make out the motionless figure of King Arthur. "Is he going to be okay?"

Morgan pointed at a shelf on the wall on which a row of crystal orbs rested. Five of the six glowed fiercely, and the sixth shone dimly. Gleipnir iron connected the orbs to the window in the floor.

"I've poured enough magic in there to hold the spell for an hour or so before I have to replenish it," Morgan explained. "There's no time to waste."

"Okay." Julie moved closer. "What can I do?"

Morgan switched off the Bunsen burner and peered into the cauldron. Its contents were still brightly colored. "What do you know about the role of blood in magic, Julie?"

Julie frowned. "Nothing."

Morgan raised an eyebrow.

Julie held her hands up. "Human-raised, remember? Bite me."

Morgan chuckled. "I don't think that would be pleasant for either of us." She lifted the vial and turned it this way and that so the blood caught the light. Julie thought she saw fragments of silvery brightness inside the blood, or maybe that was just a reflection on the glass. "Blood holds life," Morgan murmured. "Without blood, sentient life cannot exist."

Don't say it, Hat growled. *Don't you—*

"What about dryads?" Julie asked. "And naiads?"

Hat sighed. *You said it.*

Morgan grinned. "A valid question."

A stupid question, Hat muttered.

"Dryads and other species don't have blood as we know it. They have sap, for example," Morgan explained. "But all sentient beings can bleed."

Julie nodded.

"Biologically, blood is magical." Morgan swirled the blood inside the vial. "It connects the outside world with our innermost parts. It both feeds us and cleanses us. It keeps us alive and helps us grow. It can even heal us."

She grinned. "But there is a deeper magic to blood that goes far beyond biology. Consider the power of spilled blood."

Julie thought about the black stain on the stone floor in Lockerfell the night Chester died. "I think I know what you mean."

Morgan's mouth turned down at the corners. "I'm sad that you do."

"It makes sense." Julie pushed the memory away. "Everything changes when someone is killed."

Morgan nodded. "When blood is drawn unwillingly, it shifts everything. People, relationships, beliefs, and nations. Even entire worlds, often for the worse."

"It's how wars begin," Julie agreed.

"Exactly. That's why some mages succumb to the dark temptations blood brings." Morgan met her eyes. "Blood can bring out the worst within us."

Julie shuddered, remembering how close she'd come to murdering Chester's killer.

"Harnessing blood in your magic? That's one of the most dangerous things you can do as a mage. It might drag you down or darken you." Morgan paused. "It can change everything."

"So, how do you not give in to that temptation?" Julie asked.

Morgan smiled. "One thing is far more powerful than spilled blood. More powerful than anything in any dimension."

Julie tipped her head to the side. "What's that?"

"Innocent blood, willingly given." Morgan lowered her eyes to the vial. "There is no greater power, Julie. There is no greater love."

Chester filled her thoughts again, and her chest tightened. "I understand that too," she whispered.

Morgan unstopped the vial with a soft clink. "A single drop of the queen's blood is enough to make this spell possible," she explained. "Not easy, but possible." She nodded at the cauldron. "I need you to heat it for me. A spell like this requires a huge amount of energy."

Julie stepped forward and set her hands on fire, then cupped them around the cauldron and lifted it. It was heavier than it looked. "Like this?"

"Yes." Morgan met her eyes. "Don't let it get cold, whatever you do."

Julie nodded seriously.

Morgan glanced at one of the whiteboards and muttered under her breath in a language Julie didn't recognize. "Ready?"

Julie grunted. "Ready."

Morgan tipped the vial, and a single drop of blood tumbled into the cauldron. Morgan set the vial aside and held her hands over the cauldron, chanting. The rainbow colors began to swirl as though they were being stirred, and the cauldron cooled in Julie's hands.

She frowned and clenched her fingers, urging hotter flames to her hands.

"Keep going!" Morgan encouraged her.

The colors changed. They turned darker and more serious. Julie poured heat into the cauldron until she was gasping for breath. Her selenite glowed fiercely, and she channeled its power, but the cauldron still didn't boil.

Morgan was everywhere. She flitted this way and that, sometimes on her feet, sometimes fluttering when her feet weren't fast enough. She muttered under her breath, grabbed random objects and powders and fluids from the drawers and added them to the cauldron, and repeated her chants in deeper tones, then higher ones.

"What's taking so long?" Julie asked.

"Shhh!" Morgan hissed. She grabbed a book from a nearby shelf, flipped to its index, and searched it. Sweat trickled down her smooth, pale brow.

The liquid in the cauldron was now gray. Julie gritted her teeth and summoned fireballs, then balanced them on her palms, but even they couldn't bring the contents of the cauldron to a boil.

Morgan yanked open a drawer and seized a unicorn hippomane. It was a tiny, flat object like a mermaid's purse, and it shimmered with a rainbow of colors. "More heat!" she boomed and chanted again, louder this time and fiercer.

Julie gritted her teeth, closed her eyes, and summoned rage. She thought about what had happened to Chester, Blake, the Woodskins, Sylvie Mackintosh, Mina Nox, the Fernwood refugees, and everyone else who had suffered in the war.

"More!" Morgan yelled, then continued her chant.

Aloe vera juice, Hat whispered in Julie's mind.

Heat surged through Julie's hands.

"There!" Morgan cried.

Julie's eyes snapped open as a cloud of rainbow steam poofed out of the cauldron. When it dissipated, the contents were clear.

CHAPTER NINE

Morgan leaned over the cauldron, breathless. "It worked. You can put the cauldron down now. It's stable."

Julie slowly lowered the still-boiling cauldron onto the Bunsen burner, which was off. She flexed her fingers, and the flames disappeared.

"That was intense," she commented.

Morgan grabbed a tablet, the electronic kind, from a nearby desk. "Any minute now," she muttered.

Julie leaned closer. Runes appeared on the motionless crystal-clear surface of the cauldron's contents. Morgan's tablet beeped.

"What's it doing?" Julie murmured as more runes appeared, then scrolled across the surface of the cauldron.

"It's giving me the names and locations of all Lunar Fae alive in the human world and in Avalon," Morgan told her. "The tablet is inputting everything into a searchable database."

"That's very cool." Julie wiped her stiff, tired hands on her coat.

Morgan raised an eyebrow. "That's all you've got?"

"What can I say?" Julie grinned apologetically. "It's been a long day. So, anything look suspicious?"

Morgan chuckled. "Let's see." She swiped the tablet and scrolled through a list. "The database contains location data for all Lunar Fae in both dimensions," she explained. "Workplaces, homes, and their usual spheres."

Julie raised her eyebrows. "Privacy violation much?"

"Not if ordered by royal decree." Morgan frowned, smoke forming between her fingers. "Ugh, that's frustrating."

"What is?" Julie leaned closer.

Morgan showed her the tablet and scrolled through a list of names that seemed painfully short to contain an entire species. Julie was almost disappointed to see her name as Maj. Julie Meadows. She'd hoped the tablet would know her true name. All of the names were in green except one, which was underlined in red: Vivienne. There was no last name.

"So," Julie guessed, "all the Lunar Fae are in their usual places?"

"All those we know of except Vivienne, who's in the para-ER." Morgan pressed her lips together. "I'd hoped to find an anomaly. Someone we could question."

"That doesn't mean they're all innocent." Julie sighed. "It just means no one's out of place. Like you say, no one we *know of*."

"Exactly," Morgan agreed.

Julie folded her arms and shuffled to the window in the floor. She gazed through it, seeing the bright pink of cherry blossoms and the outline of the sleeping king. From here, it was impossible to see the ghastly wound in his side, which would claim his life if he was taken out of the stasis that both bound and preserved him.

"That means that the traitor could be a Lunar Fae we know and trust," she murmured.

Paranoia won't help anyone, Hat cautioned. *That's a dangerous rabbit hole to go down, Julie.*

Dangerous but necessary? Julie wondered.

Morgan laid a hand on Julie's shoulder. It was still warm from her frustration. "It's far more likely that the traitor was one of the Lunar Fae who went into hiding when our people were targeted."

Julie laughed harshly. "What do you mean, *were*? We still are, aren't we?" She threw up her hands. "There still isn't a viable heir to the Eternity Throne, and Lunar Fae councilors and princesses are still missing in action."

"That's true, although things have stabilized since the Pendragon Wars and the last uprising of the Dark Moon League," Morgan reminded her.

"I guess." Julie took a deep breath, counted to five, and let it out. Her palms cooled. "When you say some fae went into hiding, do you mean your magic can't find them?"

Morgan shook her head. "Not if they're under concealment spells as deep as yours was, for example. You only showed up on my location spells when you grew wings."

Julie chewed the inside of her cheek. "I'm not the only changeling out there, am I?" She shuddered. "You mean concealment spells don't just wear off over time?"

"They don't," Morgan confirmed.

The thought made a tremor run through Julie's spine. "So, if the IRSA 4000 hadn't accidentally drafted me into the OPMA, I might never have found out that fae even exist, let alone that I am one."

Morgan laughed. "Oh, I bet you would have found your way to the place you belonged, no matter what."

Julie smiled, and something inside her unclenched. "Are there other ways for Lunar Fae to hide?"

"Of course. Pocket dimensions my spell can't reach would be one way," Morgan suggested.

Julie frowned. "But if one of the lost fae resurfaced, your spell would have found them, right?"

Morgan nodded.

They stared through the glass at King Arthur. "Basically," Julie summarized, "we're left with more questions than answers. As usual."

Morgan grimaced. "Pretty much."

The king slept on beneath the cherry blossoms, unaware of the chaos that still ruled the world he'd tried to save.

Julie hurried across the carpeted entrance hall of the NYHQ and almost bumped into Ellie Feathertouch, the intelligence agent who'd been her first recruit.

Julie paused. "Oh, hey, Ellie!"

Ellie looked up from the tablet in her hands and smiled. "Julie! It's so good to see you." Her smile vanished. "Wait, what happened to your head?"

Julie touched a hard, painful scab on her forehead. "Crap. Is there blood?"

"A fair amount." Ellie grimaced.

"Shit. Sorry. Do you know where the drow prisoners are being interrogated?" Julie asked.

Ellie nodded. "In the containment unit. Same place as usual. Should I call Olena for you?"

"It's cool. I'll deal with it later." Julie waved. "See you."

She jogged to the elevator, now conscious of all the stares aimed her way.

You couldn't have told me I had something on my face when I reported to Her Majesty at the Palace, Hat? she grumbled. *I wondered why the griffins were staring at me.*

I don't think it had anything to do with "something on your face," which is a quite nasty cut, Hat grumbled.

Why were they staring, then? Julie snapped.

Hat hesitated. *You single-handedly defeated a drow. Word gets around.*

Julie took the elevator to the containment level twelve floors below ground. The doors opened on a solid iron door with a small barred window and glowing blue runes on its surface. Baleful yellow eyes glared at her through the window.

"Uh, hi?" Julie began. "Major Julie Meadows."

"Let her in, Fearghus," Bianca ordered from the other side of the door.

Someone grumbled, then heavy bolts clanked. The runes winked out and the door creaked open, hauled aside by a huge, hairy minotaur. He saluted sharply as Julie stepped into the bleak, sanitized hallway, all tiles and cream-colored paint. Fluorescent strips on the ceiling shed a brutal, unforgiving light on the featureless space.

The second door on the right was open, and Bianca sat on an uncomfortable steel chair inside. She waved Julie over. "Hey, girl. How'd it go at Tintagel?"

Julie strode into a small, bare observation room. The steel chair, its matching table, and its twin made up the furniture. A scrying screen on the table recorded every movement on the other side of the one-way glass. The interrogation room beyond was cold and empty except for another steel table and two chairs. There was a hefty ring in the steel table and another in the tiled floor beneath it.

"Inconclusively." Julie pulled up the empty chair and sat.

Bianca hissed in frustration. "We're just about to start the second round of interrogations. Maybe this will finally be our break."

"You okay?" Julie asked. "You seemed shaken up after the fight."

Bianca tapped a bruise fading on her temple. "Just got my bell rung, that's all. Nothing the medics here couldn't fix in time for me to get started on these interrogations." Her expression darkened. "I'm going to break them, Julie. They don't have any geasa on them."

Julie sat up. "They don't?"

"Nope. None of those self-immolation amulets either, as far as we can tell." Bianca gave a savage grin. "We have a real chance to get the truth out of those bitches."

Julie leaned forward as the door to the interrogation room clanked open. "We need this break before something else happens to Her Majesty or one of the councilors. Or anyone else, for that matter."

"Don't I know it." Bianca got to her feet as two sturdy satyr guards wrestled the male drow into the room.

"You break his ass." Julie held out a fist.

Bianca bumped it. "That's the plan." She headed to the other room.

Julie interlaced her fingers and squeezed them tightly together as the satyrs sat the drow down and shackled him to the heavy steel table. They nodded at Bianca on their way out. She didn't take the chair facing the drow. Instead, arms folded, she walked a slow circle around him.

The drow didn't acknowledge her presence. He glowered at the one-way glass. Julie felt like he was meeting her eyes. She narrowed hers and clenched her fists. Wisps of smoke escaped them.

"I'll keep it simple to start with." Bianca's tone was light and cheerful. "What's your name?"

The drow continued to pretend she didn't exist.

She stopped by the chair opposite the drow and leaned her elbows on the back of it, her curls tumbling over her shoulders. "Is that question too difficult for you? Should I draw you a picture?"

The drow's lips twisted in a sneer, but he said nothing.

"Okay, so you're not into giving up your name. I get that. Privacy is hard to maintain these days." Bianca pulled out the chair and settled comfortably into it, then lifted her high-heeled boots onto the table with a thump. "You think you're just giving your number to a friend, and the next minute, people keep trying to reach you about your doom chariot's extended warranty."

The drow ignored her.

"Thing is, guy, you have way bigger problems than spam callers on your plate." Bianca folded her arms. "I mean, whatever happens, your life is never going to be the same. You can kiss your freedom goodbye. But there are different ways to serve your sentence."

The drow continued to stare through Julie. She resisted the urge to wave. He couldn't see her, could he?

"So, you have one last chance of seeing the Mr. Nice Guy side of the Eternity Throne." Bianca abruptly lowered her feet to the floor, leaned forward, and rested her elbows on the table. "I'm going to make this *extra* simple."

The drow's eyes narrowed.

"You've got a choice." Bianca shrugged. "Either you can tell me right now who sent you to attack us and how they knew where we were." She tossed her curls back. "Or you can have Captain Jack Kaplan interrogate you. He's vicious. You might be familiar with him. Seven feet tall, turns into a tiger when he's pissed?" Bianca leaned closer and lowered her voice to a conspiratorial whisper. "Lately, Jack's always pissed."

The drow scoffed and finally spoke in a low, sibilant voice with a sharp accent. "I know your weak and foolish laws, woman," he growled. "You won't kill me. Your laws do not allow it." His smile was as mirthless as the curve of a scimitar. "That is why you cannot win."

Bianca leaned back and inspected her fingernails. "Okay. Weird take, given that you're the one in chains right now, but okay."

"Not for long," the drow hissed. "Soon, all those who are deserving will be free."

"Oh?" Bianca arched an eyebrow. "Thanks for that detail. Free how? And who are these 'deserving' paras?"

The drow sat back. "I will tell you nothing."

"Fine. You're right. We won't kill you." With disconcerting suddenness, Bianca threw herself forward and slammed her fists on the steel table with a clang that made Julie jump. "But mark my words, you son of a bitch," she hissed, inches from his face. "We *will* send you to the prison realm. I hear the beings there have a special hunger for dark magic."

The drow didn't blink. "I will gladly go," he murmured, "and be with the one true king until the day of his return."

Julie shuddered hard. *No prizes for guessing who that is.*

Hat was cold on her head. *There is not one fiber of kingship in Mordred.*

Julie's phone buzzed. Bianca sat back, studying the drow.

Bugger, Hat growled.

What? Julie asked.

Hat sighed deeply. *Read the message.*

Julie fished her phone out and frowned at the text. It was from Cassidy.

Julie, help. It's Mina. She's gone.

"Shit."

She scrambled to her feet and hurried out into the hallway as her phone rang: Malcolm. Julie swiped the screen and raised the phone to her ear.

"Julie? *Julie!*" Malcolm squealed even before the screen touched her face.

"Cassidy texted me," Julie told him. "What happened?"

"Dad's going to kill me!" Malcolm moaned. "He left me in charge while he went to a council meeting, and now she's gone!"

Julie sighed. "Take a deep breath, Mal."

"She was my responsibility. She's dangerous *and* vulnerable!" Malcolm cried. "Anything could happen to her. *She* could happen to anyone!"

"Did she disappear while you guys were helping me fight the drow?" Julie asked.

"There's a crazed vampire scrambled by dark magic on the loose in New York City!" Malcolm howled. "I can't track her. The dark magic is too strong. How will I find her?"

"Deep breaths, Mal," Julie coached. "It's okay. We'll find her. Just tell me what happened."

Malcolm took a shaky breath. "Okay." He cleared his throat. "No, it wasn't while we were fighting the drow. We got them and Bianca back to Avalon HQ without incident, and Cassidy and I went home. I checked on Mina, and she seemed fairly chill."

"Okay," Julie soothed. "Then what happened?"

Malcolm sighed. "I don't know. Cassidy was downstairs, watering that weird plant of Dad's that needs to be sprayed a million times a day and texting him the hourly updates he always wants—"

"Focus, Mal," Julie coached. "Mina."

Malcolm swallowed. "I went up to sit with Mina. Just to give her some company, you know? We were watching a harmless documentary about the hippocampi in Fernwood's lakes, and the next minute, Mina freaked. I tried to control her, but when Perkins ran in with the potion, she overpowered me and got out under the silver grille."

"Shit," Julie muttered. "Did you see which way she went?"

"No," Malcolm wailed, hyperventilating again. "Julie, she's going to kill someone or get herself killed! What if those kidnappers come back for her? What if there are more drow out there? We have to find her! I'll just have to follow the trail of bodies she's going to leave in her wake—"

"Malcolm. *Malcolm!*" Julie yelled. "Snap out of it!"

He shut up.

"You're not alone. You've got the OPMA, remember?" Julie spoke more gently. "You can lean on us. We're here to help you."

Malcolm took another shaky breath. "Thank you. Are you coming?"

Julie tugged the brim of her service cap. *Hat, would you open a line to Kaplan, please? On my phone so Malcolm can hear you.*

What am I, a wireless router? Hat grumbled.

That's not how that works, Julie pointed out.

Hat was already humming, and a phone rang in Julie's ear.

"Who are you calling?" Malcolm asked.

"The captain," Julie told him.

Malcolm let out a wail. "*No!* Not Uncle Jack!"

"Kaplan," the tiger shifter growled.

"Hey, Cap. How's it hanging?" Julie chirped.

Kaplan sighed. "This was a perfectly fine day, Meadows. In what way are you about to screw it up?"

"No biggie." Julie smirked. "I just need a Were unit to meet me at the Nox mansion. My guys from Griffin Seven would be great."

"Why?" Kaplan asked.

"No reason," Malcolm blurted.

"Is that Nox?" Kaplan barked.

"Yes, sir." Julie paused. "In all seriousness, Captain, Mina Nox escaped. We need to find her. Quickly."

"Really quickly," Malcolm moaned. "Do you have any idea of the amount of damage Mina could cause to the humans in this city? She could kill hundreds in a single night, and it's pitch-dark out here!" He groaned. "Dad's going to have my hide for this!"

"You didn't do anything wrong, Malcolm," Julie soothed. "She overpowered you. That dark magic is scary. There was nothing you could have done."

"But she's going to get hurt. Or hurt someone," Malcolm cried.

"Nox, stop that," Kaplan snapped. "Meadows is right."

"Are you feeling okay, sir?" Julie asked with mock concern.

"Shut up, Meadows," Kaplan ordered. "Nox, this isn't your

fault. I've seen how Mina can be when she has one of her episodes. She could overpower the best of us. Stop beating yourself up and do something more productive. Am I clear?"

Malcolm swallowed. "Yes, sir." The tremor in his voice had vanished.

"Good," Kaplan growled. "I know you will personally lead the search to find her," he snarled. "Preferably *before* she causes irreparable damage."

"Absolutely, Uncle Jack," Malcolm confirmed. "Just send me those Weres."

"They're on their way. Good luck, and try not to get your ass kidnapped. Is that clear?" Kaplan snapped.

"Crystal clear, Uncle Jack," Malcolm spluttered and hung up.

Kaplan sighed. "Still there, Meadows?"

"Yes, sir, I'm here," Julie responded.

Kaplan was silent for a moment. "How long do you expect to take with your investigation into Her Majesty's poisoning?"

Julie scratched her chin. She'd guessed Droppelheimer would tell Kaplan what she and Bianca had been up to for the past few days. "I don't know. We keep hitting dead ends."

Kaplan cleared his throat. "I'm going to offer you some friendly advice," he growled.

Julie stifled a grin. "Yes, sir."

"I understand that nobody's in direct danger, given the improved security around Her Majesty's meals. Also, you've apprehended some suspects," Kaplan declared.

Julie nodded. "That's right, sir."

"Then get some rest, Meadows," Kaplan told her gruffly. "Come at it from a fresh perspective."

Julie smiled. *"Friendly advice," my ass. That's not a suggestion.* "Yes, sir." She paused. "Thank you for looking out for me, sir."

There was a long silence. Julie thought the line had dropped until Kaplan spoke.

"I want you to remember that those closest to you will always have your best interests in mind." He sighed. "That might ease what's waiting for you at Avalon HQ."

"What do you mean, sir?" Julie asked.

Kaplan huffed. "Just get your ass there, Meadows." He hung up.

Julie frowned at her phone. *That was rude.*

That was Kaplan, Hat pointed out. *You* have *met him, right?*

Something's up. Julie gritted her teeth. *Better go find out what it is. Hopefully, it won't take too long, and hopefully, Horusiris will show up at some point. I'd love to spend the night with Eggy.*

Hat sighed. *Something tells me you might not get the chance.*

Before Julie could protest, her phone buzzed with a new text. It was from her boss, Droppelheimer.

Major Meadows, my office. Immediately.

Julie swallowed hard and set off down the hallway at a dead run.

CHAPTER TEN

Droppelheimer's office usually felt spacious, and it was roomy enough for four desks. One belonged to Julie, the others to Droppelheimer's office staff, Doris, Emmeline, and the questionable Vlad. Now, it felt like there wasn't enough room to breathe.

Julie paused in the doorway, recognizing several of the NCOs she'd worked with on her promotion to corporal. She delivered a bright smile to Corporal Brooklaugh, the perky Aether Elf who'd always been in her corner, but he glared at her, arms folded. Every other officer in Tactical Command was crammed into the room, and none of them looked happy.

First Sergeant Cadmeus Droppelheimer stood in front of everyone, jaw clenched. The tall, well-groomed orc seldom looked stressed, but now was one of those times.

"Meadows." Droppelheimer cleared his throat. "There are some...grievances against you."

Julie shut the door behind her, even though doing so made her feel pinned. She glanced at Doris. The wereelk gave her a sympathetic look, plucked a leaf from the hapless peace lily attempting to bloom in a pot on her desk, and stress-ate it.

"What sort of grievances, sir?" Julie asked.

"What sort of *grievances*?" Brooklaugh burst out. "What do you *think*, Major Meadows?" He scoffed. "As if you are worthy of that title."

Julie's eyes narrowed. "Excuse me?"

"You heard him." Lieutenant Erin Norman, an elegant elf, stepped forward. "You are too immature to be in Tactical Command, and we all know it. Your actions of late have proved it. You've put the entire OPMA in jeopardy. The whole of Avalon!"

"Enough." Droppelheimer didn't raise his voice, but it silenced everyone in the room.

"Sir, what's this about?" Julie asked. Her hands were shaking, and she took deep breaths to cool her palms.

Droppelheimer clasped his hands in front of him. "Your removal of the dragon heir from the Deep has caused great concern among your fellow officers, Meadows."

"Great concern?" Norman scoffed. "More like fear for our lives!"

"You've always been a loose cannon," Brooklaugh spat. "Now you're risking an all-out war with the Deep. They would be well within their rights to retrieve the heir by force!"

Heat scorched Julie's palms.

"They would not, Corporal," Droppelheimer snapped. "In the eyes of the law, Meadows committed no crime."

Julie took a deep breath, and her palms cooled.

"Committed no crime? She kidnapped the dragon heir!" Norman burst out.

"By the dragon heir's order!" Emmeline shot back, hedgehog spikes rising on her scalp.

Norman snorted. "Does it matter? You can quibble morality and ethics all you like. It won't help any of us if we're reduced to ashes by dragonfire!"

A burly Were added his voice to the mix. "She should never

have been made a corporal so quickly, much less a major. She doesn't belong in Tactical Command."

"We all knew this would happen," Brooklaugh hissed.

Vlad rose to his feet and held up shriveled, bony fists. "You wanna fight me, huh?" he demanded, brandishing them. "You wanna piece of me?"

"Nobody wants a piece of you, Vlad." Julie laid a hand on his shoulder.

She turned to the officers, whose baleful glares pierced her chest. *I've saved all of your asses more than once,* she wanted to scream. Instead, she forced her eyes away from them and onto Droppelheimer.

"I stand by everything I've done as a Tactical Command officer," she announced. "I've done good work, and all of you know that. What's more, I did the right thing by removing the dragon heir from a toxic environment, regardless of what anyone thinks."

Norman spat. "So, endangering your fellow officers just doesn't matter to you?"

Droppelheimer made a scything motion with one hand, and the officers fell silent again.

"Let it be known," he growled, "that I stand by Major Meadows' choice. In her shoes, I would have done exactly the same thing."

"Sergeant!" Brooklaugh burst out.

Droppelheimer shot him a look. The elf fell silent.

"Nonetheless..." Droppelheimer sighed. "Tactical Command cannot afford to be divided at this time." He turned to Julie, the corners of his mouth drooping. "Major Meadows, I have no choice but to temporarily suspend you from active duty. But make no mistake." He glared at the officers. "This suspension is no reflection on Meadows' merits as an officer of the Para-Military Agency."

Norman's grin was smug. "If you say so, sir."

"Leave us," Droppelheimer commanded.

The officers shuffled out of the room, shooting venomous glances in Julie's direction. She said nothing. The door clicked quietly shut. For a few moments, there was no sound except loud crunching as Doris seized the peace lily, pot and all, and shoved it into her mouth.

"I'm truly sorry, Meadows." Droppelheimer's shoulders sagged. "I need you, but I truly have no choice."

"I understand, sir." Julie held up a hand. "And thank you for your support. Really." She looked around the office. "All of you."

"I'll still give them what for if you let me," Vlad hissed.

"It's okay, Vlad." Julie laughed. "Their actions sting, I'm not going to lie, but I'm not super upset."

Droppelheimer frowned. "Regardless of what anyone says, you deserve your position, Meadows."

"And I'm sure I'll get it back, sir." Julie spread her hands. "Right now, I've got enough on my plate to fill a Frost Giant. After I figure out who tried to poison the queen, get the egg to hatch, find the crazed vampire currently stalking the streets of New York City, and have a two-minute conversation with my boyfriend, I'll probably get bored and annoyed."

Droppelheimer chuckled and patted Julie on the shoulder. "Always be yourself, Major Meadows. I hope you're able to get some rest, and I look forward to seeing you at your desk again."

"Thank you." Julie smiled. "Have you seen Horusiris around, sir?"

"Not lately, but if you're looking for him, one generally has some luck finding the Sphynxes in the cafeteria at the NYHQ. I'm told there's salmon on the menu tonight. They're almost guaranteed to be there." Droppelheimer winked.

Julie laughed. "Thanks, sir."

"One thing. Take the Central Park portal, Meadows," Droppelheimer added. "The Avalon HQ portal to the NYHQ is for official use only." He sighed. "I'm afraid, since you're suspended, that you cannot use it right now."

Julie shrugged, trying to hide the pain in her chest. "That's okay, sir. I could use a drive."

"Good luck, Meadows," Droppelheimer murmured.

Julie retrieved her favorite pen from her desk, shoved it into her pocket, and strode toward the lobby. She paused at her quarters to change into street clothes and pack an overnight bag. It felt weird to pick out normal clothes that weren't pajamas. She stared at the pair of black jeans covered in studs that used to be her favorite.

They're not you anymore, Hat commented.

Julie grimaced. *Were they ever?* She tossed them aside and picked out two old favorites, a pair of bootcut stonewash jeans and a nice black blouse. She put on the pair of well-worn shoes she'd worn during her time as a recruiter, but they didn't feel right, so she switched to a pair of calf-length military-style boots. Hat turned into his black fedora shape for the occasion, and Julie felt strangely light as she left the fortress, her backpack slung over one shoulder.

Shouldn't you be wearing your armor? Hat nagged as she strode into the inner ward.

I'm just going to the NYHQ, Hat, not a battle zone. Julie looked around for Genevieve and was unsurprised to see the Mustang rolling toward her, windshield wipers waving in excitement. *Might as well check on Vivienne while I'm there.*

Vivienne? Hat growled. *Why would you want to see that crazy old hag? She can't give you any more information. Olena promised to call you when she's recovered enough to tell you anything useful.*

Maybe I just think she's cool, and I'd like to see if she's okay, Julie retorted.

Cool? Cool? Hat spluttered. *She's not cool! She's a slimy hag!*

Julie tossed her backpack on the passenger seat and slid into Genevieve. *I think she's nice.*

Hat sniffed. *I think she's horrifying.*

Your protests are telling, Julie shot back. *And you didn't seem to think she was horrifying when it looked like she'd gone missing.*

Hat was silent.

Thought so. Julie smirked.

A tap on the window made her jump, causing the earth below Genevieve to rumble in warning. She looked up at the magnificent face of Axl. His features would have made a Renaissance sculptor swoon.

Julie rolled down the window. "Hey, Axl. What's up?"

"We heard you were going somewhere." Livius' head popped over Axl's shoulder. "We wanted to join you."

"For your protection," Axl rumbled.

Julie smiled. "I'm just going to the NYHQ, guys. I'll be fine."

"You don't know what is out there." Livius shuddered. "We're obliged to go with you."

Axl gazed at him vacantly.

"And you?" Julie asked, raising an eyebrow at him.

"Not sure what 'obliged' is." Axl shuffled his feet, which were enclosed in ginormous leather sandals. "But I still feel bad for attacking you. I think we should go along to make sure you're okay."

Livius drew himself up to his full, if bony, height. "It's a matter of honor for us." He glanced around and lowered his voice. "Besides, it's our penance for attacking you."

"You really don't have to," Julie protested.

Axl's sunny blue eyes widened sorrowfully. "But we *want* to make up for it, Julie of the Meadows."

"Okay, then." She laughed. "Get in."

Livius was bold enough to take shotgun while Axl squashed his mighty frame into the back seat. They drove under the portcullis and into Avalon Town, and Julie noted that there were more paras than normal hurrying down the streets. The brief stalemate the Breaker had caused in the war seemed to have brought a spark of life back to the town she loved.

She glanced in the rearview mirror. As usual, both dragons wore togas. Livius had a shabby knee-length robe under his blue toga. Axl wore the toga only, with one shoulder and an impressive pectoral bare. It was barely long enough. Michelangelo's *David* flitted through Julie's mind, and she averted her eyes from the rearview mirror before more impure thoughts could occur.

"You guys sure you don't want hoodies and jeans or something before we go into the city?" she inquired.

"Are we going to see humans?" Axl boomed. "I've never seen a human." He grinned with puppyish delight.

"Uh, yeah, let's not stop." Julie laughed. "Togas will be fine."

They drove through the crackling portal on the far side of the colorful plaza and popped out underneath the 110th Street Bridge in the middle of Manhattan. It was dark except for the harsh electric glow of the streetlights, but the streets were crammed with cars.

"Wow," Axl muttered.

Livius folded his skinny arms and tried not to look impressed.

"Never been Earthside, huh?" Julie asked.

Axl leaned forward, staring through the windshield as Julie turned right and headed down the street. Central Park was dark and quiet on their right. "Earthside? We hadn't even seen the surface before we followed you."

Julie frowned. "Why *did* you follow me, anyway? You had a life in the Deep. Nothing would have changed for you if you had stayed."

Livius stared at her. "But we wouldn't have been able to make things right with you after what we did to you."

Julie grinned. "As I recall, what you did to me ended with both of you trapped in frozen lava while I watched. Julie, one. Dragons, zero."

Axl boomed out an earthquake laugh. "You kicked our butts!"

Livius glanced at Julie, then back out the window. "No, but the intention was there. We would have hurt you if you'd let us."

"We were never gonna kill you," Axl assured her for the ten thousandth time.

"No, but what would have happened if we'd handed her to Sisiath?" Livius snapped. "He didn't hire us to capture her because he wanted to invite her to a tea party, Axl."

"Of course not." Axl stared at him. "We're dragons. We don't drink tea."

Livius face-palmed.

"Hey, it's okay, guys," Julie interjected. "Sisiath was going to win that land dispute, and your poor mom would have been left with nowhere to go. I get why you did what you did." She shrugged. "I can't say I wouldn't have done the same thing if it had been *my* mom who would have found herself on the street."

A pang of guilt shot through her chest at the thought of Rosa. It had been months since she'd seen her mom. Since she'd been benched, maybe she'd have the time to set up a dinner date. She made a mental note to text her mom when they reached the NYHQ.

"You wouldn't have," Axl told her sincerely. "You're too nice."

"She's too *honorable*, Axl," Livius lectured. "And that's what dragons are. Honorable." He folded his arms. "We're going to serve you until we prove our honor."

"You already have." Julie patted his clammy, bony knee and instantly regretted it.

Livius shook his head. "Not in our eyes."

"Not even a little bit," Axl agreed.

Julie smiled. She hadn't asked for two bumbling dragon bodyguards, but she didn't mind their company.

Livius and Axl waited outside the door of the private room in which Vivienne was resting. Julie realized it was the one Qtana had occupied after she was badly injured by her asshole boss Qbiit.

Qbiit was also a traitor to the Eternal Throne, Hat pointed out.

Julie gently pushed the door open. *"Asshole boss" also fits.*

The room was comfortable and bathed in warm light from the bedside lamp. Vivienne sat up, propped on her pillows, covers tucked around her waist. She wore a pink nightie that was a little too lacy to be decent, one strap dangling off her shoulder.

Hat got warm on her head.

Ew, Julie protested. *Keep it in your non-existent pants, you creepy old man.*

Hat sputtered incoherently.

Vivienne looked up from under sweeping eyelashes, the beginnings of a sultry grin forming on her face. It faded at the sight of Julie.

"Oh, hello, Julie." She closed the book she'd been reading and put it on the nightstand, face down. "Did you bring that wonderful specimen of yours?"

"Taylor?" Julie laughed. "Not this time."

"Oh, well. It is how it is, I guess." Vivienne tugged up the strap of her nightie and gave Julie a wide grin.

Lillie would have liked her, Julie thought.

Hat scoffed. *Lillie had much better taste than that.*

"Still, I'm glad to see you." Vivienne shifted and patted the mattress beside her.

Julie sat. "How are you doing? You still look pale."

"Okay, for the most part." Vivienne grimaced. "Olena will skin me if she finds out I'm reading, but what's a girl to do? I'm not supposed to read, watch TV, or be on my phone." She threw up her hands. "Or do anything productive."

"Audiobooks?" Julie suggested.

Vivienne brightened. "That's a good idea."

"I'll bring you earbuds when I come again." Julie paused. "No new memories of what happened or anything?"

Vivienne shook her head, winced, and raised a hand to her temple. "I'm sorry. Not quite there yet. Qtana tells me that both the geas and the process of lifting it can be very hard on the mind."

"I thought geasa didn't have long-term effects if they were lifted quickly," Julie remarked.

Vivienne shrugged. "So did we all, right? But Qtana reminded me that she's never lifted a geas from a Lunar Fae before. I guess we're different."

Julie smiled. "I'll bet." She paused. "It's been really good to spend time with other Lunar Fae."

Vivienne rested a hand over hers. "I'm sure it is, Julie."

"Now I just need to find out who my birth family is," Julie murmured.

Vivienne patted her hand. "It will come. Mark my words." She smiled. "It will come."

Vivienne's lewd expectation of Taylor bounced around in Julie's mind as she headed out of the NYHQ building toward the covered parking area on the side. Livius and Axl followed her at a respectful distance, arguing about the meaning of the word "accompany." Axl was convinced it had something to do with business.

Julie pulled out her phone and felt a pang of guilt when she had to scroll down to get to Taylor's chat. She'd opened his last message, a funny goat video, without responding. When she opened the chat, she realized it wasn't the only message she'd ignored lately.

"That poor man," she muttered. "Hat, what time is it in Avalon Town?"

"Nine in the morning," Hat supplied.

Julie stifled a yawn. "Sleep is overrated." She shot off a text.

Hey, babe. Sorry. Crazy few days. You OK?

She added six goat emojis to make him feel better.

She'd barely reached the parking bay when her phone chirped.

Heyyyy!

Three red hearts followed.

I'm fine. How are you?

Julie smiled.

All the better for hearing from you. Can you get a few hours away from everything?

There was no immediate response. Julie slipped her phone into her pocket and tried to crush her disappointment. She could hardly be mad at Taylor if he couldn't get away, but she fiercely hoped he could.

She fished Genevieve's keys from her pocket and unlocked the driver's door. Her phone buzzed as she was sliding into the driver's seat. Livius and Axl had almost caught up.

Actually, I can!

Taylor sent a grinning emoji and a gif of a tap-dancing goat.

Julie grinned.

I'm thinking romantic picnic by the river in Avalon Town.

Sounds perfect. I'll bring food. See you soon!

Taylor sent a bunch of hearts.
Julie chuckled and responded with a few kissy faces.

Love you.

Love you!

Julie leaned out the door as Livius and Axl approached the car. "Hey, guys, change of plans. I'm meeting Taylor in Avalon Town for a picnic. Mind if I drop you off on the plaza?"

"Can we come to the picnic? I love picnics!" Axl exclaimed.

Livius elbowed him in the ribs. "She doesn't want us to go along, idiot."

"Why not?" Axl asked indignantly.

Livius seized him by the toga. "Because it's a *date*, okay?" he hissed.

Axl's eyes widened. "*Ohhhh.*"

Livius released him and turned to Julie, then bowed extravagantly. "You go enjoy your date." His grin stretched widely across his face. "We'll find our own way back to Avalon Town."

Julie stared at them in their togas. "You sure you want to be left in the human world?"

"We'll be fine," Livius reassured her.

Axl gave his Greek deity grin. "We're *dragons*," he reminded her.

"That's exactly what I'm worried about," Julie muttered.

"What was that?" Livius asked.

"Nothing, nothing." Julie waved. "If you're sure you'll be okay..."

"We'll be fine." Livius smiled. "Have a good time with Taylor."

Axl chortled. "Have a *good* time."

Julie rolled her eyes and closed the door, then started the

engine. Its satisfying roar was a nostalgic sound as she drove through the parking bay, and she put her foot down as soon as she left the gates, waving goodbye to Fred, the Copper dwarf gate guard.

It was high time she hung out with Taylor again.

Julie leaned into the embrace of Genevieve's bucket seat as she cruised through the streets of Manhattan. Though this was the city that never slept, traffic was far quieter at this time of night. The red taillights in front of her were a string of beads instead of a solid wall. Genevieve effortlessly wove between them, and Julie gently braked to stop at a red light a block from Central Park.

You sent Livius and Axl away, but what are you going to do with me? Hat demanded peevishly. *Do I have to sit through another of your dates?*

Put yourself in sleep mode or something, Julie suggested.

Sleep mode? Sleep mode? Do I look like a mobile phone to you? Sleep mode, my— Hat ranted.

Shhh! Julie froze in her seat.

Don't shush me! Hat protested. *I'm—*

Hat, shhh! Julie snapped mentally, holding up a hand.

There was a long, breathless silence. The hairs on Julie's arms rose one by one, and goosebumps crept down her back. She glanced at the streetlights, which were still shining.

Why did it feel like the block to her left had just been engulfed in darkness?

Julie? Hat whispered.

Do you feel that? Julie asked.

Hat shuddered on her head. *You mean the overwhelming feeling of an evil presence?*

Yes, Julie whispered.

The light turned green. Behind her, a car honked. Julie put on her left blinker and turned.

Where are you going? Hat squawked. *Are you seriously heading toward that?*

The last time I felt this, I was near Mina Nox, Julie told him. She'd turned down a narrow one-way that felt more like Brooklyn than Manhattan. Graffiti splashed the bare brick walls. Garbage lay in the gutter, and a ribby stray cat picked at a discarded KFC box, disappearing through a hole in the wall as Genevieve purred past.

Exactly! Mina Nox, who is partially possessed by dark magic! Hat spluttered.

Mina Nox, who needs my help, Julie shot back. *Hat, can you text Taylor's phone and tell him what's happening?* She grimaced. *And tell him how sorry I am. I hope I'm not about to stand him up again.*

Dogs barked hysterically as Julie drove down the street. When their owners yelled at them to shut up, they sounded more irritated and on edge than they should have been.

Send a text to the group chat with Morgan and Bianca, too, Julie added.

All right, Hat mumbled, *but for the record, I still think you shouldn't be doing this. At least wait for backup.*

Text Malcolm, too. Julie's breath caught. *We're close.*

The streetlights still gleamed, but Julie felt like she'd driven under a dark cloud. A bridge crossed the street just ahead, and a train thundered over it, its squeal as harsh as a dying scream. Julie fought to keep the flames from her hands and took deep breaths to tame the fear in the pit of her stomach. The last thing New York City needed was an earthquake.

A hundred feet from the bridge, Julie spotted a huddled figure tucked in the shadow of the bridge's concrete support, which was splashed with profane graffiti in harsh pink and neon yellow.

She brought Genevieve to a halt as quietly as she could and cracked the door.

Ca— Hat began.

Careful. I know, I know, Julie grumbled. She almost summoned fire to her hands but remembered just in time that there might be humans watching. When she glanced at the windows overlooking the street, she didn't see any faces, but she decided against fire. She reached into her boot and pulled out her Bowie knife.

Julie, your armor, Hat hissed as she approached the bridge.

No time for that. Julie ignored his protests and took slow, measured steps toward the huddled shadow. The last train car rattled past, and light spilled down from the tracks.

It *was* Mina, and she wasn't alone. Someone lay at her feet—a bundle of ragged clothing, so muffled that their gender was indeterminate, topped by an unkempt mop of dirty gray hair. They weren't moving.

Julie's gut clenched. She gripped the knife tighter and approached in a wide arc so Mina could see her. You couldn't surprise a vampire. If she acted nonthreatening, maybe she stood a chance of talking her down. She kept the knife low and close to her thigh.

Julie was several yards away when she realized the vampire was sobbing.

Mina's knees were drawn up to her chest, and her arms were wrapped around her shins. Her body shook with every gulping sob. Her coat was torn and dirty, she was missing a shoe, and her face was streaked with blood, dirt, and tears. Dried blood was crusted around her mouth.

"I'm sorry," she choked out, crying hopelessly. "I'm sorry. I'm sorry. I'm sorry."

Julie edged nearer. The homeless person at Mina's feet was dead. No one could be that shade of gray and be alive. There were two large punctures in their neck, right over the carotid artery, but they did not bleed.

Julie swallowed and tried to speak calmly. "Mina?"

The vampire raised her head. She had black shadows under her red eyes. Tears poured down her cheeks. "Julie, what happened?" she whimpered.

"I'm not sure, but I know everyone's worried about you." Julie stopped six feet away, half-hiding the knife in her shadow. "Are you okay?" It was hard not to stare at the bloodless corpse.

"I don't know!" Mina let out a choking sob. "I-I was on the couch with Malcolm, watching TV, and then…then I was here." She stared at the dead person at her feet. "And *he* was here. Julie, did I—"

"Don't worry about that right now. You weren't yourself," Julie soothed.

"I don't even remember what happened." Mina sobbed. "I'm so scared, Julie. What's happening to me?"

Julie's heart stung. It was easier to look Mina in the eye in the face of her horror. "They're going to figure it out, Mina. They'll help you."

"I killed him, didn't I?" Mina cried. "I killed him!"

"Shhh. It's okay, Mina." Julie inched nearer. "It's not your fault." She held out a hand. "Come away from him."

Mina slowly straightened and wrapped her arms around herself in a desperate hug.

"That's it." Julie moved the knife back two inches so that Mina wouldn't see it, praying she wouldn't need to use it. "Let's get out of here."

Mina shuffled a step forward, but her toe bumped the corpse, and she moaned.

"It's okay. Step over him. Let's get you home," Julie murmured.

Mina's head snapped back. When her eyes met Julie's, they glowed scarlet.

"*Home?*" she hissed.

Julie held up a hand placatingly. "Or wherever you want to go."

"You want to take me *back*," Mina growled, a guttural sound. "You want to *imprison* me."

"No, no. It's okay, Mina. We're not going to do anything you don't want to," Julie promised rashly.

It wasn't enough. Mina's eyes narrowed.

"Mina, it's okay," Julie soothed.

The vampire lunged.

CHAPTER ELEVEN

The lights were much too bright.

Julie squeezed her eyes tightly shut as fierce pain lanced through her head. She gritted her teeth and rode it out until it eased to a steady, dull throb just behind her temples. There was something on her neck, too, wrapped around her throat. Julie wanted to pull it away, but her hands felt like they were a long way off.

All she could do was open her eyes just wide enough to peer through them without the piercing light. White tiles on the ceiling, and a metal, shiny thing. A drip stand.

A bag of blood.

She was in the para-ER, but why?

Julie! Eglantine gasped in her mind.

Terror and relief surged through Julie's body with an intensity that could only come from a dragon mind. Eglantine's emotions spun her like a whirlpool, and Julie felt them suck her back down toward unconsciousness. She fought to keep hold of her mind, and her hands clenched into fists. A gasp escaped her, and Eglantine abruptly let go.

"You're awake!" Warm fingers closed around her hand, and

she heard a sob that tore through her own heart. "Oh, Julie, my love."

Julie forced her eyes open. Taylor was slumped over the edge of her bed, her hand wrapped in both of his, fingers pressed to his lips. Tears streamed down his cheeks, and his eyes were tightly closed. "You're awake," he whispered.

Julie swallowed and tried to squeeze his hand, but her fingers only twitched faintly.

"Am I hurting you? Sorry." Taylor raised his head, relaxing his grip on her hand. "Julie, you scared the shit out of me." He laid a hand on her cheek. "Are you okay?"

Julie didn't know what she was doing here, much less if she was okay.

"I'm sorry, love. I'm sorry. I'm not trying to be pushy." Taylor's face crumpled, and a sob shook his shoulders. "I just…I was so scared."

"Okay, grieving boyfriend, that's enough." Olena appeared at the edge of Julie's vision and gripped Taylor's arm in a capable hand. "Out of the room, please, so I can assess her."

"Okay. Sure." Taylor stepped back, but his touch lingered on Julie's hand until the last second, and he looked back twice as he shuffled to the door.

Olena leaned over, pressed a button on the monitor near the bed, and squeezed Julie's fingernail, then watched with interest as the color returned to the tip of Julie's finger. "Take a couple of deep breaths," the doctor recommended. "Let yourself wake up."

Julie closed her eyes and took deep, slow breaths. She could still feel Eglantine's terror at the edge of her consciousness.

Eggy, where are you? she whispered, finally able to form words, if only internally.

Safe in the Sphynx realm, Eglantine quavered. *I felt your mind go dark.*

I'm okay, Julie told her, although she wasn't sure. Now that she was more awake, she could feel the sharp tugs of pain in her throat when she swallowed.

"Eyes open for me," Olena instructed.

Julie obeyed as Olena turned down the harsh lights. The Sylthana Elf shone a penlight into her eyes, then straightened and smiled. "I won't ask how you're feeling since you've got to be feeling like crap."

Julie cleared her throat, winced at the pain that stung her neck, and croaked out a word. "Headache."

"That's to be expected. Your vitals are much more stable than they were." Olena rested a hand on her arm. "You're going to be okay."

"What...happened?" Julie wheezed, fishing in the recesses of her memory. "Was it Mina?"

"I'm afraid so." Olena's face fell. "But you're safe now. Malcolm, Taylor, and those two buffoons are outside the door."

Julie's lips twitched. Smiling hurt, but only a little. "Livius and Axl." She frowned. "Hat?"

"He's with Taylor. He's okay," Olena reassured her.

Julie raised a hand, tethered by IVs, to her throat and felt thick bandages. "She bit me?"

"I'm sorry. Hat told me you were trying to talk her down when the switch flipped. She attacked you." Olena let out a shaky breath. "You were all but drained of blood when Taylor got there. If he hadn't commandeered Sleipnir, it would have been too late."

Julie managed another faint grin. "Good old Slippy." She frowned. "Taylor fought..." Pain made her pause. "Fought her off?"

"He did. Pulled her away from you and defended you against her." Olena grinned. "I know he's freaked out right now, but don't be too hard on him. He *did* just pull a crazed vampire off you, then protected you until she fled. Not a lot of boyfriends would try that, and not a lot of elves would succeed."

"Mina fled?" Julie whispered.

Olena nodded. "She was gone by the time Malcolm got there."

"Shit," Julie muttered, but she wasn't surprised.

"Taylor tells me your Mustang went a little crazy." Olena grinned. "Did you know she could turn herself invisible?"

Julie chuckled, then winced. "Nothing is impossible." She swallowed. "With Genevieve."

"I'm glad of it." Olena squeezed her arm. "Even with Genevieve flying you here, you'd lost a significant amount of blood. Luckily, Vivienne was a match for your blood type."

Julie raised her eyebrows. "Vivienne?"

"Don't worry. Donating a few pints won't affect her recovery." Olena smiled. "She was more than happy to help."

Julie glanced at the clear plastic line running into her arm, filled with bright red blood.

"In short, you'll be okay. I've done what I could for the wounds on your throat, but vampire bites take a while to heal, even with magical help. And you're going to need to take it easy for a while, thanks to the blood loss," Olena added.

Julie grimaced.

"I know, I know." Olena squeezed her arm again. "Now, do you want me to let Taylor back in here, or do you want some rest first?"

"Taylor," Julie rasped. "Please." She swallowed. "Malcolm too."

"Okay, but only for a little while. You need to rest," Olena cautioned.

Julie grinned. "How well...do you know me...Doc?"

Olena rolled her eyes. "Far too well."

Laughing hurt, but Julie did it anyway.

The ring box in Taylor's pocket felt like it weighed a ton. If he'd trusted anyone else in the room—Livius, Axl, Malcolm, and Hat —to keep a secret, he'd have taken it out and turned it over and over in his fingers. Maybe opened the lid to look at the perfect moonstone dragon.

Instead, Taylor clutched his knees, digging his fingers into the thick fabric of his hunter-green suit. He bounced his legs on the balls of his feet, heels tapping the tiled floor in the waiting room.

The last time he'd been in a hospital waiting room, he'd been with his sister Amaryl, who'd been wounded during the attack on the Aether compound. He'd lost two brothers and both parents that day. His belly rolled with nausea.

Beside him, Malcolm was slumped in a chair, head in his hands. Hat drooped on Taylor's lap, silent. He was a cocky black fedora, the shape he'd been when Julie carried him out of the Warehouse a lifetime ago. Even then, Taylor had known there was something special about the crazy-ass human he'd been saddled with.

Tears stung his eyes. Livius and Axl stood guard at the door to Julie's room, motionless and resolute, except that Axl's lower lip trembled.

The door swung open. Taylor leaped out of his chair with a force that flung Hat across the room.

"Doctor," he croaked.

"She's okay." Olena patted the air and smiled reassuringly. "A little weak and sore, but she'll be fine."

Taylor's knees buckled. He fell into the chair, covered his face with his hands, and took deep breaths to compose himself. The bandages on his hands tightened as he pressed his fingers into his hair.

"Thank Merlin," Malcolm whispered.

"No," Hat muttered bitterly, righting himself so that he was brim-down on the tiled floor. "Don't thank him."

Taylor raised his head. "May I see her?"

"Of course. She asked for you." Olena paused. "You too, Malcolm. But don't agitate her."

"I promise." Taylor rose.

"You go first." Malcolm retrieved Hat from the floor. "I'll give you a minute alone before I come in."

Taylor patted the vampire's shoulder. "Thanks, Mal." He took a breath, wiped his face with his sleeve, carefully composed his smile, and stepped into the room.

Julie looked tiny, lost in the vastness of the hospital bed, her wings sprawled on her pillow, their veins still pale. Her face was ashen too, but it lit up above the bandages on her throat the moment she saw him. She raised her arms—so buff, yet trembling with weakness—against the tubes and wires that tethered her.

"Taylor," she croaked.

He crossed the space between them in two long strides and bent to wrap his arms around her in the gentlest embrace he could manage. She shook as she pulled him closer. He pressed his face into her neck, smelling that uniquely spicy scent that always hung over her, and felt a wave of intense gratitude that he could hold her again. When he'd seen her lying on the street with Mina's teeth in her throat, her pale form brilliantly lit by Genevieve's headlights as the Mustang honked and revved frantically in a useless bid to chase the vampire off...

He pushed the memory away and pulled back, then sat in the chair beside her bed in which he'd been holding a quiet vigil for hours.

"How do you feel?" he asked, wrapping her hand in both of his.

She winced as she spoke. "Like shit." A faint grin lit her bright eyes. "Bet I look...like shit, too."

"You never do." Taylor kissed the back of her hand, meaning it. Her hair was mussed, and there was an ugly graze on her cheek, but she was still the most beautiful thing in his world. "You don't have to talk. Just rest. I'm right here."

Julie closed her eyes and sagged against her pillows, which

scared him. She should be trying to get out of bed and single-handedly capture Mina, save the queen, and end the war.

Taylor stroked the back of her hand with his thumb, feeling the ring box in his jacket pocket bump his hip every time he moved. He'd nearly lost her.

He could still lose her at any moment. She was an officer in the OPMA, and this was war. He'd made his peace with that long ago. Gazing at her motionless face, he wondered how much time they really had.

He was certain of one thing. Whatever time he had with her, he wanted it—all of it, as long as he could. His free hand strayed to his pocket and clasped the ring box.

He'd already spread out the picnic blanket when he'd gotten the message from Hat. Everything had been arrayed just right: the perfect secluded spot among the fronds of a willow by the river, the champagne peeking out of the picnic blanket, the naiad singing hauntingly behind a handy rock. The script was playing out in his mind. He'd let Julie reach the picnic site first.

"What's the champagne for?" she would ask. Taylor could hear the sassy lilt in her voice even now.

He would kneel and produce the ring. "This."

She'd hear that something was different in his voice and spin, and she'd see the ring...

But none of that had happened. Instead, Taylor had found her half-dead in an alley, and he'd fought for her life with a ferocity he hadn't known he possessed. It had almost not been enough. He couldn't stop staring at those glaring white bandages on her throat.

He could ask right here, right now, before anything else could happen to her.

He lifted his hand, but before he could remove the box from his pocket, he stopped and let it go. No. No matter how long it took to find the right moment, he'd wait. She knew he loved her, and that was what mattered. Julie deserved a proposal worthy of a fae.

The door creaked, and Taylor started. Julie's eyes fluttered open.

"Sorry, babe." Taylor leaned over and kissed her cheek. "Go back to sleep."

"I was awake," Julie croaked. Her eyes strayed to the door, and she forced a tiny smile. "Hey, Mal."

Malcolm stood in the doorway, clutching Hat in front of him like a talisman. "Should I go?"

"No," Julie rasped.

The vampire stepped into the room and pushed the door closed. "Julie, I'm so sorry."

Julie shook her head, then flinched.

"If I hadn't let her escape, none of this would have happened." Malcolm swallowed hard. "I can't believe she did this to you. I'm so sorry."

"Not your fault," Julie assured him.

Malcolm let out a breath. Julie patted the bed opposite Taylor, and Malcolm hesitantly perched on its edge. "Here's your hat," he blurted, putting the fedora on Julie's chest.

"Your hat? *Your hat?*" Hat spluttered. "I'll have you know—"

"We all know," Julie whispered. She wrapped her free arm around Hat and cuddled him close like a teddy bear. Hat made a grumbling noise but turned into a plush goat, which made Julie let out a faint version of her little-girl giggle—the one she didn't know she had.

Taylor squeezed her hand. "Doc says it's going to take a while to get back to your full strength."

"Pfft." Julie scoffed. "Back on my feet...in no time."

"Seriously, Julie. You need to listen to her," Malcolm told her.

Julie rolled her eyes. "Things to do," she protested.

"Please, babe! This is serious." Taylor pulled his chair closer to the bed. "We need you to get better, and to do that, you've got to rest."

Julie glared at him. She could do as well from a hospital bed as anywhere else. "The queen needs me to find her poisoner. They're still out there, and I need to catch them. And Mina—" She stopped, her face crumpling in pain, and raised a shaky hand to her throat.

"You okay?" Taylor's heart squeezed. "Should I call Olena?"

Julie relaxed on her pillows. "No."

Malcolm shot Taylor a worried glance and got to his feet, but Taylor shook his head.

"We know the world needs you, babe, but it needs you functioning," Taylor told her flatly. "Not in this state."

Julie scowled, a sure sign he'd won the argument.

"Don't worry about Mina." Malcolm relaxed slightly. "I promise I'm going to find her. I might not have captured her this time, but the Weres have a fresh scent. We'll track her. We'll get her, Julie. Don't worry."

"I'll help him," Taylor added.

Julie stared at him. "T, you've...got things to do."

"I know, but nothing more important than this." Taylor realized he was squeezing Julie's hand too tightly and relaxed his grip. "We need to get Mina under control before someone else gets hurt."

Before anyone else has to see someone they love on the brink of death, he added silently.

"Bianca and Morgan can keep searching for the poisoner," Taylor added. "They're pretty capable."

Julie tilted her head, her eyes glassy, and Hat stirred in her arms. They were having one of their maddening private conversations. After a few seconds, Julie scowled again, relenting.

"Okay," she croaked. "I'll stay. For now."

Taylor let out a breath. "Good."

Julie held out the goat. "Hat goes with."

"I think he should stay with you," Taylor told her, although he was sorely tempted to hug the plush goat. It was so soft. So *goat*.

Julie shook her head firmly, and there was something final in her eyes. Taylor knew when he was beaten.

"Okay, I'll take him." Taylor reached for Hat, but before he could squeeze that delightful goaty softness, Hat disappointingly turned into a knitted hunter-green scarf. About to protest, Taylor met Julie's eyes and decided against it. He wound the scarf around his neck.

Olena popped her head around the door. "I hope you two aren't keeping my patient awake."

"We *are* princes, you know," Malcolm protested weakly.

"Yeah? I'm an ER doc. Try me." Olena winked.

Julie asked. "Dragons?"

"Still at the door." Taylor leaned over her and kissed her forehead. "You're safe."

She pressed into his kiss like she didn't want it to be over. Taylor kissed her again, squeezed her hand, and turned to leave with Malcolm.

"Taylor?" Julie quavered.

He stopped in the doorway and looked back.

"I love you," she whispered.

Taylor smiled. "I love you, too."

Taylor tugged on Hat, trying to get some air to his sweaty neck as he and Malcolm walked across the NYHQ campus toward the parking bay to which Genevieve and Sleipnir had taken themselves. The eight-legged stallion, capable of such speed and height that he could hide from human eyes, had jogged beside the Mustang as though they shared the species their name suggested.

Taylor tugged again. Hat tightened.

Could you stop that? Taylor spluttered. *It's borderline too hot for a scarf right now. Can't I have a hat, too?*

I'm afraid not. Hat firmly settled into place around Taylor's neck. *Julie made me promise to protect you.*

From the cold? Taylor retorted.

Allow me to clarify. Hat paused. *Julie's exact words were, "If you allow Mina to snack on my boyfriend, I'll put you back in the Warehouse myself."*

Taylor stopped messing with the scarf. *Oh. I see.*

"We can take my car," Malcolm broke in. "The Mustang scares me."

Taylor chuckled. "Me too, to be honest."

The two princes headed into the parking bay, avoiding the pair of eagles harnessed to a gilded throne. They tended to nip.

"Where's it parked?" Taylor asked.

Malcolm produced a set of keys from his pocket. Taylor spotted a familiar brand name on them.

"Wait." Taylor stopped, a grin spreading over his face. "What *is* your car?"

Malcolm chuckled, his eyes alight with boyish pleasure. "Let's just say you're going to enjoy this. Wait here."

The vampire jogged off, and Taylor waited in the parking bay. When he heard the engine roar, he crammed his fist into his mouth and let out a whimper.

I'll tell Genevieve, Hat threatened.

No other car will ever be Genevieve. Taylor nearly swooned as the sleek shape turned the corner and hummed toward him. *But this comes pretty close.*

The pitch-black Pagani Huayra braked to a silent stop in front of Taylor. It was flat and fierce, and its curves snarled. When Malcolm touched the gas, it let out an unearthly shriek.

The passenger door opened upward like a wing. Malcolm grinned in the driver's seat. "Ready?"

Taylor slid inside and closed the door, then beamed at Malcolm. "Absolutely."

Nothing could ease the stress of what had happened last night, but the howling, gear-crunching, zipping-past-traffic journey from the NYHQ to the bridge where they'd found Julie came pretty close.

Taylor's knees were wobbly as he stumbled out of the Huayra, laughing. "What a rush!"

Malcolm chuckled. "She's no Genevieve, but she's a real beast." He slammed the door.

Taylor stood very still, staring at the spot under the bridge where it had all gone down. His hand throbbed where Mina's claws had slashed it, but he raised his fingers to his unharmed throat.

Malcolm clapped him on the back. "Don't dwell on it, Taylor. We've got to find her."

Taylor nodded.

The Weres were guarding the scene to keep wayward humans or animals from messing up the scent. Isaiah's face was a grim mask as he stepped from the shadows, clasping an automatic rifle to his chest.

"Teddy and Blake are quartering," he growled.

Noah and Austin stood guard nearby, grim-faced and imposing in their uniforms, which would look like FBI uniforms to passing humans, thanks to the Veil. Blake and Teddy would look like German shepherds instead of what they truly were: large wolves, working back and forth across the scene as mirror images of one another. Teddy was short and squat with russet-brown hair. Tall, leggy Blake moved fluidly even though one of his front legs was a Copper dwarf-made prosthetic, its joints making a faint hydraulic noise as he moved. Their tails were high and waving, noses to the ground.

"Have you found her scent yet?" Taylor asked.

Malcolm and Isaiah burst out laughing. Malcolm slapped his knee, and Isaiah wheezed. Taylor stared at them.

"Oh, wait, you're serious." Malcolm sobered with an effort.

"Elves." Isaiah shook his head. "What good is your fancy eyesight without any sense of smell to speak of?"

Taylor folded his arms, affronted. "I have a sense of smell."

"This whole area reeks of Councilor Nox," Isaiah explained, his lip twitching. "We're not looking for her scent. We're trying to figure out which direction she went in. Once you'd left with Julie, she doubled back and crisscrossed the scene a few times to throw us off."

"Did it work?" Taylor asked.

A long, eerie howl echoed from under the bridge. It was Teddy, nose thrown skyward.

Isaiah grinned. "No, it didn't." He seamlessly shifted into a huge golden wolf. "Better get in the car if you want to keep up."

Teddy howled again. In wolf form, his four comrades joined him, their high-pitched song rising against the crowded Manhattan buildings.

Taylor and Malcolm piled into the Huayra, and Malcolm revved the engine as the wolves peeled out of the alley at a dead run and bolted down the sidewalk, utterly silent. The hypercar had no difficulty keeping up with them, and their speed was breathtaking as they wove seamlessly between pedestrians plodding to work. The Veil protected the humans from the truth, but several looked startled at the sight of five large police dogs running down the street, pursued by a Pagani Huayra. Only a little, though. This *was* New York City.

"They're heading for Central Park." Malcolm slammed on the brakes as traffic thickened. He squeezed the hypercar into an improbable gap between two sedans, causing horns to blare around them, and skipped a red light in a way that made Taylor dig his fingers into his seat.

Taylor hadn't missed Manhattan traffic since he'd moved to Avalon Town. Manhattan traffic navigated by an irate vampire with superhuman reflexes piloting a vehicle that could go from zero to sixty in three seconds was one of the most terrifying experiences in his entire existence. Blocks zipped past. The Huayra bucked left, then right. The wolves darted across the street to a cacophony of squealing brakes and shrieking rubber. Malcolm swung around the oncoming traffic to dodge a school bus and nipped back into his lane with inches to spare as a guy in a truck braked hard in front of them.

The vampire *was* right. The wolves were heading for 110th Street.

Taylor's stomach flipped as Malcolm put his foot down. The Huayra screeched and shot across a red light, cars swerving wildly to dodge it. The sidewalks were thick with pedestrians, and Taylor searched them for the wolves.

"Where did they go?" Malcolm asked.

"There!" Taylor barked, his elven eyes picking out the flick of a golden tail as the last werewolf dove down the street to their left.

Malcolm twisted the wheel and the Huayra skidded, screaming, pinning Taylor to his seat. Dead ahead, the 110th Street Bridge curved over a footpath into Central Park North. The wolves bounded beneath the ancient gneiss bridge, and without hesitation, Malcolm drove after them.

The world spun briefly, then they were in Avalon Plaza, the golden light of late afternoon spilling across the multicolored cobblestones. The wolves had come to a halt.

Malcolm slammed on the brakes. Taylor threw his hands out to catch himself on the dash, but Hat beat him to it. The scarf flung out its ends and braced them, shoving Taylor back into his seat. The hypercar came to an efficient, silent halt a few feet behind the wolves.

Taylor opened the door and stumbled out, faintly nauseated even though Julie and Genevieve had trained him for this.

"What's going on?" he croaked.

Isaiah raised his head, panting heavily. The other werewolves set off, noses to the ground, in a steady back-and-forth pattern across the plaza.

"We've lost her scent." Isaiah shook his head. "There's too much foot traffic here."

Taylor looked around. Avalon Town hadn't yet recovered from the economic hits the war had dealt it so far, so the plaza was quieter than it had been before the war. Still, it was evening rush hour, and paranormals hustled to and fro across the plaza. A wereelephant mom plodded patiently toward the all-you-can-eat vegetarian joint with her calf's trunk curled around her tail. A gaggle of teenagers, earbuds inserted, moodily stomped home. Three pixies laden with shopping bags giggled and shoved one another as they hailed a taxi.

"You tracked her through morning traffic in Manhattan!" Taylor exclaimed. "How's this any different?"

Isaiah gave him an unoffended look. "Manhattan reeks of humans," he explained patiently. "Their food, their clothes, their cars. Earth's scents are simple compared to Avalon." He cocked his head. "How many species are in this plaza alone? Far more than in any city block in Manhattan."

Taylor ran a hand through his hair. "Sorry. I understand."

"*I* understand your anger," Isaiah countered. "We'll keep trying."

"It really is a shitshow," Malcolm confirmed as Taylor sagged against the Huayra. "It's not their fault. Mina's trying to evade us." His mouth pulled down at the corners. "She headed straight for the Central Park portal, knowing we'd have trouble tracking her in the plaza."

"So, she's not lost and wandering." Taylor grimaced. "She's purposely avoiding us."

"It's got to mean the dark magic still has hold of her." Malcolm sighed. "And if she's actively trying to escape us, we're not going to find her, Taylor, not even with a unit of Weres. She's too good at getting around unnoticed."

"He's not wrong," Hat added. "The werewolves might never find her scent, and even if they do, she's buying herself time to disappear magically. If she uses a scent-masking spell or takes a portal, there's no way of tracking her."

They watched in silence for a few minutes as the werewolves searched, leaning on the hood of the car, but Malcolm was right. The wolves had no luck, and as they worked, more paras spilled across the plaza, muddying Mina's scent further.

Taylor's legs were numb from standing when he straightened and turned to Malcolm. "I have an idea."

The vampire raised an eyebrow. "Let's hear it."

Taylor paused. "The Eternal Guard is all over Avalon Town. They're the most likely paras to have seen her."

Malcolm nodded sharply. "Let's ask them."

CHAPTER TWELVE

Julie rolled onto her side, then her other side. She longed to lie on her belly, but the IV in her arm wouldn't let her, even though Olena had detached the monitor's wires from her other arm, hand, and chest. Her head throbbed no matter what she did with her pillows, and every time she swallowed, a fresh pang of pain trickled down her throat despite the medication Olena had injected into her IV.

She lay on her back instead, propped up on her pillows and staring out the window that overlooked the NYHQ campus. Two rookie elves, wearing their navy uniforms like new skins, strutted across the well-kept lawn with their service caps at a jaunty angle. They saluted when they nearly ran into Sergeant Derek Adamos, a towering shirtless minotaur who guffawed in delight at their starstruck awe.

Julie huffed as the rookies kept walking. She needed to be out there doing things. Catching the poisoner, helping Eglantine, trying to smooth things over with the officers at the Avalon HQ.

This is bullshit, she announced.

No one responded. It took her a second to remember she'd

sent Hat with Taylor and Malcolm. She sighed and pillowed her head on her arm, trying to ignore the echoing silence in her mind. Eglantine had gone quiet. Julie gently probed for the unborn dragon, but long-distance telepathy tired her. She must be napping.

Julie's eye caught the blank screen of the TV on the opposite wall, and she fumbled for the remote on the nightstand, then switched it on.

"Treaty negotiations between the dwarf clans continue," announced a skinny Starlight Fae, glaring intensely into the camera as she clutched a microphone in front of the featureless mountain that hid the Copper Stronghold. "While Ard Righ Yondal Mackintosh has argued ceaselessly that signing the treaty is in the best interests of all dwarves, in the light of recent civil conflicts, some dwarf clans remain unsure that dwarfkind is ready to do battle with enemies of the Eternity Throne."

Julie grimaced. She'd heard enough about the war, and in the picture displayed in the corner of the screen, poor Mack looked stressed out of his mind. She flicked to the next channel.

This time, it was a scrawny Aether Elf standing in front of a fancy private school who squinted into the camera. "Three young griffins were attacked outside their school yesterday morning," he reported. "Unknown assailants launched magical stink bombs at the youngsters. Although uninjured, the griffins will have to remain in isolation until the smell wears off. Hate crimes against griffins, who have been staunchly loyal to the Eternity Throne, have become more common in the past several months as—"

Julie growled and changed the channel again.

A long-nosed weredog lounged in a kitschy red armchair, clutching an obviously empty coffee cup as she smiled vacantly at her guest. The burly satyr sat in a similar armchair opposite her.

"The fact remains, Brumilda, that we the people are entitled to answers." He tucked a curl behind his horns. "The state of the queen's health has been hidden from us for long enough. We deserve to know if we're going to have a stable monarchy for much longer."

"According to social media sites, many Avalonian citizens are concerned that Her Majesty is too weak to rule at a time like this," the weredog chipped in. "Do you have anything to say about that, Alderman?"

"I do. I have a *lot* to say about that. How come she hasn't appointed a regent?" The satyr threw up his hands, waving his empty cup. "Is the queen losing her mind? Some of her policies of late make us wonder if she's added dementia to her long list of secret ailments."

Julie snorted and switched off the TV. She had hoped to find a trashy, relaxing show like *Real Housewives of Avalon Town* or *Selling the Eyrie*, and all she got was more of a headache for her efforts.

Julie? Eglantine mumbled sleepily.

Eggles! Hi, moondrop. Julie pressed into her connection with the dragon, though it felt muddled and distant. *I'm okay. You can go back to sleep. I know you're tired from talking to me earlier.*

Worried about you, Eglantine whispered.

Julie closed her eyes and pressed her face into her pillow, but she couldn't pretend it was the dragon egg's smooth shell. She longed to wrap her arms around Eglantine or fall asleep curled in the nest beside her. *I'll be okay.*

I know you will, but I miss you. Eglantine's thoughts filled with an image. Julie caught glimpses of the unborn dragon's limbs and scales.

She longed to see the whole thing, but Eglantine was far away in the Sphynxes' pocket dimension. Tears stung her eyes. They felt silly, and Julie blinked them away, but the ache in her chest was real.

Frustration burst through Eglantine's thoughts, suddenly replaced with excitement. A second later, the image pierced Julie's mind, brilliant in its detail: Eglantine, fully hatched, her limbs wrapped around Julie, neck between Julie's wings as she pulled her close.

Julie gasped and sat up. A hairless cat sat at the foot of her bed, a small portal still fizzling in the air beside her.

"Finally, some peace and quiet." The Sphynx yawned and kneaded Julie's feet, her claws popping on the covers.

The portal winked out of existence, and Julie's connection to Eglantine disappeared.

"Cleo?" Julie asked. "What are you doing here?"

"Trying to escape from our noisy house guests," Cleo grumbled, kneading with more aggression.

Julie smiled. "You mean Eglantine?" She drew up her knees, turned on her side, and formed the covers into a nice nest in the crook of her legs and torso.

Cleo padded over Julie's legs and inserted herself in the nest. "If you are referring to the dragonet who refuses to hatch, yes."

Julie scoffed. "I'm sure there are advantages to having a giant dragon egg for company. That temple was pretty gloomy without her."

Cleo curled up, wrapped her tail around herself, and purred with her eyes closed for a few moments before answering. "I suppose her heat is a bonus."

Julie adjusted her pillows, considered petting Cleo, and decided against it, not only because the cat's bare skin was weird to touch. "Can I ask you something?"

"You *can*." Cleo didn't open her eyes. "Whether you *should* is up to you."

Julie hesitated. "I know you Sphynxes have perception and magic that nobody else does."

Cleo opened her eyes a crack. "Flattery. An excellent start. Go on."

Julie bit her lip. "Now that Eggy is so close to hatching, are you able to see through my concealment spell?"

Cleo stared at her like a hairball she'd just thrown up. "That's for us to know and you to wonder about, little fae."

Julie snuggled into her pillows and decided to pet the Sphynx anyway. "Charming," she muttered good-naturedly.

Cleo's purring intensified and she tipped her head sideways, guiding Julie's fingers to an itchy spot on her left ear. "Being charming is one of my many talents." She turned on her side and stretched her legs out, kicking Julie painfully in the stomach.

Julie sat up and nearly fell off the other side of the bed. "Along with somehow taking up half a huge-ass hospital bed?"

Cleo opened one lazy eye. "I *am* a cat."

"Most cats don't open portals in the aether at will," Julie pointed out. She started tickling Cleo's chin instead.

The Sphynx chuckled. "How do *you* know?"

Julie thought about Fluffy, Lillie's enormous white cat, whose favorite pastimes had included getting stuck behind the couch and needing to have his butthole shaved because he was too fat to clean it. "I'm pretty sure, although you could prove it to me if you brought me a half-eaten space rat from another realm."

"Space rat." Cleo scoffed. "As if we've been to *space*."

"Forgive me. I thought you three were *from* space," Julie teased.

Cleo opened both eyes and laughed. She stretched luxuriously, then rolled onto her back, paws in the air. "You're going to need that sense of humor when you finally break the concealment spell."

Julie stopped petting her. "What do you mean?"

Cleo glared at her but said nothing.

Julie resumed petting her, and the Sphynx's loud purrs filled the room. There were no answers in them.

<hr>

Malcolm brought the Huayra to a smooth halt in the inner ward of the Avalon HQ. As Taylor got out, a massive shadow swooped out of the sky, and a leonine creature the size of a horse landed on the stone with a click of talons. Commander Stormstar's wings spanned twelve feet and were patterned buff and brown like those of an eagle. He folded them with a thick rustle of feathers and turned to Taylor. Above the plate armor that enclosed his broad chest, the griffin's mane was thick and golden and tipped with black. It stirred when he spoke.

"I apologize that none of my guards have seen Councilor Nox," he rumbled. "Hopefully, Sergeant Droppelheimer can help us."

"Thank you for offering to escort us to his office." Taylor inclined his head. "Not a lot of people have that kind of access."

"Certainly." Stormstar set off for the double doors at the front of the fortress. "I understand the need for her to be found quickly and quietly without involving whole armies. It is the only chance the councilor has of returning to her former life after she is healed."

Malcolm and Taylor scurried after him into the lobby, staying beside the enormous griffin as the ever-present crowd of busy paras parted unquestioningly before him.

"Thank you for calling her that," Malcolm murmured.

Stormstar glanced over his shoulder. "Calling her what?"

"Councilor." Malcolm paused. "It gives me hope that she could be one again someday."

"That is who she was," Stormstar returned. "If nothing else, that deserves honor."

They walked through the grim, stone hallways in silence, winding down to the heart of the Avalon HQ, Tactical Command. Taylor felt incredulous eyes on him as he gaped at the vast command center, magically soundproofed, scrying screens and crisply uniformed paras everywhere as they commanded missions all over both dimensions. In this place, Julie, who had just turned twenty-one, had held her own. A wave of pride rushed through him, and he reached into his jacket pocket and wrapped his fingers around the ring box.

You're right, you know, Hat intruded on his thoughts. *She does deserve a fairytale.*

Hat! Taylor jumped. *You can't tell her! Promise you won't!*

And ruin it for her? Hat chuckled fondly. *Not a chance.*

They turned into another hallway, and Stormstar paused in front of a wooden door. He raised a curled talon and tapped the door sharply. It swung open, and Taylor recognized Vlad from Julie's descriptions of him.

"What you want, huh?" the bony old vampire demanded.

"Vlad! How many times do I have to go over etiquette with you this century?" Droppelheimer demanded from inside the office. "Commander, please come in."

Vlad shuffled out of the way, and Stormstar squeezed his massive bulk into the office. Taylor smiled at Doris and Emmeline, who recognized him the same way he knew them—from what Julie had said about them.

Droppelheimer stood in the doorway of his office. He bowed formally to Stormstar, who returned the gesture.

"How may I help you, Commander?" the orc asked, folding his well-groomed hands in front of him. His dress uniform looked like it had just been ironed, although the day was coming to a close.

"You can help my young friends here, Sergeant," Stormstar rumbled. "I have other business in the fortress, and they requested my escort to your office."

"Very well. Thank you." Droppelheimer bowed again.

Stormstar returned the formality, then turned around—no mean feat in a space designed for humanoids—and paced out of the office. He gave Taylor a wink as he left.

"Prince Taylor, Prince Malcolm." Droppelheimer nodded at both. "How may I be of assistance?"

"Sir, we need access to some, uh, resources." Malcolm cleared his throat. "Resources you command."

"Come into my office." Droppelheimer led them into the smaller space and closed the door. "What do you need?"

Malcolm hesitated.

Taylor took a deep breath. "We need an adder stone."

Droppelheimer raised both eyebrows. "An adder stone? Only the Para-Military Agency has access to that kind of magic. It's not to be trifled with. What do you need to use an adder stone for?"

Taylor and Malcolm exchanged glances, and Malcolm gave a barely perceptible nod.

"It's for Ilsa, sir," Malcolm explained.

Droppelheimer frowned. "Ilsanthia? If Her Majesty needs any assistance from the OPMA, we stand ready."

"It's...unofficial business, sir." Taylor clasped his hands. "But still quite important."

Droppelheimer folded his arms. "What do you mean?"

"Well, sir, you know Ilsa has had no luck in finding a boyfriend," Malcolm began.

"A king," Taylor interjected hurriedly. "He means a king."

Droppelheimer sat back in his chair. "I can't say that I do."

"Woodskins have notoriously bad luck in love," Malcolm told him. "Look at Taylor. It took him forever to find a girlfriend."

"I wouldn't say *forever*," Taylor spluttered.

"Ilsa's no different," Malcolm went on. "Until last night."

Taylor shot him a glare but played along. "Until last night," he echoed.

Droppelheimer stared at them. "What happened last night?"

"Taylor took Ilsa to 230 Fifth, one of their favorite restaurants, sir. She was feeling the weight of her queenship and needed to unwind." Malcolm warmed up to his tale. "And while they were there, they saw him."

Droppelheimer leaned closer. "Who?"

"An Aether Elf. The most magnificent male Aether Elf in the world," Malcolm went on.

"I wouldn't say—" Taylor began, offended.

Malcolm kicked him sharply.

"The most magnificent Aether Elf in the world," Taylor mumbled.

"He was sitting at the table next to the Woodskins, and when Taylor was in the bathroom, he and Ilsa got to talking," Malcolm went on. "Like a good wingman, when Taylor got back from pee—"

Taylor glared at him, but Malcolm continued, unfazed. "He hung out by the bar, letting them talk. It was clear they were a match made in heaven."

"And he was king material," Taylor grumbled, remembering his lines. "He would be perfect for Ilsa and for the Aether Elves."

"It was love at first sight, sir." Malcolm clasped his hands under his chin. "They were both smitten!"

"What happened next?" Droppelheimer asked, starry-eyed.

"The guy wrote his number on a napkin for Ilsa." Malcolm beamed. "Then he left, and Taylor went back to the table...and knocked a pitcher of water onto the napkin."

"No!" Droppelheimer glared at Taylor.

"What can I say?" Taylor held up his hands. "I'm clumsy."

"So clumsy." Malcolm shook his head sorrowfully.

"The number was illegible." Taylor sighed theatrically. "I don't know if we'll ever find him again unless we use an adder stone. I know Qtana came up with a way to link adder stones to Ariadne's thread and track someone by their magical signature. I remember his name, and with a little Aether Elf blood, I could find him, sir."

"He has to!" Malcolm burst out and fell to his knees, clutching the edge of the desk. "Or Ilsa will never again see her true love!"

Overact much? Taylor snarled. *He's going to blow it!*

Hat snickered. *Actually, I don't think so.*

He was right. Droppelheimer had fallen for it hook, line, and sinker.

"No!" the orc cried. "That cannot happen!"

Taylor stared at him.

Droppelheimer shouted, "Emmeline!"

The Woodland Fae appeared in the doorway. "Yes, sir?"

"Call the brownies!" Droppelheimer ordered. "Have an adder stone and a troll who can work it brought to my office at once!"

Emmeline raised her eyebrows. "An adder stone, sir?"

"These gentlemen need one." Droppelheimer slammed a hand on the desk. "It is a matter of grave importance. Do not delay!"

Emmeline's eyes widened. "Yes, sir!" she exclaimed and rushed back to her office.

"The troll will be here forthwith. She'll be able to help you use the stone and a military-grade telechip to find the princess' lost love." Droppelheimer gave them a serious nod. "I wish you all the best. May love triumph!"

"May it indeed, sir." Taylor bowed.

Malcolm scraped himself off the floor. "Thank you, sir." He paused. "Oh, and I'm sure you understand Ilsa's desire for discretion in this matter, sir. She would be mortified if anyone was to find out. Say, Uncle Jack."

Droppelheimer nodded. "Of course, Prince Malcolm. My lips are sealed. Even Captain Kaplan will know nothing of this."

They left the office to wait in the hallway, and after the door closed behind them, Taylor turned to Malcolm. "'One true love?'"

Malcolm sniffed and straightened the front of his jacket. "It worked, didn't it?" Seriousness returned to his eyes. "Now we need to find Mina. Fast."

Cleo was fast asleep, curled in a ball with her hairless tail over her nose. Julie had wrapped her body around the sleeping

Sphynx, and with her head propped up on pillows, the worst of the pain had subsided to a dull throb.

She pressed her face into the pillow and let out a long breath, wishing she could sleep as peacefully as Cleo was. Her hand still rested on the Sphynx's back, warm and toasty. Every time she moved her fingers, sleepy purrs vibrated Cleo's chest.

Her words ran circles in Julie's mind. *You're going to need that sense of humor when you finally break the concealment spell.* What was that supposed to mean?

Queen Esmerelda had told Julie she was of noble blood. Clearly, the Sphynxes knew that, and probably more.

Am I more important by birth than I thought? Julie wondered.

Eglantine's melodic laughter rippled through her mind. *I could have told you that you're important.*

Cleo's portal was still faintly visible as a shimmer in the air, and their connection was clear for now.

Julie smiled despite herself and closed her eyes. *You're biased, Eggles.*

Maybe a little, Eglantine teased, *but the Sphynxes seem to think so, too.*

Have they said anything? Julie opened her eyes.

Not that I could decipher. Eglantine huffed. *They're a grumpy bunch.*

Julie rolled onto her side, careful not to disturb Cleo, and stared at the ceiling. *Eggy, do you know if any of...of Mordred's descendants are still alive?*

Eglantine paused. *I don't. It's not in any of my ancestors' memories. Why do you ask?*

Julie sighed. *No reason.*

She thought about waking Cleo to ask her, but she was fairly sure the Sphynx would be less than forthcoming. They'd known she was a Lunar Fae before anyone else had, and they hadn't told her then.

No one had answers they were willing to share, and Julie had spent her frustration on the idea. Now, she just felt tired and worried. She fumbled for her phone and opened Taylor's chat, but there were no new texts, and she didn't want to bother him. He and Malcolm were probably hot on Mina's trail.

Mina wasn't the only fugitive, though. Julie scrolled through her official OPMA email, but there was nothing new on the poisoning, just her official notice of suspension.

She huffed in annoyance and selected Bianca's number from her contacts, then held the phone to her ear.

It took several rings, and Julie was about to give up when Bianca answered.

"Hey, girl!" the succubus chirped, sounding out of breath. "How are you doing? Taylor told me what happened. Sounds shitty!"

"I'm fine, thanks, Bee." Julie frowned. "What's that noise in the background?"

There was a distant explosion on Bianca's end of the line.

"Just something we've got going on," Bianca replied. "What's up?"

"I was just wondering if there's been any progress in finding out who poisoned the queen and set Vivienne up," Julie admitted. "I wanted to—"

"Hold on one second, girlfriend." Bianca took a deep breath. "*Fire at will!*"

There was a boom.

"Everything okay?" Julie asked, concerned.

"Yeah. Actually, can I call you back?" Bianca paused, and there was a dull crackle, the sound of her firing magic from her palms. "Little busy here, babe."

"Sure. Do you need help?" Julie added, but Bianca had already hung up.

Julie stared in disgust at her phone, then flung it onto the nightstand and threw herself back onto the pillows. She was so bored she was ready to scream.

The soft knock at her door felt like a reprieve. Julie sat up. "Who's there?"

The door opened a crack, and Livius popped his head around it. "Julie of the Meadows, you have a visitor."

"A visitor?" Julie asked eagerly. "Who?"

Axl shoved past Livius. "It's the Great Lady," he told her in a stage whisper.

CHAPTER THIRTEEN

"I'm right here, Axl," Lady Ennowen growled from the hallway.

Julie's hands clenched on her sheets.

"We disavowed her," Axl snarled. "We will fight her if you want us to."

"Fight me?" Lady Ennowen demanded. "I would like to see you try!"

The two dragons scattered, and the door swung wide to admit Lady Ennowen, imperious in her green, gray, and white robes. She held her chin high and shoulders back, and her jade-green eyes looked into Julie's soul.

"Julie of the Meadows." Lady Ennowen inclined her head. "I was sorry to hear what happened to you."

Julie leaned against her pillows and folded her arms. "I'm sure you were dismayed to find out I hadn't been killed."

"Why would you say such a thing, my dear?" Lady Ennowen purred. She crossed the room smoothly, moving with a slowness that suggested immensity, although she was a little old lady in this form. "I'm simply here to express my concern that you were so brutally attacked."

"I'm okay. Thanks for asking. You can piss off now," Julie retorted.

Lady Ennowen perched on the edge of the bed, which woke Cleo. The Sphynx sat up and watched expressionlessly.

"My dear, I don't understand why you are so insolent." Lady Ennowen sneered. "I'm showing you kindness and courtesy by visiting you in your fragile, vulnerable state." Her eyes wandered to the IV in Julie's arm. "Such damage caused by a simple vampire bite!"

Julie shrugged. "She caught me off-guard. I was trying to help her."

"I suppose it's only to be expected with your soft skin." Lady Ennowen laughed. "If Mina Nox had attacked a *dragon*, her fangs wouldn't even have pierced their scales."

"Mina Nox wouldn't have attacked a dragon because, thanks to you, all the dragons are holed up in the Deep instead of out here in the real world, helping the paras who need them," Julie snapped.

Lady Ennowen's eyes flashed, but she held onto her composure. "The dragons are safe, young one. They're in the protection of other dragons." She raised her eyebrows. "Perhaps if your kind had done the same instead of meddling with the affairs of other paranormals, you wouldn't have found yourself in the trouble you do now."

Heat flashed through Julie's palms, but she was too weak to summon even a wisp of smoke.

"Of course," Lady Ennowen went on evenly, "if you had not acted with such total disregard for the dragon heir's safety, my granddaughter would be safe among them now, too."

Julie snorted. "As if Eggy isn't perfectly safe where she is."

Lady Ennowen bared her teeth. They were unnaturally sharp in her human face. Julie had never noticed that about humanoid dragons before, no matter how many times Alugon smiled at her. "Nonsense!"

"I'll see your 'Nonsense!' and I raise you a 'Bullshit!'" Julie countered. "I promise nothing will happen to Eggy where she is right now."

Lady Ennowen's eyes narrowed. "I find that very difficult to believe, considering that her so-called guardian is laid up in hospital with a simple vampire bite. You are too fragile and far too foolhardy to defend the Great Lady-in-Waiting of the Deep, child."

Who says that I need to be defended, Grand-smother? Eglantine demanded loudly.

Lady Ennowen's eyes widened. *Granddaughter! Where are you, moondrop?* She frowned. *And who is this 'Grand-smother' you speak of?*

It means you're the reason I haven't hatched yet! Eglantine snapped. *You think you're keeping me safe, but you're keeping me from being who I am. Now leave Julie alone!*

Tears glimmered in Lady Ennowen's eyes. She blinked them away fiercely and shook her head hard. *Please, moondrop, tell me where you are, and I'll bring you home.*

Never! Eglantine raged.

"Your granddaughter is exactly where she wants to be," Julie growled. "I suggest you leave her alone the way she asked and respect her wishes like you would have done long ago if you *really* loved her."

Lady Ennowen bridled. "Excuse me?"

"You're excused." Julie folded her arms. "Bye now."

Lady Ennowen drew herself up to her full height. "This is *not* over!" she roared.

It's very much over, Eglantine growled.

"If you want to talk some more, you can do it via my attorney," Julie snapped.

Lady Ennowen took a deep breath, and Dr. Olena burst into the room. Her stethoscope swung around her neck, her long white hair bounced in a braid down her back, and her normally sand-colored cheeks were scarlet with fury.

"What are you doing in my patient's room?" the Sylthana Elf thundered. "Major Meadows is on strict bed rest, and I demand you leave at once!"

Livius and Axl appeared in the doorway. Axl's hands were bunched into fists, but his eyes were huge.

"Yes!" Livius clenched a skinny fist. "You should leave!"

Lady Ennowen rounded on him, and he cowered.

"You made a mistake by coming here," Dr. Olena growled. "I can push one button and summon half the OPMA. Leave before I'm tempted to do it and wake some of my sleeping patients."

Lady Ennowen shot Julie a last ferocious glare. "Mark my words, fool," she hissed. "There will be repercussions for this." Then she spun in a swirl of dragonscale robes and stormed out of the room.

Julie sagged against her pillows.

"I'm sorry about that, Julie. I have no idea how she got past Security." Olena hurried to her side. "How do you feel?"

"I'm okay. Just tired," Julie mumbled.

Cleo stretched, flicking her tail up over her back. "Well, that was enough excitement for one day." She yawned and disappeared into the aether.

Livius and Axl hovered in the doorway while Olena took Julie's vitals. Her headache was back as a numb pain behind her temples.

"Your vital signs are fine." Olena let out her breath. "I'll speak to Security and get the captain to send us more guards for your door." She glanced at Livius and Axl and lowered her voice. "Truth be told, I thought two dragons would be more than enough."

Julie chuckled faintly. "I only let them stand guard because it makes them feel better," she confided. "Not because I expect them to protect me from a real threat."

"Well, I'll make sure that Lady Ennowen won't be able to get in if she comes back for Round Two," Olena promised.

"That was actually Round..." Julie pursed her lips. "You know, I've lost count. Talk about bonding into a nightmare family." She gritted her teeth. "There's no way she's getting her claws on Eggy."

Axl shuffled nearer. "Julie?"

Julie sighed. "Yes, Axl?"

"You have another visitor," Axl mumbled.

"Is she back?" Olena growled, clenching her fists. Purple light glowed behind her fingers.

"No, Doctor." Axl shook his head. "It's a faerie."

Olena glanced at Julie. "I'm not sure you need another visitor right now."

"Please, let him in." Julie struggled to sit up. "It'll be good to see him. Besides, I'm bored out of my skull."

Olena sighed. "I guess I'd rather you had visitors than jumped out of bed and ran off to find an assassin to fight." She waved a hand. "Let him in."

Axl and Livius retreated, and a pint-sized faerie buzzed into the room on slender wings. His hair was gelled up in spikes, and his skin was moonlight-pale. When he grinned at Julie, his mouth was a black hole with spiky gray teeth.

"Major Meadows!" He turned a somersault in midair. "It's nice to see you."

"You, too!" Julie burst out. "Chatting on scrying screens just doesn't cut it."

Olena smiled. "Hello, Mr. Faerie. It's nice to see you looking so well."

The faerie bowed. "Nice to see you too, Doctor. All thanks to you."

"See you both later." Olena hurried for the door. "I've got patients to attend."

The door swung shut behind her, and the faerie fluttered over to perch on the foot of the hospital bed.

"She's right," Julie told him. "You *are* looking well. Really well."

The faerie crossed his legs. "Olena worked her magic. I'm just sorry I couldn't tell you anything about the para who killed my family."

"You had a head injury. It's not your fault that you couldn't remember, even after the geas was lifted," Julie pointed out.

The faerie shrugged. He pointed at the bag of blood hanging from the drip stand next to Julie. "You using that, or can I drink it?"

"Please don't," Julie squawked, alarmed.

"Suit yourself." The faerie chuckled. "Looks delicious. Not as delicious as *you* looked to that vampire."

Julie laughed. "Charming."

The faerie grinned.

"How did you know I was in here?" Julie asked.

"Oh, I have my ways," he told her airily. "Besides, I don't have much to do other than look for trouble."

Julie grinned. "It doesn't surprise me that you came to find me, then."

"Exactly." The faerie leaned forward. "I'm here to offer you my services."

"Services?" Julie raised her eyebrows.

"Yes." The faerie lowered his voice. "I understand you have a...dragon problem."

"If by that you mean that I've made an enemy of the queen of the dragons, yeah, a little." Julie tilted her head to one side, genuinely curious. "What do you propose?"

"I'll hide in the scales of one of her bodyguards, ride him into the Deep, follow her to her bed, and rip out her throat while she sleeps," the faerie explained calmly.

"What? No!" Julie sat up. "Please don't do that!"

"I thought you might not like the idea." The faerie sighed. "Fine. I *do* have another service to offer you, however."

"Does it involve ripping out throats?" Julie asked in dismay.

The faerie chuckled. "That's up to you."

Julie relaxed slightly. "Go on."

"I know you're bored stiff in here, and you want answers about what's happening in Avalon." The faerie folded his arms. "I can be your eyes and ears. I can report to you and keep you updated in real-time like my family did when we followed Pedro Sanchez." He tapped his ear. "I have a stolen telechip we can use to communicate."

"You stole OPMA thaumatech?" Julie raised her eyebrows.

"Of course I did. Doesn't everyone?" The faerie inspected his fingernails, uninterested.

Julie shook her head. "I really appreciate your offer. It's kind of you, but you don't owe me a thing. You were medically discharged with the highest honors, and you've done more for the Eternity Throne and lost more in the process than anyone ever should."

"You're not wrong," the faerie replied calmly. "No one should have to lose their family the way I did."

His words sent a knife through Julie's gut. She had been the CO on the op on which his wife and two daughters were brutally killed by the mysterious paranormal who was behind the war being waged on the Eternity Throne. *I was responsible for them, and they died in front of him.*

"No one should," Julie murmured, "and I'll always be sorry for what happened."

"You? Sorry? You have nothing to be sorry for." The faerie smiled. "It was the cloaked para who killed them, not you. If I blamed you for their deaths, I would have killed you and impaled your body on the highest tree in the Fernwood long ago."

"Uh, thanks?" Julie guessed.

"No, it was that cloaked para, the one who placed them under geasa that made them explode." The faerie's face darkened. "I will not rest until I get vengeance for their deaths."

"Vengeance?" Julie swallowed. "You mean justice, right?"

"What's the difference?" The faerie smiled, showing his teeth, which were as sharp as snake fangs. "I'll drink their heart's blood either way."

Being my eyes and ears feels a lot less dangerous than this quest for blood, Julie noted silently.

She cleared her throat. "Actually, your offer sounds great. I've been worrying about Taylor and Malcolm, and I was wondering if you could follow them and give me updates."

The faerie whooped, jumped into the air, and performed a pirouette that scattered faerie dust on the covers. Every mote burned a hole through the sheets with a sizzle.

"Yes!" the faerie crowed. "I will do that, Major Meadows, and I'll let you know how they are. And protect them with my life, if need be."

"I don't think it will be," Julie told him hurriedly. "They'll be fine. Just, uh, offer them your assistance."

"Of course." The faerie bowed extravagantly. "You'll hear from me soon!"

He swooped out the door with a maniacal cackle, and Julie nestled into her pillows. She could only hope that sending the faerie after Taylor and Malcolm would keep him off the mystery para's trail and prevent him from getting killed.

The Pagani Huayra was fast and beautiful and brilliant in Manhattan traffic, but as it bounced down the beautiful oh-so-uneven stone path, Taylor's kidneys pled for mercy. He was pretty sure he'd felt every bump and wobble, and even Taylor, who'd grown up in the Aether Compound, had to admit the driveway was much longer than necessary.

"Do you think Qrell will keep quiet?" Malcolm wondered, braking to slowly navigate around a small pothole.

"She thought the whole thing was hilarious." Taylor gritted his teeth as the car hit a loose stone. "I'm pretty sure she won't tell anyone as long as we capture Mina quickly and efficiently."

"That's the idea." Malcolm swallowed and took one hand off the wheel to pat his coat pocket. "I've got a few vials of the sleeping potion with me. All we need to do is to get her to swallow some."

"So, we just need to pour some fluid into a violent vampire's mouth?" Taylor queried.

Malcolm grimaced. "When you put it that way..."

Taylor's phone chirped. He fished it out and grimaced. "It's Isaiah. They've had no luck picking up Mina's scent, so they've started canvassing to find out if anyone's seen her."

Malcolm shook his head. "We'll just have to hope Qrell was right and Mina *did* flee to this estate."

Taylor could see why Mina would feel at home here. The place reeked of ostentation. Green fields stretched in every direction, glittering with wards to keep their occupants—which looked like thoroughbred racing pegasi—from flying away. There were huge barns among the fields, with soaring homes with tennis courts and swimming pools.

Those homes were nothing compared with the main house, visible when they crested a low rise. It was brutally modern, all glass and steel, out of place among the elegant gardens and green lawns that surrounded it. Two enormous wings branched off from the main part of the mansion, enveloping the Huayra as Malcolm drove to the parking space near the east wing.

"Swanky," he commented.

"Right?" Taylor grimaced. "And we're *princes*, so that's saying something."

"Any luck finding the property's owner, Hat?" Malcolm asked.

Hat was still wrapped securely around Taylor's neck, and he tightened. "No."

"Is that unusual?" Taylor asked.

Hat sighed. "*Very*. Be careful, both of you."

Taylor glanced at Malcolm, who shrugged. "Only one thing for it, I guess."

They stepped out of the car, glancing around warily. Taylor strained his ears, but there was an eerie silence on the estate. Too much silence. With huge gardens and many trees surrounding them, birdsong should fill the air, but Taylor heard only the thumps of their footsteps as Malcolm approached the front door.

"What are you going to do, Malcolm?" Taylor hissed. "Ring the bell?"

"Sure." Malcolm shrugged. "Why not?"

Taylor didn't have a good answer for that one. He unsheathed the long, slender daggers he wore at his sides, traditional Aether Elf weapons, and stayed a step behind Malcolm as they approached the double door. When he peered through the glass, the mansion was just as fancy within as outside. A pricey original sculpture stood in the entrance hall, which had mismatched walls, one brick, one stone.

Malcolm waved a hand in front of a sensor near the front door. There was a distant chime inside the mansion.

"What do we say?" Malcolm whispered. "'Hi, we're looking for a vampire who's either on a killing spree or acting lost and scared. Are you hiding her in your wardrobe?'"

"You should have thought about that *before* you rang the bell," Taylor shot back.

Malcolm whimpered. "I'm no good at this sort of thing. It's Julie's thing."

Taylor's hands tightened on his daggers. "Yes, and it nearly got her killed. We're going to finish this."

Malcolm's eyes narrowed, and his nails lengthened into claws.

They waited for a few moments, but nothing happened, nor

was there any movement in the house. Taylor noticed that apart from the Huayra, which looked at home in these surroundings, there were no other cars or vehicles of any type.

"Is it just me, or is it *way* too quiet?" Malcolm whispered.

"I agree. Something's up." Taylor jerked his head to the side. "Let's go around the back and see if we can figure it out."

Or you could call for backup and wait, Hat suggested.

Taylor and Malcolm exchanged glances.

You're not going to do that. Hat sighed. *Are you?*

"There's no time." Malcolm nodded. "Let's go."

They slipped around the east wing of the house. That took time, some shoving through manicured shrubbery, and a painful few minutes of scrambling over an elegant rockery dotted with statues and fountains. Still, there was no sign of movement in the house. Not even a pet or a footman stirred.

"It's still too quiet," Taylor whispered as they approached the back corner of the mansion.

Malcolm nodded in grim agreement. "Do you feel something?" he murmured. "Something...dark?"

Taylor swallowed. "I thought I was just anxious."

"There's something back there." Malcolm's hands were shaking. "If it's her, she's still not herself."

The vampire hugged the wall at the corner of the mansion. Taylor edged up beside him.

"Ready?" Taylor whispered.

Malcolm gritted his teeth. "Ready."

They leaned around the corner of the house. Taylor's daggers slipped in his sweaty hands as he clenched his fists on them, ready to fight.

There was nothing *to* fight, just an immense lawn trimmed to perfection and bordered by pine trees. Nothing moved.

"Merlin's tits," Malcolm cursed. "She's not here." He huffed and stepped forward.

"Malcolm, stop!" Taylor gasped.

He grabbed Malcolm's arm and yanked him back when the vampire's foot was inches from a stone lying on the grass. It looked innocuous, except for the blue glow that bled from deep within its heart.

Malcolm's eyes widened. "Is that…"

Taylor glanced around. A few yards away, a ring glittered in the grass, then another stone.

"Those are Eluned amulets," he gasped. "Julie told me about them. They're used to create a perimeter of invisibility around a battle. Military-grade."

Malcolm's eyes widened. "She's in there." In a burst of unusual bravery, he tore away from Taylor and charged past the Eluned stone.

"Malcolm!" Taylor exclaimed.

He ran after the vampire, and as he crossed the amulet perimeter, he felt a faint resistance as though the air was elastic. It snapped with a feeling like a cobweb breaking, and the sound of battle clanged in Taylor's ears.

The lawn was torn, churned, and trampled into mud and blood by the paras who clashed a few yards away. On one side were vampires, dwarves, and Sylthana Elves in black cloaks. On the other were the navy uniforms of the OPMA.

Dead ahead, disoriented by the boom of violent magic and the shrieks of the wounded, was Malcolm. He stood motionless, hands at his sides, mouth open as he stared at—

"*Malcolm!*" Taylor screamed.

A crackling, hissing ball of electric magic hurtled toward the stunned vampire.

Taylor slammed his daggers into their sheaths and flung himself forward. His shoulder crashed into Malcolm, and they went down hard on the grass. Taylor felt the heat of the magic ball scorch his shoulders, and it slammed into the dirt a few feet away, showering them with mud.

"Get up!" Taylor yelled, hauling Malcolm to his feet. "*Run!*"

They bolted toward the thickest concentration of navy uniforms Taylor could see. He kept one hand on Malcolm's back as the vampire sprinted across the battlefield. Bullets and Sylthana fire filled the air. A few yards away, a dwarf fell to his knees, blood spraying from a bullet hole in his neck. Malcolm dodged him, slipped, and almost fell to his knees. Taylor made a flicking motion with one hand and dragged Malcolm to his feet.

They crashed through a line of soldiers—Griffins, Taylor realized, spotting their arm patches—and a shoulder-height barricade of raw earth lay straight ahead. Gun barrels bristled around the barricade, but a woman shouted, *"Let them through! Let them through!"*

Malcolm reached the barricade first. Taylor gave him a telekinetic boost over it, accidentally tipping the vampire ass over tea kettle. Malcolm fell face-first into the mud on the other side, and Taylor vaulted over the barricade and landed lightly beside him, then crouched as guns cracked behind them and bullets thudded into the barricade.

"Get back!" Taylor yelled in Malcolm's ear.

The vampire didn't need to be told twice. He scrambled into the shelter of the barricade, and Taylor flopped down beside him, panting.

"Oh, hey, guys," Bianca chirped. "Fancy running into you two here."

CHAPTER FOURTEEN

Taylor raised his head. The succubus sat a few feet from them, reloading her automatic rifle. Around them, Griffins did the same.

"*Bianca?*" Taylor frowned. "What are you doing here?"

"Could ask you the same thing." Bianca cocked the rifle without effort. "We had a distress call from one of the pegasus grooms who spotted some dark-cloaked paras heading in this direction. I had a hunch, so I responded."

"Is it—" Taylor began.

Bianca held up a well-manicured finger. "One second." She got to her knees, braced her automatic rifle on the top of the barricade, and clamped down on the trigger. The roar of gunfire made Taylor clap his hands over his ears.

"Get some, bitches!" Bianca roared, continuing to fire at their attackers.

There was a click as her rifle ran out, and Bianca crouched to reload. "What are *you* doing here?" she asked conversationally.

"We tracked Mina here." Malcolm's voice was hollow. "Seems like we found her."

"We did?" Taylor stared at him.

Malcolm pointed.

Rising to his knees, Taylor peered cautiously over the top of the barricade. A handful of Griffins was engaged in a bitter hand-to-hand fight with a line of vampires a few yards away, steel clashing with fangs, sword against claw. Beyond that was a line of Sylthana Elves and Silver dwarves throwing plumes of blue fire and clumps of heavy earth, countered by dwarves and naiads in the Griffins' ranks.

Through the chaos of dirt and flames, Taylor could make out a pale figure, but her voice was unmistakable. It was twisted and guttural, but it belonged to Mina Nox.

"Forward!" she shrieked. "*Forward!*"

"What is she *doing*?" Malcolm whimpered. "She's commanding them to fight us." Tears glimmered in his eyes.

Bianca paused to put a hand on his shoulder. "It's not her, Malcolm. It's the darkness that's overtaken her." She cocked her rifle.

"Wait." Malcolm inhaled deeply. "Maybe I can talk to her. I'm her nephew. She might listen to me, even when she's like this. If they stop, I can go out there and speak to her."

Bianca's blue eyes widened. "Malcolm—"

"That was an order, Major Hartshorn, on my authority as Crown Prince," Malcolm growled.

Bianca stared at him for a second, then grinned. "Yes, Your Highness." She touched her telechip. *Cover me.* Her words crackled through the borrowed military telechip in Taylor's ear.

Copy, a dwarf growled. Taylor recognized Korin, the leader of Julie's old unit.

Bianca fished a small metal cylinder from her pocket, then crouched on her high-heeled boots and opened her wings. With a powerful leap, she threw herself into the air. The wind from her wings buffeted Taylor as she rose into the air, waving the cylinder above her head. With a *poof* of magic, a white flag unfurled from the cylinder, flashing in the blue sky as she held it aloft.

The rain of earth and fire from the rogues' ranks stuttered to a halt.

Surrender? Taylor asked.

No, Hat replied. *Negotiation. She's giving Malcolm his chance.*

"Halt! Halt!" Mina rasped. "Behold the white flag, friends! We have triumphed!"

There was a ragged cheer from the rogues. Bianca fluttered to the top of the barricade, still holding up the flag.

"Mina Nox!" she called.

Taylor peered over the barricade. The fighting had ground to a halt, and several yards of open space separated the tired, panting line of OPMA soldiers from the vampires, Sylthana Elves, and dwarves in black cloaks. Korin was in the front lines, her face grim and splattered with blood and soot, clutching a magic hammer in each hand. She eyed the rogues with the same distrust with which they stared at her.

Shit, Taylor realized. *There are a lot of them compared to this small Griffin unit. Several dozen, at least.*

Hat grunted in agreement.

There was movement near the front lines of the rogues. Mina Nox emerged from among them, flanked by a pair of Sylthana Elves, the hoods of their black cloaks drawn over their faces. Mina walked with her head held high. Her features were familiar, but the look in her glowing red eyes was alien.

"Come then, fools," she snarled. "Surrender."

Hold your positions, Bianca hissed over the telechip.

Malcolm got to his feet and cleared his throat, then brushed dirt and grass from his expensive suit.

"Mal, let me come with you." Taylor gripped the vampire's arm.

Malcolm shook his head. "No. She knows me. She'll listen to me."

He brushed Taylor aside and walked in the unnatural hush, weaving between the motionless soldiers as he headed for the bare strip of no man's land. Mina stood at its edge, smirking, her fangs protruding over her lower lip. She flexed fingers whose claws curved as cruelly as scimitars. The soldiers glared at the rogues, but Malcolm's head was down.

Taylor scrambled out from behind the barricade and edged up to the front row of soldiers, Bianca beside him.

"I don't like this," he muttered.

Bianca gritted her teeth. "None of us do, but he's right. She deserves one more chance."

Malcolm stepped in front of the soldiers, leaving their protective presence behind. His swanky shoes squelched in grass that was drenched in blood, and he came to a halt a few yards from Mina.

"Auntie Mina," he murmured. "It's me. Malcolm."

Mina hissed. "I know who you are, boy."

Now that he was closer to the rogues, Taylor could see their eyes beneath their deep hoods. Something about them made a shiver roll down his spine like an ice cube. There was no rage or fury in them. They were blank, and the rogues stood motionless like rows of de-animated golems.

"I know you're scared." Malcolm held out a hand. "It's going to be okay. We can fix this." His free hand crept into his jacket pocket, in which the crystal vials of potion nestled. "I just need you to come with me."

Mina laughed. "And go back to imprisonment? Never!"

"We're not trying to imprison you. We're trying to protect you," Malcolm murmured. "Dad's very worried about you. Won't you come home for him?"

"For Julius Nox?" Mina cackled. "That weakling? That *fool*? He could have ruled the entire world, let alone the vampires." She spread her arms. "Instead, he fools around with democracy and freedom. Idiot!"

"This isn't you talking." Malcolm's voice broke. "You love your brother."

"My brother is a fool," Mina hissed, "and I know what you're planning. You fear power. I have embraced it. You will take me nowhere."

"Please, Auntie Mina." Malcolm edged a step closer. "Nobody's going to hurt you. We just want to help you. You nearly killed Julie last night. She saved your life, remember? It's time to stop this and come home." He spoke gently, but his words rang with authority.

Mina flexed her claws and hissed. Taylor took a step nearer despite himself.

"It's going to be okay." Malcolm extended his hand. "Please, Auntie Mina, come with me."

Mina lowered her hands. Her mouth closed, although her fangs were still visible, jutting under her top lip.

"That's it." Malcolm smiled. "Come home with me. We'll take care of you."

Mina took a step forward, held out a hand to Malcolm, and shrieked, "*Now!*"

"*NO!*" Taylor roared.

Blue fire roared from the elves that flanked her. Taylor charged, crying *Hat, help me!*

He reached Malcolm seconds before the flames did, threw his arms around the vampire and spun him, and threw up a hand as though he could stop the fire through sheer willpower. He felt the scorching heat on his skin and then the sturdiness of a leather strap in his hands.

A shield sprang out of nowhere. Its weight wrenched Taylor's shoulder, but he yanked it over his face instinctively. The flames punched into it, but he felt no heat. Taylor crouched, driving his feet into the ground, and the force of the flames pushed him back, skidding through the mud, one arm still around Malcolm.

Engage, engage, engage! Bianca screamed.

The ground juddered beneath Taylor's feet, and the flames abruptly stopped. He lowered the shield, panting, and glanced at the wide-eyed Malcolm.

"You okay?" he yelled.

"Let's get out of here!" Malcolm screamed.

Taylor kept the shield up to cover them as they sprinted behind the barricade and stumbled into its shelter. Two Griffin wereeagles were spitting bullets into the battle with automatic rifles.

"Shit. *Shit*! I thought that would work," Malcolm stammered. "I thought it would work."

Another burst of gunfire from the nearest wereeagle almost deafened Taylor.

"Did you see those rogues?" Taylor shouted. "Their eyes."

Malcolm nodded. "It was like they weren't there."

"I saw something like it in the yetis," Taylor yelled. "Only they're not mind-controlled. They're brainwashed."

Malcolm shuddered. "We have to stop them, Taylor. We've got to end this battle before they all get killed."

"We need to get that potion into Mina." Taylor ducked as a plume of fire slammed into the barricade, making it shudder and filling the air with smoke. "That's the only way we'll stop them. Are you with me?"

Malcolm clenched his jaw. "I'm with you."

"I'll use my magic to hold her still." Taylor handed Malcolm the shield. "You get the potion into her when I've done that."

"Got it." Malcolm took the shield. "Where did this come from, anyway?"

"I think I know." Taylor unwound the scarf from around his neck. "Hat, was that you?"

"I can neither confirm nor deny—" Hat began.

"Do it again," Taylor barked. "I could really use Robin of Loxley's bow and that quiver that never runs out."

There was a brief pause.

"Oh, all right," Hat grumbled.

There was a soft *poof*, and a six-foot yew longbow appeared in front of Taylor, patterned with runes. Taylor grasped it, and the strap of a quiver appeared over his shoulder. He felt the weight of it on his back. He didn't have to look to know that the quiver was filled with glowing blue arrows.

"Oh!" Malcolm squeaked. He held the round wooden shield on his left arm; it had a stylized gold sun painted in the middle. Deep scratches were scored in it, but it showed no damage from the Sylthana fire.

Svalinn, Hat announced. *Capable of protecting the world from direct sunlight. Sylthana fire is nothing to that baby. You might as well have this too.*

A Viking sword appeared in Malcolm's hand. He gasped at its weight, then steadied his arm and swished it a few times. "It's amazingly balanced."

Taylor pulled out an arrow and nocked it. "Let's do this."

Malcolm met his eyes and grinned. "Come on!" He brandished the sword. "For the Eternity Throne!"

"For the Throne!" Taylor echoed.

They scrambled over the barricade and charged into the chaos. The orderly lines of soldiers and rogues were gone. Now, the lawn behind the mansion hosted a mad free-for-all with knots of soldiers scrambling to hold their own, hopelessly outnumbered by the rogues. Taylor spotted Jae on her back a few yards away, grappling with a vampire who straddled her chest. He drew the bow and let the arrow fly straight for the vampire's heart. At the last second, the vampire ducked, but Taylor flicked one hand, and the arrow curved in mid-air and buried itself in the vampire's back.

"Look out!" Malcolm yelled.

Taylor spun as a roaring dwarf swung a battleax in his direction. He ducked, and Malcolm shrieked and plunged the Viking sword into the dwarf's neck. The dwarf collapsed, gurgling, blood splattering Malcolm's suit.

"Keep going! Just keep going!" Taylor bellowed. "Where's Mina?"

There! Hat cried.

In the thick of the fighting, across the battlefield from them, was Mina, still flanked by the two Sylthana Elves. A bold Woodland Fae with the sweeping antlers of a moose charged her, head down, clutching a knife in each hand. The elves were too late. Mina dodged, and the Woodland Fae barely missed her. He spun, tossing his antlers, and Mina moved with serpentine speed. She seized his face and slammed her claws into his cheeks. He threw back his head and shrieked in agony.

"No!" Malcolm screamed.

Taylor drew his bow, but his hands were shaking as he aimed for Mina's heart.

"Don't!" Malcolm cried.

Taylor hesitated too long. Mina sank her fangs into the fae's neck and ripped out his throat with an efficient jerk of her head and an eruption of arterial blood.

Malcolm grunted in dismay and charged at Mina, flailing his sword, heedless of the Sylthana Elf who swung toward him and raised her hands. Taylor aimed at the elf's arm, and she fell to her knees with a scream. A dwarf stepped in front of Malcolm, hammer at the ready. Malcolm swung the sword in a brutal chop that slammed into the dwarf's sturdy helmet and sent him flying. A vampire charged Taylor, and another dwarf was rushing at Malcolm with a battleax.

Taylor nocked two arrows and fired, then made two slicing motions with his hand. The arrows separated, and each found its target. The vampire and the dwarf fell to the ground.

"There are too many, Mal!" Taylor yelled, nocking two more arrows as Malcolm swung his sword wildly at the wall of Sylthana Elves advancing toward them.

One of the elves punched out both arms and blue fire crackled through the air. Malcolm held up his shield and crouched. The fire splashed harmlessly over its surface, but another elf was upon him, hacking at Malcolm with a two-handed broadsword. Its blade clanged on the shield. Taylor fired two more arrows and both elves fell, but another elf charged. As Malcolm tried to rise, she swung her broadsword. It met Malcolm's shield with a crash, and the vampire cried out and fell to his knees.

Another vampire hissed inches from Taylor. He spun, yanked an arrow from his quiver, and barely dodged as she swiped at him with her claws. Taylor brought his arm up sharply and plunged the arrow into her ribs.

"Taylor!" Malcolm cried. He was on his back, holding up the shield with both hands, sword lost as blows poured down upon him from a swarm of elves that got thicker.

Before Taylor could react, a bolt of brilliant red light shot through the air and struck the shield. Malcolm gasped as the light reflected in all directions. Taylor cowered, but when it touched him, he felt only a pleasant heat.

It was different for the Sylthana Elves. The light slammed into them like it was physical, and their screams were cut short as they were flung aside like they'd been bombed.

"Need some help, boys?" Bianca called.

She hovered over them, grinning, her hands enveloped in red magic.

"We need to get to Mina!" Malcolm shouted, scrambling to his feet. He fished his sword out of the mud.

"I got you. *Go! Go!*" Bianca roared.

She flung two bolts of red light dead ahead, opening the way, and Malcolm and Taylor charged. Taylor's blood rushed in his ears, his bow slipping in his sweaty hands as he ran. With every bolt of red light, rogues scattered before them. Panic spread among them, and screams rose in all directions, cries of terror instead of pain.

A group of vampires scattered before the red light, and Mina Nox was dead ahead.

"Now, Taylor!" Malcolm yelled.

Taylor stuck the bow into the quiver and clenched both fists, summoning all of his power. He'd never immobilized a person before, but he knew he could do it if—

You haven't? Hat squawked. *You might have mentioned that earlier!*

Shut up! Taylor snapped. *I need to concentrate!*

Mina whipped around, but her feet didn't go with her. She gasped and stuck out an arm, which froze.

"Almost!" Taylor ground out.

Malcolm sheathed his sword and reached into his coat pocket.

Bianca! Hat screamed.

A mushroom cloud of fire flooded the battlefield with brilliant blue light. Taylor looked up. Three Sylthana Elves stood beneath Bianca, combining their magic into a plume of fire that reached for the succubus. Occupied with shooting magic into the paras surrounding Malcolm and Taylor, Bianca hadn't noticed.

"Bianca, go!" Taylor yelled.

Bianca looked down, but it was too late. She only had a split second for panic to register on her features. She slammed her wings down and propelled herself higher, but the fireball was faster, and it swallowed her whole.

"*No!*" Taylor screamed.

He let go of Mina and heard her guttural shriek of triumph, but his eyes were on the fireball as it dissipated, leaving a scorched humanoid figure frozen in midair. Her wings were limp. She fell like a stone toward the waiting Sylthana Elves, who had drawn their swords.

"Hands off my girlfriend's bestie!" Taylor yelled.

He yanked out his bow, nocked three arrows, and fired them.

The three elves fell in silent unison, one arrow through the center of each elf's heart. Taylor flung the bow aside and stretched out both hands toward Bianca. She slammed against his telekinesis like he was catching her physically, and he fell to his knees with a jarring thump. He had her, though. Six feet above the ground, Bianca's fall slowed, and she landed on the ground as gently as if she'd been laid there by loving arms.

She didn't move. Her armor glimmered in the sun. Her uniform was burned off in places, revealing a waxy mess of flesh and molten skin. Her wings had ragged holes ripped in their thin membranes, and her golden hair was gone.

"Bianca!" Taylor cried.

A roar of triumph rippled through the rogues.

Retreat! Korin screamed in Taylor's telechip. *Back to the barricade!*

The Griffins fled, and the rogues gleefully gave chase. Taylor fumbled in the mud for his bow and held it up, but none of them paid him any attention as they surged past, black cloaks rippling. They had eyes only for the Griffins they were pursuing.

Taylor wildly looked around for Malcolm and heard a buzz like a huge cloud of hornets approaching.

The rogues stumbled to a halt and looked at the skies. A black cloud blotted out the sun.

Taylor grinned.

Not hornets, he realized. *Faeries.*

The buzzing came from their wings, underlined by a droning chant. "Blood for blood! Blood for blood! Blood for blood!" At the head of the faerie crowd, Taylor spotted a familiar figure: the male faerie who'd served with Julie in the Griffins—the one who had lost his wife and daughters in the Cave of Altamira.

"Take them!" he hissed.

The faeries drew back their lips and screeched, all black mouths and pointed teeth. Then they fell upon the rogues. Acidic faerie dust sparkled in the sun and scorched holes in black cloaks, and rogues screamed and clutched their melting faces. The Griffins rallied around Bianca, a wall of navy surrounding their fallen leader.

Taylor tightened his grip on his bow and looked for Malcolm. The vampire was a few feet away, cowering under his shield, ashen and terrified. Blood trickled from a cut on his chin.

"Malcolm!" Taylor yelled. "Where is she?"

Malcolm pointed as Mina Nox strode through the ongoing battle, slapping faeries aside with her claws, heading straight for Bianca.

"Last chance!" Taylor shouted and focused his powers on Mina.

She stopped as though she'd walked into a brick wall. Her face twisted with fury, and she fought his telekinesis hard, her limbs dragging through the air in slow motion. Taylor gritted his teeth and dropped his bow to extend both hands toward her. She froze in place.

Her scarlet eyes found him, and their glow pierced his soul. His control of his powers wobbled, and he shook his head sharply.

"Oh no. Uh-uh!" he yelled. "None of those hoodoo voodoo juju cooties!"

He clenched both fists and lifted his hands, and Mina rose off the ground. She tried to scream, but her face was frozen.

"Malcolm, *now!*" Taylor gasped.

Malcolm charged. Mina struggled as the young vampire yanked a vial from his pocket and pulled out the stopper.

"Look out!" Taylor cried as Mina ripped one arm free of his telekinetic grip.

Malcolm saw her claws coming and lunged forward. Her claws raked his chest, leaving behind lines of blood, but that didn't stop him. Malcolm stuck the vial between her teeth, and the potion splashed onto her tongue.

Taylor's strength ran out. He fell to his knees, a rush of air escaping him, hands buried in the wet, bloody mud. Malcolm landed on his side and skidded, but when Mina landed, she only swayed briefly.

Panic clutched Taylor's heart. Then Mina staggered, the potion taking hold.

She locked eyes with Taylor.

"You cannot win," she hissed. "The Lady of the Lake has fooled you all."

Her knees buckled, and she collapsed.

Oh, shit, Hat muttered.

What does any of this have to do with Nimue? Taylor wondered.

Before Hat could respond, there was the distant blare of a horn.

"Faeries, fall back, fall back!" Korin yelled.

The faeries ignored her and continued to drop acidic dust on the panicking rogues.

Hoofbeats thundered in the distance. Korin waved her magic hammers. *"Fall back!"*

"Our work here is done, brothers," the familiar faerie called. "Let's watch them writhe in agony!"

The faerie cloud rose and soared over the battlefield in a vast murmuration. Taylor scrambled over to Malcolm, who was on his hands and knees. He grabbed the vampire's arm and pulled him to his feet.

"Look!" Malcolm croaked, blood soaking his shirt. He pointed.

The top of the nearest hill swarmed with cavalry. Taylor narrowed his eyes, and his heightened senses allowed him to recognize the gray stallion that led the charge, his rider leaning over his neck.

It was Sleipnir.

"It's more Griffins!" he exclaimed.

The rogues realized the same thing. They all rose, even the most gravely wounded, and turned toward the charging riders.

"Surrender now, and no harm will come to you!" Korin called. "Put down your weapons!"

The rogues ignored her. In eerie unison, they reached into their black cloaks and withdrew tiny objects. Taylor glimpsed the nearest one: a crystal amulet no bigger than a coin, shaped like an eagle.

They all spoke at once as the ground shook with the charge.

"Mordred for Eternity."

As one, the dark-cloaked paras clenched their fists, and Sylthana fire erupted over their bodies. Their eerie silence broke. They staggered around the battlefield, shrieking as the flames consumed them, pain and loneliness tearing through their voices as they woke from their brainwashing a moment too late. Malcolm held up the shield, and he and Taylor sheltered behind it as blue fire raged around them. A burning elf, eyes naked and tortured in a face robbed of skin, staggered toward them, screaming through a lipless mouth. Malcolm jerked the shield, and the burning elf crashed into it with a meaty thud, then fell to the ground and was abruptly silent.

When the cavalry reached them, not a single rogue was left alive. There was only ash trickling down from the sky like snow.

CHAPTER FIFTEEN

Julie?

Julie rolled onto her other side, wincing as her IV pulled in her arm. *Not now, Hat. I just got to sleep.*

Her eyes snapped open. *Wait. Hat?*

She sat up and reached for the lamp on her nightstand, then realized it was daylight. Blinking and disoriented, she looked around. Her mouth was sticky on the inside. There was no one in her room. Maybe she'd been dreaming.

We're outside, Hat murmured.

They'd only been apart for a day, but hearing his voice in her head was amazing.

May we come in? Hat added.

Yes! Please do. Julie smoothed the front of her favorite unicorn pajamas, which Sally had kindly brought over, and patted a few wayward hairs.

The door to her room opened, and Taylor, Malcolm, and the faerie piled into the room, accompanied by the smells of battle: gunpowder, smoke, blood, and steel. The faerie was the only one without a mark on him. Taylor's suit was ripped and stained with mud and blood. His hair was singed on one side, and there was a red burn on his cheek and the back of his left hand.

"Taylor!" Julie gasped. "Are you okay? What happened to you?"

Taylor strode up to her, cupped her face in his grimy hands, and planted a kiss on her lips. She kissed him back. Though he reeked of sweat and soot, she could still detect hints of petrichor.

He pulled back after a long moment. "I'm fine, babe." He still wore Hat as a scarf around his neck, although he was singed and stained.

Malcolm followed slowly. He wore a hospital gown, and through the neck, Julie spotted white bandages on his chest. There was a burn on his cheek and a bruise on his temple.

"Mal, you're hurt." Julie struggled to sit up. "What happened?"

"We have good news, bad news, and...news," Hat told her aloud for the benefit of everyone in the room.

The faerie fluttered down to perch on the end of her bed. Malcolm winced his way into a chair, and Taylor sat on the edge of her bed.

"Give me the good news," Julie suggested.

Taylor squared his shoulders. "We captured Mina. She's still unconscious. Malcolm knocked her out with a sleeping potion. We've got her in the containment level here at the NYHQ."

Julie let out a breath. "That's great news." She glanced at Taylor's singed hair. "It doesn't look like it was easy."

"No." Taylor shook his head. "Which brings me to the bad news."

Julie's breath caught.

"We tracked Mina to an estate outside Avalon Town, where she'd rallied a few dozen rogue paras. Vamps, Sylthana Elves, and dwarves, mostly." Taylor paused, and his eyes were distant.

"Was there a fight?" Julie whispered.

Taylor cleared his throat, snapping out of it. "Yes. Bianca and some Griffins responded to a distress call, and when we got there, they were fighting Mina and the others." Taylor paused. "Bianca was hurt in the battle, Julie. It's pretty bad."

Julie's guts turned cold. *Would this have happened if I had been there?* "How bad?" she croaked.

"Olena's working on her right now. She says Bianca's strong, and she thinks she'll be okay with time." Taylor shuddered. "She took a terrible hit. It would have killed anyone else in your old unit."

Julie realized she'd pressed both hands to her mouth. She lowered them into her lap. "But she'll be okay?"

"Olena thinks so." Taylor squeezed her hands. "Olena was able to heal the burns on her body, and she's in a hyperbaric chamber for the smoke inhalation."

"Okay." Julie swallowed hard. "You got Mina. Is she okay?"

Taylor looked away. "She's unhurt."

"What does Kaplan say?" Julie asked. "Do they have any treatments or anything they can try?"

"Kaplan doesn't know yet." Taylor grimaced. "Hat insisted we brief you first."

Julie raised her eyebrows. "Why?"

"Because of the...news," Hat mumbled.

Taylor frowned. "Does this have anything to do with what Mina said before she collapsed?"

"What did she say?" Julie asked.

"She said, 'The Lady of the Lake has fooled you all,'" Malcolm recalled. He frowned. "That was strange. Hasn't Nimue been missing for centuries? Besides, she was a victim in the Second Pendragon Wars. Mordred kidnapped her and forced her to make the dragon-slaying blade, as well as Morgan. Arthur had to rescue her."

"Just part of this crazed Mordred cult's mythology, I guess," Julie speculated.

Hat took a deep breath. "No, it's not. It's very real. *She's* very real, and she's right here among us, inside this building."

"Nimue?" Julie demanded. "Where?"

Hat paused. "In the hospital wing." He swallowed. "You know her as Vivienne."

There was a long silence.

Julie leaned forward. "*What?*"

"Vivienne is Nimue?" Taylor spluttered.

"I'm afraid so." Hat sighed. "All these years, we've all believed what you just said, Malcolm. That Nimue was captured by Mordred, along with Morgan, and forced to forge the dragon-slaying sword that wounded Arthur."

"Then she went into hiding at the start of the Second Pendragon War, when the Seven Families united to hunt Mordred down." Malcolm frowned.

"That part is true," Hat murmured. "She changed her name to Vivienne and hid in plain sight in Avalon Town when the war was over."

"So you knew all this time?" Taylor asked.

Julie's mind raced.

"Yes, but I never thought she would be dangerous." Hat sighed. "I thought she deserved peace and quiet after everything she'd been through with Mordred, but now it seems that Nimue was working with him all this time. The 'kidnapping' and rescue were a ruse."

"Hat, you and Nimue were lovers," Julie blurted.

Hat unwound from Taylor's neck and flopped onto the bed in front of her. "Yes."

"But that would make you—" She stopped. "No. You *can't* be. Can you?"

There was a tense silence.

Hat assumed the shape he'd been in when they first met: a blue wizard's hat covered in embroidered gold and silver moons and stars.

"I'm afraid so. I hope you can forgive me for deceiving you." His voice broke. "I'm still your Hat."

Julie let out a sound that was part laugh, part scream and scooped Hat into her arms. "This is amazing!"

"Wait. What is happening?" Taylor demanded.

"Don't you see?" Julie laughed. "He was Nimue's lover. He's thousands of years old. He talks about the Pendragon Wars like he was there for them." She grinned. "He was the stone from the Sword in the Stone, and do you remember how Vivienne kept trying to call him by the wrong name, Taylor?"

Taylor's eyes widened. "It started with 'Em.'"

"It was Emrys." Julie held Hat out and gazed at him. "Hat is *Merlin!*"

Taylor's jaw dropped. Malcolm stared at Hat.

Hat spoke quietly. "I am."

The faerie yawned and drummed his heels against the foot of the bed.

"But...but Merlin turned himself into a salmon and was caught and eaten," Taylor squawked.

Hat chuckled. "I'm particularly proud of that fabrication. Nobody thought to look for me after that."

"Why, though?" Julie asked. "Why did you go into hiding...and when?"

"If you'd stop interrupting and let me tell the story, you'd find out," Hat grumbled.

Julie laughed. She crossed her legs and set Hat down gently on the foot of the bed. "Go ahead."

"I'm going to do this telepathically to stop you all from interrupting," Hat grouched.

He paused, and the air flickered above him like the start of an old movie. Colorful shapes appeared in midair: a glamorous court, knights in shining armor around a circular table, the king seated among them with a gold crown gleaming on his head. Julie recognized Arthur, whole and healthy, not the pale, sleeping king she'd seen at Tintagel.

The Golden Age, Hat told them. *King Arthur ruled Avalon, and much of the human world, too. His knights ensured peace and justice, and he was the first king to work toward freedom and equality for all paranormals. He established the Veil to keep humans and paras safe from one another. It was a wonderful time to be one of his subjects.* Hat paused. *And through it all, I was by his side.*

Another figure swam into focus: Merlin. Julie had seen him in a training simulation when she was promoted to corporal, and she recognized his flowing robes, long white beard, and sparkling blue eyes. Her breath caught. Why hadn't she recognized the mischief in those eyes?

Our greatest worry back then was that the king would have no heir, but we saw him falling in love with Morgan, a powerful local mage, and believed all would be well. Hat sighed. *As the Royal Warlock, I advised the king, taught him magic, and served the Eternity Throne and its subjects with all the magic I had, but my life was empty until I saw her.*

The image showed a rush-strewn floor some distance from the Round Table. Julie recognized the young brown-skinned fae dancing with a faceless nobleman. Her face, transfixed with joy, made Nimue seem even more beautiful.

She was the daughter of the Duke of Brocèliande, one of Arthur's allies. Hat gave a wistful sigh. *She was the loveliest thing I had ever seen. I made bold efforts to court her. I made myself look younger, for a start, although I knew she always saw through me and didn't care about my age. What's a hundred years' difference when you're a Lunar Fae and a warlock? It just means a few gray hairs.*

In the image, Merlin turned away from the Round Table and made for the dance floor. His beard shortened and darkened as he went, and he bowed to Nimue, then held out a hand to her. She gave him a coy grin and refused to take it.

She wanted nothing to do with me, but she was interested in my magic and begged me to tutor her. Her father knew she had talent, and he allowed her to stay. I believed it was the only way I'd ever get close to her. Hat laughed softly. *I was right. I taught her everything I knew, and as the years slipped by, we fell in love.*

"Then something happened between you two," Taylor observed. "You talked about it when I asked Vivienne to find Julie when she'd been portaled out of Avalon."

Yes. It was so stupid, so petty. Although by that time, there had been enough stupid and petty arguments that the relationship was struggling like the proverbial camel. Hat groaned. *By this point, Nimue was my partner in work as well as in love. That was how she got her nickname, the Lady of the Lake. After Arthur was disarmed in battle with King Pellinore of the Sylthana Elves, Nimue got Excalibur back, broke its dark enchantments in the magic waters of the lake, and returned it to Arthur.* Hat chuckled. *That was quite an adventure.*

Julie smiled. "Sounds like you guys had a good time together."

We did...until I ruined it. Hat's tone saddened. *She was working on a new type of ward to protect Camelot, or so she told me. She met with Mordred alone. She said she was getting his military perspective on her spell. I didn't handle it well. I was jealous and angry, and we both said things we shouldn't have. That was the end of Nimue and me.*

Nimue's smiling face faded.

She returned to her father and became his court mage at Brocèliande. I believed I'd never see her again. Hat swallowed. *Then it all went wrong.*

The image darkened and focused on a face at the Round Table: angular, with a thick mustache and glittering black eyes.

Mordred was King Arthur's nephew and a knight of the Round Table. Nobody knew back then that he was also a traitor, Hat explained.

The colors swirled and ran together, then turned black and scarlet. A battlefield appeared: horses and riders, swords and lances, screaming faces. Above their heads were two banners: the gold and red dragon and the yellow and black eagle, both rampant.

Arthur left Mordred on the Eternity Throne while he defended the borders of Avalon against marauders, Hat went on. *As always, I accompanied him. When we returned, we found the banner of the black eagle over Camelot. Mordred had usurped the throne and brainwashed many of the knights. He had the army at his command.*

And so the First Pendragon War began, with Mordred on one side and Morgan, Arthur, and me on the other. The dragons rallied behind us. The drow rallied behind Mordred. Mordred's goal was to enslave Avalon and Earth under his rule. Arthur's was to restore the peace we'd enjoyed until the war began.

The battle scene faded to black. Julie frowned.

You know what happened next. Hat was holding back tears. *We received word from the Duke of Brocèliande that Nimue had been kidnapped. Morgan was gone too. By the time we rescued them, it was too late. Mordred had forged a blade that could kill a dragon. He slew Eglantine's mother, and in retaliation, Arthur gathered his forces at Camlann in one great charge against Mordred and his army. That dragon-slaying blade was too strong for us.*

An image appeared through the darkness. The shore of a dark sea on a black night. Merlin, on his knees, his arms wrapped around the fallen king, cradling him in his lap as Arthur's blood seeped into his robes.

It was too strong for me, Hat whispered.

Julie's chest ached for him. She brushed her fingertips over his brim.

"Why have you been masquerading as an artifact all this time?" Malcolm asked gently.

I didn't know where to go without Arthur. Hat swallowed hard. *Mordred was going to take over the world. There was nothing but darkness and chaos. Morgan took Arthur to Tintagel, where his last few loyal knights guarded him while she tried to save him. Her healing magic was stronger than mine, and I felt I'd failed him one time too many. So I became a salmon. I became no one. I didn't want to be in the world anymore.*

"Hat, I'm so sorry," Taylor croaked. There were tears on his cheeks.

Being a salmon took too much energy in the end, Hat murmured.

So I became a hat. Centuries later, one of the knights—this was before the Knights of the Round Table became the Para-Military Agency—stumbled upon me washed up on the shore, and he took me to the palace. I was put in the Royal Treasury, and eventually, I found a use for myself in the recruitment department. At least it made me feel I was doing *something* again. *That's when I found out about Vivienne and knew she was alive and well in Avalon Town.*

"Then Qtana's IRSA 4000 made you obsolete," Julie commented. "And that's how you ended up in the Shrine of Previous Technology and Magic."

Exactly. Hat's brim curved as if in a smile. *And that's how I ended up with you.*

"Why, though?" Julie asked. "Why did you choose me?"

The door crashed open, making all of them jump. The picture in the air above Hat disappeared abruptly.

Kaplan blasted into the room, all seven feet of him, the backs of his hands bristling with orange and black hair.

"What in Merlin's name is this?" he roared.

"Oh!" Julie turned to Hat. "*That's* why you hated me talking about your testicles!"

There was a pregnant pause.

"I should have known." Kaplan threw up his hands. "I should have *known* that having you back in my headquarters would exponentially increase the amount of ridiculous and confusing moments in my day, Meadows."

"Don't look at *me*, sir!" Julie raised her hands. "This time, I was just here in bed, not doing anything."

Kaplan jabbed a huge finger at Hat. "You messaged me. What do you want?"

"Sir, we need to brief you." Taylor swallowed. "About a recent battle."

"You certainly do, Woodskin!" Kaplan bellowed. "Considering that Mina Nox is in my containment level, and I have no idea how she got there!"

"That's not important right now," Hat snapped. "What's important is that we've found the Lunar Fae traitor."

"Who is it?" Kaplan demanded.

"Nimue." Hat paused. "Vivienne. She was no victim, Captain. She was the perpetrator all along."

Kaplan's huge, bushy brows knotted. He touched his telechip, and there was a moment of silence for Julie, who wasn't wearing one.

He's summoning a fae team, Hat explained.

"Let's go get her," Kaplan growled.

Taylor got up, and Julie threw back her covers and leaped out of bed, then nearly face-planted on the floor.

"Whoa, easy." Taylor caught her and gently propelled her back into bed. "We'll be right back. You sit this one out."

He rushed out of the room, followed by Malcolm and the faerie. Julie and Hat were left alone. She reached for him, pulled him into her arms, and squeezed him so tightly that his seams popped.

Hey! What are you doing? Hat spluttered. *What was that for?*

Julie cuddled him closer. *I'm sorry you had to go through all that, Merlin.*

Hat relaxed in her arms. *Thank you for your compassion, Julie. And please don't call me Merlin.* He chuckled. *I've been Hat for so long that I've grown to prefer it.*

Okay. Julie smiled. *That's cool with me.* She paused. *But if Viv...I mean, Nimue is really the traitor, why didn't you tell us right away?*

Hat snuggled down into her arms. *Because you deserved to know the truth first. I'm sorry I kept this from you for so long, Julie. I thought it was for the best.*

Julie stroked his crown. *I know you did. It's okay.*

She held him in her lap for a few minutes, listening for shouts or the sounds of battle. But there were none. A few moments later, Kaplan, Taylor, Malcolm, and the faerie returned. Kaplan's face was scarlet with fury.

"What is it?" Julie asked. "Did you find her?"

Kaplan shook his head. "No." He held out a small white card. "Her bed was empty. We only found this." He frowned. "It's addressed to 'Emrys.'"

Julie took the card. The words were written in a smooth, flowing script.

I should have known you would betray me again.

Julie bobbed, sidestepped, and barely dodged a scything kick from Taylor's left foot. As it skimmed past her, she stepped close and blocked the returning leg with both hands, then swept with her right foot. It caught his supporting ankle and knocked his feet out from under him. Taylor landed on the mat with a heavy thump and a grunt.

"*Still* want to treat me like I'm made of china?" Julie asked, planting her hands on her hips. She was only breathing heavily.

"I wasn't," Taylor wheezed, rolling to his feet. "I know better than to hold back when I'm sparring with you."

He turned to face Julie, hands held close to his face. She grinned and raised her fists, then moved quickly. Jab, hook, jab. Taylor dodged and blocked. A wicked gleam sparkled in his eyes, which crinkled at the corners, and he made a come-hither motion with one hand. An invisible force seized Julie by the waist and slammed her against him, pinning her arms around his waist.

She chuckled and hugged him closer. "I thought you said no powers in this sparring match."

Taylor planted a kiss on her forehead. "I thought you weren't one for following rules."

She snuggled against him. "It's good to be able to spar with you again."

"Good to see you looking like yourself again." Taylor's telekinetic grip on her relaxed, replaced by his encircling arms. "That was a scary month."

"It's over now, though." Julie pulled back and smiled. "Everything's okay."

He leaned closer, and their lips met. Hat made loud gagging sounds that echoed around the gym at the back of the Avalon HQ.

Get a room! he complained.

Julie laughed.

"Maybe we should do that." Taylor's eyes sparkled.

"Sorry. Not now." Julie kissed his chin. "I need to meet with Stormstar about our progress on looking for the poisoner now that I can take a more active role again, and then I need to check on Bianca during visiting hours."

"How is she?" Taylor asked. They walked off the mat, ignoring a minotaur who was pummeling a stone pillar instead of a punching bag. His enormous fists left indents in the stone.

Julie smiled. "Recovering better than anyone expected. She's pissed that her hair's taking so long to grow back."

Taylor laughed. "Sounds like Bianca."

Julie scooped up Hat, who she'd left guarding her gym bag, and cradled him in one arm. He was in his wizard hat form and drooped contentedly from her elbow as they headed for the door.

Before they reached the door, a candle appeared in front of Julie. She stopped and waited patiently as the candle changed into a small wrinkled humanoid with enormous pale eyes.

"Major Meadows." The kobold drew out the words into an eerie hiss.

"Hello, Gemma." Julie smiled. "What's up?"

"There are dragons at the portcullis." Gemma's pale eyes didn't waver. "They're asking for you."

"Dragons plural?" Taylor wondered.

Julie grimaced. "Better go and check it out. Thanks, Gemma." The kobold had disappeared.

"Shit, shit, shit." Julie jogged to the elevator, Taylor right behind her. "I didn't think Lady Ennowen would take it as far as coming to the gates of the Avalon HQ."

"This is war." Taylor's jaw clenched.

Julie swallowed hard. *What if those officers are right and she's here to take Eglantine by force?*

Then we'll fight her, Hat growled. *Eglantine cannot be allowed to return to the Deep.*

Julie reached into the side pocket of her gym bag and pulled out a tiny silver disc. She attached it to her chest and unzipped the gym bag. As the elevator hummed upward, her dwarf-made armor clanked out of the bag piece by piece and attached itself to her, cinching tight around her waist, arms, and legs.

She raised Hat to her head, and he transformed into a helmet, visor and all.

"You carry that around with you these days?" Taylor asked, impressed.

Julie flipped her visor up. "If I'd been wearing it when I went after Mina, things might have gone a little better."

"Maybe." Taylor chuckled. "Might want to cover it unless you want everyone to know you're the Knight."

"One step ahead of you." Julie fished her dragonscale robe out of the gym bag and draped it over her shoulders to hide the armor.

When the elevator doors opened onto the lobby, it was even more chaotic than usual. Officers yelled commands, a troop of dwarves clattered across the room to the main doors, and the paras at the reception desks looked harassed as they grabbed phones and frantically typed on their computers.

In the middle of the chaos, Sergeant Levin Shulme stood out. The massive centaur with his brilliant white coat stood motionless, a finger pressed to his ear as he spoke on his telechip.

Julie jogged up to him. "What is it, Sarge? Is it Lady Ennowen?"

Shulme shook his head. "It would appear not." He paused. "They're calling for you, Major Meadows."

Julie squared her shoulders and glanced out the main doors. The inner ward was in chaos as navy-uniformed soldiers deployed on the walls. She glimpsed the shimmer of dragon scales on the other side of the portcullis.

Taylor took her gym bag. "I'm right behind you, babe."

Julie took a deep breath and strode out of the fortress, smoothing her robe, which was still white and featureless. Around her, archers were deployed to the battlements, and their rhythmic footsteps rocked the inner ward. She stopped a few feet from the portcullis and peered through the gaps between the bars.

The street beyond was filled from sidewalk to sidewalk with dragons.

There were silver dragons with elegant horns from the golden mountainsides and a huge black dragon with the spines and snout of a crocodile from the lava river and shimmering blue and green dragons from the deep lichen forests. Even a few furry white dragons from the snowy peaks, and a handful of fist-sized flower dragons, tucked between the scales of the larger dragons. None of them spoke, nor did they move. They simply stood on the street, exhausted and silent. Some were bleeding. A sinuous six-winged dragon was draped over the shoulders of the lava dragon, unconscious.

The dragon at the head of the group had ice-blue wings and thick white fur that tumbled in silky profusion over her neck and chest. It was streaked with blood.

Julie opened her wings and flew over the wall, which bristled with archers.

Our relations with the Deep must have gotten a lot worse over the past month, she mused.

Hat sighed. *They have. There are no regular communications now, and Danijah missed the last council meeting.*

Julie frowned, troubled. She landed lightly on the street a few yards from the group of dragons. All of the homes and businesses had their doors and windows locked, but Julie saw a few nervous faces peering from their windows.

"I am Julie of the Meadows." Julie lifted her chin. "You asked to speak to me."

The white dragon stepped forward, and her icy eyes searched Julie's. Then she lowered her head and bent her forelegs until she was on her elbows. Her long white tail curled gracefully around her body, and her eyes closed. Behind her, one by one, the other dragons bowed as well.

Julie's heart thudded in her throat. *What is happening?*

Remember your dragon etiquette, Hat urged.

She returned their bows. "Please, friends. Don't bow to me."

The dragons rose. The white dragon spoke in tones like a rushing avalanche. "Hail, Julie of the Meadows, Heirkeeper of the Deep. We have escaped the Deep and come to pledge ourselves to the unborn Great Lady of the Deep."

Eglantine, Julie realized.

"You speak for the only leader we wish to follow," the white dragon went on. "Thus, we pledge our loyalty to you also."

Julie swallowed. *I wasn't expecting this.* She took deep breaths but could feel the earth shaking under her feet. *Hat, what do I do?*

Hat gasped. *Are you asking me what to do?*

Yes! Julie squawked. *Help!*

Accept their pledge. They're right. You represent Eglantine, and if they want to follow her, they need you. Hat's tone softened. *Look at them, Julie.*

Julie's eyes dwelled on the dried blood in the white dragon's fur. She stepped forward, forgetting etiquette. "I'll do anything I can to help you. What happened to all of you?"

The white dragon hung her head. "The Great Lady would not allow us to leave." She closed her eyes, and Julie felt her reaching for her mind. The white dragon gave her a glimpse of chaos: fireballs raining through the dark mountains, a chaotic flight toward the Maw of the Deep, watching one of her friends fall in a cloud of fire, her cry cut short.

"I'm so sorry." Julie touched the white dragon's long, soft nose.

The white dragon leaned into her touch. *We were forced to vote in favor of staying out of the war, but we could no longer submit to Lady Ennowen's rule,* she murmured into Julie's mind. *She grows more and more maniacal. She has a strange new adviser, one we never see, but it is as though she has been gripped by madness.*

Do you know who the new adviser is? Julie asked gently.

The white dragon sighed. *No. We only hear Lady Ennowen speak of them, and we have begun to fear that, thanks to this adviser, she will join the war...on the side of the Mordred cult.*

Julie's stomach clenched. Dragons as outright enemies in the war? The thought was horrendous. It was world-ending. She couldn't help the tremor that ran through her body and spread cracks like cobwebs through the asphalt at her feet.

You are not wrong to be afraid, the white dragon told her. *We want you to show us how we can help end the war before that can happen.*

Julie raised her head and looked into the dragon's blue eyes. *What's your name?* she asked.

Evrah, the dragon told her. *Daughter of Methunoch.*

Julie smiled. *I don't know how yet,* she promised, *but I'm going to help you.*

She turned back and looked through the portcullis at the stunned faces within, then raised her hands.

"Let them in!" she called. "They're no threat to us. They're refugees from the Deep."

"Let them *in?*" Shulme squawked.

Twenty minutes later, Julie understood his trepidation. Even though all the vehicles had been cleared out of the inner ward, the dragons filled it from edge to edge. OPMA medics in purple scrubs hurried among them tending the wounded, but they barely had room to get past with their response bags. They had to turn sideways to slide between the scaly bodies.

Julie grimaced. "Sorry, Sarge. I didn't think this through."

Droppelheimer ran a hand over his bald, tattooed head. "When Kaplan told me the chaos factor in my office would increase tenfold with you as my aide, I didn't know what to expect, but it wasn't this, Major Meadows. Even your suspension does not appear to have gotten in the way of your ability to create dragon-sized difficulties."

Julie's toes curled, but when the orc looked at her, he was grinning.

CHAPTER SIXTEEN

Julie tried not to fidget as she sat at one end of the long table in the upstairs conference room in the Avalon HQ. The arched stone window at one end overlooked the training grounds, where a group of pegasus rider recruits were sky-jousting. The crash of lances and the *poofs* of parachutes opening were distant compared to the turning of pages inside the conference room.

Droppelheimer, Kaplan, Taylor, Alugon, and Shulme were present in person, as was Eleni, the gorgon who ran the refugee center on the outskirts of Avalon Town. She wore wraparound sunglasses and a headscarf, from which tiny adder heads occasionally poked out in curiosity. Everyone except Julie and Taylor was absorbed in reading the files Julie had handed to each of them when they came into the conference room a few minutes ago.

Julie realized she was tapping her heel on the stone floor and stopped. *This better work.*

It's a good idea, Hat told her. *It's going to.*

Eleni finished first. She put the file on the table and grinned. "This is a good idea."

Kaplan lowered his file. "I'm not so sure," he growled. "The last thing we need is another Pompeii."

"That's just it, sir." Julie leaned forward. "This is designed to *avoid* an Avalonian Pompeii. The last time dragons went to war, they had a single mission: capture and stop Mordred. They were hunters and killers because they had to be."

Kaplan's brows knitted. "And they killed thousands of innocent people in pursuit of Mordred, even though they eventually got him."

"Exactly, sir." Taylor cleared his throat. "That kind of collateral damage isn't acceptable to any of us."

"We presented this proposal to Lady Ennowen months ago, but she rejected it out of hand because it came from me and not from the dragon heir. I still think it can work." Julie raised her chin. "If we utilize the dragons as protectors and defenders, innocent people don't have to get hurt. In fact, innocent people can be kept safer."

"If we put this plan into place, dragons won't go out to pitched battles," Taylor chipped in. "They won't be involved in manhunts—"

Julie cleared her throat.

"Apologies. Parahunts." Taylor shot her a grin. "They'll be assigned to peaceful communities under threat from the war, and their only role will be to keep ordinary paras safe."

"If Fernwood Deep had been surrounded by dragons, it would not have burned," Julie offered quietly.

Droppelheimer laid the file down and nodded. "It could work."

Alugon spoke up. "It *will* work. If this option had been presented to the dragons when the Heirkeeper came up with it, it would have reduced conflict among us, as well as with the outside world. Especially since you plan to use only volunteers."

Julie nodded. "Absolutely. Only dragons who volunteer will

be assigned communities to protect. Other refugees from the Deep will be given shelter elsewhere."

"Everyone will volunteer." Alugon's eyes narrowed. "We left because we want to help."

"We all feared that dragons would increase fatalities in the war." Shulme gave a rare grin. "But this will *reduce* them."

Kaplan cleared his throat. "As Augur, you represent all of the refugee dragons," he told Alugon. "If you agree, we'll implement this plan. It's a good one."

Julie glanced at Taylor, and they exchanged grins.

"Where will the dragons be deployed?" Shulme asked.

Julie nodded to Eleni. "That's where you come in. I know you're planning to repopulate Fernwood Deep and the Deadwoods."

Eleni tucked a snake back into her headscarf. "I am, but we don't have the resources to ensure that the people will be safe when they go home. Still, many of my refugees want to go back to their homelands, and those forests are suffering without their woodland paras. Fernwood isn't Fernwood without the dryads, and the Deadwoods need to be brought back to life after what the Green Man did to them. I don't want to send refugees back into danger, though."

Julie grinned. "The dragons could change that. They could help rebuild *and* protect the people who return to the enchanted forests."

"We have magic that will help with rebuilding and bringing life back to the Deadwoods." Alugon smiled. "We will jump at the opportunity to make a useful home for ourselves while we wait for a true Great Lady to return to the throne of the Deep."

There was a brief silence. Kaplan broke it by slamming a massive hand on the table in front of him, which made everyone jump. Eleni's headscarf slid over her eyes, and snakes spilled everywhere. Alugon knocked his glass of water over on his file, and Julie accidentally cracked the stone under her chair.

"Well, what are we all waiting for?" Kaplan roared. "Let's make this happen!"

Ancient dryads spread their enormous limbs overhead, their interlacing arms blocking out all but the gentlest rays of dappled sunlight. Julie took a deep breath and leaned back between the spines on Alugon's back, enjoying the cool breeze on her face.

Enjoying the country air, are we? Hat snarked.

I haven't been in Fernwood since the battle, Julie admitted. *It's good to see it at peace again.*

They followed a narrow lane, overgrown with ferns and roots and strewn with dead trees that had been half-reclaimed by vines and moss. Alugon's claws crunched softly in the leaf litter. Evrah and Methunoch led the way in front of Alugon, carrying Taylor and Malcolm on their backs. Horusiris was curled up in Methunoch's thick fur, fast asleep.

Peace, yes, young one, Alugon rumbled in Julie's mind. *But there is much work to be done. The air here smells lonely, and the trees are sad.*

Julie looked back. *We're about to change that.*

As far as she could see, refugees, dragons, and OPMA officials and soldiers followed them. The line of dragons was punctuated by UMMVs—magic-powered military vehicles—that hummed and glowed blue as they hovered over the ground. The window of the nearest one was rolled down, and a goat's head stuck out of it. The goat was chewing its cud, and a determined female ogre had a firm grip on the rope around its neck.

Julie grinned. *I can't wait to see them home again.*

Alugon came to a halt. Ahead, Methunoch and Evrah had their heads down, trying to push a huge log out of the way. Julie felt a chill roll down her spine as she recognized the fronds on the dead branches.

"Stop. *Stop!*" she yelled.

The two dragons ceased their efforts and looked up.

"That's not a tree." Julie stood up on Alugon's broad back. "That's…that's the corpse of a dryad."

Leaves rustled, and a dryad who was only a century old strode up to Alugon, wearing an OPMA uniform.

"We know, Major Meadows." He held an automatic rifle in his twigs. "She fell during the destruction of this village, striving to protect its inhabitants and its wild creatures."

Julie cleared her throat. "Then let us bury her according to your customs."

"We bury nothing." The dryad soldier walked up to the moss-draped body and rested a twiggy hand on it. "Her remains feed the woods that gave her life. Young dryads will rise from her richness. Move her from the path, and let her body crumble and feed this forest."

Alugon stepped forward, and Julie slipped back into position between his spines. He reached out an enormous paw, wrapped it around the fallen trunk, and lifted her body gently out of the way.

Methunoch and Evrah led them a few hundred feet forward, then stopped.

"We are here," Methunoch announced.

Alugon extended a leg, and Julie slipped down off his back, hopped onto the paw, and stepped to the ground. It took her a few moments to realize that there had been a village here. There was no clearing and no buildings, just a forest overgrown with ferns and brambles and draped in moss. Then her eyes picked out the indentation through the middle of the space where a stream had run. She spotted a tiny birdhouse-like home nestled in some branches, overtaken by creepers. Then she saw an earth mound with a rotten door hanging from its hinges—a werebadger's home. The tangle of trees to her left had an arch like an empty doorway in them.

"We *are* here," she mused aloud.

The UMMVs fanned out, and woodland paras spilled out of them, carrying their belongings in small trunks or snazzy new suitcases from Avalon Town or little carts pulled by goats or children. The adults stared around them in bewilderment like they didn't recognize this place either. Some wandered over to their homes. Others stood in empty patches of grass and wildflowers and looked lost.

Julie's stomach twisted. *Have we done the right thing?*

A butterfly fluttered over the grass, its wings patterned in jade green, deep purple, and shocking yellow. There was a happy squeal, and a young Shajara Elf tugged his hand out of his mother's and ran across the grass, reaching for the butterfly. Other children pulled away from their parents and joined him in a wild game of tag: bumbling werefox kits with white-tipped tails, Woodland Fae youngsters on tottering limbs, and faeries no bigger than Julie's fist, only able to fly short distances on tiny wings.

Their laughter filled the clearing, and Julie grinned at Taylor. He came up to her and wrapped his hand around hers. A few feet away, Malcolm pulled out his phone and snapped discreet pictures.

"Sorry," he mumbled, reddening when Julie caught his eye. "I *am* here to do PR, remember?"

"It's okay, Mal," Julie told him.

"It's more than okay." A familiar young faun stepped forward, goat horns peeking from his tight, golden curls. "Let the world see that the paras of Fernwood Deep are not afraid."

He strode onto a grassy knoll, and his high, bleating voice echoed around the ruined village.

"The last time we saw this village, it was ruins and ash." His brown eyes scanned the assembled crowd. "There was smoke and fire everywhere. Our homes and schools and churches were burning. We ran because we had no choice. Our stream dried up, and our dryads fell. All of us lost somebody that day."

Several of the woodland paras drew nearer to one another. The ogre husband put his arm around his wife, who cuddled her baby.

"We left because we had to." The faun clenched his fists. "We return because this is our home. It might not look the way it did. *We* might not look the way we did either, but we survived, and we'll rebuild it as beautiful as it was before. Except, this time, there will be one difference." He spread his arms. "There will be dragons!"

Julie looked at the dragons who surrounded them: Methunoch, Evrah, and Alugon, their scales glittering in the sunlight. They stood around the village like a wall.

A ragged cheer rose from the woodland paras. It ended abruptly when Julie stepped up beside the faun.

"Not all of you who left this village have returned." She spread her hands. "Not all of you could. Some chose to stay in Avalon Town where they feel it's safer. Those who did come are the best and bravest of Fernwood Deep. You're showing the world that there is strength in unity. You're reclaiming your homes." Julie clenched a fist and held it above her head, flaming. "I stand with you in refusing to accept that our enemies can take away our homes!"

The ensuing cheer was loud and full-throated, and the dragons blew plumes of smoke skyward in salute.

"Now let's rebuild!" the faun yelled.

Everyone set to work. Julie, still commanding her grassy knoll, assigned tasks. A unit of OPMA infantry patrolled the woods, searching for signs of recent rebel activity, although they'd received reports that this area was safe. Methunoch and Evrah pulled stubborn creepers and overgrown saplings away from the woodland paras' homes. The Shajara Elf family took the uprooted plants away and planted them deeper in the woods. A naiad crouched and pressed her fingers into the dry streambed, and clear water welled up.

Julie strode up to the werebadger sett. Methunoch had cleared away the overgrown vegetation, and the entrance was visible: a hump in the earth with a rotten wooden door that made Julie think of *The Hobbit*. She pulled the door open and peered into the gloom at crumbling earthen steps that led down into a cozy chamber. Broken furniture jutted like shattered bones in the gloom. One side of the chamber had caved in, and the corner of a crushed TV was visible under the rubble.

"This was our house." A small, serious-faced child with a button nose and glittering black eyes had appeared beside Julie.

"This is going to be your house again." Julie grinned. She closed her eyes and reached for her earth magic. She could feel the thick, rich, dark earth of Fernwood Deep, teeming with roots and life, and she shaped it carefully. The child beside her gasped as a quiet rumble echoed through the sett, then the hiss of settling dirt. Julie opened her eyes as the steps rebuilt themselves. Dirt from the pile at the bottom rushed to fill the crumbled edges until they looked as though they'd just been carved by skillful hands.

The child laughed and scampered down the steps. Julie was about to follow him and rebuild the living room when her telechip beeped in her ear.

Bogies approaching, east flank! the commander of the patrolling unit squawked in Julie's ear. It was Private First Class Sky Miller, a weremule who'd been recruited at the same time as Julie.

"What's wrong?" the child asked, looking up at Julie.

"Stay here," Julie ordered. "Everything's going to be okay."

She cursed herself for saying those words as she flung her wings open and flew across the bustling clearing, heat throbbing in her palms. Her wings hummed as she rose and hovered above the clearing, looking around. The paras were a happy swarm over their homes, already presiding over a glittering stream and several cleared spaces.

Alugon lay in a smooth curve around the south side of the village. His bus-sized head rested on his claws, but his eyes were open.

Where are they, Hat? she demanded.

There! Your one o'clock! Hat called.

Julie's head snapped to the right, and she spotted the navy splash of patrollers creeping through the heavy undergrowth. Less than a klick beyond, she saw a collection of paras in black cloaks.

Julie's hands burst into flame.

"Methunoch! Evrah!" she roared. "To me! Civilians, send your children and elderly into cover, then enact your emergency plan the way we rehearsed!"

Screams echoed through the clearing as children ran to their mothers. Taylor stood by the werebadger sett, beckoning paras inside. Malcolm helped a tottering old Woodland Fae cross the village to safety. Alugon rose to his feet, branches crackling and popping as he moved.

I am with you, Julie of the Meadows, he rumbled in her mind.

Julie made a swift motion with one hand. *Stay where you are unless I call for you. I want these civilians to see that they'll be safe with Methunoch and Evrah. You and my unit must hang back for now.*

Alugon's amber eyes found hers, and he nodded, then settled back into place.

The civilians were rushing for their half-built homes when Methunoch and Evrah joined Julie, hovering beside her, their white fur stirring in the wind.

I see them, Methunoch growled. He drew his lips back to reveal sharp white fangs.

Evrah, hang back and watch over the village, Julie ordered. *Methunoch, with me! Private Miller, hold your position.*

Yes, Heirkeeper. Evrah flew in a broad arc over the village.

Julie folded her wings and dove, arms and legs at her sides. Flames licked her dragonscale robe as she swooped down on the dark-cloaked paras. Methunoch was close behind her, and they dodged and wove between the broad branches until Julie saw a flash of black ahead. She threw her wings open and hung in mid-air a couple of hundred feet from the leader of the group. He was an Aether Elf, she realized with a pang of shock.

"Stop!" she roared. "By order of the Eternity Throne!"

The paras jerked to a halt, and Julie was suddenly faced with a bristling mass of spearheads and drawn arrows. Sylthana fire bloomed in the hands of several elves, and she saw the dull glow of earth magic being summoned. The flames in her hands intensified, and no one fired.

"There is no Eternity Throne here," the Aether Elf leader hissed. His eyes had the flat, dead look of one deep in the throes of a geas.

Julie raised her burning hands. "Wanna bet?"

"Leave now," Methunoch snarled, "and no harm will come to you."

The elf made a cutting motion with one hand, and the air filled with the hisses of arrows flying. Flames engulfed Julie's body, and the arrows burned to ash in front of her face. Several pinged harmlessly off Methunoch's scales, and he batted one aside.

"That's insulting." Julie cackled.

"Take them!" the elf screamed.

The paras scattered into the woods.

"Now, Methunoch!" Julie yelled.

She dove toward the Aether Elf leader, remembering just in time not to use fireballs in the living woods. Instead, she summoned a burst of wind that hit him in the chest and knocked him flat on his back. He skidded and rolled to his feet, cloak covered in leaves. Julie took advantage of his disorientation and threw up a wall of earth in front of the scattering paras. They stumbled to a halt and spun as Methunoch spat a wall of ice at them, trapping them.

The elf shrieked in fury. He raised his hand, and his telekinesis grabbed for her throat. She dodged his power, rolled out of the way, and felt for the earth under his feet. It bucked, throwing him into the air, and he landed with bone-jarring force on his face.

"Give it up, asshole," Julie spat. "And don't even think about grabbing one of those amulet thingies."

"Heirkeeper, the woods!" Methunoch roared. More dark cloaks melted into the trees.

"They're making for the village," Julie shouted.

She reached for the earth and opened a hole beneath the struggling elf. He fell into it, and with a shower of dirt, Julie buried all of him except his face.

"Stay," she told him, then spun. "Let's go, Methunoch. After them!"

Flashes of Sylthana fire suggested the trapped paras were melting their way through the ice, but she had no time to worry about them. Julie ran into the thick woods, following the waving branches and disturbed undergrowth.

Where are they? she asked.

At the edge of the village! Hat cried.

Panic clutched Julie's chest, and the earth juddered under her feet. *Alugon!*

Alugon chuckled, an earthquake of a sound. *Wait until you see the village before you call me in, Heirkeeper.*

Julie burst out of the trees, Methunoch hot on her heels, and stumbled to a halt.

A wall of blue ice ran across one side of the village, courtesy of Evrah, who coughed out more ice wherever Sylthana Elves tried to melt it with blue fire. Methunoch bounded over the wall, arrows clattering harmlessly off his scales, and landed beside his daughter, and they continued to build the ice wall.

Julie opened her wings and fluttered into the air for a better view. Sky Miller and the rest of her infantry patrol unit were holding position, ready to join the fight if they needed to. When a battle cry echoed through the boughs of Fernwood Deep, it didn't come from the OPMA. It came from the villagers.

A heavy crate of weapons, courtesy of the OPMA, stood open and empty in the middle of the clearing, and the villagers charged as a unit, led by the curly-headed faun. He carried a short sword and a buckler, and his bleating yell tore the air as he rushed the ice wall. With an agile leap, he front-flipped over the wall and landed with his blade buried in the chest of a dark-cloaked vampire. His fellows poured over the wall after him: faeries with faerie dust rifles, werebadgers and werefoxes with claws and teeth, Shajara Elves with fistfuls of hemlock and deadly nightshade. They were not fighting folk, but for their village, they would be warriors.

The dark-cloaked paras were caught off-guard. The werebadgers dragged an elf to the ground and tore out his throat before he could scream. An irate dwarf drew back his bow to fire at the faun, but a swarm of faeries and ogres descended upon him before he could let the arrow fly. He fled screaming, pursued by faeries, the ogres slamming their tiny clubs into his ankles.

"Don't pursue!" Julie called. She spotted a Sylthana Elf with flaming hands turning toward the Fernwood paras and sent a tongue of fire into his chest, knocking him to the ground. "They won't be back!"

The elf scrambled to his feet, his cloak burning, and bolted into the woods. The rest of the dark-cloaked paras were not far behind. They scattered into Fernwood Deep, and a roar of triumph rose from the villagers, who brandished their new weapons over their heads. Methunoch and Evrah jumped over the ice wall and joined them, intertwining their necks in a dragon hug. Their songs filled Julie's mind, silent yet achingly beautiful.

She grinned. *Hat, I think we've done it.*

Hat chuckled. *For once, Julie, I don't disagree.*

Children and elderly paras spilled from the safety of half-rebuilt homes as the dragons led the victorious villagers back into the village. Julie landed beside Taylor and twined her fingers with his as she watched moms and dads scoop their children up and spin them around. Everyone took turns pounding their faun leader on the back, and the whole village gathered around the dragons, all talking and laughing at once.

Malcolm snapped more pictures.

"They did it." Julie squeezed Taylor's hand. "They chased those assholes off on their own."

Taylor smiled. "Sure did. Another brilliant idea, babe."

"Not so bad yourself." Julie nudged him with her hip.

Alugon gave a low, warning growl in her mind. *This is not over, Heirkeeper. They will be back.*

They will, Methunoch agreed, looking over the happy crowd at Julie.

Of course they will, but when they do, you'll stop them. Julie smiled. *For now, these villagers feel good about coming home.*

"Friends! Friends!" The faun vaulted back onto his grassy knoll, arms outspread. There was a smear of blood on his bare chest, but he didn't seem to mind. "This calls for a celebration!"

There was a loud cheer.

"Uh, we're supposed to be rebuilding," Julie called.

The villagers didn't hear her, or if they did, they ignored her. A huge table that was missing one leg was carried out of the werebadger sett. The Shajara Elves grew a sapling to replace the missing leg while faeries disappeared into the forest and returned with armfuls of fruits, nuts, and berries. Werebadgers set the table with large leaves for plates, and the next thing Julie knew, three kids had grabbed her and Taylor and propelled them onto mushroom seats by the table.

Julie didn't recognize half the fruit on the table, but all of it was good, exploding in her mouth with bursts of tart sweetness. She'd cleaned her plate when a trio of werefoxes returned from the woods with a whole deer, skinned and ready for the fire the faeries built for the second time. The gamey scent of cooking meat filled the air as the shadows grew long and the light golden.

"Come on, everyone." Julie got up from her mushroom, laughing. "Let's get a little work done while we wait for dinner!"

There was a great rush of wind, and the mighty dryads around them bent and hissed. Dead leaves swirled around Julie's feet. She looked up to see a giant leaf soaring in the wind and laughed.

CHAPTER SEVENTEEN

The leaf settled lightly on the ground nearby, and a jolly, sturdy, six-foot-tall person stepped off. He spread his arms wide and let out an earth-shaking laugh. Bright blue eyes twinkled at Julie over a thick tangle of beard composed of leaves. Grass spilled over his eyes like bangs.

"I heard that some of my people were returning to Fernwood Deep," the Green Man announced, "and I am here to help."

"Ember!" Julie beamed. "It's so good to see you."

"It's good to feel life in my forest again." Ember bowed to Julie. "Now, I might know nothing about building homes, but I *can* help you all bring the woods and fields back to life. Have you Shajara Elves? Naiads and dryads? Then come with me, and let us grow your crops again!"

A gaggle of woodland paras trotted after him as Ember strode to the nearby clearing, the ice wall still melting inside it. A young faun brought up the rear, playing a merry tune on wooden pipes.

"Okay, everyone." Julie turned to the rest of the woodland folk. "Let's rebuild these houses!"

They gave a cheer, and Taylor, Malcolm, Julie, and the other paras started working. Malcolm fetched twigs, thatch grass, and small stones for the faeries to rebuild their houses in the trees. Taylor opened a box of nails, courtesy of the OPMA, and got to work replacing wooden planks in a werefox cottage.

Julie returned to the ruined werebadger sett, and her earth magic cleared away the rubble and sculpted the walls of each tunnel and chamber back into place while the werebadger family combed through the newly-repaired rooms. She could hear their cries of surprise and delight when they found tiny treasures in each room as she finished it: a wedding picture, a grandmother's recipe book, or toys the werebadger children had thought were long gone.

When Julie emerged from the repaired sett, the sun had gone down, but the village was alight. Will o' the wisps hung among the branches, and swarms of fireflies, summoned by Shajara Elves, perched in the trees. The fire under the deer on the spit crackled and leaped high, and an elderly Woodland Fae trimmed off succulent cuts of meat and placed them in a giant wooden bowl.

Ember and the rest of his group were in the stream, washing their hands and hooves in the clear water. Irrigation canals, winding as naturally as any tributary, ran out of the village and into the fields beyond. The trees had been cleared, and a crop of wheat stood knee-high, green and stirring in the soft breeze.

Up and down the single street of the village, lights turned on in the little homes, on the ground, and in the trees. They weren't yet done, but the village felt alive again.

Taylor walked up to Julie, his hair mussed and a band-aid on one thumb. "Pretty cool, huh?" He put an arm around her shoulders.

She leaned into him. "Pretty amazing, if you ask me."

"I'm so hungry," Malcolm complained. "And I hurt my finger." He held it up. Julie had to lean closer to see the tiny scratch.

"Let's feast!" Ember called.

A faerie band, perched in the trees, struck up a tune on their tiny harps. It was cheerful in an eerie way, and laughter filled the village as everyone took their places at the long table. The were-boars had dug up potato-like tubers, which had been roasted in the coals, and there were more delicious mounds of fruit. Julie couldn't remember when she'd last been this hungry. The venison was fresh and rich and unseasoned, and she couldn't stop eating.

"Now all we need is wine!" a dryad boomed.

"Did someone say wine?"

The voice came from nowhere and everywhere at once, and everyone fell silent. Even Alugon raised his mighty head and listened.

A fluting note echoed through the woods, followed by another. Then they came all at once, spilling over the village like a stream over rapids, playful and silvery, and Bacchus danced into the firelight. Apart from a few carefully placed leaves, his bare body was a lithe composition of solid muscle. Wild curls spilled over his black eyes, and he played a gleaming flute, fingers faster than they had a right to be. There was a staff dotted with white flowers under his arm, and he stepped in time to his music.

Ember let out a deep chuckle. "Hello, old friend." He held up a wooden goblet.

Bacchus' song didn't change as he took one hand from the flute and touched a finger to the goblet. It filled with mead, as did every other empty receptacle on the table.

Taylor grabbed his tin cup and laughed. "*Now* it's a party!"

"Easy there." Julie chuckled and put a hand on his arm before he could drink. "Some of us need to stay alert in case those rogues come back."

"Bummer." Taylor put down his cup. "But you're not wrong."

They didn't drink, but when everyone left the table and followed Bacchus in a dizzy circle around the village, they did dance.

Dawn broke richly gold through the thick canopy of Fernwood Deep. Julie blinked at it, surprised, as she looked up from the end of the street she'd just finished paving. Laying the stones with earth magic was easier than doing it by hand, but her back still ached when she straightened and looked across the village.

In the morning light, it was hardly recognizable compared to the day before. Little gardens, profusely flowering, surrounded the homes. The wheat crop covered the field in a thick carpet of abundance. A mattress of springy ferns and soft mushrooms had been laid out under the feast table, now set with boiled eggs and more fruit, and the village children lay like sardines under the table, covered with a blanket of moss. The smell of baking bread wound through the village, and from somewhere came the thump of a hammer. A werebadger knelt in the vegetable patch beside her home, planting onions.

Methunoch and Evrah came to stand on either side of Julie so quietly that she didn't see them until Methunoch butted his long nose into her hand.

The Deep has long been the home of dragons, he murmured, *and I think I can make my home here, too.*

Julie pressed her fingers into the thick fur of his neck. *You've done an amazing job, both of you.*

All of us have, Evrah agreed.

They bounded away, their white shapes sinuous in the dawn light, and curled up in the roots of a gigantic dryad to sleep.

Julie smiled and stretched her sore back. *This isn't much compared to what you've seen, huh, Merlin?*

Don't call me that, Hat grumbled. His tone softened. *Just because I've seen a lot of magic doesn't mean I'll ever tire of what it can do.*

Julie had to agree.

Twelve straight hours of sleep did wonders for Julie, although her back still complained a little. She snuggled closer to Taylor on the couch, letting her head rest on his shoulder.

The couch faced a huge window overlooking Avalon Town, content and colorful in the afternoon light. The TV screen levitated in front of the window, glowing with blue magic. The coffee table between the couch and the TV was covered with the remnants of Julie's favorite meal, Sylthana fish and chips from Meggie's.

On the screen, a beat-up blue SUV screeched to a halt on a bridge, facing a slew of police cars, their lights glittering.

"I love this part," Julie mumbled.

Taylor's arm was draped lazily over her body, his fingertips tickling her thigh as he gently dragged them over her fluffy pajamas. "It's pretty romantic for an action movie."

"Maybe that's why Lillie loved *Baby Driver* so much." Julie smiled.

Taylor kissed the top of her head. "Lillie would be proud of you, you know. You're becoming quite the hellion."

"Thanks, T." Julie cuddled closer.

Taylor took a deep breath. "I hope she'd be proud of me, too," he whispered.

Julie looked up at him. "What do you mean?"

Taylor's free hand was tucked into the pocket of his hoodie, and it looked like he was holding something, turning it around and around inside his pocket. Something small and square. "Tell you later," he muttered and gave her a grin that crinkled the corners of his eyes the way she loved.

Julie scoffed but turned her attention back to the screen. Baby was walking out of prison, color bleeding back into his world the moment Debora smiled.

The credits rolled and Taylor straightened, gently dislodging Julie. "Julie, I—" he began, about to pull something out of his pocket.

Julie's phone buzzed noisily on the coffee table. The first notes of Beyonce's *Run the World* blared through the room.

"That's Bianca's ringtone," Taylor observed.

Julie reached for her phone. "I can ignore it. It's okay."

"No, no. Didn't she have a doctor's appointment today?" Taylor squeezed Julie's hand. "Take it. We've been worried about her."

Julie flashed him a grateful smile and lifted the phone to her ear. "Hey, Bee! How'd it go?"

"Go?" Bianca demanded. "How did what go?"

"Uh, your doctor's appointment? To check on the progress of your wings?" Julie raised her eyebrows at Taylor, who shrugged.

"Oh, that! Yeah, that was fine." Bianca paused. "That's not why I'm calling." A growl crept into her tone.

Julie sat very upright. "What's up?"

"I have a lead on Nimue," Bianca snarled.

Julie's eyes widened. "Tell me."

Taylor raised his eyebrows. She gripped his hand.

"Morgan has proof that she's in the Deep," Bianca explained. "Can you meet me at Tintagel ASAP? She said she'd tell us more when we got there."

"Hold on a second." Julie lowered the phone and put it on mute, then turned to Taylor. "Babe, Morgan thinks she's got proof that Nimue is in the Deep. Bianca wants to meet me at Tintagel, but—"

"No buts." Taylor kissed her forehead. "Go do your thing."

"I'm sorry, T." Julie grimaced.

"Sorry for what? Saving the world?" Taylor chuckled. "I'll pack you an overnight bag."

"You're the best. Seriously. You know that, right?" Julie squeezed his hand.

Taylor flashed her a grin and got to his feet.

Julie returned to the call. "I'll be there as fast as Genevieve can take me. And you should know that my boyfriend is the most excellent being in any world." She raised her voice as Taylor padded into the bedroom. "And has an outstanding ass. Ten out of ten for the ass."

"With you on that one." Bianca gave a throaty chuckle.

Julie got to her feet. "I'm just going to take a shower. Then I'll be on my way."

"See you there. Be safe," Bianca added. "Don't get attacked by drow or anything."

"I'll do my best," Julie retorted.

She hung up and headed for the bathroom. When she stepped out of the shower, Taylor had laid her dragonscale robe, arming doublet, and the amulet that summoned her armor on the bed. She pulled on the doublet, then placed the amulet on her chest and touched it. Her armor rose from its stand in the corner of the room and attached itself to her with a series of metallic clanks.

Should call you Iron Man, Hat observed as she grabbed him from the nightstand. *Where are we going?*

Tintagel. I'll explain on the way. Julie tugged him onto her head and swung her robe over her shoulders, then hurried out of the bedroom. Taylor stood waiting by the front door, her backpack in one hand and a steaming go-cup in the other.

Julie took both and stood on tiptoe to kiss his cheek. "I'm really sorry about this, babe." She paused. "You seemed like you wanted to say something before the phone rang."

"Don't worry about it. It can wait." Taylor wrapped her in a hug. "Be safe. I love you."

"I love you, too." Julie returned the embrace. "And whatever's on your mind, we'll get to it as soon as paranormally possible, okay?"

"Okay." Taylor opened the door for her, a gesture she'd only recently begun to allow. "Go kick ass."

"See you soon," Julie promised.

She heard the soft click of the door closing behind her as she headed down the hallway. Not for the first time, she left a chunk of her heart behind in Avalon Town.

As Genevieve soared over the hills, Julie leaned forward, squinting through the windshield.

Are those dragons? she asked.

Tintagel loomed on the horizon, its twin sandstone towers gleaming in the last golden rays of the sinking sun. The sea shimmered vermilion and blue behind it, reflecting brightly in Julie's eyes, but she could still make out soaring shapes that swooped and dove around the towers and the bridge that connected them. A scaly host perched on the top of one of the towers, their wings fluttering, serpentine shapes silhouetted against the sky.

Looks like it, Hat agreed.

Wow. Julie blinked. *What are they all doing here?*

She steered Genevieve toward the road leading up to the portcullis. A lithe green-and-brown dragon with three pairs of wings flew alongside the Mustang, and Julie recognized Minatarva, one of the dragons who'd left the Deep with Alugon. She took one hand off the wheel to wave and Minatarva smiled, her bluer-than-blue eyes sparkling.

Genevieve landed with the faintest squeak of rubber and rolled up to the portcullis. Minatarva loped alongside as the portcullis rose and Julie drove into the inner ward. Bianca was already there, leaning against the pedestal of the giant statue of King Arthur. She was on her phone texting, and she absentmindedly blew a bubble of bright pink chewing gum.

Julie brought Genevieve to a halt and stepped out. "Hey, Bee!"

Bianca turned to her, grinning. Her golden ringlets hugged her head Marilyn Monroe-style, and the tip of one of her gazelle horns had been broken off. Soft new fur covered parts of her leathery wings, but it was still startling to see the splashes of pink and red where the membrane was still healing. In two places, white bandages covered the holes that hadn't yet closed.

"How's it hanging, girl?" Bianca gave her a firm hug.

Julie returned it. "You never did tell me what the doctor said about your wings."

"Nothing new." Bianca shrugged. "The holes are still closing. He reckons they'll be okay, but I'm still not allowed to fly, which is a real pain in the ass."

"How did you get here?" Julie asked. Behind her, the portcullis clanked shut with a rattle.

"Took a cab. Taxiport. Not bad service, although the driver was a little road rage-y." Bianca looked around. "What's with all these dragons?"

"I was hoping you'd know," Julie admitted. "I've never seen so many at Tintagel."

Minatarva stepped forward. "We feel it is our duty to assist the keeper of the Quest with the protecting of the once and future king."

"Wouldn't kill you to use their first names." Bianca chuckled.

Minatarva smiled. "We are still unused to terminology in the surface world. Things were different in the Deep." Her smile faded.

Julie rested a hand on the dragon's scaly shoulder. "They really were. I'm sorry."

"It is better this way," Minatarva acknowledged.

"Why would Morgan need help protecting Arthur?" Bianca asked.

Minatarva shuddered, and the yellow spines along her back paled. "Lady Ennowen was on a dark path even before this week's press release."

"That was crappy, if not unexpected," Julie agreed.

"Who calls a hunt for a real and dangerous war criminal a 'witch hunt?'" Bianca spat the words. "Stupid old crone."

"Her support for Nimue is concerning. If the Deep attacks

Tintagel, even Morgan's magic would be hard-pressed to protect Arthur," Minatarva told them. "We consider it safest to fight dragons with dragons, so to speak."

"*Apparent* support," Bianca corrected her. "Do you think it'll get to the point where the Deep attacks? They'd be fools to try to bring Tintagel down."

Minatarva inclined her head. "It is best to be safe."

Julie rubbed her chin. "I wonder if that support is voluntary."

Bianca raised an eyebrow, still thin and downy after recently growing back. "You think she's under a geas?"

"I'm not sure. Maybe?" Julie shrugged. "It would explain a lot."

Couldn't have happened to a more deserving dictator, Hat muttered.

Julie smirked.

"Let's go talk to Morgan." Bianca pushed off the pedestal.

Minatarva flew away, and Julie and Bianca made their way to the orchard in which King Arthur slept at the center of the tower. There were more cherry blossoms on his glass casket than usual and no sign of Morgan. Julie swept away some of the blossoms while Bianca texted Morgan. The slumbering king looked the same as he always did, eyes closed, face porcelain-pale, his hands folded over the gleaming blade that lay next to his body. The ghastly wound in his side, blackened and rotten, was shocking no matter how many times Julie had seen it.

"She's up in her study." Bianca pocketed her phone.

They climbed the spiral staircase and found Morgan peering into a microscope, or the approximation of a microscope. It had a glowing crystal ball in its guts instead of a slide.

"Hey, bestie!" Bianca crowed. She leaned over Morgan and hugged her.

Morgan looked up from her microscope thing. "Bestie, Julie! You both got here fast."

"We're eager to hear what you've found." Julie interlaced her hands in front of her. Hat was cold on her head.

Morgan nodded, her lips pressed into a grim line. "I'm hoping I can prove our hypothesis that Nimue is spending a lot of time in the Deep."

"Hypothesis?" Bianca scoffed. She flopped into a nearby office chair and put her high-heeled boots up on the nearest table, next to a magic mirror under a gold cloth. "We *know* she's in the Deep from the way Lady Ennowen talks, for one thing. She's got to be the mysterious adviser the dragons keep talking about, especially now that Lady Ennowen has withdrawn her support for the Eternity Throne's war effort."

"*And* there are rumors that something's off about Danijah now that he's back at council meetings," Julie pointed out. "Almost like there might be a spell on his mind."

"Yes, but that's just speculation," Morgan grumbled. "We need cold, hard proof, and I think I might have found it."

Julie moved closer as Morgan pushed her chair away from the microscope thing. "What is it?" she asked.

"The presence of the dragons has boosted my magic to the point where I don't have to spend as much time on keeping up the spells that protect and maintain the king." Morgan glanced fondly at the window in the center of her floor. "It means that I've been able to devote more time to finding Nimue."

Her hands flashed with heat, and flames licked the edges of her fingers. Julie stepped back, startled. She'd never seen Morgan lose control, even for a moment.

"Sorry." Morgan shook her hands, and the flames went out. "I'm double-pissed. I was with Nimue in Mordred's dungeon, and she looked so afraid." Her eyes narrowed. "But it was all a lie. I thought we had a bond of friendship. I guess I was wrong."

She's not alone in that, Hat murmured.

Julie ran a reassuring hand over his brim.

"What's even worse is that this isn't the first time Nimue has caused panic, chaos, and death in Avalon *and* the human world." Morgan gritted her teeth, and smoke curled from her palms. "We thought she was helping us stop Mordred during the Second Pendragon War, but all those times that he slipped through our fingers, all those times when we thought we were winning, only to find he was one step ahead? That was all because of her." Flames licked her hands. "*Pompeii* happened because of her!"

Bianca popped a bubble. "Chill, bestie. You're not doing yourself any favors."

"I know, I know," Morgan grumbled, shaking her hands out again. "But I risked my life to help rescue Nimue. It was all just part of the act."

"There had to be a reason 'Vivienne' got my back up." Bianca enclosed the name in air quotes.

"I wondered why you didn't like her." Morgan sighed. "Her disguise was so good that even I didn't see through it. I didn't recognize Vivienne as Nimue, and even if I had, I didn't know Nimue for what she truly is, not then."

"You say you've found proof that she's spent time in the Deep?" Julie asked.

Morgan nodded and turned back to the microscope. "I believe I have. Captain Kaplan granted me access to the evidence from Nimue's home. What was left of it after the fire, anyway. I've spent hours magically reassembling bits and pieces." She gestured at the microscope. "Have a look."

Julie peered into the eyepieces at a scrap of fabric, neatly cut from what looked like a hem. It glowed with a faint blue-green light that looked familiar.

"What is it?" Julie asked.

"It's a piece of cloth from a coat I reconstructed from Nimue's closet," Morgan explained. "Took me all day to get the coat done. The glow is the interesting part." She touched the microscope. "The thaumascope shows us the magic signature of things, trace evidence magic leaves behind on anything it touches."

"Makes sense," Julie conceded.

"The blue-green you see? It's a very specific magical signature." Morgan smiled. "It only comes from the Deep."

Julie's eyes widened. *"That's* why it looked familiar to me. It's the same color as some of the bioluminescent fungi in the Nest Garden."

"Exactly. Nimue, or Nimue's coat, has been to the Deep. And not just the Deep, but the area around the Nest." Morgan rubbed her hands. "Why would she have a reason to go there except for a nefarious purpose?"

"Tourism?" Julie guessed.

Bianca chuckled. "The dragons don't allow tourists into the Deep, Julie. Only diplomats, and that grudgingly."

"Few surface paras see the Nest," Morgan agreed.

Brownie magic must be stronger than I thought if they could get into the Nest, Julie mused.

Hat chuckled. *Brownies have been underestimated for centuries, except by you.*

"So, she's been in the Deep." Bianca played with one of her short curls. "That supports our theory, but it doesn't prove it."

"No. We need more proof. A lot more," Morgan agreed.

Hat went cold on Julie's head again. She sank into a nearby chair and pulled him off, then held him in her lap.

"Can we try a location spell again?" Bianca asked.

Morgan shook her head. "The queen is too weak to donate more blood. I wouldn't risk it."

All this is because of me, Hat whispered.

Hat, no. Why would you say that? Julie stroked his crown.

Because if I had revealed that Vivienne was Nimue earlier, I could have saved dozens of lives. Maybe more. Hat sighed. *I'm so sorry, Julie.*

You couldn't have known she was a traitor, and you thought you were doing the right thing by protecting someone you once loved. Julie cuddled him. *We can only do the best we can with the information we have.*

She did *once trap me in a magically-induced coma and bury me alive,* Hat pointed out. *I'm aware of her capacity for duplicity.*

She did what? Julie's eyebrows shot up.

It was part of her training. We were working on blood magic, and it took hold of her. I thought it was only temporary. I thought she'd overcome its corrupting effects. Any Lunar Fae should have been able to do so with all the safeguards I'd put in place. Hat sighed. *But now I see that I was a fool to think that she* wanted *to resist the temptation of blood magic. I was a fool to think she could change.*

Julie fished for words but struggled to find any. *I want to comfort you, but I don't know how,* she admitted helplessly.

Hat sighed, and Julie heard the sigh of an old man with a broken heart. *All you can do is catch Nimue before she wreaks even more havoc, Julie.*

Julie squeezed his crown. *Whatever it takes.* She hesitated. *Have you told Morgan who you are?*

I would rather not. Hat turned cold in her hands.

It's okay. Your secret's safe with me. Julie slipped him back onto her head.

"I have made preparations for the day when we *do* manage to track Nimue down." Morgan opened a small wooden chest on a nearby table and pulled out a tiny glimmering object that looked like a wadded cobweb.

"What is it?" Julie asked, holding out a hand.

Morgan dropped the shiny thing into her palm. "A binding spell, the most powerful one I've ever crafted. Not even a dragon could break free of it."

Julie weighed it in her hand. "Feels lighter than a ball of cotton."

"It's made of Gleipnir steel, triple refined and woven in the style of the net of Rán," Morgan explained. "If you cast this over Nimue, not only will her magic be nulled, but she'll be physically bound, too."

"All we need to do is find her." Julie sighed.

"The Deep is warded by dragon magic. I can't look into it, even with my crystal ball. Possibly not even with a location spell." Morgan folded her arms. "Magical means are not going to find Nimue. We need witnesses. We need eyes on her."

Bianca leaned back in her chair, hands behind her head, lips pursed. "So we need to go to the Deep."

Morgan raised her eyebrows. "I'm not sure that's possible."

"What, infiltrating a hostile land populated by dragons?" Julie shrugged. "We've done harder things."

Bianca chuckled. "Valid."

"You don't understand, Julie. The Maw of the Deep is inaccessible now. The dragons sealed it with lava magic when Evrah and the others barely escaped with their lives," Morgan explained. "I doubt even the Sphynxes could open a portal to the Deep."

"I'm sure the dragons can open a portal *out* of the Deep." Julie chewed the inside of her cheek. "Since Danijah has been traveling back and forth."

Morgan frowned. "What are you getting at?"

Julie and Bianca exchanged glances.

Bianca grinned. "I have an idea, but you are not going to like it."

CHAPTER EIGHTEEN

Taylor flung himself on the couch and stared at the ceiling for several moments before letting out a long groan.

He fished the ring box out of the pocket of his hoodie and flipped it open, then gazed at the shimmering moonstone dragon. Tracing his thumb over its smooth surface, he imagined it on Julie's slender finger. The dwarves had assured him that the ring wouldn't be affected by her fire. The moonstone would even store magic for her like her armor did.

She'd love it. Well, he hoped she'd love it. It was probably a good thing that Bianca had phoned when she did. Had he *really* been about to propose to her on the couch?

"Really, Taylor?" he demanded, then snapped the ring box shut. "You're an idiot."

He rolled onto his side and wrapped his arms around his torso, staring at the credits of the movie as they kept rolling, the lyrics to the Simon and Garfunkel song resounding through the apartment. Taylor gave himself the rest of the song to feel sorry for himself. When it ended, he sat up, grabbed his phone, and dialed his best friend's number.

Iris Wingfinger answered on the first ring.

"What did she say?" Iris shrieked in his ear. "Did she say yes?" Her voice dropped two octaves. "Did she say *absolutely yes*? When is the wedding? Can I make the dress?"

"Iri! Slow down." Taylor chuckled, feeling the tension ease in his shoulders. "I haven't asked her yet."

"Tay! What are you doing?" Iris moaned. "You've been trying to ask her for nearly three months."

"I know, I know." Taylor pulled a pillow over his face and growled into it. "I'm just…I can't find the right moment. I put on *Baby Driver* because it's her favorite romantic movie—"

"Romantic?" Iris groaned. "*That's* her definition of romantic?"

"Just roll with it, okay? I know it's no *Notting Hill*." Taylor sighed. "Anyway, when it finished, I was going to ask her right here in the apartment."

"Taylor!" Iris barked. "Remove your head from your ass right now! You are *not* going to ask that wonderful girl to marry you on your couch!"

"She deserves a fairytale," Taylor wailed. "How am I going to give that to her? There's a civil war on. I can't even get a reservation at the cabin I took her to for the break last year. It's too near the Fernwood conflicts."

"There's got to be a way," Iris told him firmly. "We just need to think creatively." She paused. "What's her favorite activity?"

"Setting bad guys on fire," Taylor answered instantly. "Making snarky comments at inopportune moments. Verbal aggravation."

"True, but unromantic," Iris pointed out.

Taylor leaned back into the cushions, trying to think. "Driving Genevieve."

"So use the car somehow. Take her on a romantic drive or something," Iris suggested.

"I don't trust Genevieve. She'll give away the surprise," Taylor grumbled.

After pausing in surprise, Iris spoke slowly. "Genevieve is a car. You know that, right?"

"You'll understand if you ever go anywhere in her." Taylor grimaced. "She's...not normal." He ran a hand through his hair. "I *could* use that. I could make Genevieve fly through the air above us with a banner attached to her that says, Will you marry me?."

"Uh-uh. That's a cop-out." Iris snorted. "That's for guys who don't have the guts to ask a girl with words."

"Yeah, I guess. And I-I have a speech planned." Taylor's cheeks flushed.

"What about the place you first kissed?" Iris suggested. "Or where you went for your first date?"

"A random harbor in New York City and a mid-range steakhouse near the NYHQ? I don't think so." Taylor closed his eyes, mind racing. "Wait. She loves Sleipnir, right? I could borrow him. I'll train him to do a whole dressage routine. In the end, he bows down in front of her and holds the ring in his teeth while I give my speech."

Iris turned that down with a flat "No."

"I'll book a room at the Eternal Hotel near the palace. The penthouse. I'll fill it with will o' the wisps." Taylor opened his eyes. "When she opens the door, they all come spilling out to reveal me, kneeling in the center of an ocean of rose petals. I hire three cupids to sing and play harps—"

"Cupids?" Iris groaned. "Really?"

"Okay, here's a better idea." Taylor sat up, hugging one of the couch cushions in his lap. "I take her to the beach, the little one near Avalon Town where civilians can still go safely. We go for a long walk. I hire Poseidon and his chariot. He arrives in all his majesty, kidnaps me, and disappears into the ocean. When she inevitably comes after me, Poseidon welcomes her into the chariot on the ocean at sunset, and I'm there on one of Poseidon's foaming horses, holding the ring."

"You do *know* that you can't just hire Poseidon, right?" Iris pointed out.

Taylor huffed. "I don't know how to do this, Iri. I want it to be perfect for her."

"Then you need to talk to someone who knows her even better than you do," Iris told him gently. "They'll be able to give you the best advice."

The idea flooded Taylor's mind with light.

"Iris, you're a genius." He hugged the cushion tighter. "Thank you! I have a perfect idea!"

"Good!" Iris laughed. "Okay, love-you-bye!"

She hung up, and Taylor scrolled through his contacts. It was time to call in the big guns, a power beyond anything he could find in Avalon Town.

Julie's mom.

Alugon shuffled into Morgan's study, eyes narrowed suspiciously.

Smart dragon, Hat observed.

Shhh, you, Julie grumbled.

"Al!" Bianca simpered. "Have a seat!" She pulled one up for him and plumped its pillows, an impressive feat given that it was a desk chair.

Alugon's eyes narrowed further. "Thank you, Bianca of the Hart's Horn." He perched on the edge of the chair. "You wished to speak with me, Morgan?" He bowed to her.

"I did." Morgan leaned against the nearest table. "We have a request, Augur."

"One that might save the entire world from this war," Julie chipped in.

Alugon's eyes became slits. "What is your request?"

"That you hear us out in full before interrupting." Morgan folded her arms. "Even if you want to."

Alugon looked at the three of them, then folded his arms with a swish of his many-colored robe. "I suppose I owe you three that much." He nodded at Julie. "Go on."

"Good." Julie grinned. "Al, we need to get into the Deep."

Alugon opened his mouth.

Bianca held up a finger. "Ah-ah! You promised."

Alugon closed his mouth and glowered.

"It's the only way we'll be able to prove that Nimue is Lady Ennowen's new adviser. When the dragons learn a traitor is controlling their queen, they'll turn against her," Julie explained.

Alugon raised his eyebrows but said nothing.

"If we can get proof that Nimue is the adviser, we could make peace between all dragons." Bianca leaned forward. "But the only way we can do that is if you help us."

"We need you to take us into the Deep." Julie grinned. "To do that, you'll have to convince Lady Ennowen that you had a change of heart. You never wanted the dragons to get involved in Avalonian affairs. You're sickened by what you've seen—"

"Nothing could be further from the truth!" Alugon burst out.

"Al, work with me. It's pretend," Julie lectured. "You just need Lady Ennowen to believe you really want to come back to her and that you've brought Bianca and me to the Deep as prisoners. She knows you. She trusted you. She'll bring you to the Nest, and then we'll have a chance to lay eyes on Nimue. We could use a memory ball to prove it. We could put a stop to everything!"

There was a breathless silence. Everyone stared hopefully at Alugon.

He cleared his throat. "Have you finished?"

"Yeah." Julie sat back. "That's it."

"Very well. I heard you out as you requested." Alugon raised his chin. "My answer is no."

"Oh, Al, come on!" Julie cajoled.

"Think about this. Wouldn't it be great to have proof?" Bianca asked. "You're the only way we can get into the Deep."

"I do not disagree that proving the adviser is Nimue will

change everything." Alugon shook his head. "But we don't know that. What is more, your plan is as ridiculous as it is foolhardy."

"Bullshit," Julie protested.

"I think it could work, Augur," Morgan told him gently.

"I think it could fail spectacularly," Alugon growled. "I shall do no such thing."

"Come on, Al." Julie pushed down the bubble of frustration in her chest and felt her palms cool slightly. "We need you to work with us on this. The whole plan hinges on Lady Ennowen believing you've had a change of heart."

"Good." Alugon grunted. "That means you won't be risking your lives since I won't do it, and there is nothing you can say that will change my mind."

Julie planted her hands on her hips. "You love Lady Ennowen. You always have."

Alugon dropped his gaze. "I am unwavering in my choice to follow you and the unborn heir."

"Yes, but you still care about her. Don't do it for us, Al. Do it for her. She might be acting this way because Nimue has her under a geas," Julie urged.

Alugon sighed. "You enjoy seeing me make a fool of myself far too much, Julie of the Meadows."

"Aw, Al, you know that's not true. *And* you know that's not what this is about." Julie went over to him and rested a hand on his. It was colder than she'd expected. "If we can confirm that Lady Ennowen is under a geas, that will prove she's innocent."

Alugon looked at her sharply, his amber eyes suspicious.

"And if we can *dis*prove the theory, at least we'll know what we're dealing with," Julie added gently.

Alugon leaned back in his chair and let out a long breath. Julie reached under her robe and poked a finger past the edge of her breastplate, feeling the tiny Gleipnir net hidden under her arm.

Aren't you going to tell him the rest of the plan? Hat asked.

What, that I plan to throw this thing the moment I set eyes on that bitch Nimue and drag her to justice, dragons or no dragons? Julie snorted inwardly. *I don't think he'd be receptive to that idea. We'll break it to him later.*

"This plan comes with very real advantages if we can pull it off," Bianca summarized.

"They do, Bianca of the Hart's Horn, but those benefits do not nullify the dangers," Alugon murmured.

Julie squeezed his hand. "They might outweigh them."

Before Alugon could respond, a shrill beep penetrated Julie's mind. She jumped and grabbed Hat's brim.

There's an OPMA-wide alert on the telechip network, Hat explained before Julie could yell at him. *I thought you'd like to hear it.*

"Bee, are you wearing your chip?" Julie gasped.

Bianca shook her head. "What's going on?"

Julie held up a hand as Shulme spoke into her mind.

Attention, attention, attention! Bowden Hill is under attack. Civilians are threatened. All units respond!

Julie jumped to her feet.

"What is it, young one?" Alugon asked, alarmed.

"Where's Bowden Hill?" Julie demanded.

Morgan looked up. "It's a small village about an hour's walk from here."

"It's under attack. I've got to go." Julie hurried for the door.

"Wait, young one. Let me come with you." Alugon got to his feet.

Julie shook her head. "You stay here, Al. The rest of OPMA is on its way. I'll keep them away from the civilians until they get there."

"Why would anyone attack Bowden Hill?" Morgan wondered.

"Why do those assholes do anything?" Julie retorted.

Bianca got up. "I'll go with you."

"No way. Don't compromise your recovery, Bee. It's not worth it." Julie hurried for the door.

"But you're suspended!" Bianca protested.

Julie grinned. "I never said I was going as an OPMA major." She shrugged off her dragonscale robe. "It's time for the Knight to ride again."

When Julie strode into the inner ward, Genevieve was ready and waiting. Her headlights flashed in happy recognition as Julie strode toward her.

"Quick, Gennie." Julie gestured at her armor. "I need you to do that thing again."

Genevieve's engine hummed with pleasure. A blue glow enveloped the classic Mustang, and she rose into the air. Then she began to change. Tires flipped around, transforming as they did so. Her nose elongated. Her paintwork darkened, and bright red GT stripes bled down the length of her body.

When Genevieve lowered herself to the ground again, the black-and-pewter 1971 Mach 1 had been replaced by a gleaming 2022 Shelby Mustang GT500, a purring monster of speed and power. The front door banged open, and the 5.2 liter supercharged V8 engine let out a dragonlike roar.

"Let's do this, girl." Julie slipped into the driver's seat as the portcullis clanked up.

The seat belt clipped over her body, and Genevieve charged.

Bowden Hill lay at the bottom of a dale, surrounded by small, square fields that were a startling presence in the moorland. Julie guessed the village, which was little more than a handful of streets, was usually sleepy and quiet.

Now it teemed with monstrosities.

She stabbed the brakes, and Genevieve hummed to a halt on top of the nearest hill.

"What is going on down there?" Julie asked.

Screams rose through Genevieve's open windows. At the eastern end of the village, worried paras peered out of their doorways. On the western side, chaos reigned.

A mass of creatures swarmed from the ruined earth of a nearby field, its crops destroyed, scars ripped in the dirt. Some creatures were still dragging themselves from beneath the ground: horrible, grayish things with pale eyes and disfigured bodies. Above their heads, a swarm of transparent beings flew in circles, screeching like ravens feeding on the dead.

"Ghouls and wraiths?" Julie muttered. "I haven't seen those since the Haunted Hill."

A handful of brave civilians stood their ground on the main street, clutching hammers, axes, and rusty swords.

They don't stand a chance, Hat stated.

Julie grinned and tightened her fingers on the steering wheel. *They do now.*

She slammed her foot down on the gas pedal, and Genevieve bellowed down the quiet country lane, heading for the main street. At the same moment, the cloud of wraiths formed into a single fierce mass and charged at the civilians.

Genevieve rocketed down the main street. The leader of the civilians, a round-faced weredog, raised his rusty sword. Julie saw his expression change from terror to determination as the first wraith swooped toward him, its transparent cloak-like body hardening to solid gray. It would hit him like a falling boulder.

Julie threw the door open as Genevieve skidded to a halt inches from the civilians. She leaped out of the car, summoned fire, and blasted the wraith. The creature shrieked and exploded into ash, showering the civilians.

"It's the Knight!" the weredog cried, his eyes huge.

Julie punched out two tongues of flame and grew them tall,

building a wall of fire across the street. The wraiths shrieked, ash filled the air, and the attackers pulled back.

"Get to cover!" Julie bellowed. "I'll hold them off!"

The civilians scattered as a breath of icy wind screeched toward them, ripping the flames apart in the center of the wall of fire. Wraiths poured through the gap. They looked like disembodied cloaks, but there was only darkness where their faces should have been, except for glowing white mouths that snarled as they swooped toward Julie.

She took out three with rapid fireballs, but the ball of flame that shot from her fist bounced off the fourth. Its body had solidified, and it plunged at Julie with a piercing shriek. She yelped, tapped into her fear, and called up a pillar of earth that shot from the ground and slammed into the wraith's guts. Its shriek was cut short, and it exploded into a cloud of ash, buying Julie a precious few seconds to seal the wall of fire again.

Where's the OPMA, Hat? she cried. The ground rumbled beneath her feet, and it wasn't because of her.

Trying to get in touch with them, Hat assured her, *but they must be en route. You only need to hold them for a few more minutes.*

The asphalt erupted at Julie's feet, showering her with rubble and dirt. She leaped back as a ghoul crawled out of the earth, its limbs bending the wrong way, round mouth snapping with blackened teeth, white eyes expressionless but fixed on her. It lunged for her ankles, and she stomped on its head. There was a satisfying pop under her heel before it turned to ash.

More ghouls were coming, tearing up the street as they crawled toward her with gurgling shrieks. They'd tunneled beneath the wall of fire. Julie called on her magic and tried to bury them, but they dug faster than she could summon earth.

"Shit!" Julie yelled as a ghoul's twisted fingers closed around her ankle. She gave it a fireball to the face, and it exploded. More of them poured from the ground. The street had become a writhing mass of limbs and teeth and sickly gray skin, ash leaking from cuts in the ghouls' flanks as their claws tore one another in their haste to get to Julie. Two grabbed her legs. One snapped at Julie's calf and wailed when its teeth clanged on dwarf-forged steel. She kicked it in the face and stumbled when the second ghoul yanked on her leg. Her arms flailed, and she landed on a mass of squirming, screeching ghouls.

They smelled triumph and plunged at her, their hands closing around her arms and her neck, claws scraping the visor of her helmet. Ghouls swarmed over her back, and the more Julie's fear fueled her earth magic, the more the ground trembled as additional ghouls poured from under the surface. She was suffocating in a sea of the monsters.

"Screw this!" Julie screamed.

She summoned fire, and her gauntlets erupted in flames. The ghouls fell back, shrieking, and ash filled the air around her. Flames licked her shoulders and torso, and she was suddenly free. She scrambled to her feet, flames on her legs now, and focused on channeling the heat into the ground around her.

The very dirt caught fire. Ghoul screams filled the air as flames pooled around her like she'd flooded the street with gasoline and tossed a match. Ash created a cloud over the burning street.

Julie stood up, panting, teeth gritted. The whole street was ablaze, but the wall of fire she'd built at the end of the street was gone, and the wraiths shrieked their displeasure as they formed a swirling vortex of fury over her head.

"Come on!" Julie roared at them. "Get some!"

She flung her wings open and jumped into the air, her body still shrouded in fire. The cloud above her turned gray as the wraiths solidified. Julie stretched her arms above her Superman-like and beat her wings as fast as she could. She shot into the dark cloud of monstrosities like a rocket of flame, and everything she touched turned to ash as she punched through it.

Julie broke free of the wraith cloud and rose into the air,

panting with effort, only blue sky above her. When she looked down, the wraiths were after her, their white mouths wide as they snapped at her feet. She bent down and punched fireball after fireball into them.

"This is what you get for attacking innocent people!" Julie bellowed, fireballs flying from her fists.

True, yet not particularly snappy, Hat commented.

I didn't ask for your feedback! Julie snapped. *See any OPMA units yet?*

Not yet, Hat growled.

Crap. Julie dodged a fast-moving wraith and hit it with fire before it could attack.

Hat gasped. *Julie, look! On the street!*

Julie blasted a hole through the cloud of wraiths. In the few seconds before more wraiths flooded to fill the gap, she saw an elf no more than eleven or twelve years old bolting across the scorched main street, his feet kicking up a cloud of ash.

His high-pitched scream reached her ears, and the wraiths stopped, then hovered, transparent, each a gray outline of a cloak. Their hoods all turned toward the fleeing child.

"*No!*" Julie screamed.

The wraiths charged, plunging in a vortex of horror toward the elf kid.

"*No!*" Julie screamed again.

She folded her wings flat to her back, stretched out her arms, and fell like a stone. Time slowed. Having the advantage of mass, Julie fell faster than the wraiths could fly, and she zipped past them. As Julie dove past the rooster weathervane at the top of the church steeple, the elf kid looked over his shoulder, face ashen and eyes wide with fear.

When she glanced over her shoulder, the wraiths behind her were rock-solid. They'd pulverize the kid like a ripe plum.

Julie flung open her wings and let out a defiant scream. She flung one arm around the kid and curled her body around him, then turned back to the wraiths, her free arm burning, and sent up a plume of fire. They slammed into the flames with a physical force that flung both Julie and the kid to the ground. She desperately rolled onto her back, arm still outstretched, flames filling her world. The child was screaming. Ash filled the air as wraiths plummeted into the fire.

Then there was silence. Julie and the kid sat in a cloud of ash, choking.

Hat, tell me there's backup nearby, Julie begged.

I-I can't get in touch with HQ. Hat turned cold on Julie's head. *I don't know what's happening.*

The ash began to clear. Julie rose to her feet and gave the kid a shove. "Get inside!" she barked.

He bolted. Julie summoned flame to both hands, her heart hammering wildly in her chest as she looked left and right. The ash was as thick as mist.

I've tried again. I can't get through to them, Hat cried. *Or to Tintagel. My communications are compromised!*

Julie's eyes narrowed. *I can think of only one person with the power to do that to you, Hat.*

He got colder.

"This was a trap," Julie growled aloud.

The air fizzled to her left. Julie whirled, burning fists raised, as a portal opened in the ash. There was darkness beyond the portal, then the sound of slow clapping.

Vivienne stepped out, her dark eyes glittering, still applauding sarcastically. She wore a gray dress as light as mist and a cloak that spilled over her shoulders like a waterfall, and she was as pretty as she'd ever been, even with her hair piled on top of her head and secured in place by two daggers. Had she always had that cruelty in her eyes?

"*Nimue,*" Julie hissed.

"That's not very nice." Nimue adopted a hurt look. "Don't you know me as Vivienne?"

"I know better now," Julie snarled. "And I know you endangered all these paras' lives just to lay a trap for me."

"Clever little fae." Nimue chuckled. "Unfortunately for you, cleverness won't save you."

"Oh, I wasn't counting on cleverness." Julie held up her burning fists. "I can shoot fireballs and shit."

Nimue threw back her head and laughed wholeheartedly. "How old are you, child? Twenty? Twenty-one?" She cackled. "I have had thousands of years to hone my skills."

"Cool story, ho," Julie sassed. *Hat, can you reach* anyone?

No, Hat panicked. *I'm sorry, Julie. She's done something to me!*

Nimue's lip curled. "I bet some people think your irreverence is cute, but I don't."

"Really? Who would have guessed?" Julie glanced at the houses behind her and took a few steps toward the open fields, where there would be no collateral damage. "I totally didn't get that from how you're trying to kill me."

It's okay, Hat. She took a deep breath and a few more paces toward the fields.

"Kill you?" Nimue sneered. "I have grander plans than that for both of you."

"Touch Julie, and I *will* murder you," Hat snarled.

Nimue rolled her eyes. "Really, Emrys? I thought we'd been over this." Smoke curled from her fingertips, thick and dark and toxic. "We all know who's the better mage."

It's not okay, Julie! Hat cried. *What are we going to do?*

Julie stifled her smirk. *What Nimue doesn't know is that you're not my only avenue of mental comms.*

Hat gasped.

"Greater mage, huh?" Julie's flames intensified. "Come over here and say that to my face."

Nimue chuckled. "Are you *really* going to fight me, Julie?"

Eggy! Julie yelled. *Eggy, are you listening?*

Eglantine's voice curled sleepily through Julie's mind. *Julie?* She gasped. *Is that Nimue?*

"Fight you?" Julie snickered. "I'm not going to fight you." She crossed her arms over her chest, and flame enveloped her. "I'm going to kick your ass."

Can you get in touch with other dragons? Julie asked sharply.

I think so, Eglantine whimpered.

"I don't appreciate your tone." Nimue sneered. Flames covered her hands, too. They were deep orange, and thick smoke billowed from them.

Good, Julie told her. *We're going to need them.*

CHAPTER NINETEEN

Eglantine's heart throbbed in her chest. She squirmed, feeling the vague twitches of limbs that seemed to be a long way away, responding only sluggishly to the despairing fury in her mind.

Through Julie's eyes, she saw Nimue raise her burning hands.

Julie! she screamed.

Get help, Eggy! Julie shouted, and the world filled with fire.

Eglantine longed to fling herself against her shell. She could feel everything that separated her from the outside world: the thick fluid, the veined membrane, and the sturdy obsidian of the shell. Still, she knew that when the day of her hatching came, she would shatter the egg like porcelain. Every memory told her that.

She wanted to kick out and burst free, but her limbs stirred only feebly when she tried.

In her head, Eglantine opened her jaws and let out a dragon roar, earth-shaking, castle-toppling, and edged with smoke. No sound emerged.

Julie! she screamed in her mind.

Julie didn't respond. Eglantine felt flashes of fire and the pounding of her heart, plus the knowledge that she'd never had to fight anyone this powerful before.

Sphynx claws pressed into her shell, painless pinpricks. *Stop wiggling,* Cleo grumbled. *I'm trying to take a nap.*

Julie's in trouble! Eglantine gasped. *I need to help her!*

Horusiris, who was curled up close in her nest, chuckled. *Julie's always in trouble.*

This time feels different, Eglantine protested. *This time she* needs *me.* She tried to roar again. *I am the Great Lady-in-Waiting of the Deep! I should be in battle with my fae bond!*

She probed the memories of her ancestors, seeking the reason she had not yet hatched. None of them remembered waiting like this. They only remembered the glorious moment of breaking free, breathing real air, and spreading their damp and sticky wings for the first time.

Why have I not hatched? she demanded angrily. *I thought I would hatch when I was free of Grandmother and the Deep!*

Cleo rolled onto her back, purring, her soft skin pressed against Eglantine's shell. Ranubis walked up to her and rubbed against her. Even Horusiris was moved to give her a tender headbutt.

It will happen when the time is right, he told her.

I wish everyone would stop saying that! Eglantine roared. *When will it be? Julie needs me* now!

Horusiris chuckled softly. *Julie needs* dragons, *Eglantine. Remember that she isn't the only one you can reach with your mind.*

Eglantine hesitated. *She's not?*

Of course not. You are the Great Lady-in-Waiting, like you just said. Horusiris purred, a thrum that ran through the entire egg. *You have the ability to touch the minds of every dragon who has sworn loyalty to you. It's a magic that runs as deep as fire in the blood of dragons.*

Eglantine's heart hammered. *Julie?*

Julie didn't answer. When Eglantine looked into her mind, her world was a chaos of flames. She saw Nimue's dark eyes, a sneer of triumph, and a ball of blazing fire...

Then nothing.

Julie! Eglantine screamed.

There was only darkness.

Fear shot through Eglantine's body, red-hot. Her limbs spasmed with it, and she threw her head back until she felt the hard shell against her nose. A wave burst through her. It felt as though her limbs were drenched in liquid fire.

For an instant, Eglantine thought the shell had shattered, but it was only that her senses had gone beyond her obsidian prison. She could feel the tiny dimension of the Sphnyxes' realm, their warm bodies, and their pedestal. Then she could feel beyond the borders of this world into the vastness of Avalon, its marching mountains, its spreading forests, its winding coastline. The landscape was distant and blurred. Far clearer was her sense of the dragons. They stood out like bright stars in her senses, crystal-clear. She understood with a deep ancestral certainty that these were the dragons who had sworn loyalty to her.

These were her people.

She arched her neck and roared in her mind, and her thunderous voice echoed across dimensions.

Dragons! Dragons! Dragons! Your Lady-in-Waiting calls upon you!

Surprise, joy, and panic. The emotions of her people buffeted her like ocean waves. She faltered and felt her magic wobble. Then a calm, clear voice spoke into her mind, one she knew well.

Great Lady-in-Waiting, speak, Alugon boomed. *Your servants are listening, and your commands shall be obeyed.*

Hope pulsed through Eglantine's body. She leaned into the bond, and her magic strengthened. Hatched or unhatched, these dragons knew her as their ruler, and none of them would disobey her call.

My fae bond is in great peril, she cried. *Find her and save her!*

Kaplan hunched over his keyboard, muttering angrily to himself as he slammed his large fingers down on the keys. They crackled and thumped satisfyingly under his fingers. Would Qtana never understand that typing an angry email wasn't as much fun on one of her new-fangled touch-screen thingies?

Don't push me. Do it or face the consequences! Kaplan.

He pressed send without proofreading and scrolled to the next message in his inbox. As if sending emails was going to win this accursed war. Kaplan scoffed as he opened a message from his new head of recruitment, asking for a way to fast-track recruitment paperwork since new recruits were pouring in from all over Avalon now that the treaty negotiations were coming to a close.

He was in the midst of typing a grumpy reply to ask the IT trolls instead of wasting a superior officer's time when all the hair on the back of his neck stood up at once. Kaplan felt a tingling in his fingernails and at the base of his spine as his tail attempted to grow. He growled, his canine teeth stretching with a satisfying feeling of pressure, and looked up from his screen.

It felt like there was someone in the office with him, but the door was still closed, and his hopeless assistant was nowhere to be seen. He turned his chair to look out of the large window overlooking the NYHQ campus. A bull moose galloped across the manicured lawn, soaking wet, and almost crushed a cloud of faeries with his antlers. The faeries started jabbering furiously and the moose turned into a buff, apologetic man in a brown uniform, then sprinted for the cover of the building when the faeries started pelting him with acidic dust.

Nothing out of the ordinary. Kaplan rubbed the backs of his hands together. His skin itched as tiger fur threatened to creep through. Shrugging off the feeling, he turned back to his computer and saw Horusiris walking across his keyboard.

Kaplan bared his teeth and hissed. Horusiris flattened his ears, his rat tail lashing, and let out a long yowl. His mincing paws pressed more keys.

What are you asking me for? Get in touch with uhiew;jn[oreg09h'boDSNJDKMSA

"Get *off*!" Kaplan snarled, digging his elongating claws into the armrests of his chair.

"Make me!" Horusiris yowled, baring his teeth.

Kaplan drew his lips back and let out a deep snarl. Horusiris lashed out with his front claws and yowled louder.

The door of Kaplan's office swung open, and a young Starlight Fae peered inside. "Um, sir?"

Kaplan looked up. "*What?*"

The Fae eyed Horusiris. "It, uh, sounded like there were cats fighting in here, sir."

Kaplan smoothed the front of his jacket. "Piss off, kid."

"Yes, sir." The fae withdrew.

Horusiris sat down, pressing send with his asshole, and gave Kaplan a slow blink.

Kaplan huffed and rubbed his hands, smoothing away the hair that had sprouted on the backs of them. "What do *you* want, Sphynx?" he grumbled. "I have things to do." His hands were still itchy, so he licked them.

"I thought I should inform you that there is considerable trouble in Avalon," Horusiris purred. "Since you don't seem to be aware."

Kaplan paused and raised his eyebrows. "I'm *well* aware, pussycat. There's a war on if you hadn't noticed."

Horusiris stood up and jumped into Kaplan's lap. Kaplan hissed. Horusiris ignored him.

"I mean specific trouble." Horusiris sat down and started kneading Kaplan's thighs. "Trouble that involves Julie Meadows."

"Is that supposed to surprise me?" Kaplan batted Horusiris with one hand.

Horusiris dug his claws into Kaplan's thighs. "It's bigger trouble than usual."

"Bigger trouble than usual," Kaplan grumbled. "How much bigger?" He slapped Horusiris again, knocking him off.

The Sphynx landed on his feet. "Big enough to involve Nimue."

Kaplan leaped to his feet. "*Nimue?*"

"Yes." Horusiris sat down and wrapped his tail around his paws. "You might want to send her some backup. She's in Bowden Hill."

"Merlin's stinking hemorrhoids!" Kaplan grabbed his phone. The fur on his hands had returned, and he could feel it trailing down his back, every hair standing bolt upright. It took him a moment to remember that the phone wasn't the fastest comm he had anymore. He slammed it into its cradle and touched his telechip.

Griffin Regiment, emergency deployment. To arms immediately! he ordered. *Gather in the portal room and wait for my command.*

Yes, sir, Shulme replied.

Kaplan paused to think about what he'd heard and seen when it came to Nimue's powers. He touched his telechip again.

High Magic Division, he growled, *prepare for battle.*

Taylor was more nervous than he'd expected to be. He shifted in the expensive velvet chair, glancing around the Palm Court. Its high glass ceilings let in a soft glow, complemented by crystal chandeliers, white tablecloths, and the Roman-style statues in every niche. Orchids bloomed opulently on every table, and silent waiters in black suits drifted across the floor.

He wiped his hands on his pants and told himself he was

being a nincompoop. The edge of his palm grazed the ring box in his pocket, and his heart thudded faster. Should he have talked to her before he bought the ring? What if she saw it and thought Julie would hate it? What if she didn't give him permission? Was he supposed to ask permission? Did humans do that? Had they ever?

There was movement across the room, and Taylor spotted Rosa's mass of sprayed black curls. The portly middle-aged woman was intercepted by a tall waiter, and she said something that made him blush and her guffaw.

Taylor couldn't help smiling, and the knot in his guts unraveled.

Rosa pushed past the waiter and strode toward Taylor's table. She wore excessively red lipstick, mom jeans, and a sweater that had been in fashion twenty years ago and toted an enormous bulging handbag.

"*Taylor!*" she sang, jingling her bangles and earrings.

Taylor got to his feet, and Rosa flung her arms around him, almost crushing him in her embrace. Mom had never hugged him like this. Despite her overpowering perfume, Taylor leaned into the hug, pressing his face into her comfortingly soft shoulder.

"Hey, Rosa." He hugged her tighter.

"Aw, hi, baby." Rosa stepped back and pinched his cheek. "How are you doing, my poor honey?"

Julie had told her his parents had died in a car accident. The story wasn't true, but the empathy in Rosa's eyes was real.

"All the better for seeing you," Taylor answered honestly.

"Oh, listen to you." Rosa chuckled and swatted at him. "This place is swanky!"

"My treat," Taylor assured her as they took their seats.

"I should hope so, dear, given that that's an Armani suit." Rosa grinned and opened her handbag. "I have something for you!"

Taylor cupped his chin in his hands, delighted. "You do?"

"You know I do, baby!" Rosa pulled out a small bottle of something green. "Aloe vera concentrate!"

"Concentrate, huh?" Taylor raised his eyebrows.

"Much more practical than the juice, and with all the benefits!" Rosa gushed. "You'll never have trouble pooping again!"

"Wonderful!" Taylor exclaimed.

Rosa beamed and held out the bottle. "Here, honey. All yours. I have plenty more."

"Thanks, Rosa." Taylor pocketed it. It would join a collection of sealed bottles in the bottom of a kitchen cabinet.

Rosa put a hand over his. "I've been thinking about this for a long time, baby. I didn't want to say anything right after you lost your real mom, but..." She paused. "If you want to call me 'Mom,' I'd like that."

Taylor looked into her brown eyes. They were crazy, sure, but the love that poured from them was undeniable.

"I would love that," he murmured. "I really would...Mom."

Rosa's eyes lit up. "That's my boy." She pinched his cheek again.

The waiter arrived with delicate teacups and an elegant circular metal stand containing rectangular white plates stacked with an afternoon tea that rivaled even Meggie's. There were tiny delicate sandwiches: cucumber and smoked salmon, trout caviar, brioche, egg, and goat cheese, plus buttery scones with clotted cream and jam, macarons, tiny tarts with raspberries, and chocolatey delights.

Rosa giggled. "I feel like the queen of England!"

Taylor grinned. "That was the idea."

"Sweet boy." She chuckled and took a caviar sandwich, which she popped into her mouth with irreverence. "Mmm, this is good!"

"I'm glad you're enjoying it." Taylor stirred a sugar cube into his tea and took a sip.

Rosa took another sandwich. "What's on your mind, honey? I

know you didn't invite me here without Julie just because you wanted to spoil your future mother-in-law."

Taylor sprayed tea everywhere, and the other diners turned to stare. Three waiters hurried over, but Rosa beat them to it. She opened her handbag and withdrew a wad of crumpled paper napkins from KFC, with which she mopped tea droplets off the pristine tablecloth. The waiters skidded to a halt and watched in horror.

"There you are, dear." Rosa dropped the napkins back into her handbag. "Like nothing ever happened."

Taylor leaned closer. "How did you *know?*"

Rosa patted his hand. "Oh, honey, did you really think I didn't know the moment you asked me to come and mentioned Julie wouldn't be here?" She grinned, eyes sparkling. "So, where is it?"

Taylor hesitated, but the Veil would do its job, right? He reached into his pocket and pulled out the ring box. When he popped it open, Rosa gasped and pressed both hands to her lips.

"Oh, *Taylor!*" she cried.

"Is it that bad?" Taylor quavered.

"Bad?" Rosa laughed. "Honey, this is the most beautiful thing I've ever seen!" She reached out and touched the dragon-shaped moonstone with a finger. "*How* did you find someone to shape it like that?"

"Do you think she'll like it?" Taylor pressed.

"Of course she will, honey." Rosa beamed at him. "It's not about the ring, you know. It's about the person she's going to say yes to."

Taylor swallowed hard. "Do you...do you think she will?" he croaked. "Say yes, I mean?"

Rosa squeezed his hand. "I can't answer for her, honey, but I've hoped for years that someone like you would come into her life."

Happy tears stung Taylor's eyes. As he wiped them, Rosa took the opportunity to eat two lavender macarons.

"So, how are you going to ask her?" Rosa asked eagerly. "Any grand plans?"

"No," Taylor admitted. "That's why I asked you to come see me." He smiled. "I just can't seem to get the timing right, and everything just felt wrong. Now I'm starting to think it might be because I need to make you part of this."

"I'm honored, honey." Rosa squeezed his hand. "And I've got plenty of ideas for you."

"Please, tell me. I'm desperate. I don't know what to do." Taylor leaned forward.

Rosa chuckled. "When Julie was a little girl, she was not one of those who dreamed about her wedding, you know?"

Taylor grinned. "I can imagine. She doesn't seem the type."

"Oh, no. She was always reading books. You know how she is." Rosa waved a hand. "But she *did* tell me one time about her perfect proposal."

Taylor clutched the tablecloth. "What was it?"

"She was fourteen, and she'd just had her heart broken by a boy for the first time. Graham Burton." Rosa's expression darkened. "What a turd."

Taylor gasped. "Rosa!"

"He left her on the threshold of the winter dance that year," Rosa growled. "He should be glad I haven't seen him since, or I'd have given him a piece of my mind. Poor Julie was in tears. Sat in the backseat sobbing in her cute little poofy dance dress. It wasn't just about Graham, you know. It was the year after we lost David, and it was just so hard on her." Rosa smiled. "That was when she told me that she'd dreamed that one day, Graham would ask her to marry him."

Taylor leaned closer. "How?"

His phone buzzed, making him jump. When he pulled it from his pocket, Kaplan's name flashed on the screen.

"I've got to take this," he muttered apologetically.

Rosa waved a hand and helped herself to a scone. Taylor swiped the screen and raised the phone to his ear. "Sir?"

"Woodskin," Kaplan growled. "Where are you?" His tone made shivers run down Taylor's spine.

"New York City, sir." Taylor swallowed. "What's wrong?"

Rosa looked up, cheeks bulging with the scone.

Kaplan paused. "I'll keep this short. Nimue has Julie."

Taylor dropped his phone. It clattered noisily on the table, and Rosa stared as Taylor rescued it and held it back to his ear. "*What?*"

"I'm not sure myself. One of those hairless cats appeared and told me," Kaplan snarled. "She's in Bowden Hill. We're going to get her."

Taylor swallowed hard. "What can I do, sir?"

"Nothing yet, Woodskin. Just sit tight." Kaplan's voice was gruffly gentle. "I just thought you should know."

"Yes, sir. Thank you, sir." Taylor hung up and stared at the blank screen. His belly felt like he'd swallowed a block of ice whole.

"Taylor, honey." Rosa was wide-eyed. "What's the matter?"

Taylor forced a quick smile. "Oh, nothing, Mom. Just work." He laughed.

Rosa's eyes narrowed.

"Anyway, I was thinking." Taylor tugged his collar, loosening it slightly. "Would you like a glass of wine? They have a nice selection here. Or a cocktail?"

"Don't lie to me, boy." Rosa raised her chin. "I've raised teenagers. It's not worth trying."

Taylor's protests died in his throat as he stared into her burning eyes.

"Tell me the truth." Rosa gripped her fork tightly. "Is my baby girl in danger?"

"Mom, she's…It's just…just in a work situation," Taylor babbled.

Rosa's eyes narrowed. "Honey, don't think for a moment that reassures me. Did you *really* think, after all this time, that I believe you two are working in insurance?"

Taylor said nothing.

"I know my baby girl, Taylor." Rosa sat back. "I've seen the change in her."

"Y-you have?" Taylor asked nervously.

"Of course I have. She was a pale, weedy little thing who spent all day reading. Now she's got biceps like Lara Croft." Rosa snorted. "Did you think I wouldn't notice? And there's that scar on her forehead. That was never there before. It's small, but I saw it."

"She, um—" Taylor attempted.

"Bumped her head?" Rosa raised her eyebrows. "Sure she did, honey. I'm no fool. I don't know what you two are up to, but I know insurance isn't it." Her face crumpled, and her lower lip trembled. "I don't know why you two are hiding the truth from me, but...but I have a right to know if my baby girl is in trouble." Her voice cracked.

Taylor stared into her eyes, saw the white-knuckled grip on her fork, and something broke inside him. He would have given anything, *anything*, to have a mom like this. To have a mom right now.

He knew what he had to do. It could backfire, but any other decision would be the wrong one. He had to follow his heart on this one.

"Can you take a few days off work?" He wrapped his hands around Rosa's. "It's time you visited us at home."

Moonlight.

Julie felt it soaking into her skin, cool and soft. Where it reached her blood, it crackled with power. She was propped up against something hard, reveling in the incredible feeling of moonlight soaking into her.

Dimly, she was aware of her lungs aching, but the moonlight was soothing the pain. Each breath she took came more easily than the last. She tipped her head back, felt her skull scrape rock, and let the moonlight soak into her face.

Her thoughts grew clearer. She was sitting on something soft. Grass?

Fear rippled through her. *Where am I?* She groped for her memories, but they were slippery, like trying to catch fistfuls of water. There had been a village...an attack...a fire.

Nimue.

Fear and anger jolted through Julie, and she had to fight her feelings down to keep the earth from trembling. She kept her eyes closed and carefully slowed her breathing. Wherever she was, Nimue must have brought her here, and she needed to think.

This is the second time in six weeks I've been knocked out and woken up not knowing where I am, she grumbled. *Pisses me off.*

There was no response. She felt something heavy around her wrists.

Hat, where are we? she hissed.

Still nothing. Julie carefully opened her eyes a crack and spotted Nimue. The fae stood with her back to Julie, wings folded and glittering in the moonlight. Her head was tipped back, arms extended, and she murmured something Julie couldn't quite hear, but the words rustled over her skin like bat wings.

They were in a forest glade with green grass and trees clustered nearby. It didn't look like Fernwood Deep or the Deadwoods. Mistwood North, maybe?

Julie glanced at her hands. Sturdy steel shackles enclosed her wrists, and a heavy chain, each link thicker than her thumb, ran over her lap. She was sitting on the grass, propped against a rock.

It took no great leap of intellect to suppose she was chained to the same rock.

At least we don't have to go through Lady Ennowen to get to Nimue, she mused.

There was no response from Hat. Julie closed her eyes again, trying to ignore the frantic thudding of her heart. She needed to get in touch with him if she was going to face Nimue.

Hat, dude, serious. Where are you? she hissed. She couldn't feel anything on her head. He wasn't with her.

The realization made her feel like she was standing on the edge of a cliff.

Hat! she screamed. HAT!

The ground stirred beneath her, and Julie took a breath, trying to calm her fears, but the tremor spread. Hat! she screamed.

Julie!

It was Eglantine. The dragon's deep, musical voice flooded Julie's mind, stilling her throbbing heart. The trembling of the earth stopped. Julie hoped it hadn't gone far enough to catch Nimue's attention.

Eggles, moondrop, what's going on? Julie tried to keep her thoughts calm. *Are you okay?*

I'm fine. I'm safe with the Sphynxes, Eglantine reassured her.

Julie let out a breath. *Where's Hat?*

I don't know, but help is on the way. Eglantine's voice rang with determination. *I've sent the dragons. They're coming, Julie.*

Thank you. Julie fought for another slow, deep breath. *Do you know where I am?*

Not exactly, Eglantine admitted. *I can guide them to you, but I don't know where that is.* Her voice hardened. *The tiger man sent more soldiers than I could count. We're going to get you back.*

Julie took a breath at the thought of Kaplan. If he knew what was going on, he'd find her. *Thanks, Eggy. I—*

"I know you're awake, Julie."

Julie opened her eyes. Nimue was done with her creepy-ass chant, and she faced Julie, her wings jutting over her shoulders, glimmering like broken glass. The same hard glitter was in her eyes.

She smiled, dazzling as ever.

"Good for you," Julie spat. "I know you're a traitor. Where's Hat?"

Nimue gave a tinkling laugh like sleigh bells. "You mean Merlin?" She looked up. Her voice turned harsh and guttural. "He's undergoing a change."

Julie followed her gaze, and her heart froze solid. A whirling vortex of dark magic, swirls of black and deepest purple and the red of venous blood, spun and sparkled in midair over their heads. Julie could feel a throbbing forcefield of menace surrounding the vortex, a pulsing invisible aura of hatred and malice.

At its center, glimpsed through the swirls of palpable evil, was Hat in his wizard's hat form. His brim fluttered and frayed as the magic tore at him. His tip was whipped back and forth, and flashes of electric-blue magic burst against the darkness of the vortex as it tore at him. The flashes grew duller as Julie watched.

"*Hat!*" she screamed, flying to her feet. Her wings burst open, and she jumped into the air, reaching for him. She felt shocking pain as the dark magic aura scorched her fingers like fire. Then her chains tightened and the shackles yanked her back, wrenching her shoulders. She almost fell, her wings fluttering madly, but strained against her bonds instead. "*Hat!*" she shrieked.

Nimue laughed again. "Scream all you like, dear." Her smile widened. "His wards are protecting him for now, but those defenses won't last forever!"

Thunder rumbled as Julie's sorrow ripped through her chest. Cracks appeared in the grass a foot below her feet as she strained against the chains.

"*Hat!*" she howled.

"Keep screaming." The swirling vortex and the gleaming moonlight cast flickering shadows over Nimue's smile. "His wards *will* fail, and when they do, my spell will shred him."

Julie stared at her. "*Shred* him?"

"Oh, I'm no murderer, Julie." Nimue's eyes narrowed. "He'll have a choice."

Julie stared at Hat.

"He can come back as his true self." Nimue laughed.

"Or he can be destroyed."

CHAPTER TWENTY

His true self. Hat would never turn back into a warlock, not after what he'd been through. Terror ripped through Julie's chest like a beast's claws.

Hat would choose death.

The ground quaked, and the trees surrounding the glade tossed and shuddered with the movement. Nimue swayed easily, keeping her balance. "Scared, are you?"

"Not just scared," Julie snarled and clenched her fists. "Pissed."

Nimue's grin fueled the rage in Julie's chest. Fire burst from her hands, then her forearms, then from every pore of her body. It engulfed her, the flames tickling as they danced over her eyes, bathing the moonlit clearing in flickering gold light. The shackles on her wrists softened like melting butter and she spread her wings, flames roaring. She strained against her bonds as they lifted her into the air. The shackles melted, and Julie shot into the air.

Hat, can you hear me? she cried.

There was no response from Hat, struggling in the dark vortex. Julie reached toward it, but dark magic seared her fingertips, and she pulled back with a yelp. The flames winked out.

"Don't touch that!" Nimue barked. She rose into the air, her diaphanous wings humming, eyes narrowed. "How did you break those iron bonds?"

Julie spread her arms, moonlight soaking into her skin. "Maybe I'm more powerful than you thought."

Nimue sneered. "Don't flatter yourself, little fae." She spread her arms. "Don't you see *my* power?"

Julie glanced at the vortex. "What, that thing?" Her eyes narrowed. "Not that you'd know, but there's no power greater than love." Her fists ignited. "Add pissing me off by hurting those I love, and you'd better be ready for an ass-kicking like you've never experienced."

Nimue threw her head back and laughed again. "You may be more powerful than I'd thought, but you're nowhere near my level." She spread her arms. "Look around, little fae. Don't you see where we are?"

Julie risked a quick glance around. The forest spread as far as she could see in every direction, but the constellations were Earth's. The glade hosted a stream, and she realized she hadn't been chained to a single rock. A ring of standing stones, their tops worn to jagged points by the passage of time, stood beside the smoldering remains of her chains.

"This is Hotè de Viviane." Nimue's smile widened. "The House of Nimue. We're in Brocèliande, you foolish whelp. This is *my* turf."

"You know what else they call this place?" Julie growled. The flames of her fists roared up to her elbows.

"Do enlighten me." Nimue smirked.

Julie gritted her teeth. "Tombeau de Viviane."

Something flickered in Nimue's eyes.

"That's right," Julie hissed. "The Tomb of Nimue."

"You can't hope to defeat me," Nimue snarled.

Julie summoned wind. It roared around her in a howling,

whirling tower, whipping the trees and ripping chunks of grass from the earth. She grinned and cracked her flaming knuckles. "I guess we'll find out how wrong you are."

Nimue's face twisted in fury, and she let out an ear-splitting shriek. Flames swallowed her hands.

Julie yelled defiantly and beat her wings harder and faster, then reached toward Nimue. The whirlwind surged toward the other fae. The vortex sputtered as the whirlwind passed through it.

Nimue closed her fists as the whirlwind reached her, and the flames turned to thick black smoke. She thrust out her hands and the whirlwind froze, howling and swirling in place, wads of grass and earth and branches ripping through the air. Julie tried to push it forward, but she'd lost control. The thick smoke filled the whirlwind, so dense that Julie could see only the wicked gleam of Nimue's smile. Then the whirlwind surged back toward her.

Julie fell back, flailing for control of the wind, but it was too quick. The thick smoke surrounded her, choking her. Dirt sprayed her face, a thousand pinpricks of pain, and the wind plucked her out of mid-air and spun her. Eyes streaming, gasping for breath, Julie threw her arms over her head to protect it as leaves and twigs lashed her armor.

Julie! Eglantine gasped in her mind. *Here!*

A surge of power blazed through Julie's veins. Dragon power. She took a breath that burned fiercely, ignored the pain in her lungs, and summoned earth. There was a deafening crack as a wall of dirt burst out of the ground. It slammed into Julie's boots, and she fell to her hands and knees on it. The whirlwind sputtered, and Julie's pillar of earth bore her up, shattering the whirlwind and lifting her clear of the smoke.

She sucked in a glorious breath of fresh air, then the earth between her fingers turned scorching hot. With a yelp, Julie kicked away from the pillar, her wings humming as they took her weight. A deep red glow burst from the heart of the pillar, and it erupted into boiling, spitting lava. Tongues of molten earth reached toward her.

Julie chuckled. "I've seen this before, you old bitch."

Nimue hovered across the glade from her, face contorted in concentration. The lava rose, and Julie held up her arms and summoned rain. The moonlight disappeared abruptly as black clouds swarmed across the sky like locusts. Rain poured over Julie's shoulders, splattering the lava. It hissed and spat, tiny bursts of steam curling into the air, and turned black and inert.

Nimue shrieked in frustration. The rain stopped, and as moonlight poured between the scattering clouds, Julie punched both arms at Nimue. Fireballs left her fists, hissing and crackling. Nimue dodged two but not the third, the one aimed between the first two. It slammed into her chest with a thud that knocked the air from her lungs, and she fell.

Julie flattened her wings to her back and streaked after the falling fae, flames guttering on her hands as she flew. Smoke billowed from Nimue as she crashed into the trees on the far side of the glade. Wood splintered, trunks cracked, and she disappeared into a cloud of smoke, splinters, and torn leaves.

Julie hovered above the smoke cloud, her burning hands clenched by her sides. "Had enough yet?"

There was a whoosh of flame, and it didn't come from Julie. She glanced to the right. Fire surged through the treetops near the spot where Nimue had fallen, white smoke pouring into the sky as the flames surged through the forest.

Julie summoned rain, but before the clouds could form, there was a hiss in the air—the sound of a missile. She looked up a second too late. The flying rock slammed into her chest with a devastating crack. Julie tumbled backward, her world spinning, throat closing with terror when she felt steel on her chest. Her breastplate was damaged.

She landed on her back hard, grass and earth spraying around her as she skidded across the glade. She came to a stop in one of the shallow streams, winded. Her lungs felt flat and empty; her mouth was open, and cold water soaked into her hair and seeped into her armor.

Laughter boiled around the clearing. Julie struggled to her knees, still desperate for breath. The air was thick with smoke as the forest burned. Two points of scarlet light glowed behind the smoke, and Julie made out Nimue sashaying toward her like she was on a catwalk.

"You're making a good effort. I'll give you that," Nimue called. "But did you really think you could stand against *me*?"

Julie's lungs finally responded. Air rushed into them, and she staggered to her feet, water, blood, and mud dripping from her armor and dragonscale robe. She clenched her fists, and flames engulfed them.

Nimue stepped out of the smoke, one eyebrow arched and a smirk on her face.

Julie spat blood and glanced up. The solidified lava pillar towered over her. "We're not done yet," she rasped.

She reached for the fear that threatened to melt her spine, and the pillar behind her collapsed into a pool of glowing lava. It rushed across the ground, spitting and steaming where it crossed the stream, and rippled toward Nimue.

The fae blanched with fury and clenched her blazing fists. Thunder snarled in the sky, and Julie knew she had to move fast. She let out a scream of rage and charged at Nimue, pushing all her fear and anger into the lava that bubbled at her feet. It rose like a tidal wave, flames bursting across the grass where drops of lava fell to the earth and splashed toward Nimue.

She didn't try to step aside. She met Julie's eyes and smiled.

The sheet of rainwater came down first, turning the lava black. Before Julie could react, lightning followed, and the world turned white.

Taylor wasn't sure Rosa had fully understood the term "visit" as opposed to "move in." His shoulders ached from the straps: the duffle bag on one shoulder, the enormous heavy laptop bag on the other, and the backpack over both.

How did she fit this in here? he wondered, tugging at the massive suitcase she'd somehow wedged into the trunk of the taxi. The driver fidgeted nearby, no doubt acutely conscious of this promisingly busy evening in Manhattan.

With a final desperate lunge, Taylor hauled the suitcase out of the trunk, almost falling over backward. The taxi driver slammed the trunk, jumped into the driver's seat, and drove off.

"What a lovely man," Rosa observed with no trace of sarcasm.

Taylor wrestled with the suitcase and finally pulled out its handle. He bent to pick up the *other* suitcase—there were two of them—and stumbled onto the sidewalk, heavily laden.

"Can I help you with those, honey?" Rosa asked.

"It's okay, Mom. Thanks," Taylor told her. He shrugged the duffle bag higher on his shoulder.

Rosa looked around. "Are we here for an airport shuttle or something?" She chuckled. "Not that I'd know. I've never been on a plane. I thought the airport was in Queens."

"Not...not exactly," Taylor admitted. "We're nearly there."

"Nearly there?" Rosa raised her eyebrows. "Taylor, honey, we're at the edge of Central Park."

Morning traffic swished past Taylor's back. In front of him, the 110th Street Bridge slumbered, its fine-cut gneiss the warm color of hazelnuts. The perfectly round arch below it beckoned toward the lovely green lawns of Central Park.

Taylor turned to Rosa. "Mom, things are about to get weird."

"Weird?" Rosa asked. "What do you mean?"

Taylor didn't know. He'd never heard of a human being brought into Avalon. He reached into his pocket and wrapped a hand around the vial inside it, his heart thudding painfully in his ears. He wasn't certain this was going to work; it was Aether Elf magic so old that Taylor hadn't heard of it before he went digging in the library at the Aether Compound last night.

He was only sure of two things: first, this was the right thing to do, and second, it was illegal.

Rosa's brown eyes widened. "Taylor, what's happening?"

Taylor's grip tightened on her suitcases. "I need you to trust me, okay?" He swallowed. "Please. Can you do that? Just trust me."

Rosa put a trembling hand on his arm. "Of course I do, honey."

Taylor's gut clenched. He could only hope he was worthy of that trust, but this was his only choice. He pulled out the crystal vial and held it in one hand. With the other, he made a faint turning motion with two fingers. The stopper left the vial and floated in midair.

"What's that?" Rosa asked.

To her human eyes, he'd taken the stopper out normally. That was about to change.

"I'll explain everything in a moment." Taylor took a deep breath. "Please take your sunglasses off for me."

She eyed him, then slipped them off.

Taylor reached telekinetically for the water inside the vial and brought it out in a shimmering ball. It sparkled with a faint, dark purple hue, affected by Aether magic. He felt the magic activating inside the ball of water, took a deep breath, and gently splashed two droplets into Rosa's eyes.

"Oh!" Rosa gasped, rubbing her eyes. "What was that?"

Taylor dropped the water back into the vial. "Water from a faerie well."

"A *what?*"

"You'll see in a moment." Taylor held out his arm. "Hold on. This might feel strange."

Rosa shot him a sideways glance but did as he asked, still clutching her sunglasses. Taylor took a deep breath, adjusted his sweaty hands on the suitcases, and walked through the portal to Avalon.

There was a moment of dizziness as portal magic swept them from one dimension to the other. As Julie had the first time, Rosa squealed, and her grip tightened on Taylor's arm.

"It's okay!" Taylor called. "It's okay."

Solid ground returned under his feet, and Rosa wobbled, nearly wrenching his arm out of its socket. Taylor steadied her. Rosa raised her head, ashen with shock, and her eyes got so wide that he could see the whites.

They were standing in Avalon Plaza, the heart of Avalon Town, from which its six main streets branched like the legs of a dragonfly. Its cobblestones glittered in different colors: warm sandstone, bright amethyst, harsh granite, gleaming diamond. Shops and businesses lined the plaza on all sides. Bright banners hung from every facade, and the music that threaded through the air, light as mist, had a cheerful medieval quality.

Taylor smiled, waiting for wonder to fill Rosa's face as she gazed at the paranormals who went about their business: a centaur ducking his head to step into a nearby barber shop, a naiad with a lyre busking on the street corner, a wereduck in a fluffy white dress waddling down the street with three yellow-haired little boys in a tidy row behind her.

Rosa's eyes locked on a minotaur sitting at a small wrought-iron table outside Meggie's, sipping delicately from a china cup and enjoying a cucumber sandwich with the crusts cut off.

"What is *that*?" she shrieked, pointing.

Taylor let go of the larger suitcase and hastily pushed her arm down. Clearly, Rosa was quite capable of seeing through the Veil. He smiled. "Mom, welcome to our home. Avalon."

Rosa didn't appear to be listening. "Where's my Julia?" she demanded. "Tell me she's not here in this terrifying place!"

Taylor looked around the plaza, wondering if he'd missed something. A Sylthana Elf juggled four fireballs for the amusement of a tiny orc in a stroller. The baby's mom chatted on the phone with a friend, showing off her tusks as she laughed.

"Look at that thing's *teeth*!" Rosa hissed.

Hooves clattered on the sidewalk nearby, and Rosa leaped sideways with a shriek as a contingent of pegasus riders cantered past, each carrying a horse bow and a longsword slung over their backs.

"Those people have weapons!" she wailed. "Where's my Julia? Is she safe?"

"She's…she's safe here," Taylor answered delicately.

"Safe *here*!" Rosa squawked. "Are you telling me that this is where you *live*?"

Taylor swallowed. "Yes."

"How could you bring my baby girl here?" Rosa cried. "How can she survive here without being gobbled up for breakfast by all these…these *creatures*?"

"They're not dangerous, Rosa," Taylor attempted.

"Not dangerous? *Not dangerous?*" Rosa wailed. She pointed. "How can *that* not be dangerous?"

Relief flooded through Taylor when he followed her finger to a leggy, dark-haired Woodland Fae strolling across the plaza, accompanied by an enormous russet-brown wolf. The wolf had a metal foreleg that moved with stilted grace compared to his other limbs.

"It's a bionic wolf thing!" Rosa howled. "How do you know it hasn't eaten my poor Julia?"

"He would never eat her, Mom." Taylor smiled. "He works for her."

Rosa stared at him. "*What?*"

Taylor raised his hand and waved. "Hey, Blake, Ellie! Come on over here."

The wolf looked up, and his long tail wagged. He trotted

toward Rosa, who screamed and grabbed Taylor's arm. Blake stopped and cocked his head to one side, then let out a confused whimper.

Ellie, his Woodland Fae fiancée, put a hand on his shoulder. She smiled with the quiet confidence of a half-para who'd grown up in the human world. "Maybe turn into your humanoid form, babe."

"Oh, right," Blake rumbled.

Rosa stared. "Did it just *talk?*"

Blake's outline stretched, hair and tail receding. His prosthetic shifted with him, metal clattering quietly as it changed from wolf leg to human arm. A second later, he walked toward Rosa on two legs, his brown hair falling over his face as usual, wearing jeans and a button-up shirt in pale gray.

"Mom, this is Blake." Taylor gently tugged Rosa out from behind him. "Blake, Ellie, this is Julie's mom Rosa."

Blake gave a gallant bow and extended a large callused hand. "Nice to meet you, ma'am."

Rosa looked into his soft brown eyes and slowly stretched out an unbelieving hand. Blake shook it with the utmost tenderness.

Taylor privately thanked his lucky stars that they'd run into Blake instead of Teddy or Austin.

"Why don't you tell Rosa a little about what a wonderful leader Julie is?" Taylor asked.

Blake gave Taylor a confused look but obligingly turned to Rosa. "She's really wonderful, ma'am."

"You work for her?" Rosa gasped. "Julie...Julie's in *charge?*"

"Oh, yes, ma'am. Everyone here respects her. I know there are some who don't like her, but it's only because she speaks her mind and she's not afraid to get things done." Blake smiled. "I'd follow her anywhere."

Taylor gave him a fierce look. *Don't talk about dangerous shit!* he willed silently.

"So." Rosa glanced at Taylor. "Those promotions were real."

"Of course they were, ma'am. She's been on a fast track since she joined the OPMA," Blake told her sincerely.

Things were straying into military territory. Taylor grabbed Rosa's arm. "Why don't we get you settled in at the apartment?" he suggested.

"The OPMA? What do you mean?" Rosa demanded.

Blake smiled. "She's a major, ma'am. She's gotten us out of some real nasty situations. Saved our lives a lot of times, too. One time, with an army of dwarves—"

Taylor waved his hands desperately. Blake stuttered to a stop, staring at him.

"An *army*?" Rosa spluttered. "A *major*?" She whipped around and glared at Taylor. "Is Julia in the military?"

Taylor took a deep breath and decided to rip off the Band-Aid. "She's a major in our military, Mom, and she's brilliant. She's saved us from our enemies more times than most of us can remember."

Rosa's eyes narrowed. "These enemies. Are they like *them*?" She jerked a thumb at the bustling plaza full of paras.

Taylor shuffled his feet. "Something like that." He decided it was best not to mention dragons.

Rosa grabbed the front of Taylor's jacket. The movement was so sudden that it made him jump, but she tugged him closer, her face ashen with fury.

"You take me to the leader of this two-bit militia right now," she snarled. "I need to give him a piece of my mind about putting a defenseless human girl on the front line of battles that have nothing to do with her!"

"Um…" Taylor began.

"Defenseless?" Blake burst out laughing.

Taylor and Ellie both glared. Blake immediately stopped laughing.

"Did you hear me, Taylor?" Rosa demanded, giving him a shake. "I want to see him. *Now!*"

She released Taylor, turned on her heel, and strode off across the plaza.

"Taylor, I'm so sorry," Blake began. "I didn't—"

"It's okay. It's not your fault. Talk later," Taylor told him and jogged after Rosa. "Mom. *Mom!* Wait up!"

"Where is he?" Rosa demanded. "Is that him?" She pointed at the minotaur, who was finishing his tea.

"No. But we can go talk to him if you want," Taylor blurted, desperate to appease her. "Just…maybe not right now."

"Why not?" Rosa snarled.

"Because, uh, because we need to drop off your luggage at my apartment first!" Taylor held up the smaller suitcase, his arm trembling with exertion. "We wouldn't want the juice you brought for Julie to go off in the sunshine, would we?"

Rosa relented. "Okay, but I'm not letting it go, do you understand?"

"Of course not. I know you better than that," Taylor soothed.

"A *major!* My baby girl!" Rosa muttered fiercely. "How could anyone allow that?"

"I'll explain everything," Taylor promised.

Rosa snorted. "I think her boss needs to explain! Where is he?"

"We'll go to him. I promise. Let's just get you settled in first, shall we?" Taylor asked.

Rosa sighed. "Well, okay." She frowned. "But what about that phone call you got earlier? What about my Julia? She's in danger?"

Taylor grinned. "Trust me. She's more than capable of holding her own in any fight."

"Even a fight with *these* creatures?" Rosa asked in disbelief.

Taylor freed a hand and laid it on her shoulder. "Of course she is. You raised her, didn't you?"

Rosa's frown vanished, and she grinned.

Taylor held up a hand, and a carriage drawn by two

hippogriffs clattered to a halt beside them. Rosa didn't bat an eye at the gigantic half-horse, half-eagle hybrids as Taylor loaded her luggage inside.

"Magic Way Homes, please," he told the driver, a pixie.

"Sure thing, guv," the pixie replied.

Taylor helped Rosa into the carriage, and after the doors swung shut, she settled back in her seat and pulled out her phone.

"She still hasn't answered my texts," Rosa muttered.

Worry gnawed Taylor's stomach. He pushed it down as well as he could, knowing it wouldn't help.

"Can I ask you something?" he ventured.

"Sure, dear. What is it?" Rosa looked up from her phone.

"Can you see clearly here?" Taylor asked.

Rosa glanced around. "Clear as I ever do, honey. They gave me reading glasses, but I don't need them anymore. I've been taking ginkgo biloba for that. It's a natural antioxidant with amazing properties, and improving eyesight is one of them. Do you want some, dear? I notice you're looking a bit squinty lately." She started digging through her handbag.

The ancient tome in which Taylor had read about the faerie water and the sketchy gnome who'd sold him the vial had both told him the magic would work slowly and to varying degrees, depending on the subject.

"You don't seem all that bothered by the existence of another world," Taylor noted.

Rosa arched an eyebrow. "Bothered? What do you mean?"

"Just that you..." Taylor hesitated, thinking about the aloe vera juice gathering dust in his apartment. "You seem very willing to expand your beliefs."

Rosa chuckled and waved her hand. "Oh, honey, you're silly." She closed her handbag again and held it on her lap, fixing him with an indulgent smile. "Why wouldn't I believe in another world? I saw a miracle with my own eyes when my little Julia came back almost from the dead."

Taylor cocked his head to one side, listening.

"She was a sickly baby when she was born." Rosa smiled, but her eyes were damp. "We stayed in the hospital for weeks, my poor little Julia and me. Her father was a doctor, a trauma doctor, and every time the other doctors told us about her condition, I would watch his face since he knew what they were saying. Every time he would look more worried."

"I'm sorry," Taylor murmured. "That must have been more difficult than I can imagine."

"It was terrible, honey." Rosa dropped her eyes to her hands, clasped tightly on her handbag. "Losing David was awful, but fearing for my baby's life? That was the worst time I can remember." She shivered. "The doctors kept saying there was nothing more they could do, and I was watching my baby waste away. Every time I fed her, she seemed weaker and more floppy, so I looked for other possibilities. Natural things, you know. She was surrounded by tubes and wires and things, so I thought something from nature might help her."

Taylor thought about that aloe vera juice again.

"I gave her homeopathic drops. Easy to get into a tiny baby with no appetite." Rosa's eyes lit up. "And just when we were all sure she wouldn't make it, a miracle happened. They *worked*."

Taylor smiled, trying to hide the sadness curling through his chest. The baby Rosa had given birth to *hadn't* made it. Julie was the fae baby who'd been placed with the Meadows to keep her safe.

"One morning, I went into the NICU, and there she was, all pink and wriggling, looking up at me with those big eyes." Rosa beamed. "We went home two days later. The doctors couldn't explain it, but I could. My homeopathic drops had worked. They gave me back my baby girl." She dabbed her eyes and laughed. "If my baby could come back from near death, then all this? Well, it's nothing. Belief saved my Julia. I've never had trouble believing."

Taylor put a hand on Rosa's knee. Julie and Rosa would have

to work out the truth between them. It wasn't his place, but there *was* something he could say. "You're an amazing mom, Rosa," he told her. "Julie is the way she is because of the way you love her."

"Oh, honey." Rosa laid her hand over his. "What a sweet thing to say."

Taylor met her eyes. "I mean it."

CHAPTER TWENTY-ONE

Julie's mouth tasted like copper. Her cheek was pressed against the muddy earth and smoke filled her lungs, but she couldn't cough. Everything hurt too much.

She tried to move her limbs, but it felt like they were a long way away, and for a horrific moment, Julie thought they were gone. Her eyes snapped open. The first thing she saw was her gauntleted hand, clenched and resting on the mud beside her face. Her fingers twitched.

"Your armor must be inlaid with selenite," Nimue called. Thunder muttered behind her words. "Clever, but it won't take another hit."

Despite the moonlight filtering through the scattered thunderclouds, Julie saw that the crystals in her armor were dull and lifeless. Nimue was right. She forced herself to her hands and knees, then to her feet, and stood swaying on the mud.

The glade was unrecognizable. Brocèliande was burning. The red glow of the flames danced in the puddles of mud that were all that remained of the peaceful streams. Smoke and thunderclouds choked the stars, and huge scars had been ripped in the earth. The grass had been churned into mud. Solid lava had formed shiny black pools all over the glade. Fragments of leaves, still burning and driven by wind, showered down on the glade like glowing bits of fire. Only the stones—the tomb—were untouched.

Nimue hovered in the air, grinning. Soot streaked her face, and each tooth was outlined in blood, but her eyes shone with triumph.

Julie clenched her hands, trying to summon fire. A shower of sparks fell from her fists.

"Didn't know we could command lightning, did you?" Nimue yelled, moving closer.

Julie groped for her powers. She needed full, direct moonlight. The clouds above her responded sluggishly, but she began to push them aside. She had to keep Nimue talking if she was going to buy time.

"Alugon didn't mention it, no," she shouted back. Heat flooded into her palms as moonlight finally reached her.

Nimue chuckled. "Of course he wouldn't. Lightning has been our birthright for centuries, but the Pendragon kings deemed it illegal because it draws on dark magic." She spat on the earth. "Fools that they were."

Julie took slow, measured breaths. She glanced at the vortex above their heads, half-wreathed in smoke. The flashes of blue coming from Hat were only dull pulses now. He was almost invisible, almost lost to the darkness.

Thunder rolled and Nimue raised her hands, her eyes gleaming.

"The time of the Pendragons is over," she hissed.

Julie clenched her fists, and they burst into flame.

Nimue laughed and called the lightning. It crackled through the clouds above her head, blinding white and almost too fast to see. Julie felt its power surging through the sky.

There's no better protection than dragonscale, Morgan had told her. *Powered by a dragon's heart, it can repel even the darkest magic.*

Eglantine! Julie cried out. *Help me!*

Lightning snapped through the sky, and Nimue stretched out a hand. The bolt danced on her fist, and she focused on Julie.

Love and fury surged in Julie's heart, and it wasn't her own. Eglantine had heard her call. Julie felt power surging through the bond as though electric moonlight had drenched her blood. But it wasn't her skin that began to glow silver.

It was the robe.

Lightning flashed. Julie ducked and threw up one arm, drawing the robe over her face before the lightning slammed into her. The impact sent her skidding, but she dug her feet into the mud and stayed upright. She smelled burning hair. For an instant, she saw the lightning crackling through the robe. She felt its dark power like something that wanted to seep into her skin.

No! Julie raged in her heart. *This isn't who I am!*

She stepped forward and let out a scream of effort. Fire enveloped her, and the lightning rebounded.

"Impossible!" Nimue shrieked.

Thunder ripped through the air. Julie lowered her arm as the bolt of lightning, intensified threefold, slashed across the glade and slammed into Nimue's chest. She screamed and fell to her knees. The lightning crackled over her skin, fragments of jagged white light dancing all over her, and she screamed again.

This was Julie's chance to get to Hat.

She leaped into the air and flew toward him, but it was too late. The blue light that flashed from him was so dull it was nearly invisible. His brim was hopelessly frayed, and the tip had been blown away, leaving only tattered, smoking threads.

"Hat!" Julie screamed.

She thought she saw him turn toward her. Then the dark magic swallowed him, and the vortex swelled like it was sated.

Nimue's laugh was a harsh caw. She rose to her feet, her gown hanging in blackened, tattered ribbons. Her skin oozed black. "He was never a match for me!"

"No!" Julie screamed. "Hat! *No!*"

The vortex was pitch-black and sparkled, and there was no sign of Hat.

Julie's wings faltered, and grief flooded her like a physical blow. "Hat!" she sobbed.

She didn't see the pillar of earth coming until it was too late. It slammed into her ribs, brutally forcing the air from her lungs, and she tumbled to the ground. Her wings wouldn't respond. She landed face-first, and skidded through the mud.

There was blood in her mouth. Her ears rang. She dragged her hands underneath her shoulders and forced herself to her hands and knees, then to her feet, gasping desperately for air. Reeling, Julie turned to face Nimue.

"That won't be necessary," the fae hissed. "Stay down."

The ringing in Julie's ears had subsided, and her vision had cleared enough that she could see the glowing ball of magic forming in front of Nimue. She held her hands a foot apart, and between them, something dark crackled and sputtered like it was being caged. It grew slowly, and Nimue grinned.

That's a geas, Julie realized.

Don't be afraid! Eglantine's voice pierced Julie's mind like a brilliant beam of sunlight. *They're coming!*

Julie felt her connection to the unborn dragon open wide. She gasped, clutching her chest as she felt the distant thunder of wings. When she looked up, the skies were so thick with smoke that she could see nothing.

But she knew they were coming.

Julie clenched her fists, ready to ignite them.

"Uh-uh, none of that," Nimue called. "Down, little fae!"

The geas surged forward as a ball of black magic, swift as a shadow. She gasped and stumbled back, trying to escape, but there was nowhere to go.

Brilliant white light shot from Julie's armor. Dazzling beams poured from the selenite crystals inlaid in the steel and the geas flinched, smoke curling from the black cloud where the light struck it.

"You don't have the magic to resist me!" Nimue snarled.

She extended her arms, and black magic poured from her hands, pulsing into the geas. It grew larger, and pressure gathered around Julie's mind. She reached for her power and poured it into the selenite. The white light intensified, but her head began to spin.

"You can't win," Nimue hissed.

Hold on! Eglantine called.

There was a deep chorus of powerful voices rushing through Julie's mind like a flock of birds. *We are coming!* the dragons called. *We are coming, Heirkeeper!*

Just hold on a little longer, Alugon growled. *We are on our way, Julie of the Meadows.*

Dizziness swamped Julie and she staggered, gasping for breath. The white light from her armor flickered.

"That's it," Nimue growled. "Just let it take hold."

The geas felt physical, like it was forcing her down. She fell to one knee, pressing a fist into the mud to keep from falling on her face. The dragons were coming, but they wouldn't be here in time. She couldn't keep this geas at bay for much longer.

"Yes," Nimue crowed. "You're mine now, little fae!"

The pressure of the geas was steady, but the ropes of black magic pouring from Nimue's hands had grown thinner.

She thought she was winning.

I need to buy time. Julie smothered a grin. *And I know exactly how.*

How? Eglantine cried.

By letting baddies do what baddies do best. Julie's eyes narrowed. *Monologue.*

She inhaled, ribs aching, and spoke as loud as she could. "Why would you do this?" She sobbed dramatically. When Hat didn't comment on her overacting, the weight in her chest grew.

Nimue sneered, but it was working. Only wisps of black magic oozed from her hands to the geas.

"The fact that you have to ask only proves how little you know. How *pathetic* you are," Nimue spat. "Why would I not?"

Julie hung her head and sank down on both knees. Her tired limbs trembled, and the geas grew heavier. Her head was still spinning.

"You all talk about freedom and unity." Nimue shook her head. "As though there's any world in which those two things aren't mutually exclusive. Nobody *wants* to work together. Everyone wants what's best for *them*." Her eyes glittered. "But only a few of us have the balls to go out and get it."

"Mordred," Julie wheezed, her vision blurring. "Mordred was what you wanted."

"Don't let the name of my beloved into your filthy mouth," Nimue hissed. "My king has a vision of peace for all dimensions. Look at your precious human world. Look how it's always tearing itself apart, how there are *always* wars. Humans aren't meant to rule themselves. They're meant to *be* ruled. We hide like we don't have the power to hold the entire Earth under our command."

Julie wanted to rail against her, but she reminded herself to keep buying time. "Peace in slavery."

"You could call it that." Nimue shrugged. "It's still peace. Paras are more like humans than they like to admit. Both are happiest with someone else calling the shots. With my geasa, I have freed them from the chains of responsibility for their choices." She took a step nearer. "Soon you, too, will feel that freedom."

The rustle of scales in the dark night. The hiss of wings against the stars. Julie felt them as the dragons grew nearer.

"I've grown in power with every soul under my command." Nimue's smile glittered like a drawn blade in the firelight. "You'll be one of the most powerful yet. Thanks to you, I'm close to accumulating the power I need to free my love from the eternal punishment he was so unjustly given."

Cold fear curled in Julie's belly. She slammed her other fist into the mud in genuine weakness. The geas felt like it would pin her to the ground and overcome her. She knew that if her face hit the dirt, it would be over.

"That's right." Nimue chuckled. "I have you now. Your armor might still be glowing, but you and I both know you're *mine*."

Julie's vision darkened, but in her mind, she saw a dark forest spread out below her as she flapped her massive wings, surrounded by her brethren, scales shimmering in the moonlight. She saw a plume of smoke on the horizon. She was looking through Alugon's eyes, and he was close.

"You will never escape," Nimue hissed. "You may think your friend's little machine can conquer my magic, but you're wrong. They call it the Breaker, don't they?" Her face was twisted, almost unrecognizable in the flickers of black magic and the fierce fire-light. "*I* am the Breaker, and you are mine now."

She lowered her hands, and the geas snapped and crackled over Julie's head. Nimue smirked.

The dragons were close enough that Julie could feel their power. No, *Eglantine's* power. As the dragons grew nearer, Julie's connection with Eglantine strengthened, and dragon magic flooded her veins.

She clenched her fists.

"Bring out the portal device that will take you to the heart of Tintagel." Nimue spoke calmly. "It's time I paid the old king a visit."

Fear clutched Julie's chest like a cold hand. Were the dragons close enough? Could she refuse, or should she stall?

Nimue's eyes narrowed. "I *said*, bring out the portal device!"

Julie reached into the pocket of her dragonscale robe. As always, the little round device rested there. Right beside it, she felt something small and soft, like a tangled cobweb.

The binding spell.

"Come on," Nimue snapped. "I'm ready to finish this."

Julie could hear the distant rustle of dragon wings. Through Alugon's eyes, she saw nothing but smoke. *We can't see you,* he rumbled. *We need a target.*

She grinned. *I can arrange that.*

"Why aren't you doing as I say?" Nimue ranted.

"Yeah, well." Julie raised her head and smiled. "What can I say? I've never been one for following orders."

She rose to her feet, and her magic surged. Bolts of white light sprang from the selenite in her armor and wrapped around the geas, trapping it. It sputtered and fizzled.

"*No!*" Nimue shrieked. Her face twisted with fury, and black magic oozed from her hands and feet.

Julie crossed her arms over her chest, and fire roared over her fists.

"Breaker?" She scoffed. "You're nothing but a hag."

Nimue lost her shit. The fae screeched, a sound that tore Julie's ears like giant fingernails down a resonant blackboard. Dark energy poured from her open mouth, then shot from her skin, black lightning crackling around her.

The geas above Julie's head grew heavier. Her flames guttered and she stumbled, the pressure almost crushing her.

"My power is beyond your imagination!" Nimue shrieked. "Look at me!"

A bolt of black magic burst from Nimue and surged into the sky, blowing a hole in the clouds of smoke.

Panting with pain and effort, Julie smirked. "Yeah, we're looking at you."

Nimue stared at her. "*We?*"

Alugon burst through the smoke, the firelight brilliant on his scales, his maw wide open. Julie staggered back a step. The forest fire flared around her, fed by the wind from the dragon's wings, and Alugon spat a waterfall of dragonfire onto Nimue.

Nimue screamed, lost in a cloud of fire.

Julie's heart hammered as Alugon swooped over her. A massive white dragon was close behind him. She opened her jaws and breathed blue flames. Then more dragons were pouring fire onto Nimue, and the fae's screams echoed through the glade.

Julie pulled her robe around her. If she jumped into the stream, would she be safe?

You are *safe, Julie.* Eglantine laughed. *Dragonfire can't hurt you.*

It can't? Julie gasped. *Not even where the robe doesn't cover me?*

No. You are dragon-bonded. Eglantine's tone hardened. *You can't be harmed by dragonfire, but Nimue can.*

Julie let her hands fall to her sides. The vortex of black magic that had swallowed Hat still swirled around her. If she wanted to save him, she needed to stop Nimue.

"For Merlin," she whispered and strode forward.

The dragons continued to spit fire at Nimue. Hands blazing, Julie squared her shoulders, ignored her thundering heart, and strode into the pool of flames consuming the glade. A tongue of red fire splashed toward her. She hesitated, but it played lightly over her hands and face, tickling like her flames.

Her steps quickened. She strode to the thickest part of the flames and found Nimue at the center. Her head was thrown back and she screamed, arms straining sideways. Dark magic swirled around her like blood in water. Wherever the flames touched, her skin bubbled. Then black magic bled from it, repairing the damage.

Even so, Nimue was barely holding on. The fae fell to her knees, still screaming. There was no sign of the breathtaking woman who'd first greeted Julie. Her dress was gone, replaced by bloody rags that barely clung to her body. There was no sign of that burnished skin. Nimue's body was doughy and misshapen, covered in hairy growths, her ribs standing out like hoops.

"Nimue!" Julie yelled.

The fae turned her face toward Julie. The eyes were as gray as those of a dead fish, her toothless mouth was a black, puckered hole in her face, and thin wisps of gray hair whipped around her head in the midst of the flames.

Julie recoiled. "He was right. You really *are* a hag."

Nimue sneered, but another cloud of dragonfire surrounded her. It was as light as a playful kiss on Julie's skin. Nimue screamed, and more dark magic bled from her as she fell to her hands and knees.

Al, that's enough, Julie called.

Understood, Alugon confirmed.

The dragonfire stopped coming. Julie took a deep breath, focusing on the pent-up rage that snarled in her belly, and reached for the flames that surrounded Nimue. They weren't hers, but they obeyed. They fell back, leaving the hag panting and trembling, half-naked in a circle of soot and ash.

Julie pulled out the binding spell.

"You cannot win," the hag hissed. "You cannot stand against him. He will become the ruler of this world and all worlds, and —" She was fumbling in her rags for something.

Julie saw the flash of a crystal amulet and swooped in. She snatched the self-immolation amulet from Nimue's weak, shaky hand and dropped it into the pocket of her fireproof dragonscale robe. "Nuh-uh. You are *not* doing that right now."

Nimue bared her teeth. "Imbecile! Fool! You shall not—"

"Kiss my ass, bitch," Julie snapped and tossed the binding spell at her. The ball unraveled into a net of gleaming silver threads and enveloped Nimue, and she collapsed to the ground, unconscious.

Julie looked up as a blue-scaled dragon swooped over the forest, a river of water frothing from his open jaws onto the flames. The flames began to die, and the smoke cleared. The glade was a black husk. Nothing lived there except Julie and the motionless hag.

Julie turned to the vortex of dark magic still swirling over the stones of Le Tombeau de Viviane, but before she could move, the air fizzled a few hundred feet away, and a portal opened with a dull crackle.

There was a familiar roar—the sound of three hundred seventy-five horses thundering together. Genevieve plunged through the portal, headlights glowing, black and pewter paint gleaming in the firelight. Mud spun from her tires as she charged into the glade.

"Go, go, go!" Kaplan's voice yelled.

More portals opened around the glade, and a three-hundred-pound tiger plunged through the nearest one, jaws wide. The roar that emerged from behind his yellow fangs shook the earth. Bianca followed him, bandaged wings wide and hands glowing with red magic.

Griffins poured through the portals, weapons at the ready, solid and reassuring in their navy uniforms. They surrounded Julie and fanned out through the glade, looking for something to fight. Kaplan led them, muscles rippling under his striped coat, and Bianca swooped over to Julie.

"You okay, girl?" she yelled.

Julie grinned and gave her a gauntleted thumbs-up.

More paras stormed out of the portal in uniforms Julie didn't recognize: black suits with obsidian body armor decorated with swirling moon and star shapes in bright gold. She watched with interest as they spread out around the glade.

"Come on, you." Julie bent and grabbed a fistful of the Gleipnir steel, hauling Nimue to her feet. The hag groaned. "You've got somewhere to be."

She half-supported, half-dragged Nimue to Kaplan, who was in the middle of the glade. Every hair on his body stood upright, making him look twice his already considerable size, and his tail lashed his flanks.

"Hey, Captain!" Julie called.

The tiger whipped around to face her. In the reflection of his huge eyes, Julie saw that she was glowing. Moonlight and flames poured from her body. The power made her hands shake.

"*Meadows?*" Kaplan growled.

Julie threw Nimue down at his paws. "Thanks for the backup, sir, but I had it handled."

Kaplan's amber eyes narrowed, and his coat settled. "Why am I not surprised?" he grumbled. "Is that..."

"Yes, sir." Julie folded her arms. "This is Nimue."

Kaplan transformed and stood over her in human form. He prodded Nimue with a toe and yowled in the depths of his throat, then eyed Julie.

Julie's stomach swooped. She was still wearing her knight outfit.

"We're going to have a conversation about this, Meadows," Kaplan growled. "As soon as Nimue has been drained of all of her magic," he added louder, "and sent to the prison realm."

Nimue could only summon a faint groan.

"Take her away," Kaplan growled.

Two of the black-and-gold-uniformed paras, both Aether Elves, strode up to Nimue. They levitated her into the air and strode toward the nearest portal.

CHAPTER TWENTY-TWO

Julie didn't watch the elves take Nimue through the portal. She bolted back to the last place she'd seen Hat.

She'd thought the black magic would end when Nimue was bound, but as her boots squelched in the mixture of mud and ash, the vortex still swirled as it had done before.

"Hat!" Julie called. She stumbled to a halt beneath the vortex, cupped her hands around her mouth, and yelled as loud as she could. *"Hat!"* Her throat ached with her scream, but there was no response.

Her hands were shaking. *Hat, come on!* she cried in her mind. *Talk to me. Say something! Merlin! Emrys!*

That snarky British voice didn't speak.

Nausea boiled in Julie's gut. She fell to her knees, mud seeping onto her skin, her face tilted toward the vortex. The clouds of smoke had all but dissipated as the dragons continued to extinguish the forest fire, and moonlight poured onto her skin.

A sob choked her. *Hat, please, come back to me. I don't care what form you take. I just need you back.*

She bowed her head and raised both hands toward the vortex. Moonlight surged within her, growing stronger with the force of love that pounded in her chest. It flowed from her glowing skin, wisps of silver light coalescing into a ball of liquid magic.

Please, she whispered. *You're my friend.*

Bolts of light shot from the shining silver ball. They pierced the vortex, and Julie thought it slowed down.

"Hat! *Merlin.* Whoever you are. Come back to me!" Julie sobbed again. More magic pulsed from her fingertips and beamed into the vortex. "Emrys. Come to me. Please!"

Hot tears coursed down her cheeks, and the magic's glow intensified. Blinded by the light and her grief, Julie closed her eyes. Spasms gripped her. It took a few seconds before she could yell the words that rose in her throat.

"Merlinus Ambrosius, get your star-spangled ass back here!"

There was a dull boom, and the light seeping from her fingertips became twin beams of brilliance. They punched into the vortex and it exploded, torn apart from the inside by her lunar magic. The shockwave knocked Julie on her ass, and her hands plunged into the cold mud. There was a flash of silver light, and then the sky was empty above her except for the distant stars.

Julie's heart turned to ice.

Then she caught a glimpse of something small and floppy falling. With a faint *thwap*, a piece of scorched fabric struck Julie's lap.

She clutched it. "Hat?"

He was in his wizard's hat form, the brim still frayed, the tip still missing. Black scorch marks covered his insignias, and he drooped in her hands.

Hello, Julie, he whispered.

Hat! Julie cried. She held him close, pressing her face into the fabric, which smelled of smoke. *Hat, I was so scared.*

I wasn't. Not a bit. Hat scoffed.

Julie laughed, tears seeping into his crown. *Sure, you weren't.*

Of course not. Hat chuckled softly. *I knew you had my back.*

Always, Julie promised. She lowered him into her lap, staring. *Are you okay?*

As she watched, Hat repaired himself. The frayed brim knitted together. Threads wove themselves to replace his point, and he straightened, the scorch marks fading.

I'm fine, he assured her.

Julie held him up by the brim. *The spell was supposed to reveal your true form or destroy you. Why are you still a hat?*

That's just it, Julie. It was meant to reveal my true *form, not my* original *form. There's a difference.* Hat's brim curved in a smile. *I've always told you that who you really are is up to you. I'm still your Hat.*

Julie buried her face in him and cried. They were tears of joy, but she didn't have to explain that to Hat. He knew.

A heavy hand landed on her shoulder. "Meadows," Kaplan growled. "It's time to go."

When Julie stepped through the portal into the Avalon HQ, the portal room was chaotic. Griffins, officers, guards, and dudes in the black and gold armor seemed to be everywhere, milling through the room, shouting and gesturing.

The dudes in the black and gold armor are the High Magic Division, Hat explained. He was a helmet again, tucked under her arm.

Julie grinned. *I missed that.*

We were separated for, what, an hour? Hat pointed out.

Still missed you. Julie raised her voice. "Clear a path!" she shouted. "The prisoner's coming through!"

The room fell silent, and a path opened to the door. Every eye was on the portal.

They've all gathered to see Nimue brought in, Hat told her.

Two members of the High Magic Division pushed through the portal, followed by Nimue. The hag's reddened eyes darted around. She was still draped in the binding spell and shuffled under its weight, and her hands were cuffed with magic-nulling bonds that glowed with blue runes. A third High Magic soldier walked beside her—a Starlight Fae with one hand clenched by her side, leaking wisps of white magic.

"There's no escape now, Nimue," Julie growled.

The hag glared at her and opened her mouth to shout.

"None of that," the Starlight Fae snapped, clenching her fist tighter.

Nimue's lips were pinned together like they'd been sealed with glue. Her eyes burned, but another soldier in black and gold stepped through the portal behind her and gave her a light push. "Move along."

Nimue shuffled forward, followed by more Griffins, then Bianca and Kaplan. The crowd of OPMA personnel closed behind her. Paras were shaking hands, grinning, and thumping each other on the back.

"As if they were the ones who captured her," Kaplan growled. He'd halted beside her.

Julie shrugged. "I'm just glad we got her, sir."

Kaplan nodded. "Her magic is nulled now, Meadows, and it'll be drained soon. She'll be under constant supervision until she's banished."

Julie was pretty sure the hag wasn't going anywhere this time. Relaxation made her shoulders slump, and she realized how much her body ached. When she reached up to wipe a bead of sweat off her brow, her hand came back bloody. She'd taken more of a beating than she'd realized. Her wings folded flat against her back.

Are you okay? Hat asked.

Tired and sore, Julie admitted, *but nothing a long bath and a big hug from Taylor won't fix.* She looked around. *Is he here?*

She scanned the crowd and spotted him a moment later, trying to shuffle politely through a tight-knit group of disappointed Griffins who hadn't gotten the chance to see the epic battle they'd expected. He was tapping an orc on the shoulder, trying to get him to move.

Julie turned toward him and opened her mouth to call his name, but a familiar voice cut through the hubbub.

"*Juliaaaaaaaaaaaa!*"

Julie's stomach fell to her boots. "*Mom?*" she squawked.

The orc stumbled forward, shoved aside by the curvy woman. Rosa burst through the crowd of paranormals, a wide grin splitting her face and her brown eyes sparkling.

"What the..." Julie and Kaplan blurted in unison.

"My baby!" Rosa cried and disappeared behind two centaurs as they clattered across the room.

Julie's toes curled. "Sir—" she began, turning to Kaplan.

He held up his hand. "My office."

"*Julia!*" Rosa yelled.

Kaplan cringed. "As soon as you've dealt with... Who is that woman?"

Julie sighed. "My mom, sir."

Kaplan raised his bushy eyebrows. "You have twenty minutes." He folded his massive arms, biceps bulging like boulders within his uniform. "Then I want explanations as to why your *human* mother is here in Avalon and why you saw fit to take up moonlighting as a vigilante."

The weretiger turned on his heel and stalked away, and Julie turned back to the commotion. "Trust me, sir," she muttered, "I'd like to know the answer to that first question too."

Rosa elbowed her way between the two centaurs and bounded across the floor to Julie, her curls bobbing wildly.

"Oh, Julia, my sweet, sweet baby!" she shouted in a room full of Julie's colleagues.

"Mom!" Julie protested.

Rosa flung her arms around Julie's waist and pulled her into a tight embrace. "You're all beaten up, you poor thing!".

Julie could feel every gaze in the room on her. When she

looked up, Taylor was standing a few feet away, grimacing. "Sorry, babe," he mouthed.

"My precious baby girl, trapped in this world full of creatures!" Rosa wailed.

"Mom. *Mom!*" Julie placed her hands on Rosa's shoulders and gently pried herself free. "I'm okay."

"You're bleeding!" Rosa cried.

"It's nothing. It'll be fixed in a minute." Julie took Rosa's hands. "I'm fine, I promise."

Rosa stared at her, bewildered, then took in the armor. "Julia, honey, they're saying you're in the military and that you're a major. I-I don't know what to think."

"I know it's a lot, Mom, but I can't explain right now." Julie squeezed her hands. "I need to go talk to the captain."

"That big man who was with you? He looks awful!" Rosa scowled. "Is *he* the one who's been sending you into battles in this crazy place?"

"Sort of," Julie admitted.

Rosa's eyes narrowed. "Then I'm coming with you. I need to give him a piece of my mind!"

"Mom! No. Seriously. Kaplan's cool. He's just scary to look at, that's all. He's a good guy." Julie glanced over her shoulder. "I want to explain everything, and I will, but I really need you to give me a few minutes."

"We'll wait right here for her, Rosa." Taylor put a hand on his new mother's shoulder.

Julie met his eyes and shrugged. *What were you thinking?* she hissed through their telepathic connection via Hat.

Taylor's face fell. *It was time.*

Time? What's that supposed to mean? Julie raged.

Taylor's eyes were pleading. *Trust me.*

The expression on his face made Julie pause. *I do trust you.*

Taylor's smile returned, and his shoulders relaxed.

"I don't think you should go alone, honey." Rosa's eyes filled with tears. "I don't understand how you've been coping in this world. You don't belong here, baby."

"Mom..." Julie took a deep breath, her hands tightening on Rosa's. Doubt almost overwhelmed her, but the love in her mother's eyes crushed it, and she knew what she needed to do. "Actually, I *do* belong here."

Rosa's eyes widened. Julie stepped back, allowed her hands to fall by her sides, and opened her wings. They were slender and dragonfly-like, patterned with shining silver veins, and gave off a pale glow.

Rosa's hands flew to her mouth. She stared at Julie, tears gathering in her eyes, and Julie's heart fell. *Have I hurt her?*

Then Rosa lowered her hands. She was smiling despite the tears that shimmered on her cheeks. "Oh!"

"I love you, Mom." Julie stepped closer and kissed her forehead. "And I'll see you later."

"Go, babe." Taylor grasped Rosa's arm. "I love you."

"Love you," Julie called over her shoulder as she hurried through the portal to the NYHQ.

Julie gritted her teeth as she jogged out of the NYHQ portal room and headed for the elevator. *Out of the frying pan, into the fire,* she muttered.

Oh, don't be such a drama queen, Hat chided. *You're hardly getting burned, either with your mother or with Kaplan.*

I wouldn't be so sure. Julie's stomach knotted as she stepped into the elevator and hit the button for the third floor. *I've just revealed to my mom that I'm not biologically hers, and Kaplan now knows I'm the Knight. He's going to lose his shit.*

You just fought Nimue. I think you can handle this, Hat told her.

Julie tapped her foot as the elevator rose. *Have you* seen *Kaplan when he's angry?*

Valid, Hat acknowledged. *What are you going to say?*

I guess I'll find out when I say it, Julie muttered.

The elevator doors slid open, and Julie stepped into the recruitment office in which she and Taylor had worked for so many happy months when she first discovered the paranormal world. As always, she paused for a moment, taking in the cubicles and the hum of phones and the paranormals huddled over their computers, searching for more soldiers to help put an end to the war. She'd been scared shitless the first time she'd had to go into Kaplan's office, and that was *before* she'd known that he could transform into a Bengal tiger at will.

Her hands trembled as she strode across the floor, drawing wide-eyed glances as her armor clanked and her dragonscale robe rustled. She knocked on Kaplan's door with a gauntleted hand.

"Come in," the weretiger growled.

Julie stepped inside. Kaplan glanced at his watch. "A minute to spare." He raised an eyebrow. "Impressive. Sit."

Julie perched on one of the armchairs, balancing Hat on her lap.

"Meadows—" Kaplan began.

"Sir, wait." Julie squared her shoulders. "Let me speak."

Kaplan's eyes narrowed. "Do I have a choice?"

Julie took a deep breath. "I know what I did as the Knight was illegal—"

"*Illegal?*" Kaplan's hairy eyebrows butted heads. "I could have you *court-martialed.*"

"Maybe it was crazy." Julie raised her chin. "But I saw a gap where the system was letting paras down, and I took care of it. Don't get me wrong, sir. I believe in the system. I'm *part* of the system, but it's never been perfect, and when the system fails, we have to stand up and do something. That's what I did as the Knight, sir.

"I was breaking the rules, but I was also saving lives. You can't deny that the Knight did more than just rescue some paras from gangsters. The Knight made paras believe in goodness and trust the Eternity Throne again at a time when they could easily have turned to the other side."

Kaplan's eyebrows were making out in the middle of his forehead. "It was foolish," he growled. "Impetuous."

"You got me there, sir." Julie shrugged. "But I don't regret a thing I've done as the Knight."

Kaplan sat back in his chair, steepled his fingers, and studied her. "You're not wrong, Meadows." He grunted. "The Knight *was* helpful. We can cover up the fact that the Knight was a PMA officer gone rogue, and you can avoid a court-martial."

Julie let out a breath. "That's good news, sir."

"As long as you hang up your cloak and no one ever hears from the Knight again," Kaplan finished.

Julie sat back in her chair. "You want me to stop helping paras as the Knight?"

"That's what I said," Kaplan snarled. "And that's before I get into the implications of you bringing your *mother* to Avalon. How did she get here?"

I'm pretty sure Taylor brought her, but I'm not throwing him under the bus, Julie muttered inwardly.

Agreed, Hat told her.

Julie shrugged, holding Kaplan's gaze.

The silence hung over them, then Julie leaned forward, rested her elbows on the desk, and met Kaplan's eyes.

"Sir, I know I've broken the rules." She kept her tone steady. "And I know it might get politically uncomfortable if my identity as the Knight gets out, but I'm not going to quit. I'm here to help paras any way I can, and where my reach as an officer of OPMA doesn't go far enough, the Knight is my only means of going farther. Give up one of the most important ways I have of making a difference?" Julie shook her head. "Respectfully, sir, I don't think so."

Kaplan leaned back in his chair, arms folded. His face was blank. Even his eyebrows drooped, and no matter how long Julie stared into his burning amber eyes, she couldn't make out what he was thinking.

She cringed in her chair, waiting for him to explode. The seconds slid past, slimy on her skin, and the silence stretched and stretched.

Kaplan lowered his head and let out a long breath. When he looked up, he was smiling, and it didn't show any of his teeth. It held both sorrow and pride.

"I accept your refusal to give up being the Knight as your resignation." His hands fell into his lap. "I will give you an honorable discharge from the Para-Military Agency."

Julie's heart froze. "*What?*"

Kaplan reached over the desk and rested a massive hand on Julie's. It was softer than she'd imagined, like the paw of a giant cat. "You've outgrown the OPMA, Meadows. It's time for you to move on."

Julie stared around the office, flabbergasted. This was the office in which it had all started. She had been sitting here, staring out this large window, when she'd first laid eyes on dwarves and orcs.

Kaplan's eyes were distant as though he too was reliving that moment. "The first day I met you, I told you that you were complicating everything." He chuckled. "I had no idea how right I was."

Julie felt as though her chest was being squeezed by a giant fist. "But sir, what will I do? Where will I go?"

"To the Eternity Palace, Julie." Kaplan pronounced her first name with the edge of a tiger growl in it. She hadn't often heard him say it, but she liked it. "The queen has requested your service. I've been searching for a reason to keep you under my command." His smile *was* sad. "But I now see I would only be holding you back."

Julie's eyes stung. "So, I'm not part of the OPMA anymore?"

Kaplan opened his mouth, but no sound came out. He closed it and shook his head.

Julie leaped out of her chair, rushed around his desk, and threw her arms around the burly weretiger. He was far more huggable than she'd envisioned. She buried her face in the broad, muscular chest and tried to hold back her tears.

"Thank you for everything, Jack," she choked out. "For believing in me, for pushing me, and for having my back every time it looked like I was crazy."

Kaplan's arms settled around her, his voice husky with emotion. "It's been my honor." His embrace tightened. "Keep doing great things, Julie."

Julie closed Genevieve's trunk gently. *That's everything.*

At least you can stay at Taylor's apartment until you figure things out with the palace, Hat reminded her.

I guess. Julie sighed as she walked around to the driver's side. *First I need to figure out why Mom is here and how she can see through the Veil.* She stretched, sore muscles protesting. *At least I got to take a shower while they were processing my paperwork.*

She stood by the driver's door and gazed around the inner ward of the Avalon HQ, the battlements standing out sharply against the sunset. The huge space was empty and silent at this time in the evening. Nothing stirred on the broad stone floor. The only sound was the clopping of hooves as a pair of satyrs patrolled the walls.

Julie stared up at the larger-than-life OPMA banner that hung over the main doors and saluted.

Kaplan's right, you know, Hat murmured. *You have outgrown the OPMA. You're going to do great things in the Eternal Palace.*

It feels right, Julie admitted. *But also hard.*

Hat laughed softly. *Right things often are.*

She wiped away a tear and glanced around the courtyard one more time. *I just don't understand why none of my OPMA friends came to talk to me while I was doing my paperwork. I thought at least my unit would see me off.* She shook herself. *Maybe I'm just tired and overreacting.*

Hat said nothing. Not in the mood for his cryptic silence, Julie got into Genevieve and turned the key, and the V8 Cobrajet rumbled to life. She drove under the portcullis and threaded her way through the streets of Avalon to Taylor's apartment building. Genevieve was purring happily, but Julie couldn't relax and enjoy the Mustang's power the way she normally did.

Why would Taylor drag Mom into Avalon now? she wondered. She couldn't stop thinking about the look in his eyes. He had a reason, a major reason, but Julie couldn't imagine what it was. Thinking about the possibilities made her blood run cold. Maybe her mother was sick.

That made her feel nauseous. She threw Genevieve into a parking space in front of the understated glass and granite building, then jogged through the revolving door into the lobby. The elevator ride seemed to take an age, and Julie fidgeted, heart hammering.

Finally, she ran down the hallway and hammered on Taylor's door. "It's me, babe," she called and pushed it open.

A cloud of blue butterflies burst through the door, their wings rustling as they fluttered past Julie, soft as a breath where they brushed her skin. She gasped and stepped back, and the cloud of butterflies swooped past her into the hallway, turned, and flew back again, wrapping her in a soft blue cloud.

Julie's hands flew to her mouth. Her eyes followed the butterflies back into the apartment, which was filled with light. Will o' the wisps in delicate glass orbs drifted near the ceiling, their silver glow complementing the warmer light of the fireflies that clustered on every surface.

Flowers spilled everywhere. Jasmine crept up the walls, its sweet fragrance filling the room. Hibiscus and plumeria bloomed on either side of the big window that overlooked Avalon Town, and the floor was carpeted in daisies.

"Hello, honey." Rosa laughed. "Do you like it?"

Julie dragged her eyes away from the decorations and realized that *everyone* was gathered in the apartment. They were all crowded in the living room, beaming at her. Malcolm and Cassidy and Julius Nox and Gerald Perkins, with Pookie sitting at Malcolm's feet and Fluffy—several pounds lighter and wearing a pink bow in his fur—in Cassidy's arms. Fred Orloffson and Victor Barkhands, the gate guards of the NYHQ and the Aether Compound. Ellie and Blake. Iris and Dr. Olena. Julie's old unit, including the faerie, perched on Raven's shoulder. Horusiris sat in front of a small portal that offered her a glimpse of Eglantine, moonlight oozing joyously through the egg's shell. Kaplan, standing near the back and grinning like a pumpkin. Cironeous Achilleos the centaur in his Stetson, Randkluft the yeti, Yondal Mackintosh, and Ilsa and Amaryl Woodskin. Bianca had a large glass of red wine in each hand, and Bacchus was beside her. Droppelheimer and Alugon were near the plates of finger food on the coffee table. Derek Adamos, the mighty minotaur, and Shulme. Emmeline, Doris and Vlad. Livius, grinning hugely, and Axl beside him with his mouth full. Rosa, hands clasped under her chin, her eyes shining.

Front and center, there was Taylor.

He wore a shimmering emerald-green suit as easily as his skin. His eyes were huge as they rested on her. She was wearing a PMA sweatsuit, but he was looking at her like she'd fallen from the stars.

"Taylor?" Julie croaked.

No one said anything. The only sound was the gentle throb of music playing in the background. Human music, Julie realized. Her favorite album.

Taylor crossed the floor in one movement and wrapped his hands around hers. "You must allow me to tell you how ardently I admire and love you."

Julie blinked. "What?"

"You once said those were the most romantic words in literature." Taylor smiled.

Julie looked past him at Rosa, the only person who knew about her *Pride and Prejudice* obsession. Her mother's eyes were misty.

"I didn't know how else to begin. Where else to begin." Taylor took a deep breath, his thumbs lightly brushing the backs of her hands. "I'm well aware that telling you what you *must* do never ends well for anyone."

There was a soft ripple of laughter from their gathered friends, but Julie couldn't drag her eyes away from Taylor. The look on his face was more certain and fiercer than any she'd ever seen there.

"As for the fact that I admire and love you, well, if I've done you any justice as your boyfriend, you know I do." Taylor was breathless. "The word that really struck me in that line was 'ardently.' Ardent means burning or glowing. You...you're the most ardent being I've ever come across, Julie. You're like a blazing flame. To your enemies, you're a consuming firestorm. To a world at war, you're a lighthouse beacon. To me..." He swallowed. "You've always been the place where I can come to warm my hands."

"Taylor," Julie croaked.

"Let me finish." Taylor gave her hands a light squeeze, his voice hoarse with sincerity. "You brought light, warmth, and purpose into my world, and you made me more of the person I want to be. You are a bright flame, so it only makes sense that you should be ardently loved. If you'll give me the chance, that's how I want to love you for the rest of my life. With a love that consumes and protects but also warms and shelters. I want to be the place where you can come in out of the cold forever."

"Honey." Julie stared up at him, aware of her heart fluttering like a firebird in her chest. "What is this?"

His eyes shone with tears, but he was smiling, and there was nothing in the entire world except for him: her petrichor prince with the crinkles in the corners of his eyes and the soft waves of his hair.

"Julie Meadows," he whispered and sank to one knee. One hand disappeared into the pocket of his jacket, and he pulled out a small square box.

Julie let out a strangled unromantic squawk and clapped her hands over her mouth.

Taylor opened the box. The ring was a moonstone carved into the shape of a rampant dragon.

"Will you marry me?"

AUTHOR NOTES RENÉE JAGGÉR
WRITTEN AUGUST 2, 2023

Thank you for reading through to the back of book ten. I appreciate you so much!

As I write, the US is coming out of the worst heat wave in forever. Arizona is particularly bad. People are getting burned when they fall and touch the sidewalk in Phoenix. Wow!

Fortunately, I live at a higher elevation. It's not cool here, but it's not nearly as bad as the southern part of the state. It only hit 113 one day! Yesterday, it was down to 97, and the monsoon rains hit with a vengeance. It was delightful.

My mother is visiting (not me, Jo), and when we went out to have coffee under the awning this morning, and it rained on us. Normally it rains in the afternoon, but this time we were pelted with big, fat drops at 10am. I have become one with living here since I enjoyed getting wet! We did go in when the drops started splashing coffee out of the cups, though.

New things in my life:

I have gotten the bug for canning now! I bought a kettle and everything. Last night, I canned watermelon rinds (kinda taste like crunchy, spicy apple butter), dill pickles, and red onions. Today I will do some bread and butter pickles and eggs. Everyone tells me pickled eggs are great, so I will try them. Did you know that bread and butter pickles are called that because housewives used to trade them to grocers for bread and butter during the Great Depression? Me either.

I am also obsessed with seeing another Starlink satellite train. I saw one by accident and thought it was aliens. If you haven't seen one, or heard of them, check it out. https://www.space.com/starlink-satellite-train-how-to-see-and-track-it

I and the friends I was with, drinking wine while gazing at the night sky tried to figure out what it was. I thought it looked like Santa's sleigh was being pushed by about forty reindeer. They insist it was aliens. I wish it was. New material for books!

I am enjoying the way this series is evolving, which, as some of you might know, a writer doesn't always control. Julie and Taylor have minds of their own. I loved writing the proposal. I want one like that! I hope you're enjoying these as much as I am enjoying writing them.

Until we speak again, I hope your skies are sunny and your days are filled with happiness and good books!

Renée

BOOKS FROM RENÉE

Para-Military Recruiter
(with Michael Anderle)
Drafted (Book 1)
Recruiter (Book 2)
Accepted (Book 3)
Lead (Book 4)
Recruited (Book 5)
Soldier (Book 6)
Tactical (Book 7)
Officer (Book 8)
Leader (Book 9)
Victor (Book 10)
Appointed (Book 11)

Piercing the Veil
Dangerous Opportunities (Book 1)
Dangerous Responsibilities (Book 2)
Decisions To Make (Book 3)

Reincarnation of the Morrigan

Birth of a Goddess (Book One)
The Way of Wisdom (Book Two)
Angelic Death (Book Three)
A Cold War (Book Four)
A Battle Tune (Book Five)
Broken Ice (Book Six)
A Torn Veil (Book Seven)
Sins of the Past (Book Eight)
The Wild Hunt Comes (*Book Nine*)

The WereWitch Series
Bad Attitude (Book One)
A Bit Aggressive (Book Two)
Too Much Magic (Book Three)
Were War (Book Four)
Were Rages (Book Five)
God Ender (Book Six)
God Trials (Book Seven)
The Troll Solution (Book Eight)
Winner Takes All (Book Nine)

Callie Hart Series
Thin Ice (Book One)
Cold Blood (Book Two)
Feelings Run Deep (Book Three)

CONNECT WITH THE AUTHORS

Connect with Renée

Facebook: https://www.facebook.com/reneejaggerauthor

Website: https://reneejagger.com/

Connect with Michael Anderle

Website: http://lmbpn.com

Email List: https://michael.beehiiv.com/

https://www.facebook.com/LMBPNPublishing

https://twitter.com/MichaelAnderle

https://www.instagram.com/lmbpn_publishing/

https://www.bookbub.com/authors/michael-anderle